Will Carver is 31 years old. He is married and comes from Reading. *The Two* is his second thriller.

Praise for *Girl 4*

'There is a vivid – almost cinematic – quality to the writing. It is intense and makes for uncomfortable yet compulsive reading' *News of the World*

'Will Carver's debut crime thriller centres around Detective Inspector January David's efforts to catch a serial killer. A tense and often gory read, this will have readers trying to guess who the killer is from page one' *Press Association*

'This writer will go from strength to strength and I believe we will be hearing a lot more from Mr Carver' Crimesquad.com

Also available by Will Carver

Girl 4

WILL CARVER
THE TWO

arrow books

Published by Arrow Books 2012

4 6 8 10 9 7 5

First published in Great Britain in 2012 by
Arrow Books
Random House, 20 Vauxhall Bridge Road,
London SW1V 2SA

www.randomhouse.co.uk

Addresses for companies within The Random House Group Limited can be
found at: www.randomhouse.co.uk/offices.htm

The Random House Group Limited Reg. No. 954009

A CIP catalogue record for this book
is available from the British Library

ISBN 9780099551041

The Random House Group Limited supports The Forest Stewardship
Council (FSC®), the leading international forest certification
organisation. Our books carrying the FSC label are printed on
FSC® certified paper. FSC is the only forest certification scheme
endorsed by the leading environmental organisations, including
Greenpeace. Our paper procurement policy can be found at:
www.randomhouse.co.uk/environment

Typeset in Palatino by SX Composing DTP, Rayleigh, Essex
Printed and bound by CPI Group (UK) Ltd, Croydon, CR0 4YY

For my brother, who said,
'Why don't you just write a supernatural thriller?'

Prologue

——◆——

I've come to know my mother a lot better over the last year, since she died.

We're much closer now.

She'd seen things before that terrible spring of '85; her journals tell me that much. It wasn't until the day before my sister Cathy was taken, that cloudless spring day I trustingly left her outside on her own, the day all our lives began to wither and change into something altogether darker and broken, it wasn't until the last day our family was happy that my mother saw him, the one she refers to in her journals as The Fat Man.

The vision that would haunt her.

The nightmare that held all the answers but which nobody believed.

Now I believe.

Now I understand.

With my mother gone, he is the only person who can help find my sister.

But, in my nightmares or visions or intuitions or whatever these things are, I am yet to see him.

I haven't seen anybody since Audrey, my wife, my pregnant wife, left. I stayed with her while she recovered from the ordeal with Eames but knowing she had been with him, that she had slept with the man that killed all of those people, that his child, not mine, was growing inside her and that she was going to keep it, there was no choice but to part.

She betrayed me with the villain I arrested and now she has disappeared to I don't know where. I do not care.

Ploughing through the diarised moments of my dead mother's life is part of my routine now. The piles of handwritten notepads occupy the space that was once Audrey's home office. I spend most of my time in that room when I'm home, tricking my mind into believing the house is much smaller than it really is. Cutting myself off from the reality of the dwarfing world outside.

So far I have learned nothing significant about the similarities between our abilities. The gift or curse I seem to share with my mother. The volumes from '84 to '87 are merely a chronicle of the steady decomposition of Mother's mind and the irrepressible growth of her irra-tional desperation. They chronicle the breakdown of our family following Cathy's abduction. My father's with-drawal and resignation was proportional to Mother's apparent madness and both my parents' neglect of me.

The height of her hopelessness came a year later than these entries, when she turned to the Lord.

3rd March '88: No visions last night either. Can't take this. Lit a candle for Cathy's safe return. Prayed to God or whoever will listen. Where are you, Fat Man? Tell me where my girl is. Why do you no longer visit me? Who will help us?

Now I am closer to my mother, it hurts to read her sounding so delusional. Not in regard to her visions of this *Fat Man* but because she'd lost so much hope, so much confidence in herself, that her only option seemed to be entrusting her faith to an idol she had long since forgotten.

The moment she passed on her fear to this higher power was the moment she gave up on my sister.

The moment she stopped fighting.

And I refuse to do that.

In the space of one year I have lost a father I hardly knew, a mother I didn't want to know and a wife I wish I'd never met.

Once again, I'm alone.

There is no one.

Only Cathy.

And there certainly is no God.

Litha
June 2009

Celeste

I don't move, at first.

It takes a few seconds to realise that, actually, I can't.

I'm bound, and not just physically.

As my eyes adjust to the darkness in my windowless room I can make out a tiny rectangle of light on the wall in front of me.

And I know that I've been caught.

I know that she didn't die.

Stupidly, I think it's over.

The room is as cold as you would expect a jail cell to be; the skin on my breasts goose-pimples as a numbing chill bolts down my neck, causing my shoulders to judder.

Somebody stepping on my grave.

My hands are restricted, tied to the frame of the bed, which I now register as double size. Even in the blackness, I am aware that I have been placed in the centre of the room rather than up against a wall.

Both arms are stretched out perpendicular to my body. But I'm not handcuffed. My wrists are tethered to the bars of the bed frame with what feels like satin or some other equally sleek fabric. The loops holding me in place are not tight and yet, still, I cannot seem to move my arms. The same smooth material rubs against my ankles,

7

binding them together and attaching them to the bottom bedstead.

What is this?

I focus on the strip of light, cocking my head to the right slightly to listen for voices, something, anything that confirms the police have finally captured me. The saliva in my mouth is thick from thirst, the acridity of smoke enveloping every taste bud.

I pull at the cloth that fetters me to the frame, trying to release myself.

Nothing.

Spiritually, my shackles tighten, paralysing my limbs, leaving my body crucified to the mattress beneath.

The back of my neck itches, then my lumbar, then the inside of my right thigh. I can't scratch. I can't move.

They can't treat me like this.

I wriggle my core violently, hoping to dislodge something, my limbs still heavy and motionless. The bed moves half an inch closer to the door but my situation does not improve. So I scream. With every last one of my muscle fibres twitching simultaneously and the tendons in my neck trembling, I let out a cry that warbles with viciousness.

I hold the roar for five seconds, maybe ten, then wait.

Nothing.

Nobody comes.

Again I cry out, this time interspersing my howls with 'You fucks' and 'Let me out' and 'Who *are* you?'

I wait again, catching my breath.

Silence.

I stare intently at the illuminated rectangle ahead of me, my eyes fixed on the same spot, willing the flap to open and reveal the face of my arresting officer, the man

8

to be hailed as a hero, the one who stopped the procession of mutilations and burnings and blood-draining exsanguinations.

I want to see January David's eyes, full of pride and achievement; his pathetic feeling of triumph despite the death of the five people he could have prevented if he really knew just what was going on.

But, despite my powers, I cannot open the small door to the outside of this prison.

So I wait.

Momentarily, I give up.

That's exactly what they want.

Relaxing into my restraints I take six long breaths, in through the nose, hold for five seconds then expel through the mouth, opening my eyes again on the third exhalation. On the ceiling above me I can just make out a pattern. A circle, slightly bigger than the bed that I am lying on, but it is too dark to see what is painted inside. With my vision compromised, it is only a short while before my other senses begin to compensate. I can smell the paint now; I couldn't at first. Whatever the symbol above me is, it is fresh. As if the cell has been recently decorated.

Then I smell burning. Not like something is on fire, not like the smell a few hours ago that I can still taste on the flesh inside my cheek as I knelt in front of another victim, the fire burning beneath her. Just candles. Newly lit candles, the extinguished matches still hot, the minuscule stream of smoke dancing into the air as its flame is blown out.

Then I feel something altogether alien. It's as if, somehow, the silence I have found myself in has become even more quiet. I sense something drawing closer.

The tin flap drops open, sounding like a car crash against the noiselessness of my isolation.

I hold my breath now, my body rigid in anticipation.

More light streams into my cell, forming a pathway along the dust particles floating around inside.

Initially, the opening frames a bearded chin, but that slowly descends out of sight making way for vibrant pink lips against the palest of skin tones, then a pointed nose that resembles a flat owl's beak, perfectly symmetrical, eventually stopping on the eyes. Dark and bloodshot. So dark there is little colour difference from the pupil.

He doesn't blink.

I open my mouth, the viscous saliva forming a string that connects both my lips. I want to speak but can't force myself to say anything. As if attempting to call out in a dream.

The man's eyes are unflinchingly reserved, reluctant. I feel my own widen further, trying to take in more than is possible through the tiny aperture I have been allowed.

Eventually, he blinks, and I jump. Every movement is exaggerated, every sound is amplified: his blink is like a whip cracking.

These are not the eyes of my arresting officer.

These are not the eyes of January David.

V

The traffic lights change again, illuminating my living room in an orange wash followed by a flood of green that remains until another drunken rabble passes by and presses the button at the junction, whether they need to cross or not.

The juvenile compulsions of the weak-willed.

I take a sip of red wine and watch the northern wall of my flat cycle through the colours once more.

A scraping behind the door alerts me that the bed is moving.

I don't care, though.

I've got her.

It ends tonight.

Litha marks her demise.

The wine is full-bodied, thick, like blackcurrant syrup. It coats the inside of my mouth before passing down my throat, swathing it in a fruity glaze that is almost sensual. I close my eyes and lick my teeth slowly, starting with the incisors at the top. I can still detect the changing lights somehow. I drop back into the comfort of my worn leather chair, the only piece of furniture, all I need in my near-empty room.

The muffled screams persist but I remain unmoved, allowing myself this pleasure.

She starts to wail. Long guttural bleats that develop into predictable obscenities.

This is the sound of justice. The sound of God's work.

Nobody can hear her. Nobody will ever hear her.

Moving my wine glass into my left hand I flip open my mobile phone in my right and hit 9 three times. It isn't long before a woman answers.

'Emergency Services. Which service do you require?' She sounds too chirpy.

'Fire Brigade, please.'

She doesn't speak again. The phone line clicks straight through to a well-spoken man who asks me what my predicament is. I speak in a slightly raised pitch, masking my true voice in case the call is being recorded. I don't want to sound like me; I want to sound desperate for help.

I give him the address of the fire.

'I don't know whether there are any people in there,' I lie, forcing a fake whimper of concern.

He tries to make me stay on the line and wait for the help to arrive. He says I should stay exactly where I am.

I hang up.

It doesn't require too much force to twist the phone in my hand and break it in two. The back plate falls off, exposing the inner workings. I release the catch that holds the SIM card in place and take it out. Bending this in half dislodges the chip on the front. I flush it down the toilet. Then, walking back into the living room, I see the wall is lit in red. Looking out of the window, I notice a young couple waiting by the side of the road until it is safe to cross.

Behind me the woman shouts again. A faint murmur. 'Who aaaaare you?'

I glare at the couple who have now crossed the road and paused to embrace, hoping they did not hear, waiting for them to continue with their journey, watching as his hands wander down her body.

I hold my breath.

They carry on their way, undoubtedly heading towards a night of fleeting coital ardour. Once they are far enough away I hurl one half of the broken phone across the street into the road to be carried away by traffic; the other I drop straight down into the bushes below, splitting it into two locations.

They don't need to find us.

She will be judged.

When the screaming stops I make my way over to the room I have prepared for her.

I smile, waiting at the door with my finger on the latch that will release the rectangular flap that separates us. Closing my eyes again I breathe deeply but silently to compose myself, the corners of my mouth dropping into seriousness.

Her retribution is my salvation.

I stare at her through the opening, her body tethered to the bed that will be a final place of rest. She stares back, trying to retain some power, to show she is not afraid. But, of course, she breaks.

'Who the fuck are you?'

To look at her you would see that such language does not suit her willowy, almost ethereal, appearance. But, knowing her as I do, understanding her inner evil, her masked malevolence, her odious self-determination to transform her visualisations into heinous reality, I am not shocked.

I say nothing.

She asks again, this time placating me as if I were a sub-mental buffoon.

'Who . . . are . . . you . . . and . . . what . . . do . . . you . . . want?' Her eyes widen in her annoyance, her teeth grinding.

Several years ago, I was someone else. A father, a husband. I was loved, and needed, but that man is gone. Who I am now is of no concern to you. You may know me only for my actions and you are here so that justice may be served.

You are here at the will of my Lord, so that he may have his vengeance.

That I may have my peace.

I do not tell her any of this. It is not required.

Instead, I close the hatch, drop to my knees, and begin to pray.

My work is just beginning.

This is my genesis.

January

I knew this was coming. I knew seven weeks ago when the fifth body was found in the undergrowth to mark the coming of summer.

I knew it last night while I slept. While The Two performed another merry dance, banging their drums, rolling their wheels, tormenting me with their mysterious messages in the room where The Smiling Man once stood. That dark, endless room in my mind where my subconscious is invaded by intuitive visions, cryptically pointing me towards the solution to my investigation.

I knew this was coming. And still I couldn't stop it.

When I arrive, Paulson is talking to a fireman I don't recognise, a cigarette hanging from his top lip, oblivious to the sudden irony of his habit. An ambulance is parked on the kerb, the back doors flung open. I pull up nearby and take a moment to collect myself.

My sergeant tilts his head, acknowledging my arrival, and motions for me to come over.

I scratch around my neck, pulling the uncomfortable shirt collar away from my skin. It's a humid, sticky day. Heaving myself out of the musty car, I push the door shut, trapping in the stench of Scotch and insomnia, and amble over to the live crime scene.

'Too late?' I ask, deflated, arriving in the midst of conversation, my hands in my pockets.

'Chief Archer, this is DI David.' Paulson takes care of the formalities. 'He is the lead investigator on this case.'

I sense the high-ranking fireman judging me on my appearance. I see him look me up and down as though I have just emerged from a doorway and asked him for money to get into a shelter for the night. He doesn't even realise he is doing it.

Paulson, of course, picks up on this behaviour and cocks me a knowing glance. Archer turns to survey the building, and behind his back I mouth the words 'Where's Stringer?' to Paulson, enquiring about our usual fire department contact. He shrugs his shoulders and makes a shape with his lips that says 'Gone.' Archer is new and clearly out to impress.

'A fire was called in about fifteen minutes ago,' the chief relays authoritatively, looking up at one of the windows on the block in front of us. 'Anonymous call.'

Paulson flicks through the notes in his own pad and looks up at the same window. I keep my attention on Chief Archer, staring up at his six foot five inch frame, mesmerised by his hefty moustache jumping up and down with every word.

'It's contained now. Made to look like some kids were messing around with candles or squatters making trouble. But obviously it's not.' Now he looks directly at me. 'Seems to me it's that guy you haven't managed to catch yet.'

I don't know what to say. He's right.

He turns back to the building. 'We'll know more in the next couple of days.' He continues to reel off his script, methodically, as if unenthused at the meagre blaze he and his team have been rushed out to; like he is disappointed the whole street isn't burning down. A missed opportunity to stake real ownership on his new position.

Archer offers me nothing in the way of significant information or respect but I thank him for his report and duck under the tape that cordons off the entrance to the building. Paulson ambles close behind me.

Two flights above us, I hear a clunking noise and the voice of the male paramedic telling his partner to 'Lift!' He comforts the patient saying, 'There you go, miss,' then squeezes clean air into her mouth and nose. I stop partway up the stairs and look back, wide-eyed, at Paulson.

She's alive.

I turn and leap up the stairs two at a time. Paulson, almost instantly breathless, attempts to follow, but his bloated heart can't pump the blood to his muscles quickly enough.

Three flights up I meet the paramedics who are wheeling a woman down the stairs on a gurney. I stop them.

'How is she?' I ask, catching my breath.

'Sir, I need you to move,' the male paramedic says forcefully, glaring at me, his knuckles turning white as he grips the mobile bed tighter in his frustration.

He starts to push the gurney holding the girl towards me, hoping I will step aside.

I slam my hands down on the surface either side of the girl's legs, widening my stance and leaning forward to halt proceedings.

'Sir—' The male paramedic raises his voice; his female partner jolts nervously.

'This is my witness,' I state, cutting him off. Paulson

finally gasps his way to my side, holding the banister for support. 'I am Detective Inspector David.' I lower the level of my voice, hoping to clarify the situation somewhat. I watch the tension release from the paramedic's shoulders and slowly push myself upright, taking my hands away from the victim. 'I am Detective Inspector David,' I repeat deliberately, 'and this could be a valuable witness in a high-profile case.'

I have their attention now. Neither of them tries to jump in again but I still sense their urgency.

'Is she going to make it?' I don't have time to sugar-coat it.

'She's inhaled some smoke,' the female paramedic chimes in.

'OK . . .' My tone urges her to go on.

Her partner interrupts again. 'She should be fine but we really need to get her to the hospital.' I see he wants to start pushing the gurney again.

'Take my partner with you,' I instruct uncompromisingly. I look at Paulson, who draws in another exaggerated breath; he has to tackle the three flights of stairs again after not fully recovering from his journey up.

The paramedics wheel the victim past me, reluctantly obeying my order. They have no choice. My authority takes precedence at a crime scene. I draw Paulson aside.

'Stay with her. I want to know as soon as she wakes up. OK?'

'OK, Jan,' he replies, releasing his grip from the railing to demonstrate his readiness for the task.

'As soon as she wakes up,' I reiterate.

He nods.

'I'm going to need a sketch artist ready too, so you'll have to call that in on the way.'

Paulson dutifully follows the victim down the stairs and into the back of the ambulance waiting outside. I continue up to view the scene of the crime.

But I already know what I'll find.

The smoky stench emanates through the corridor and hits me with only a few stairs to go. I smell charcoal and fruit. I smell hay, just as I had in the woods on the May Bank Holiday; just as I had for the four victims before that.

As I enter the doorway of the apartment, it is as I expected. A circle of salt large enough for someone to sit or kneel inside. Ahead of that, on the floor, a silver candlestick with the stub of a black candle. I know before it is tested that it will show remnants of essential oil rubbed on the outside.

For a brief moment, I convince myself I can smell sulphur, but I can't.

Next to the candle is a small circular fireproof dish containing a charcoal powder laced with a crumbled dried fruit.

It is the same as the others.

The dish faces the altar, the spot where the victim was found. This is the only thing that is different from the previous crime scenes; the only aspect that has changed.

But I knew all this last night.

And that's why I know there is something here I am missing.

I can understand why Archer was disappointed: this was hardly an inferno. The altar is a large wheel attached to the ceiling by chains. It appears to be a wagon wheel, wooden, with a frame of iron around its circumference. The spokes are wooden too and thread into a metal centre which undoubtedly caused heavy bruising to the victim's back as she writhed against it, attempting to free herself.

Below the hanging wheel are the remains of what appears to be a controlled bonfire. Only a couple of feet across, it explains the scent of hay in the air.

I move over to the window and see Archer below.

The fire had not roared out of control. The walls are still intact. The ceiling has some smoke damage but nothing significant. This was called in anonymously. It's not as if a neighbour saw smoke bellowing from the windows and the flames danced around the room, alerting passers-by that the building was on fire.

This is the same killer, it's clear to me; but, somehow, this time, it is different.

Standing in the centre of the salt circle, I close my eyes and think about what The Two were trying to tell me last night. What extra information were they trying to give to me that nobody else has?

My phone vibrates in my pocket.

The light flashes Paulson's name on and off.

'Paulson?' I answer the phone.

'She's awake, Jan.' He speaks in an almost whisper.

'Already? Fuck. Does she . . .'

'She remembers the face,' he says excitedly, inter-rupting me. From his tone I can tell he is smiling.

'Call the artist now. I'll meet you down there.' I hang up before he even has a chance to respond.

When I arrive at the hospital, Paulson is standing guard outside the witness's room. She is Brooke Derry, twenty-seven years old, from London. Through the window in her door I can see she is gingerly sitting up in her bed, talking to a man who is rubbing frantically at a drawing pad with his blackened thumb.

Give it another twenty minutes of softening the chin, sharpening the cheeks and widening the eyes, and we will have an accurate image. The identity of the killer that has eluded us since October last year.

The artist performs his final smudge and blows some black dust off the page. He turns it around to Miss Derry and she nods. He then swivels the drawing around to face us as we peer through the window of the ward door. We haven't been in yet. I didn't want to add any pressure to her, to influence her. She needed time to focus on the identification before I question her.

The sketch shows a woman; long, mousey hair, late thirties, high cheekbones, probably very pretty ten years ago.

An impression of the woman we will eventually come to know as Celeste Varrick, the killer we have been chasing.

Our first truly tangible lead.

I now know the face of the murderer I pursue. I can stop her before she strikes again, before The Two have another chance to torment me.

But I am hunting a ghost, a shadow. Somebody has got to her before me; she has been captured already.

I'm chasing someone that no longer exists.

Brooke

---◆---

I tell the police everything I remember.
My statement is a true account of the event of my near-death experience to the very best of my recollection.

I came straight home from work as I always do. I unlocked the front door to the building. I had my earphones in so I couldn't really hear anything other than my music. I pressed the button for the lift because I live on the top floor and I wasn't going to walk up the stairs after a full day of work. I must have only taken one step inside the lift when I was grabbed from behind.

I didn't see a face and the hand that clasped a handkerchief over my mouth was gloved. I remember them being stronger than I was but that isn't difficult: I'm pretty small. I couldn't say whether there were any identifying marks at this point or how this person smelled or whether the body that pressed itself against my back to hold me rigid as the doors closed behind us was a man or a woman; it happened too quickly.

Then I blacked out.

This is what I tell Detective Sergeant Paulson while we wait.

The second part of my story is more vivid. Though groggy and disoriented, the shock of finding myself in that position seemed to focus me somewhat.

The first thing I recall is the scent of the straw bundle burning underneath me. It wasn't a completely detestable fragrance, to be honest. It had something to it that made it more palatable than burning wood or fabric. Either way, I was certainly ingesting some of the fumes, but not choking at this point.

I hadn't yet opened my eyes. I wanted to take it in one sense at a time. As I said, I was still in a slight stupor and panicking wasn't going to help. I soon sensed that I was moving ever so slightly. Like I had been swinging back and forth but was coming to a stop and my motion had switched, twisting from side to side as momentum slowed.

My hearing was next to focus as the fuzziness in my head continued to evaporate. A woman's voice was emanating from the area directly ahead of me. It was rhythmic, almost singing. But not quite. It was soothing. Complementing the motion of the wheel I was attached to.

This was the voice of my captor, I thought.

Don't unnerve her.

I didn't want to open my eyes fully in case she noticed. I tried to see through a squint but had to fully open my eyes and blink because the smoke was making them water. She didn't see, though; she was facing to the side at this point.

'But she did eventually turn to face you?' Detective Sergeant Paulson asks abruptly, almost excitedly, as he interrupts my recounting.

'Yes, it was only a moment after that she turned to face me head on.'

'And you think you can describe this to our sketch

artist?' He waves at the door and a man with a pad enters my hospital room. DS Paulson stands up ready to greet him.

'Yes. I remember the face lucidly. That's not something one forgets,' I confirm.

DS Paulson offers his chair to the artist and leaves me alone in the room with him to describe the woman I saw at my attempted murder scene. He advises me to take my time, and assures me that he will be waiting just outside.

I tell the artist that she was pretty in a non-conventional way. High cheekbones, large eyes that were grey or green, hair that was long and naturally wavy but a little greasy – not in a bad way, though. She was tall and thin. The word I use is wispy. Her skin was pale, her lips were thin and lacked colour, but her upper lip was pronounced. The first sketch looks a bit like her but after a little smudging and rubbing, he manages to push the eyes further apart, point the chin a touch more and move the nose down; all without erasing a single line.

He flicks the pad around and I nod. That is the extent of my reaction. This is the face of the woman I am telling the police I saw at the site of my attempted murder. The person who tried to kill me; to make me her sixth victim.

Shouldn't I feel fear? Or a surge of adrenalin? Should I not be shaking?

Should this lack of reaction stand out to the three detectives? The one in front of me with a sketch pad, Detective Sergeant Paulson, who is outside, and the tired-looking one, January David, who has just arrived?

Do they think they have already captured their killer just because they have a picture of her face?

Detective Inspector David introduces himself to me. He tells me that he is not here to talk and does not want

24

me to strain my voice any further. He'll be back at some point to go over my testimony again, but he says he just wants to thank me, that my help has proved invaluable and that I should count myself extremely lucky.

That's exactly how I feel. Privileged to be here. To be alive.

And now I feel important, and crucial to the case.

I am exactly where fate designed. I am distracting the police, feeding them the information they require about Celeste. While I am here being so vital and helpful, the person I have described so vividly as the villain is receiving a similar treatment to that which I experienced only a few hours ago.

Now she is hunted.

I just made her the most wanted woman in the country.

January

—◆—

It has to be Murphy. He's the only one who's stupid enough to do it.

Not thinking further than his own ambition.

My mind has not rested since we saw the sketch of the killer we will soon come to know as Celeste Varrick. This is a concrete lead. Nothing from a dream, or a vibration felt as a candle flame dies out, or a hunch from experience. It's something we can all see and touch and use. This is real police work.

My plan was to hold on to this information, to digest it and compare it to everything else we have gleaned so far. However, something doesn't sit right. The signature is the same; the candles and salt circle are present, the aroma, the burning, but the MO has evolved. She was fastened to the hanging wheel rather than resting on her knees. Was the killer interrupted? A personality doesn't just change partway through a serial murder; I know that, Murphy knows that. It's how we catch these criminals; we see their personality, their psychology in the scenes they leave behind.

It is different. Slightly. But enough for me to notice. I know that what is being presented as reality is not always truth. Things are never exactly as they seem. Sometimes the differences are the mistakes that lead to a conviction.

But Murphy takes the picture as gospel. He idiotically thinks, or the people pulling his strings believe, that we'll find Celeste Varrick quicker if everyone in the country is looking out for her. That's not how it works. The inevitable public hysteria would prove a hindrance at best. Now we know the face of the killer, that it is a woman, we'll have people calling in with inaccurate, misleading sightings across the capital and beyond. It will slow down the investigation. The team will have no choice but to look into every claim no matter how ludicrous.

It will promote a vigilante mentality. Civilians taking the law into their own hands, attacking women who resemble the killer, detaining a lookalike. All the while, the true perpetrator continues her work, planning her next victim, or worse, fleeing and leaving another string of unsolved cases.

Leaving more families to destroy themselves through lack of closure.

Leaking the artist's impression of our suspect to the press will undoubtedly set us back when it should have taken us closer to resolution.

I only needed a day.

Tomorrow morning, when people get up to start their working week, they will be greeted by the sight of a killer they did not need to know about yet.

Archer left a message saying that this wasn't the only fire in London tonight; that his team was called out several times, that he's been trying to get hold of me since I left.

That Brooke Derry might not be the only victim of the evening.

27

V

This morning I wake up when the rolled-up newspaper thuds against my door. I sit bolt upright on the sofa, stiff after an uncomfortable night's sleep, the alcohol desiccating my brain. I missed my usual run. It doesn't seem right to leave her here alone, even though I know she's trapped.

She's not going anywhere.

I stretch my neck, first looking to the right, then to the left, then rolling my head from side to side as I look up at the ceiling. Quietly, I edge over to the door of her cell and gently release the clasp to look in on her. She is asleep on her back, fastened securely to the bed, exhausted from a night of futile ranting.

I carefully shut the flap, keeping her in the dark.

I'll miss Gail this morning. My routine has changed.

I open my front door and reach down to the mat for my morning dose of current affairs. Not everything changes. Out of habit I roll off the elastic band as I walk to the kitchen area, I lay the paper down on the work surface and reach for the fridge. I'm out of grapefruit juice, too much to think about over the last couple of days. I grab an upside down glass left to drain after the last time I washed up. The bubbles have left a scum around the rim of the vessel which I wipe off and dry with the bottom of

28

my T-shirt before filling it with tap water.

I lean against the worktop as if I am about to stretch my calf muscles, but there's no need this morning, so I just read. The front page has hardly any text. Instead it shows a life-like drawing of a woman.

A pretty woman with high cheekbones and flowing hair.

The woman I have tied to a bed only ten feet from where I stand right now.

I smile to myself. London knows the face of its demon.

You have done well, V.

This is the Lord's will, V.

I take a swig of my tap water and turn through the remaining pages. An article on national identity, something about the financial state of Britain, the usual political scandal, and before I know it I have flicked all the way to the sports section.

I feel gratified. Fulfilled, even.

I shut the paper leaving it sports-side-up on the counter. I don't need to see the picture of her face. I can see her face whenever I want to.

It won't be until tomorrow's paper that they report on the second girl they found that evening.

I float back into the living room, perch on the edge of my worn sofa, place my hands together, close my eyes and ask, 'What will you have me do with her now, Lord?'

Celeste

—◆—

He's out there. I can sense him.
I hear the murmur just beyond the door.

'. . . *sobrazod-ol Roray i ta nazodapesad, Girae ta maelpereji . . .*'

I close my eyes tightly, hoping the darkness will somehow improve my hearing.

'. . . *farezodem zodenurezoda adana gono . . .*'

It sounds Latin, maybe. But the way he speaks is so rhythmic, like a chant or a mantra. It's monotonous and continual.

He's praying.

Logically, I link the Latin with Catholicism and my situation begins to make more sense.

I see now why he cannot understand what I do, what I have been doing. That he would think my actions immoral, my rituals unnatural. That, for a righteous, devout man, there is only good and there is only evil.

That he is good and I am evil.

That he is right and I am wrong.

'. . . *eca, od zodameranu! Odo cicale Qaa . . .*'

Arabic. Maybe Aramaic. Perhaps he is speaking the language of Jesus. He is praying to a God.

He is not in control of what he does; his purpose comes from a higher place. To him, my beliefs are erroneous. My anger turns to fear.

The image of Brooke Derry strapped to the wheel as the fire burns beneath her flashes into my mind.

At least I know that my work is done.

I strain my ears to hear more but he stops. I hear the crack of bone as he stands up from what must be a kneeling position.

A second later, I am blinded.

The fluorescent bulb chugs into action, immersing the room in a bright white light, shrinking my pupils to pinheads and sending blotches of colour across my retinas.

I slam my eyes shut, sucking air through the gaps in my teeth, hissing in the pain before focus returns and the reality of my situation dawns.

Recovering from the sudden influx of light, I quickly try to examine the room, my prison.

Creased white linen on a white wooden bed frame. The walls are painted a bright white too. Everything from the door in the middle of the wall ahead of me to the straps around my wrists and ankles is white. Everything except the writing.

To the left of the door, in letters around twelve inches high, it says: *1 Corinthians 10:18–22.* The words have been handwritten in black paint.

'The sacrifices of Pagans are offered to demons, not to God. You cannot drink the cup of the Lord and the cup of demons too.'

The writing below the reference is in a smaller scrawling font, but it allows me into the mind of my captor.

It is as expected.

To the right of the door is another reference and another message.

'*2 Corinthians 6:14. Do not be yoked together with unbelievers. For what do righteousness and wickedness have in common?*'

There is good and there is evil.

He is right and I am wrong.

To my left is a missive from Deuteronomy 31:16–19. This time in two-foot letters exclaiming how 'God' is angry with me.

I shake my head and squint my eyes in disbelief, trying to avoid the temptation to look left, where I am sure the writing will allude to Thessalonians in some way.

I don't and it does.

'*The coming of the lawless one will be in accordance with the work of Satan displayed in all kinds of counterfeit miracles, signs and wonder, and in every sort of evil that deceives those who are perishing.*'

His message is clear.

His God is the light and I am darkness.

For he is good and I am evil.

I know this cell is homemade. That the authorities have failed again. That this is somebody taking matters into their own hands. A vigilante who will thwart the efforts of *the lawless one* in the name of a God.

I understand his motives even if he does not remotely comprehend mine. That he thinks Paganism is somehow linked with Satan.

But it isn't until I tilt my head up towards the painted circle I had partially glimpsed in the original darkness that I realise it is more than that.

It's not just a circle.

I see it so clearly now.

It has been painted there to keep me trapped.

V

⬥

She refuses to eat, but she will take water. Maybe to moisten her throat, which has grown sore from all her unheard, futile screaming over the last thirty-six hours. As I sit down on the side of her bed she struggles, wanting to hurt me, trying to strike out at her captor.

'I'm here to look after you,' I tell her truthfully, sincerely. 'To stop you doing what you have been doing.'

I tilt the cup so that she can take down some liquid. In three gulps the cup is empty. She stares at me, not saying anything, unresponsive to my kindness. Then she spits directly into my face.

And laughs at me.

Calmly, I stand up and walk towards the door. I could leave it open, I could untie her; still she would not be able to go anywhere. I'm just being cautious. Also, it's another layer for her yelps to penetrate, and I want to go out. I need to maintain routine, to perpetuate normality.

Closing the door shuts off the sound of her chortling, her puerile victory. I put on my trainers, tying the laces into a double-knot, and leave the flat.

I must improve on my time.

I have to see Gail upon my return.

She has to believe that nothing is out of the ordinary.

I come home, not in record time but adequate, and my neighbour is making her way out to her office job.

'Morning, Sam. Didn't see you yesterday,' she comments, instantly worrying me that she thinks something is wrong.

'Everyone needs a rest day, Gail,' I respond, smiling, looking the part of the unflustered jogger, camouflaging the role of panicked kidnapper.

'True, true,' she nods. 'I don't know how you do it.' She smiles and carries on walking. 'Have a good day, Sam,' she calls back without even looking, her thoughts shifting immediately to the working day ahead, instantly forgetting her arbitrary morning niceties.

'You too,' I oblige, but she has already disappeared around the corner.

I bend down, the lactic acid building in my thighs because I stopped to exchange pleasantries, and I pick up the paper, satisfied with my smokescreen, content with the return of regime.

Inside my flat, with the front door now closed, I tuck the rolled paper under my chin, bend my right leg so that my foot touches my gluteals, grab the ankle with both hands and stretch out my thigh for six seconds. I repeat on the left leg. Then once more for each leg again, trying to keep the lactic acid build-up at bay.

I grab the tube of tabloid articles, shake my legs one last time and head straight in to check on Celeste.

A triangle of light appears across the floor as I open the door to her dark prison.

She doesn't move.

34

I ease my way through the gap so as not to let in more light, so I don't disturb her.

She has been here less than two days and already the room is starting to smell.

Of course, I had thought about feeding her and bringing her water, but it looks as though she has held out as long as she can and has had no choice but to wet herself. Maybe this is why she doesn't want to eat.

It suddenly dawns on me that I have no idea what I am doing.

I have captured the woman who has been doing these horrible things that have been reported in the papers, but now what? How long am I supposed to keep her here? She has seen my face now; she doesn't know where she is but she can identify me, her captor, her guard. Is there any intention of releasing her?

Why do I question? Who am I to question?

I lay the newspaper down next to her on the page that describes the second incident on Litha, the other woman that was found later, the details of the fire and salt and candles still evident.

We will discuss this later.

As I leave the room I switch on the bright, blinding fluorescent lights I installed and shut the door behind me. Celeste's eyes screw up tightly before the inevitable barrage of disparagement ensues. She will then be silent as she reads her article. Straight after, the indignity continues.

But I can't hear it.

I am praying to the Lord.

I am questioning.

As I open my eyes, my knees sore from the floorboards,

the poison in my thighs refusing to back down, I am filled with new knowledge.

That I am to make a monster of her.

That only one of us will ever leave.

Samhain
October 2008

January

———❖———

I never dream of Cathy. But, most nights, I go to sleep thinking about her.

Today, she would have been thirty-four.

Sitting on the lounge carpet, my back resting against the leather sofa I used to share with Audrey, a pile of Mum's journals stacked to my left, a glass of red wine to my right – not the wine that Audrey used to buy but the kind you can afford on a detective's salary; the kind most people use only for cooking – I crane my head to the left to stretch my neck. And I think of Audrey. How I wanted to protect her. How I saved her. How I sat by her bedside until she recovered. How I tried to make things work, get them back to how they were. How she wanted to keep the baby. How I just let her go.

I can't seem to get the place warm any more.

Or tidy.

It's difficult enough to drag myself upstairs to bed each night; there appear to be more steps now I'm here on my own. Tonight is no exception.

I drop my chin onto my chest, blowing out a lungful of alcohol-drenched air as both eyelids edge closer to my softening cheeks, gravity pulling my relaxed lips closer to the floor. As I inhale, a dankness travels up my nostrils, filling my throat with a familiar acridity that jolts me backwards into a bewildered darkness I have not visited for some time.

And any thought of Cathy dissolves into nightmare.

The carpet that just cushioned me has been replaced with hard wood caked in a dense layer of dust. The legs that had been outstretched in front of me are now crossed, compelling me to sit upright. I force my eyes wider in an attempt to allow more light to hit my retinas, but in front of me is never-ending black. Realisation instinctively widens my eyes even further, but still no light enters.

This is not the same as before.

I am not tied to a chair.

There is no blindfold.

I can see.

And there are two of them this time.

Only the sound of shuffling feet permeates the eternal black nothingness; the dust displacing as they shift from foot to foot in this all-encompassing shadow.

Then quiet.

I'm paralysed. My mouth dries in anxious expectation. I find myself holding my breath. Anticipating something spectacular.

This may just be a dream. Something is telling me that, at any moment, a flood of light will engulf the room and I will be confronted by that haunting yellow smile.

Wrong.

And wrong again.

Candles ignite in circles around the two figures ahead of me. First one flame then a trail of fire spitting to life, accelerating round to end where it started. To the left I notice a boy. Dressed plainly in grey trousers and shirt, his skin is pale, his hair is dark. His eyes are closed and his fists clenched. He is motionless.

On the right, the figure is a blur. Though lit by the burning wicks, it is distorted. She is distorted. Through the haze I can still make out that it is a young girl; I cannot focus on any specifics but I recognise that much.

I flit my gaze back to the left at the boy, who still does not move, then back to the right at the girl. I squint in an attempt to sharpen her edges and, in that moment, things change.

Because I think it is Cathy.

Why would she be here?

I must deconstruct the scene, analyse my dream, but, instead, I gasp; I manage to draw some breath. A gust of air causes the temperature to drop, extinguishing one of the boy's flames, and the cold removes the dust, replacing it with the pungent scent of rosemary.

Now the boy can escape.

I am still distracted by his cloudy partner.

The boy tilts his head robotically to the side, his eyes now open and flashing, cycling through different colours, his gaze locked into mine. The girl turns slowly inside her circle, her arms outstretched playfully, her face a blur of hair and motion.

My body is glued to the floor; only my head will move. I pan back to the boy and he is making his way towards me through the gap in his ring of fire, the dead circle of wax in his left hand.

He steps through the opening, edging along a painted tightrope, never deviating his stare from my face. I do not want to avert my eyes but the girl is spinning faster and faster. I see there is a line from my circle to hers.

We are all linked somehow.

Already, I am being given answers.

The boy. He produces three ribbons: black in one hand, white in the other and red from around his neck. They are tied together and placed atop the candle in front of where I sit. Despite the proximity, his facial features seem out of focus, with the exception of the eyes.

The girl rotates at an unreal pace, the flames around her lying down with the wind she creates.

The candle on the floor in front of me puffs to life, burning the ribbons, producing a smoke that temporarily masks the herbal aroma. And I can move. The boy walks backwards into the diminishing light like a toy soldier, keeping a staccato rhythm with his laughter, a child-like chortle at first, then deeper and into a whisper.

The girl ceases her revolution and looks straight at me, screaming a silent wail before her final whirlwind blows out the lights, plunging everything back into gloom.

I expect to wake up.

Not yet.

Silence.

I feel him near me again. In front of me.

I wait.

There's nothing else I can do.

A speck of light appears. Somewhere in the distance, directly in front, between the circles of dead candles at either side of me, a light. What looks like a match being lit miles away begins to grow. It's getting closer.

Gradually, it reveals the outline in front of me.

The boy is not alone.

The girl has stealthily made her way over, directly behind the distressed boy.

The light draws ever nearer and the girl creeps closer to the boy. I punch my fists and shout in an attempt to warn him, but he doesn't move.

The light grows brighter; I can feel its heat. Something on fire.

Now the girl is directly behind him. I notice he is holding his chest, perhaps in pain. She weaves her blurry hands around his waist but he doesn't flinch.

Gently, she places her hands on his, caressing them until their fingers interlock.

The light grows redder then white again as it draws nearer.

My eyes flit between the two in front of me and the flame behind.

She is not Cathy.

The girl rests her chin on the boy's shoulder as they complete their embrace. His mouth moves into a smile. I can't tell whether he is still laughing over the sound of the approaching fire-crackle.

The heat is palpable. I see him grip her hands tighter.

He wants her there.

I resign, taking this cue to desist my violent outbursts against my unseen jail.

The glow behind is a giant wheel, ablaze and rolling towards us.

The Two squeeze each other for protection, bracing themselves for impact.

Somehow, their closed eyes seem to shut even further as the flaming wheel prepares itself to take them out. As it hits, the girl screams one last time. In this instance, it is audible. So high-pitched it seems to shatter the impenetrable bubble that holds me.

The fire engulfs the two children in a miniature supernova and continues towards me, the roar seeming to harmonise perfectly with the scream.

The last thing I remember is the light.

I wake up sweating. The ball of flame from my dream is the best way to heat me in this house, it seems.

It's the first vision I have had since Audrey left four months ago. I know that's what it is. It was the same black box where The Smiling Man always met me. But it wasn't him this time.

I know the feeling but there is still so much left to understand. I'm hoping Mother's journals can shed more light.

Where is The Smiling Man? Who are the two children?

I don't understand it yet but what I do know is that something is starting. Something evil walks the streets of London again, and I have this information before anybody else.

But it is the first vision; it has no context. The only thing I can be sure of is that in twenty-four hours, unless I can somehow decipher this cryptic message, someone, somewhere in this huge city, will be murdered.

Lily

There was that time I cut myself, drew a little blood too, but, if I'm honest, I wouldn't call it a real wrist-slitting attempt.

This was back when people cared.

The thing with the pills was stupid, I know that now. Horrible way to do it, too, in hindsight.

Lost some friends that way.

I suppose there's still that head-in-the-oven thing, or hanging. Haven't tried those. A gun is out of the question, though. Not much room for error with that one. Not many people left.

Last time it was the guy who lives in the flat above me and that girlfriend of his, who seems to be staying over more and more, rent free, who saved me.

Sometimes I lie awake at night listening to them fucking or giggling, and I cry.

It's quiet tonight, though.

The light is on upstairs. I can see it, but nobody is home. I know this because I turned off my TV hours ago and have been waiting for his key to turn in the lock so that I can pretend to accidentally bump into him. Talk to him. Talk to someone.

I live above a pharmacy on the Fulham Road. Some old lady owns the building above and rents it out as two flats.

It isn't two flats, though. So, whenever the guy who lives above me wants to get home, he has to open my front door and walk through part of my flat before getting to his own makeshift entrance.

It could be awkward if I had visitors here one night or threw a party he wasn't invited to.

That has never happened, though.

Nobody comes any more.

And it looks like even he won't be returning home this evening. Staying with that girl again, I guess. Screwing each other at her place tonight while I sit silently in my flat not putting my head in the oven, not hanging myself on the back of the bathroom door, not living.

But not being alive is not the same as being dead. I don't want that. I've never really wanted that. That should be obvious.

Tomorrow is Halloween. It's a day when people can be someone they are not. Isn't that what it's all about? Dressing up like someone else? Putting on a mask to disguise who you really are?

Hiding in plain sight.

I'll be someone completely unfamiliar tomorrow.

Instead of being that stupid girl who tried to kill herself those few times and refuses to get any help, or that stalker downstairs who listens to people having sex, or the introverted aloof loner that nobody realises is alive, I'll be an enlightened woman who is trying to save herself in any way that she can; I'll be the one surrounded by hundreds of people who haven't even noticed she is dead.

Celeste

❖

I don't decide who should be the one to die.
   That is not my role. The choice has already been made for me.

I do not believe that it is possible for everyone to know God personally in their lives; I do not trust in the power of the Holy Spirit and I do not have faith that being centred on the Holy Trinity provides the most comprehensive existence.

This is not how I work.

But I did know to be at this church at this time on this date.

And I did know that Lily would die.

I would save her.

I'm her saviour.

Something is guiding me but it isn't God.

I sense her presence in the building immediately. There are only a few people in here at this time; it's a weekday, just before lunch. A middle-aged man stands at the front, lighting a candle, muttering something, his head tilted up towards the heavens. The other five people are women. Elderly women with nothing better to do than pray their lives away.

It is no coincidence that Lily sits behind me.

We are all exactly where we are supposed to be.

Before she even speaks I know she is the one I am here for.

There is an air of melancholy, a feeling of sadness, the sensation that the pews behind me, in front of me, beside me, are now awash with desperation.

That's all I need but I let her make a fool of herself first.

'Dear God,' she says, as if she is writing a letter or email, 'I know I don't usually come to church. OK, I never come, you obviously know that, but I'm running out of options. There's no one left to turn to.'

This is pretty much how people always start.

'I'm asking for help.'

She continues with her heartfelt plea to the Lord she has never considered until ten minutes ago. The inevitable breakdown follows.

That's my cue to step in, to offer an alternative.

I look up from my fake prayer, eyeing the pathetic congregation of weekday dunces who judge me for my beliefs even though they while away the time in a man-made building they consider more significant than the natural world around them.

The man at the front still whispers to the roof; the pensioners that pepper the seating are not lifting their heads any time soon.

Nobody has even noticed me.

I turn to see her. Unexpectedly, her expression projects a sorrow that pierces my own heart.

She looks directly at me, not saying a word. Her face is pale, with no make-up, her long ginger hair falling down to her lap, lengthening her face even more, accentuating her frown; her eyes are coated in water but no tears have yet fallen. But she is infused with heartache.

'I can help you,' I say in a hushed voice.

She seems shocked that someone would be talking to her. Then her eyes tighten, the giant tears drying out instantly, and she vents. Suddenly spewing forth her woes in such a concerted burst that it seems rehearsed. I wait patiently as she moves through her list of troubles – like I've never heard it before – her voice urgent yet calm, not disturbing the peace.

'. . . and I know what I want now. I know it,' she says. 'I don't want to die alone.' Finally, a tear falls.

I place my hand softly on hers and peer straight through her.

'I can help you.'

She won't die alone.

I'll be there.

January

---◆---

It seems insane that nobody saw it happen. There were people on every section of grass, partying in some way or another. The White Horse Free House was, as always, heaving with custom, so much so that for most of the evening the crowd outside was spilling dangerously into the road. There is a hospital on one side of the square, a church on the other, restaurants along the main road, and yet nobody in Parsons Green noticed a 25-year-old woman with bright ginger hair being stabbed and gutted on the intersection of pathways in the very centre of the frivolous celebrations.

The scene of the crime is being illuminated by the four lampposts that kicked in as soon as darkness descended. She was not merely in plain sight, she was on stage, spot-lit. Still somehow imperceptible.

People are so self-involved that they are unaware of the dangers that lurk around this city.

It couldn't possibly happen to *them.*

I realise what it is immediately. Though it's far too early to link it to last night's vision, I know this isn't just another murder in the capital.

This is the start of something.

I've been here before.

In the coming weeks and months, we will refer to Lily

Kane not by her name but merely as *the first murder*. She'll be as anonymous as she felt.

She died kneeling down in the dirt, her throat collapsed, blood oozing from her stomach, the acid poisoning her insides. I don't need a forensic specialist to tell me that. I don't need my intuition.

Yet, in front of my perfectly pallid genuflecting corpse is the evidence that will convince Paulson and Murphy of what I already know. That this is something more than the usual. That this is a ritual.

And ritual suggests repetition.

Another body.

Another vision.

The circle around her is made from salt and is only around thirty inches in diameter. In the centre is a candle. For some reason this has been left burning, almost destroying itself. Around the silver candle holder are four small black stones, onyx perhaps. They are placed apart at equal distances, forming a square inside the circle. Maybe to indicate the four points on a compass, or the major integers on a clock face. At this moment I can't be sure, I just want to gather everything I can.

Are these stones even important? They were not referenced in my dream.

It's difficult to filter what is useful from what is not. For several months now I have reverted to and relied upon standard police legwork to help me understand the handful of minor cases I've attended to.

I haven't necessarily had to stretch myself too much since I captured Eames, the man responsible for the spate of zone-two killings over recent years.

I haven't wanted to since Audrey took off with his child.

I'm out of practice.

The job has not been my priority of late.

So I'm bound to make mistakes.

And that's exactly what happens.

'Looks like witchcraft, Jan,' my other sergeant, Murphy, spouts nonchalantly, biting into an apple, surveying the area, not even paying attention to the dead girl on her knees in front of him.

'Yeah. Maybe, Murph.' I dismiss him, presuming he is wrong, as he so often is; my contempt is uncensored. Despite the fact that I am his superior and despite his disloyalty during one of London's highest profile cases in decades – the capture of Eames – I can't shake him. He's still part of my team. Someone higher than me is ensuring he stays exactly where he is. Someone will ensure that he makes a name for himself.

Murphy continues to spray his glance around at the wider area; Paulson is in the pub forecourt, rounding up possible eyewitnesses. I stay with the victim, hoping there is more to this scene than the girl and the salt circle.

But there's nothing.

No obvious CCTV cameras point at this spot in the park. I send Murphy with some of the junior officers to check the cameras on surrounding buildings; the shops nearby, the school, church and pub, hoping one of them may have picked something up to give us a clearer visual idea of what occurred.

Returning to the point at which I started, I kneel down myself so that my face is level with the victim's. The corners of her mouth are turned down, like she is disappointed to be in this position. Like she is upset to be dead.

I bend over to blow out the candle. My signal that I've finished, that my investigation of the scene is over.

As my breath hits the flame, not a nanosecond before, not a picosecond after, at the instant the air from my lungs touches the blue fire of the candle, she drops. Collapsing to the side in a crumpled dead heap.

What have I done?

Lily

—✦—

He never came home.
I waited.

I start to imagine him at her place, inside her, sweating, his tongue pressed hard against his two front teeth as he pushes himself deeper. Then I imagine she is me. That I am looking up at him. I can feel his breath; I can inhale his scent.

I put my hand between my legs.

And stop.

I don't have the motivation.

If I'm honest, if I think about it, I'm not even really that attracted to him. He's just the last person on earth who still acknowledges me; who affirms I exist. I don't even mind his girlfriend. She's perfectly pleasant. Nice, even. To me, at least.

It makes it easier to hate her.

No work this morning. I have an appointment. And right now, that seems like a blessing. Being a newly qualified lawyer is not all courtroom drama; in fact, it's never like that. It's an office with files and paperwork and phone calls and a company name made up of three men's surnames and wondering why you chose this profession in the first place. It's monotony and things you don't care about at all and it's inescapable because

I owe so much money and I'm tied into this firm for years.

So, a doctor's appointment is like a respite.

I jump in the shower, leaving the door open, not pulling the shower curtain all the way around the rail. The bath mat will get wet but he might catch a glimpse of me if he comes home in the next twenty minutes.

I put in this much effort for someone I'm not even attracted to.

And I'm disappointed when he doesn't show.

I can walk to the doctor's from my house. It's on the corner of Parsons Green.

Thirty-five steps from the spot where I will shortly slump to my death.

The road opposite my flat, the one I usually walk along to get to the tube, is covered in leaves. The time of year, I guess. Pumpkins litter the doorsteps and living-room windowsills of the Victorian terrace. Some designs are particularly elaborate, not just eyes and a misshapen, jagged mouth. I heard on the news how the American tradition has spilled into our annual celebrations, making Halloween a major night on the UK calendar.

On the other side of the street I see a disabled man. I couldn't fathom a guess at his age; he looks like he may have had one stroke too many. Like he has difficulty just controlling his tongue.

He's tall but developing a hunch. His right leg drags behind him, his hands are disfigured but clenching his walking frame solidly.

He's one of the constants in my life. Every day I see him. It's always at different points along the street or main road, but he is always out, hauling himself around the block just to get out of the house, to keep his mind occupied, active, to utilise the last semblance of strength in his legs before they completely give way on him. It takes two or three hours for him to get around the block once; a walk that would take me five to seven minutes.

It's a kind of determination I have never had. Never needed to have.

Recently it has been more difficult just to raise myself out of bed. Initially I was diagnosed with depression. Seems an obvious assumption, I guess. A fairly easy diagnosis to obtain if you really want it.

It could account for the tiredness and the weight loss. If I had any friends to be worried about me, it wouldn't be out of the question to suggest an eating disorder. But it's not that. I just seem to get full very quickly.

It wasn't until the sickness and indigestion that I managed to heave myself to a doctor.

That was a couple of weeks ago.

Today's trip is not to my usual doctor. I'm off to the health centre on Parsons Green to discuss my blood-work results or something.

Whatever. Half a day at work, I'll talk about blood and bile and the years of acidity. I'll even talk about the bloody tar I left in the toilet this morning.

At least I'm not in that office staring at another file about human resources violations.

The sky is that British autumnal grey that somehow still blinds you if you look at it for too long. I feel the cold even more with my recent weight loss, and my thick coat feels heavier and harder to hold up.

For some reason I lift a hand to wave to the cripple across the road.

He manages to judder his head in response and continues with his daily workout.

The journey during the day is so different from how it will be tonight. The champagne bar will be full of fitted suits and briefcases. The tube will have crowds coming out of it with their heads up trying to locate the trendiest hang-out, rather than drones flooding into it, their heads down, hoping not to avoid eye-contact with anyone so early in the day. The pub on the corner will be bursting with people who won't sound out of place saying 'hoo-rah' and 'by Jove'. The actual Green will be alive with costume and celebration and tricking or treating. And I'll be kneeling in the middle.

Invisible.

The woman on reception is overweight. And old. Her hair is curly and purple. She doesn't say hello or ask how she can help me. She leaves me standing in front of her at the counter until she has finished tapping away at her keyboard, like she has something more important to deal with. That I'm inconveniencing her in some way, because I'm early. I'm always early.

She lifts her eyes up to me after clicking *Send*, as if to say, 'What do *you* want?'

'Lily Kane,' I say, as if she should know I'm coming. 'Nine thirty?' I prompt.

She exhales, disgruntled, and taps something into her computer.

'I'm here to pick up some results.' I don't need to give her this information; I'm just trying to reach her on some personal level.

'Take a seat. The doctor will be out shortly.' And she drops her head back down to let me know she has finished.

It isn't long before I'm taken into one of the sterile

rooms. Three white walls, one of glass. A doctor sits down behind a desk. It doesn't matter what he looks like, it doesn't matter how he sounds; all that matters is his words.

'How long?' I ask him, looking straight through his head.

'Not long. Months, maybe. No more than a year.'

I think about the invalid snailing around the block and just how lucky he is.

How I wish I could be like him.

I'm sure the doctor's wording is sensitive, his tone sympathetic, but it's not important.

I hear him say *stomach*, I register *cancer*. Then all I get is, 'You're going to die. You're screwed. That's it. All done.'

Next.

Whether or not we spoke about possible care options from that point is of no interest. If I called the blob at reception a bitch on my way out, it is of no consequence.

Months, maybe.

No longer than a year.

Walking round the block won't help.

Dazed, I wander out through the doors, across the road and onto the Green. I'm aware of my surroundings but unaware of where I am heading. On one triangle of grass a red setter fights playfully with a Labrador. The woman walking with a pram stops and looks on nervously, protective. The man on the bench reading his tabloid newspaper doesn't flinch.

I continue my dizzy jaunt, not veering off-line. I pass an oak tree on my right as I ease through the crossroads where I'll eventually be found.

Emerging out the other side of the green I see a man fishing around in the parking meter chute for change.

Behind him is a poster that says, 'Does God exist?' It has three possible boxes to tick. Yes, No and Maybe. Below, in blue, it states: 'Explore the meaning of life.'

Before I realise I've even digested this, I'm sitting inside St Dionis Church, praying for a miracle.

So, when the person on the pew in front of me turns around and tells me that they can help, I don't even ask how. I just agree to meet at the oak tree tonight at seven o'clock.

Hours maybe.

No longer than a day.

January

❖

'I'm sure it was just a coincidence, Jan.'

Back at the station, Paulson tries to rationalise what I saw, what I felt. I sense Murphy roll his eyes. Things are still sore between us since his disastrous lapse in allegiance during the Eames case, when he foolishly thought I might be the culprit. It's better, but still not the same.

I feel like I have to lower the level of my voice so that Murphy can't hear me. I don't want him listening in and reporting back my misguidances and mistakes. I don't want to make it easy for him to spy on me.

I tap Paulson's shoulder with my right hand, urging him to turn his back on Murphy, who is over at a filing cabinet pretending to do something.

'It wasn't what I saw. It was just that something struck me as she fell. It was like a kick in the chest, like some - thing pushed me backwards as I blew out the candle.' I pause to note his reaction. He looks at me as if to say *Go on*. I feel a need to fill the silence but I can't tell him about The Two that visited me last night. Not yet.

'I can't explain it just yet, but there is something more to this case, Paulson. We need to find out what it is.'

I recognise the look he gives me. He knows how uninterested I've been in my recent caseload; that I'm almost longing for another big case I can completely submerse myself in.

To distract me.

To stop me thinking about Audrey.

To prevent me from looking further into the journals.

I want to learn. But I don't want to become my mother.

'Well,' he responds reluctantly, 'we need to wait for the post-mortem results to come back. See if it can shed any light on what happened.'

But the only thing the autopsy will tell us is that she had stomach cancer at a stage that was completely inoperable and not even worth fighting. It will show that she took a sharp blow to the throat before she was stabbed, making it impossible to scream or draw breath.

It will not tell me why she was killed or who may have done it.

It will not explain what I felt as she keeled over. That this is something we have never encountered before. That we need to be looking at this in a way that will not please our superiors. That we cannot just rely on visual, tangible evidence; we cannot go simply by the book. Some things are not written in the book; some things cannot be seen.

'What we need to do is be detectives.' I raise my voice, suddenly angry, but Paulson keeps his cool. This type of thing has been happening more frequently of late, gradually loosening my grip on control, constantly test - ing Paulson's allegiance.

'We need to readdress the issue tomorrow, Jan. It's late. There's nothing more we can do tonight.' He places a comforting hand on my shoulder. I shrug it off as if he's patronising me, but he's not; Paulson is genuine.

I don't want to finish the conversation. I don't want to enter into anything with Murphy. Increasingly it seems that he is deliberately trying to come up with the most outrageous solutions to cases; to show me that he is embracing the medium that gives me my edge; that has provided me with extra insight and information. Pretending he believes. Entrapping me.

I leave the office without another word. My partners are stunned into inactivity. Paulson just wants to help. Murphy debates going over my head for a second time.

With a half-empty bottle of Glenlivet, fifteen-year, between my legs, I drive out of the station heading for I don't know where. I'm not going to drink it. It is there as my comfort blanket. My reward. My companion.

My mind tells me I should go home; maybe some sleep will do me good.

It's the best option.

So I don't take it.

Instead, I make my way back to Parsons Green. To the crime scene. Hoping I will pick up on something I missed earlier.

It's dead now. The pubs are closed, the frivolities have ceased and the square is now plunged into darkness. The street lamps around the Green only illuminate the road. I find a space outside the church to squeeze my car into, between a Mercedes and a Porsche. In fact, all of the cars along this road appear to be of this calibre. My Ford Mondeo looks somewhat out of place.

With the church irradiating the sky behind me, I cross over the precipice into the black of the common ahead. It is dimly lit but I can make out the intersecting pathways. The area is taped off and a handful of officers are still hanging round the scene ensuring nothing gets disrupted. It's cold but not the cold I felt before. This is more literal. I take a large gulp of my whisky before entering the park to keep me warm, taking me closer to the driving limit. Numbing me quicker than the air's chill.

The vibe is different.

I walk along each path in turn, hoping to glean information from feelings alone. Wanting to recreate the sensation I experienced as the first victim dropped to a place worse than death in front of my eyes only hours ago.

When I blew her over.

I walk from one end to the other several times. From the pub to the main road and back again. Diagonally from the health centre to the coffee shop two hundred yards opposite. From the all-girls' school back to the church.

It's over.

Whatever force was here earlier is not here now. At least, I can't sense it.

I'm taking a top-down approach that only considers the intangible. I'm thinking of the vision of the two children, I'm dwelling on the victim's body falling as I blew out the candle. I'm entrusting the part of me I resisted on the last case; putting too much faith in it. And I know that I shouldn't.

I should be working a bottom-up technique, trying to profile the killer, asking what happened at this crime scene. What type of person could have committed such an act? What kind of personality would this killer possess? Was it planned? The other information, the things that only I see, they should be used to support the real police work. I realise that, but I'm too busy avoiding reality to implement what I know to be true.

There are no eyewitness testimonies, probably no CCTV. I'm falling back on the esoteric because I should have used it to crack the last case sooner. I can't afford these mistakes.

I sit on a bench near the centre of the park, staring at the spot where Lily Kane's life was taken, and think of nothing.

Dropping into a drowsy emptiness I concede that tomorrow I will have to revert back to regular police work to solve this. Interviewing work colleagues and questioning the drunkards who were nearby when she was slain. Obtaining CCTV footage. Looking into any crimes reported that may match this for the rest of the country; Europe, even. Has there been anything similar in the past?

The tension in my shoulders drops as I give in to my lack of power and my eyelids increase in weight. Like a drunk with nowhere to go, I spend the night on a bench. To me, it's the same as going back to that empty house.

In the morning I can attempt to be a real detective again. A real person.

But it won't get me anywhere. I'm not in the right frame of mind yet. I'm still heading downwards.

The only thing I feel can snap me out of this lull is for Celeste to take another life.

That's her Christmas present to me.

My wake-up call.

V

Today is the same as any other.

I bound up the final four flights of stairs, expending the last ounce of energy after my regular five-mile morning run. Pushing myself.

I pass my neighbour in the corridor.

'Morning, Gail.' I smile at her.

She nods and smiles back in recognition but we both continue past each other.

The weekend newspaper is rolled up and resting on my doormat for when I return.

I don't look at it straight away.

Once inside the sanctity of my own flat, I close my eyes and take three long inhalations, forcing the air back into my lungs. I feel healthy.

As I walk to the kitchen I roll the rubber band down the tube of newspaper so that I can open it out flat and lay it on the worktop. I gulp down the bottle of water I have stored in the fridge; two of my back teeth let me know I've neglected them, and I wince with the pain.

Resting my hands either side of the newspaper, I push my feet back to stretch out my calf muscles, and start to digest the morning news.

The front page is shocking.

A simple line graph depicts the increase in knife crime

in the capital over the last ten years. Usually, in cases such as this, the paper shows a recent picture of the victim supplied by a family member, or even an old school photograph, but this girl, Lily Kane, gets a graph. Ten black dots joined by a blue line.

I read on.

I know the pub that is mentioned. And the church. There is a slight allusion to some kind of ritualism, but the authorities believe that the paraphernalia found near the victim was mostly likely left there as part of the Halloween celebrations in the area.

It angers me.

I stop reading. I stop stretching.

It just seems like another innocent victim of a random stabbing incident. Whatever emotions are starting to build within me are neutralised by the endorphins coursing through me from the exercise.

I pace into the living room and take a breath of the cold air out the window.

And calm myself.

This isn't right but there is nothing I can do about it.

Not yet.

Not this time.

I have to leave it alone until the Lord tells me otherwise.

Yule
December 2008

Totty

⊰•⊱

They all thought I'd die of a broken heart.

I thank God I never brought the grandkids with me this time.

But maybe that would have saved me.

I might not have been chosen.

I'm here for my wife today. She is the reason I've made the trip from East to Central London.

My Pats loved the West End. Musicals, mainly, but she'd drag me here for plays or some jazz pianist she fancied seeing.

'Most of the galleries are free, Reg,' she'd say, her way of enticing me.

She was the only one who ever used my real name, Reginald. Reg. Everyone else called me Totty, on account of my job as a totter in the East End during the war.

Nobody has called me Reg for four years.

She made me promise I'd still come over this way when she was gone. And I have. Every month. Today is the last time, though.

I get out at Charing Cross because the stairs lead straight up to Trafalgar Square, which is right in the middle of where I want to be. The day is all mapped out. Start at the National Portrait Gallery. It's free. Just as Pats would've wanted it. Then on to St Martin-in-the-Fields to hear some live music, and on to a place for lunch with a decent selection of whisky.

I've picked up a ticket for the latest camp musical too, but, come the curtain call, my seat will be empty. And it will remain vacant. I'll be slumped over in the middle of the square, the hole in my heart bigger than the day Pats passed on.

It should be easy for the kids to remember, though. The same day their mum died.

Well, the same date. It's a few years apart.

It's not like I could ruin Christmas any more.

January

✦

I thought about getting a Christmas tree, brighten the place up a little, but what am I going to do, buy myself a present, wrap it up and put it under the tree to open on my own Christmas morning? I can't even remember if I was still with Audrey last Christmas; time is somewhat blurred.

Things are starting to dry up in the Lily Kane case; no new evidence is coming to the fore. For a nation apparently under constant CCTV supervision, the cameras surrounding the area where Lily Kane was killed have proved as fruitless as all other lines of enquiry. Hours of footage of shop-fronts, pavements, tree-blocked views of the Green, not to mention the amount of cameras that aren't even filming – their presence acting only as a deterrent.

And there's only so many times you can ask her colleagues what kind of a person she was. Her upstairs neighbour was resistant, a possible suspect after we found pictures of him on her laptop, but his girlfriend provided a solid alibi for his whereabouts that night.

The team is stranded. Stagnated. We are at a point where it feels like waiting. Waiting for another murder instead of trying to solve this one. But that is not the case. And I know I'm being scrutinised from all directions. It's like my success affords me a great deal of leniency while somehow putting me under even greater pressure.

It's not always straightforward to profile a killer from one victim. I wonder whether Lily Kane is actually the start of something, or if it ends with her. I question whether this murderer has a plan to take another victim, so that I have something to do over the festive period, something to take my mind off my life. I want to work. I don't want to sit in a leather snuggler chair, built for two, all by myself, drinking Scotch or wine or beer until I pass out. I don't want to be that person.

I don't want to be the person who wishes death on an innocent human either, but, occasionally, in moments of despair, it can seem like the only way I'm going to get any better.

Lily Kane was not a hedonistic killing. There was no sense of anything sexual and the ritualism points to a more mission-oriented murderer – the victim was targeted, chosen specifically as unworthy of the life they were leading. If I'm right, we can catch this person before they do too much damage.

But the ritualism, the links with faith, they scare me. The last thing we need is a visionary – someone acting on voices in their head instructing them to kill. At random.

At this moment, there is not enough to go on to err on either side of the psychopathic fence.

My eyes are heavy. I try to focus on the tumbler of whisky in my hand, but there seems to be a haze hovering above the glass, which confuses me. I try to open my eyes wider to stare through it but they close instead. My chin drops to my chest. I breathe in and out through my nose for a few seconds, trying to summon the strength to pull myself out of this habit I am forming.

I yawn. A dense, lengthy yawn that pushes my head away from my chest briefly as my chin presses down hard with the force of my fatigue. The saliva in my mouth thins out and I dribble over my crotch. Tears start to form in my eyes and drop onto my legs.

I can't stop any of it.

The dribbling.

The tears.

I'm not sure I even want to any more.

Silently, I cry myself into something similar to sleep and my grip releases the glass of alcohol, spilling it into my already damp lap and jerking me back upright.

Into the darkness.

Onto the dust.

And I wait for the sound of shuffling feet.

But it doesn't come.

I hear the sound of a bell ringing.

The circle of candles ignites to my left. But the boy is not inside this time. Then, to my right, the girl's flames switch on. But she is not inside either.

Where are they?

A small bell tinkles again and a new circle of burning wicks appears to my left, forming a triangle. It rings again and, to my right, another circle materialises, forming a large square in front of me.

Still, I am the only one here.

All is silent. Four circles flicker as I wait for The Two.

Suddenly, the flames bow down, pointing forwards in my direction as if somebody opened a giant door in front of me.

Like someone has just been let in.

They're here.

A line starts to illuminate from all four clusters of light, moving diagonally towards the centre, slowly edging to a common meeting point where the boy shuffles from left foot to right, left foot to right.

I wait.

He stops moving, reaches into his pocket and produces a tiny bell on a blue ribbon. Holding his arm outstretched, perpendicular to his frail torso, he gives a sharp flick of the wrist to jingle the bell one more time.

And I start to rise.

Inside my protected tube, I lift off the floor, my legs still crossed. I levitate, higher and higher. The boy tilts his head upwards following me, his eyes now flashing through a range of colours. Higher and higher I climb; I don't panic. I feel safe in here. Nothing can get in. Nothing can get out.

He rings the bell again and I stop.

Now that I am about a hundred feet in the air, the boy looks almost helpless.

In the distance, as before, a speck of light appears. This time growing quicker, like a white sun rising in the distance. A shadow appears in front of the growing semi-circle.

The girl.

And she is running. She is running extremely quickly. As fast as she was spinning in my previous vision of her. Within seconds she seems to have covered miles of ground.

She is a blur but I know it is her.

As she nears, I start to lower, descending into a smell of damp pine. The boy's flashing eyes stalking me as I drop in height.

The girl gets closer, extinguishing some of the candles

as she passes with the breeze she is creating. Still, her identity is hidden behind a haze.

At the same time, I hit the ground again, the boy still looking directly at me. The girl halts abruptly, momentum having no place in this realm; her hands move swiftly around the boy's chest so that both hands cover his heart.

They both fall back as blood starts to drench the front of the boy, some seeping from the corners of his mouth.

He becomes an outline.

Almost invisible.

They lie there, completely still, apart from the short intakes of breath from the boy.

She takes her right hand from his chest and waves a bloodied finger in front of her face. Wagging it from side to side. Her lips are puckered as if preparing for a kiss or starting to whistle.

The boy appears to be fighting sleep. The silhouette of his head drops as his eyes begin to close, then jerking back up and opening his eyes. The flashing has stopped. With each nod his weariness grows until he finally comes to rest.

And disappears completely.

The candles die out and the sunlight diminishes behind, plunging me into complete darkness once again.

It feels as though I have been holding my breath for a couple of minutes as I wait for a ball of fire or a bell ringing or a scream or the shuffle of tiny dancing feet in the dust.

But nothing comes.

Nothing startles me back to life.

I remain in the silent black for hours. This has never happened before.

I eventually wake up in the morning; the liquid spilled or cried or dribbled on my trousers has dried or evaporated, and stained.

I have been there all night.

It feels like I haven't slept at all.

Even in my drowsy state, I realise that this second meeting with The Two is forming a pattern. The circle of candles appeared both times. In the first instance creating a triangle, this time a square. Both visions included a herbal scent and a pin-prick of light that grew in menace. The drop in temperature is leading me to think that this next murder is planned to happen outside, just as it was with Lily, the first murder.

Yet this time I felt secure; I was not at risk.

The profile is building.

But my experience of the last case, when these visions began, directs my thoughts towards the ritualist aspects of the case. They steer me in the direction of the spirituality that surrounds Lily Kane's death.

I do not want Totty Fahey to die.

I don't want to find an old man slumped on his knees, dead and unnoticed in the centre of London.

But it is the one thing that can snap me out of this.

And clear my mind.

By filling me with guilt.

Celeste

I set up in the wrong place to begin with.

Whatever is guiding me towards these people sent me to a different crossroads.

Initially I feel drawn to the Charles Statue that connects Whitehall, the Strand and Northumberland Avenue. I have my cloth, candles, a bell and four sun discs to welcome in the solar rebirth on this, the shortest day.

Totty's shortest day.

I pace more frantically as time passes, and nobody shows. A sharp edge from the holly in my bag juts out and scratches my leg as I walk.

Where is he?

The commotion across the road becomes more palp - able and I realise I have made a mistake. This is not where I am supposed to be. I hoist the bag containing my elements over my shoulder and make a dash across the road towards the square.

I can't understand it. Why would it be here? Where is he?

I bound through Trafalgar Square. The artist on the podium is bleating about the excessive use of CCTV; a mass has congregated to humour him. I head straight to the steps that lead to the National Gallery and spring up to the top, two at a time.

I reach the top, out of breath, and spin around to take everything in. I can see the whole place from this point. The well-dressed man loitering behind me waves his hands, a newspaper tucked under his arms, and says something like 'The Bible is always right.'

This sentence jars me. My father was a Christian for a while, and then a Buddhist. Mother was Catholic her entire life. Both allowed me to find my own faith but encouraged me to learn about as many others as I could. No holy book is *always right*. Sometimes, even nature fights back. What is natural for one may not be for another.

I try not to listen to him.

He is clearly convinced he is the new Martin Luther King.

He continues: '. . . this is a house built on sand. These are not my words, these are God's words.' People passing roll their eyes at his articulate insanity.

A community support officer is looking on and joking with a tourist. He then stops a girl on a bike, telling her that she is not allowed to cycle on this pavement, she needs to walk her bicycle through this area.

This is the least of his problems tonight.

He's looking at all the wrong things.

I'm trying to find the right thing. The right person.

I scan the area below me, trying to block out the preacher.

'We need to build our house on a rock,' he shouts in staccato, to accentuate every word.

I breathe. Slow breaths.

One, two, three, breathe.

One, two, three, breathe.

And it becomes clear.

The four statues that pillar the square are almost aglow to me. General Napier, Major General Havelock, George IV and the ever-changing fourth plinth; they form four points that, when linked, make up a cross straight through the centre of Trafalgar Square. And standing on the point where all the lines meet is an old man.

There he is.

Totty

—◆—

I feel my age as everybody passes me on the stairs exiting Charing Cross tube. It's not even that many steps but I have to rest halfway up.

Things will be much easier when I'm dead.

I lean against the plinth that holds a statue of King George IV above me and breathe the fresh wintry air into my lungs to re-energise myself for the journey ahead.

The buildings all around the square shield it from the wind. Next to me, two heritage wardens are nattering to one another about a soap opera storyline while I pant and cough only three or four feet away.

They continue to gossip as a young girl springs off a bench ahead of me and attempts to catch a pigeon inside her jumper. At the front of the square where Nelson's Column stands, I see the bronze lions treated as an amusement park ride rather than anything artistic or iconic.

But the unofficial guardians of the square continue to gas about nothing important.

A young lad in a hooded top puts his head inside the lion's mouth while his girlfriend takes a photograph; another little vagrant feigns bestiality while three of his gang look on, pointing and laughing while the statue is raped.

It seems you can get away with anything these days.

I opt to take the path to the Portrait Gallery rather than tackle the steps in front of the National. Most of the time I just feel like I am getting in the way of people.

I don't even know what the feature is at the Portrait Gallery until I get there. Something about Pop Art, which I've never really got on with. I don't have much of an appreciation for paintings that I feel I could have done myself. Some look like scribbles that my grandkids give me to pin on my fridge. Maybe I just don't understand it. But it's what Pats would have wanted so I go with it.

At the ticket desk an intelligent-looking lady gives me a small booklet that explains some of the paintings, and asks if I'd like to do the audio tour. I shake my head. She then asks whether I would like a ticket to the room hosting the Photographic Portrait Prize.

'How much is that, then?' I ask, expecting the worst.

'Oh, it's only a pound. It helps to showcase the work of talented young photographers.'

I can't really say no to this. Not if it's *only* a pound.

She prints off my ticket and I head to the first room, unfolding my booklet as I move.

There are seven differently themed rooms. The first explains the origins, the second goes into the aspects of style, but my booklet shows two rooms that might actually be of interest. One dedicated to Pop Art and Film, the other is simply entitled *Marilyn*. It's not so much the art I'm interested in, I do that for Pats, but the film and Miss Monroe.

In the *Marilyn* room, I see a sculpture: three hangers hooked onto a pole, string tied to the hangers draping almost to the floor, and some twisted wire on the ground next to it.

I can't understand what this is doing here. I look at the literature I was given when I entered. It says something about the tragedy of fame and how it consumes everything it touches. But I can't understand why it's a portrait.

I turn my head to the left to ask Pats what this is all about. I still do this from time to time. It makes me sadder on each occasion.

I miss her the most.

It seems like the best time to leave. I don't bother with the photography display.

When I leave there's a sign strategically placed to make you feel guilty that it's a London attraction without a cost. It suggests a £3.50 donation.

And that angers me.

Surely it would be easier to charge that small amount to get in. If they had a blank donation box I would have put something in, but I won't have someone telling how much I should give to be reminded that I am alone and don't have my wife with me any more to explain the things I don't understand.

It's the same when I go over to St Martin-in-the-Fields. A lovely church, really, it is. Gorgeous. And I sit there for free watching a Korean lad play the piano beautifully. He looks so young I can't understand how he's learned to play so well. Some kind of prodigy.

But, as I leave, satisfied with my free afternoon of live classical music, a girl thrusts a red bucket into my face, shaking it so I can hear the change rattling around inside. A sticker on the front implies that £3.50 is the preferred amount.

I throw in a pound coin. That's the same amount I gave the gallery for the exhibition I didn't see.

I need a drink.

The walk to the whisky bar would take anyone else five minutes; for me it's more like twenty after I've pushed my way through the crowds that can't see an old man struggling. I treat myself to a Macallan Select Oak and a smoked salmon sandwich, which costs nearly the same amount as the steak that I really wanted but know I would never be able to finish.

This will be my last meal.

After a second, then a third drink, I notice how dark it is through the window. At first I think it might start to rain but it soon dawns that it's night-time. The clock behind the bar says 17.26.

How long have I been here?

Where has the day gone?

I knock back the last centimetre of Scotch and pay the Italian man lurking next to my table, waiting for me to leave, with cash. There is no suggested tip of £3.50 so I leave him with the change; about twelve per cent of the entire bill. He fetches my coat and helps me thread my arms through the appropriate holes so that I may be on my way.

The city noise hits me as quickly as the drop in temperature. I adjust my scarf so that it covers more of my neck. People ahead of me cross over the road, even though the light is still red, but a double-decker bus has stopped the traffic and they think it's safe. I wait until the light turns green again.

Trafalgar Square is more alive than earlier. I can sense the hubbub, it is packed with people trying to squeeze the most out of the last few hours of the weekend. Lit high above the crowded streets is a platform. A man in a bowler hat with a giant mirror stands on top, reading out the pages of a Sunday broadsheet. He then angrily tears it into pieces, throwing it out over his audience like confetti, and delivers a speech that is meant to inspire thought or spark questioning.

Another free exhibition.

I gravitate towards the gathering horde.

Snailing closer to my death.

I enter the square from the other side, passing the statue of General Charles James Napier, and continue towards one of the fountains. There is a bustle of different voices at ground level discussing the performer on the platform above them. In the distance, atop the steps, a middle-aged man in a suit is waving a rolled-up newspaper, preaching about the Bible, trying to drown out his oratory rival.

I stop in the middle of the square so that I can flit my attention between both of them and lose a little more time as darkness descends even further.

As I turn around to take a look at the Christmas tree, the blade rips through my heart. At first it feels cold, then excruciatingly hot. I can't make a sound as my throat fills with blood. The hustle of the crowd transforms into a perpetual hum that seems to slow everything down and I swear that everybody turns away from the performances to watch me drop to my knees.

Then the hum dissipates and all is silent.

I see a light in front of me and a woman's face.

I want it to be Pats, but it's not.

The last thing I sense is somebody kneeling in front of me telling me to 'Ssh' as they light another candle.

And I know this is the end.

I say my final words and prepare myself.

We'll be together soon, Pats.

And then, all is black.

V

I've extended my morning run to six miles. I can also spring up five flights of stairs in my building at the end now. I hit the button on my stopwatch as I touch the last step, and take in several short breaths, slowing slightly with each one. Regaining my composure.

I keep moving, walking confidently down the corridor, preventing lactic-acid build-up in my leg muscles. My body feels flush with heat now that I am not jogging, and suddenly I notice my perspiration.

As always, the paper is rolled up on my doorstep, wrapped in plastic, fastened with an elastic band. Gail exits her flat at the end of the corridor, dropping her keys on the floor twice before double-locking her front door. She looks flustered this morning.

'Everything all right, Gail?' I ask.

'Oh God, it's just one of those Mondays already, I think,' she responds, continuing her walk as she fishes around for something in her bag. 'Bloody nightmare,' she mutters, trotting off to the stairs.

I laugh knowingly as I reach down for the newspaper, keeping my legs straight in case they buckle beneath me, stretching my hamstrings.

I take the key out of the zipped pocket of my hooded training top. My hands are shaking, perhaps a result of the cold weather, more likely to be adrenalin or perhaps exhaustion. It takes some effort not to mirror my neighbour's early-morning incompetence.

A wave of heat whacks me in the face as I enter the flat. I've overcompensated for the weather and left the radiators on far too high. It's difficult to breathe in through my nose, and my mouth feels like I've been feasting on walnuts.

Deciding that air is more important than liquid at this stage, I pace over to the window and lift it open, poking my head outside to suck in the winter. Below, I see Gail spill out onto the street, her head down, not looking where she is going, still rummaging through her bag.

My fingers crack as I interlock them and stretch them high above my head. As my top rises with the reach towards the ceiling, the cold from outside hits my stomach, refreshing me further.

I strip.

Kicking off my trainers without untying the laces, pulling down my tracksuit bottoms and underwear in one swift move, wrenching up my hooded top and T-shirt with equal efficiency, I stand in front of the draught, my sweat drying almost instantly. I don't think anyone can see me. I don't care.

Leaving my clothes in a pile on the living-room floor, I head naked into the kitchen with my paper. I roll off the elastic band, as I always do, take off the plastic, roll it out flat on the side, as I always do, and leave it while I turn to the fridge.

Today I take the grapefruit juice out and drink straight from the carton. Things like this don't matter when you live on your own, when you are alone. Then, as I always do, I turn back to the work surface, plant my hands either side of the paper and extend my legs to warm down the muscles I have been using.

It's happened again.

The front page tells the story of another murder. This time an old man, Totty Fahey, eighty-two years of age.

My skin goose-pimples and I close my eyes for a second so I don't have to fully digest it.

The article continues, he was stabbed through the heart in the middle of Trafalgar Square, the police are finding it difficult to round up any witnesses. Apparently people walked right by the dead pensioner, initially believing it to be part of one of the performances; ignoring his life. The police are going to examine footage of the day.

I swap positions to stretch my left leg.

A candle and four sun talismans were found arranged in front of the body, hinting at the possibility of a connection to the Lily Kane murder almost two months ago.

My cold, naked body starts to rise in temperature as I become angrier.

I drop to my knees on the tiled floor and say a prayer.

A prayer for Totty.

A prayer for humanity.

And one for myself.

This has to stop. I ask the Lord for some answers. I ask him if there is anything I can do.

I kneel in silence, my hands still pressed together. Waiting.

And he answers.

I need to paint my spare room white.

January

I knew where I would find the victim.
I knew it would be here.

Not at the time, but it makes sense now. Something clicks when I hear the words *Trafalgar Square*. I imme-diately think of the shape formed by the candles and kick myself for not imagining this place. It just seems too public. But maybe that is the killer's hallmark, maybe it is a taunt aimed at the police or possibly just at me; they want to show how much smarter they are than us.

The location of the murder, more specifically, the distance in comparison to the first, changes the profile to more of a visionary thrill-seeker but the careful con-struction of the scene points away from that. They are somehow planned yet random. Something already tells me the CCTV footage will be a waste of manpower. Again. I get it checked anyway.

I associate the candle circles with the four plinths; I relate my own elevated position in the dream with the height of Nelson's Column overlooking the square. It may be correct, I may be forcing connections onto the scene that aren't really there. I still have little comprehension of The Two but it appears their message is not the same as The Smiling Man's. They are not trying to inform me how the victim will perish, it seems they are telling me where.

The centre of the square is taped off but it's difficult to keep the people away.

Now they want to look.

Now they notice.

The candle still burns.

The old man is kneeling on the centre stone of the square, dead, but balanced perfectly. His flat cap is still sitting on his head, his scarf wrapped snugly around his neck, his arms dangling by his side in his warm raincoat, his hands bloodied, knuckles just touching the concrete.

He faces the steps that lead to the National Gallery. A middle-aged man at the top feels it is still appropriate to continue airing his thoughts about the state of mankind.

'What colour is the truth? What gender is a principle?' he trills.

'Murph, you have to go and shut that guy up. Get him out of here.' I order Murphy over there so I can clear my head. A big part of me still doesn't want him around.

Paulson arrives with his notepad and pen at the ready, his eyes scrunched slightly in contemplation.

'Nothing, Jan.' He shrugs, deflated. 'How could no-body see anything?' he asks rhetorically, then continues, 'A waiter in the whisky bar said he left half his meal, had a few drinks but was alone the entire time. Their cameras film outside the bar, some of the road, but the statues block the view of the centre of the square from that height. Fucking useless.' He shakes his head in dismay and mutters something under his breath about it being a waste of time.

Perhaps the killer is purposely performing to large crowds because he knows it will skew eyewitness testimony. People often fill in the gaps of their memories, they fabricate part of their recollection of events. With a crowd this size, stories would differ so much that we wouldn't know which was truth and which was hyperbole.

Yet, apparently, nobody saw a thing.

This killer is a contradiction.

Paulson strolls over to me despondently and places his faithful notepad back in his inside jacket pocket. I nod my head at him, motioning to follow me around to the front of the body.

He lifts the tape above his head, plods over to where I am waiting and we both squat to the same level as the victim. We can talk discreetly here.

'This is a series,' I confirm in a hush.

'Looks that way, Jan. Looks that way.' He peers around, distracted, as camera lights flash behind our barricade, still bemused that this went unnoticed for so long.

'Another hugely public place,' I continue.

'Close to another major holiday,' Paulson adds.

'Another series.' I rub my hand against the stubble that has emerged on my chin over the course of the day. 'Already.' Echoing Paulson, I shake my head in disbelief, knowing the work that goes into serial crimes. But secretly I'm pleased to have this, to be away from the one-offs and the lack of challenge that comes with having proof or witnesses or clear motive.

It's not exactly the same. Yes, the candle is lit in front of the old man but the pewter candlestick has been placed on an ice-white cloth. The four black stones have been replaced by four other stones carved into sun shapes. They are positioned around the inside of the salt circle in exactly the same way, forming a square. A silver bell sits next to the candle stick – there are no fingerprints.

The candle still burns.

I have an idea.

'I need to try something,' I tell Paulson.

'What?' he asks.

'Just wait here, I need someone to see this.'

Paulson notes the excitement in my eyes and is anxious. He grabs my shoulder as I start to edge forwards.

'Jan, what are you doing?' I know he's worried but that isn't my concern.

'Trust me.' I shrug his hand off. 'Just watch.'

I picture the girl in my vision and I realise that she doesn't want me to do this either.

But I have to know.

I move forward further, dropping into a crawl, creeping cautiously towards the corpse. My arms are shaking as I slowly close in on the subject. As I arrive, I look back over my shoulder at Paulson and exaggerate an exhalation so that he perceives my anxiety.

I turn back to the front. Nelson's Column towers over us in the background, drowning us in shadow. I count in my head. My eyes closed. My head bobbing with each passing second.

One, one thousand.

Two, one thousand.

Three, one thousand.

And I blow out the flame.

Celeste

—◆—

Is it easier to take the life of someone you know is already dying?

Or somebody who has led a long and full life?

Does it make the task any simpler if you believe they no longer wish to exist or that they would give their own life for somebody else?

Everybody dies.

I look back at Lily Kane and more recently to Totty Fahey and I still can't say whether one was more deserving than the other. Everything is circular. Death does not mean the end in the same way that life does not always mean the beginning. They walked on this Earth and will walk again on the days when our two realms overlap.

I did not take from them; this is what people will not understand. I gave them more. A chance. The oppor-tunity not to be condemned to darkness. I did not approach Lily Kane in the church proposing an easy way out; I offered her the chance of salvation. I was with her when she passed. Not everybody can comprehend, but Lily knows. She realises that I was her saviour.

The old man is conscious of this same fact.

I was present in their greatest moment of need, their most desperate of times.

*

It's too late to rescue myself.
   But I saved them.
   And I can save more.

January

---❖---

He didn't drop.

When I extinguished the flame in front of the kneeling, dead body of the old man, Totty Fahey, he stayed as he was.

The kneeling, dead body of an old man.

But I changed.

I thought he would collapse in the same way Lily Kane had. I believed that my actions had some kind of intrinsic impact on the scene, that I was part of the ritual. I allowed my confusion over these visions to affect the way I compute a crime scene. I permitted the death of my parents and my wife's betrayal to cloud my judgement. I bought into the spirituality too much.

My focus has returned.

Blowing out the candle snapped me back to reality. The focus of the investigation should be the tangible evidence: the crime scene, the victims, building an accurate profile of this killer. The visions of The Two, the faith behind these slayings, the non-material, mystic aspects should only be used as a guide, as support for what is real.

Myself, Paulson and Murphy are busy collecting any information we can, and I have assembled another team to run through the CCTV footage from the numerous cameras around the square where Totty was stabbed through the chest.

A young, enthusiastic constable enters the office and informs me that Higgs has picked something up from the tapes. I'm not certain who Higgs is but I follow him down the corridor, Paulson and Murphy in tow.

A bank of four monitors line one wall with various recording equipment dotted between. Three officers are seated and waiting anxiously in front of one screen which has a paused image of a crowded Trafalgar Square.

'We can see the victim here,' Higgs points at Totty near the bottom of the picture, 'looking in the opposite direction to everyone else – up at the column, towards the surrounding statues. Everyone else is either watching the crackpot at the top of the steps or the performer on the plinth with his mirror and broadsheet.'

He swivels around to ensure I can pick out everything he is explaining.

'This is several seconds before he is attacked.'

Then he presses play.

And we watch, holding our breath.

'Wait!' I push closer to the screen, resting my hands on the back of Higgs' chair and leaning over his shoulder. 'What the fuck was that? Where did he go? Go back. Go back.'

Higgs rewinds to the point where Totty was alive and we watch the clip again.

The old man is visible. There is a flash of light, a flare, like sunlight hitting a camera lens, only this was at night, then he is gone. On his knees, hidden by the crowd. We can't even see the crowd moving around him before the image is distorted to see which direction the killer comes from.

'What is it? A bad tape?' I ask, confused. Concerned.

'We think it may be some kind of inopportune reflection from the performer's mirror,' another of the constables explains.

'Inopportune is right. Fuck.' I step back from the chair and push my hair backwards in frustration. 'Can we enhance the image in the mirror? Will that give us anything?'

Higgs says that they can try that but it is the next part of the video that is interesting.

With the old man stooped out of sight I focus on the crowd surrounding him who continue to be transfixed by the show. Towards the top of the screen there is movement in the crowd as someone quickly darts away from the spot where Totty draws his final breath, crashing into several spectators on his way.

Higgs pauses the video again and points at the figure.

'I recognised him as Jackson Forster. He's been done for theft, GBH, drugs. He disappears down to Charing Cross tube with someone. We checked the time stamp on the CCTV and the idiot used his wife's Oyster card around a minute later.'

'Good work . . .' I pause.

'Higgs, sir. Constable Higgs.'

'Good work, Higgs. I take it you have an address for me?' He hands me a piece of paper with the details. 'Keep it up, lads. Keep going through these tapes. See if we can pick something up from another angle.'

And I walk out, heading straight for my car.

'Morning, Mrs Forster. Is Jackson home at the moment?'

I'm on my own at the front of the house. Paulson and

Murphy are watching the rear and side in case he makes a run for it.

'Who's asking?'

She is young, mid-twenties, and artificially pretty. That synthetic beauty where her tan is not real, her natural chestnut hair is dead from peroxide and her adequate eyelashes are hidden beneath such fakery that her make-up level appears moderate. She is petite, her breasts are hoisted up too high and I've seen this kind of attitude before.

He's definitely here.

'Is Jackson at home today, Mrs Forster?' I remain polite.

She steps forward and pulls the door in close behind her saying, 'No. He's not in. I'm not even sure he'll be back today. Do you want to leave a message?'

I roll my eyes and reach into my pocket to produce my ID. Before I take it out, Murphy shouts from the side of the house. I push past the diversionary bimbo and step into the hallway. The kitchen is to the right. I turn left into the lounge, which smells like sandalwood joss sticks masking marijuana. I pace through the adjoining dining area, which is clearly never used for dining as there are two mattresses pushed into the corner with a screwed-up ball of a quilt tossed on top. Turning right I am now behind the kitchen in another hallway that leads to a downstairs toilet where Jackson Forster's legs are hang - ing from the window, his torso outside being gripped by DS Murphy.

I grab his belt for leverage and yank him back into the room, hitting his head on the window frame. He slumps to the cold tiles beneath me.

'Are we done?'

He looks up at me and nods.

Murphy and Paulson join me on the three-seat sofa in the lounge. It has a hideous brown swirling effect and the material seems to be of a similar pile to the burgundy carpet it doesn't quite match. The springs are shot and we each sink low into the cushion. Jackson sits on the corresponding single-seater opposite, which looks to have been dragged out of a brick-dust-filled skip. His wife perches on the arm, straddling it in her loose-fitting, grey, dancer's tracksuit bottoms. Paulson can't help but stare at her chest.

I tell him straight that we know where he was at the time Totty Fahey was stabbed through the chest, that we have video footage of him exiting Trafalgar Square, that we can track him on the tube, that we know he met someone at Charing Cross.

And he looks relieved.

'Babe, get the bag.' He rests his hand on his wife's thigh and sits back into his armchair smiling.

She returns with a black bin-liner and hands it to me. There are eight different wallets and purses in there all belonging to different people.

'Look, I was there that day. I can't deny that. You got me on that but I wasn't there to kill nobody.' His initial arrogance fading.

He was pick-pocketing. The area was ripe for the taking that day. That's why we can clearly see him bumping into people.

He's small-time.

A nobody, waste-of-space crook.

'But I might've seen something that night. Yeah. Yeeeaaah. If we can forget this wallet business I might've seen something that night which could help you guys out.' He all but licks his lips.

'Go on.' I say this knowing that I don't want to strike a deal, I don't even care that much about taking him in for the thefts, I have bigger things on my mind.

He does go on. And on.

And on.

Describing nobody and everybody. Generic. Average. Cliché.

It's obvious he's lying, even to Murphy.

We are not looking for a man with a normal build. A man with blondish-brown hair. A man of around six feet in height, it was difficult to tell because he was kneeling down.

We are not even looking for a man at all.

We don't know this yet.

We don't realise that we should not be looking at the top of the screen at the commotion on the CCTV footage, we should be scouring for a woman on the steps at the National. We should spot her weaving through the crowd towards Totty Fahey.

What we do know is that Jackson Forster is lying.

That this is a dead end.

That we still have a long way to go.

But I am in the right mindset now. And I'm taking Jackson in regardless.

Imbolc
February 2009

Talitha

❖

I shouldn't have lived this long, anyway. The doctors said it would be a miracle to get to thirty. I've had an extra three years already.

So my family have been prepared since I arrived.

It should be easier for them to let me go.

But you can't be prepared for this ending.

My parents weren't even ready in the beginning.

I was born very early. Two months early, in fact. So I didn't have a nursery painted, or a Moses basket or clothing or a bottle or a blanket. They were waiting until the last minute so they had enough money saved.

I ruined that.

It's the reason I'm different.

The reason I'm so grateful.

I've heard that Crohn's disease is pretty popular with us. By 'us' I mean premature babies; calling us preemies doesn't make it cute, but I've never had any trouble in that area. My issue is with my heart. It's ill-formed, or something. A hole in a ventricle or an atrium or both. Something like that. Something that doesn't matter any more because I can't change it. Something I no longer talk about.

I'd already had two major medical procedures and was only allowed out of my plastic housing three weeks before when I was originally due to arrive into the world.

Dad changed my name at the last minute to Talitha because it means *little girl*. I would have been Alice if I'd have been on time. If I'd have weighed a little more.

If anyone is brave enough to ask me about it I simply tell them, 'My heart beats too fast so I'll only live half as long as you.' This usually makes them feel suitably uncomfortable so I tend to follow it up with, 'But it means I'll always stay skinny.'

I'm the only one who ever laughs at that.

Mum always tells me I'm too full of whimsy. She says I should take my condition more seriously.

That it should define me.

But, for me, life is great. I have a much clearer idea than most when it will all end, so I appreciate each day, hour, minute that I have. And that's why I want to share this feeling. It's the reason I preach. It's the reason I tell anyone I can that there's so much more to it.

I throw out a cliché like, 'You don't know how lucky you are.' Maybe something obvious like, 'You don't have to do that job if you choose not to.' Or I'll hit them with, 'You could be dead tomorrow, and I probably will be.'

If I said that today, it would be true.

I don't mind being dead. I knew it was coming.

I would have chosen a different way.

I'm just glad I had passed on before the fire.

January

◆

With the case gathering more weight as a possible series of murders, my own kudos within the station grows. I'm being left alone. Something of an expert. Somehow, a genius.

So, if I don't shave or change my clothes, if they smell drink on my breath before lunch, if my eyes are bloodshot for days because I am afraid to close them for too long, it all gets overlooked. Because I've done this before.

Because, at work, they think I'm a success story.

But, of course, in my personal life, I'm nothing of the sort.

Everything I touch dies.

Everyone I am close to is taken.

Totty Fahey's death before Christmas did something to me. It sent me back so that I could move forwards.

I've had Paulson look into the victims' names, to see if there is any connection, any correlation.

There doesn't seem to be anything yet.

As I suspected, the killer is not stupid enough to be caught out by a shop-front or museum closed-circuit camera. The footage we have of either victim is, in the main, from earlier points in the day. We see Lily walk past the station early in the morning. She was captured at the hospital too, we knew that from her records, but there is nothing that covers the part of the Green where she was left to die on her knees.

We have watched the screen as Totty dawdles into the National Portrait Gallery, moseys over to the church and hobbles across the square into the bar where we had a witness confirm his presence that afternoon. But there were thousands of tourists and spectators for the plinth that evening. It was dark. We can spot him for a moment in the crowd but the brief reflection of light from the performance has affected cameras on all angles: even when we see him we cannot make out who is with him, then he is swallowed up by a crammed audience. Later in the evening we can pick him from the bunch, but by then he is on his knees and it is too late. Whoever was there with him has vanished undetected for now.

And Jackson Forster proved a wasted line of enquiry.

I thought that, perhaps, the way they were killed had some significance. Lily was stabbed through the stomach and Totty was hit through the chest, but there isn't much to go on here either.

One was a young woman, one an octogenarian male.

One, a newly qualified lawyer, the other, a retired rag-and-bone man.

Of course, there is always the possibility that these are just random people cut down for no other reason than the thrill of killing; that they are in the way of the wrong person at the wrong time. If that is so, it will make the perpetrator more difficult to trace.

Higgs and several others are correlating and comparing footage from both murders, trying to uncover an overlap; anybody who shows up in both locations.

I have Murphy running background checks on known acquaintances.

Legwork. Thankless.

Pointless.

He doesn't think I'm an expert or a genius, neither do the people he is helping to oust me, and he makes it obvious that, whoever is pulling his strings, he's not buying into the January David mythology. Whenever I see him I am reminded that the upper ranks could still be watching me, just like before, and my own success actually brings more pressure to solve this quickly. Two people have died already. Time is closing in. But we can't do it overnight. Some cases go unsolved for weeks, months, a year. Some, like my sister's, take longer. Many are never resolved.

I am interested in the aspects that people dismiss, the things they can't understand. The things they can't see or touch or test. Anyone could see the salt circles, the candles, the bell, the cloth, the piles of herbs, the antique silver. Anyone could see that both victims were found in a kneeling position and it's this kind of tangible evidence everyone else clings to, they want me to rely on it. So that I'm not such an embarrassment to the force. So I don't draw attention to myself for the wrong reasons. They want me to ignore the things I claim to see.

But is there some weight in the fact that Lily Kane's body went limp at the precise moment I blew out the candle? Is there a reason that Totty Fahey's did not?

Why should conventional detective work and unorthodox investigation be separate and exclusive?

I don't know it, but I am doing the right thing this time.

But The Two are trying to give me more.

What I don't see is more worthwhile than what I do see.

The things that we miss hold all the answers.

The things that are no longer there.

The signs.

The symbols.

The rituals.

Oh God, I'm starting to sound like Mother.

V

I do not hear a voice.

 I'm not insane.

But I know what the Lord wants me to do and I will oblige. It is not yet the time to put an end to the things that upset me in the newspapers. I have been told. Not with the words of man, that's not how it works.

Sometimes, when I pray, there is nothing. I can ask questions which are not answered. It may only be for my own sense of catharsis. When the communication is two-way, it is very different. As though extra information has been uploaded directly to my conscience, as if, all of a sudden, I have a greater knowledge without performing any work to obtain it.

The voice of the Lord communicates through my own inner voice.

This can be anything from ensuring I maintain physical fitness to volunteering at a homeless shelter to painting my spare room white.

The spare room hurt me.

 I hadn't used it for years.

 I hadn't even been in there.

 Who am I to question the Lord?

 The room is still pristine when I open the door, this

action like releasing the hermetically sealed box of trauma that is my past. When I was still Sammael Abbadon. When my wife still loved me and our child was still alive.

I cry a silent cry as the door to the compartment in my brain, the one that has been locked for as long as this room, opens. My mouth remains in a mid-yawn position, afraid to move and develop into a quiver. I don't even realise I am holding my breath.

I look across the room to where his cot stands in the corner, glowing white, as though dust is frightened to settle on it. There is a white sheet and blanket with two white stuffed animals at the top end, resting against the pure white bumper. My gaze remains fixed on this corner of innocence for I don't know how long.

I click back into reality as two tears drop in quick succession onto the exposed skin of my right foot and divert my attention from thoughts of my son.

The Lord knows I must be stronger than this.

I pan my view over to the right, where the chest of drawers stands, full of clothes that my son will never get to wear. On top is an unused keepsake box, some books I had hoped to read to him one day and a picture of the three of us the day he was born.

I tell myself, 'That is Sammael Abbadon with his family.'

I tell myself, 'That is not you.'

The walls are currently a sky blue colour; we knew it was a boy; we were prepared for that much. To paint these all white will take several coats. I stupidly glossed the radiator a similar shade. It took me days to do it before, and that was when I wanted to be in here.

But I do not question whether this will be worth the anguish.

I know that it will.

This is only the preparation.

Misery transforms into anger as I take the first step over the border between hallway and nursery. Anger. This is the only emotion that will get me through.

To give me the strength. The energy.

I head straight to the corner where the cot sits, the muscles and tendons in my face contracting, tightening the skin and protruding the veins. The bones in my fingers tense into claws, prepared to tear apart whatever lies ahead.

I start by reaching down into the depths of the cot, screwing up the blanket into a tight ball and hurling it out through the gap in the doorway. Next, ridiculously, I throw the stuffed toys into the hallway, bouncing them off the wall.

My next adversary, the mattress, is somewhat awkward and troublesome, springing back to shape every time I try to needlessly fold it into something smaller.

The location of the Allen key I used to connect the panels that make up the cot escapes me. I test its rigidity with a forceful shake. I was hoping to lean it one way, then the other, then back again, and repeat until something snapped, but it's pretty sturdy.

Some of the anguish returns.

I want to get out of this room.

Suppressing the urge to weep again, I draw strength from the last ounce of venom I can muster, take a short step back, raise my right knee to my chest then thrust it forwards with a bellowing guttural rasp.

The pane of wood snaps at the top, in the centre, making the rest of the structure more malleable. Almost in the same movement I grab the right corner, shaking it violently, loosening the screws, then propel it to the back wall, folding the thing in half.

I do the same thing to the other side. Shouting as I do so. Willing myself to finish.

Summoning the last of my strength, I drag the thing into the centre of the room, bend my knees, gaining leverage, then lift it before propelling my dead son's bed across the room, smashing it into the radiator I foolishly glossed sky blue and watch it clatter to the floor at the same time I do.

On my knees, I scream out vowels to hold back the tears. As the anger subsides back into heartache, I drag myself out of the childless torture chamber and collapse onto the miniature mattress spread out in the hall.

I let go.

I weep uncontrollably. Remembering the time we were given the news.

The time Sammael Abbadon was given the news.

I recall the instance my wife decided to leave, how we couldn't survive it together.

And my heart breaks all over again.

Today, as I look into the room that has been painted a pure, glowing white, including the radiator which has been re-glossed, I understand why the Lord asked me to perform this task. It was a test. To discover my worthi -ness. To attach the emotion of clearing my son's re -maining items with the feelings I have when I read about these occurrences in the newspapers.

More motivation to capture Celeste Varrick.

Tomorrow, when I collect the paper after my morning run, I will be given further instructions, yet still, it is not the time to take her. There is more work to be done.

January

We've known for weeks that there's no obvious connection between Lily Kane and Totty Fahey. Paulson searched whether they or any family members had police records, whether their paths may have crossed through employment or social engagement. Nothing was found. Paulson perches himself on the edge of my desk, moving a pile of my files to one side in order to clear a space for his enormous frame. He has a stack of papers in his hands.

'I've found something that might interest you, Jan.' His voice is at a low volume and he looks over his shoulder, nervous that somebody might hear what he is about to say next.

'Go on,' I tell him, leaning forward in my chair, subtly closing the drawer which holds the copy of my sister's case file and my as yet unopened bottle of Highland Malt.

'I found out a little more about the salt circles and have dug a bit further into the other ritual elements. It's all very interesting.' He waves his wad of paper to indicate that everything I need is written in those pages.

That's when Murphy blasts his way in. The slam of the door as it swings open, the handle colliding heavily with the wall, startles us both. I jump back in my chair; Paulson clumsily drops his stack of information onto the floor.

'Waste of time and resources,' Murphy mumbles, ripping his scarf away from his neck while Paulson collects his print-offs and slots them back into order.

'What's wrong, Murph?' I ask. Humouring him. As if I care.

'Oh, it's just the background on these bloody victims,' he continues with his insensitive diatribe. 'Totty Fahey has all this family who were clearly supporting his existence all this time. There are loads of them and they're all crying and nonsensical, then you get fucking Lily Kane . . .' He emphasises the curse to demonstrate his frustration.

Paulson and I wait silently, thinking he has something more to say.

He does.

'. . . she has hardly any family and the few that I did manage to find either hadn't seen her for half a decade or said that Lily Kane had been dead for years. Unbelievable.' He throws his jacket over the back of his chair before slumping down into it himself, visibly exhausted.

'Well, that sounds pretty suspicious, don't you think?' Paulson chips in.

I divert my gaze to the information on the salt circles that Paulson has printed out.

'Yes. But I checked them out, they're clean, they just disowned her a long time ago. Nothing more than minor family disagreements evolving into life-long grudges. So, in short, I've got fuck-all,' he confesses.

But he knew all along that that would be the conclusion.

'So how's the real police work going?' Murphy asks sardonically.

Despite his attitude, he is doing what I ask of him, even though he knows it is punishment for his lack of support on the Eames case. I think he has earned a reprieve.

'Well, Paulson's been on the Internet.' I laugh, not making fun of Paulson, just lightening the mood. Bringing us back together as a team. Paulson looks at me, wide-eyed, as if to say, 'Jan, what are you doing?' But if we are going to crack this before another life is taken, we need to pull together.

If I'm going to get out of this rut fully, I'm going to need them behind me.

I know that much.

Paulson fights the urge to come back with, 'Yeah, and Jan has been having some dreams again.'

He presents his additional findings to me and Murph, telling us that these circles are sometimes used as protection; that they have to be *cast*. That they define the user's sacred area. He informs us that the use of candles makes it difficult to determine what faith or belief system these rituals are derived from. That the four points within the circle suggest Paganism or Wicca, yet the candles imply a more conventional religious belief.

'Sounds like Satanic witchcraft to me,' Murphy jumps in – with both feet – as ignorant as usual, mixing faiths together.

The easy answer.

Less effort.

'So we're adding Satanism into the mix, are we?' Paulson asks, disgruntled. 'Seems a bit easy, Murph. Sounds like something the papers would print.'

'And we don't want them interfering with this.' I interject, my focus aimed directly at Murphy.

'Oh, you know what I mean. I'm just saying that we should be wary of misdirection. It could all be nothing.' Murphy pretends to follow the official line, playing devil's advocate.

I, of course, know it isn't *nothing*. Paulson does too, which is the reason he looked into it. That's the aspect that piqued his interest.

'Let's not rule anything out just yet.' I speak and they listen. 'We don't have time to sit here and learn about every religion and break-off group in the world. Let's get someone in. Looking at this only briefly' – I hold the handful of papers Paulson has printed – 'I think we should pursue this line of enquiry.'

For now.

I tell Paulson and Murphy that there's nothing more to do today, that they can both take off. I'm going to stay for a while to look over the papers that Paulson has printed off, see whether I can find a Pagan or Wiccan, or both, maybe they're the same thing, to come into the station and act as a consultant for the day. To get things moving.

But it won't just be for the day.

She will be here until the end.

'I can stay and go through them with you if you like, Jan,' Paulson offers sincerely. 'I'll help you locate a specialist.'

'It's OK. I'll go through them tonight. I'll find someone.'

Don't be like me.

Leave me alone.

'If you want some assistance . . .' he pushes.

'It's fine,' I insist, interrupting him. 'I've got it. You go home.'

Murphy throws his coat over his shoulder and grabs

Paulson by the arm. 'Come on. Before he changes his mind.'

After they've gone, I slouch back into my seat once more and, with a flick of the middle finger on my left hand, I pull the drawer open. It slides out smoothly on its coasters and bangs to a stop at full extension to reveal my bottle of drink. The warmth I've been waiting for.

I pull it out, place it under the desk between my legs and unscrew the cap for the first time. There's something rewarding about this simple act; I like the sound it makes as you crack the seal.

I tip out the dregs of an old cup of coffee, staining the carpet further. My left eye catches the folder and a glimpse of the text, which says *confidential*. It reads *Catherine (Cathy) David*. It displays the date she was taken. I screw the lid back on the bottle and place it back on the file, covering the words.

Not at work, Jan.

Snap out of this.

What would Cathy think?

Outside I can hear a cluster of men raising their voices, then a car door slams, then another. I get out of my seat to investigate, taking the empty caffeine-stained *I heart London* mug with me.

It's dark outside. I try to remember the date when the clocks go forward an hour. At this time of year, it's dark when I head into work and dark when I leave.

It's always dark.

I use my forefinger and thumb to pry apart the blinds.

Just below, two cars and a van are filling up quickly with uniformed officers. The blue lights are already rotating before they leave the station. I stare at the top of the van, the light flashing, revolving, drawing in my gaze until my eyes zoom in to a close-up where all I can see is the flash of blue, then white, then black, blue, then white, then black.

Blue.

Then white.

Then black . . .

I'm back in the room.

The dust is already at the back of my throat, the scent of spring flowers in every direction.

This time I am standing up in my invisible chamber, waiting, for what? For the flicker of a candle? For a speck of light to appear in the distance? For The Two to present themselves?

Not this time.

The circle of tiny flames illuminates to my left, where I expect the boy to be standing, shifting the dust around his feet as he jigs from side to side. But he is not there. A pile of clothes lie neatly folded in the centre.

To my right, the same.

Light. A circle. A pile of neatly folded clothes.

My eyes dart about the blackness in a futile attempt to discover their whereabouts.

The pile on the right begins to move as if something is trying to escape from beneath.

I'm frightened to focus.

Afraid to look around.

Then, from the front of the pile of folded clothes where the girl should be standing, a snake appears. It isn't huge but it's still a snake. It slides out fully from underneath the garments and begins to circle them.

From above, a drop of liquid falls onto the centre of the

clothes. Then another. Then a third, larger drop. I can't see where they're coming from; above is as black as beyond.

The drops start to form a trickle. A white trickle.

Like milk.

The trickle soon becomes a gush, which bounces off the top of the pile, droplets hitting the snake who continues to circle.

I take a quick glimpse to my left but nothing has changed.

When I look back, the gush of milk has grown to a waterfall and the reptile forms a track behind him, where the liquid grows thicker on the floor. Splashes start to hit the candles. One of the candles flickers and dies, and the snake escapes through the dark breach.

I follow his track as he moves swiftly to the other circle and disappears under the dry mound of trousers and T-shirts.

The pile ignites instantly into a healthy blaze.

I hear someone call my name.

'Jan?'

I look behind me.

Black.

Back to the front, the milk still pouring, the fire now wildly out of control.

'January?' the voice says again.

Then white.

'JAN!' he shouts.

Then blue . . .

And I'm back in the office, the light on the van rotating. Almost no time has passed.

I release the grip on my mug as the sound of Paulson

shouting my name from behind me brings me back to reality too early. The handle breaks on the floor and a crack forms down one side of the giant cup.

'Fuck,' I say, clearly unnerved. 'What are you doing sneaking up on me like that? Jesus.' I squat down to pick up the broken pieces.

'I forgot something.' He bends down and fumbles in his top drawer. I don't ask him what he has forgotten. 'Where were you just now?'

I was busy getting clues to the next murder, which I now know must occur tomorrow, yet, unlike last time, I don't have any idea where it will be or how it will be performed – fire, flood, poison? There wasn't enough time.

So, whoever the victim is, they are certain to die before I get there.

I need to get back to that place. To my trance.

I need to get to sleep.

The vision itself won't help me solve the case but it gives me a head-start on the perpetrator. I know before they do.

'Just thinking about the case,' I lie.

He pulls a pack of cigarettes from the mess inside his drawer and smiles as he presents his findings with a relieved sigh.

'Sure you don't want me to stay?' he asks, fidgeting, awkward.

'I'll be fine. You get off,' I say, absent-mindedly flicking through the wad of paper that he printed off the Internet. 'I won't be much longer anyway. Might just take these home.'

Paulson skulks out of the office, no doubt to unwind with some late-night gambling or to drop down a dark stairwell into one of his members' clubs that you won't find in any London guidebooks.

And I head back to execute my master plan.

Sleep.

Finish the vision.

Obtain the information needed to solve the case.

But that would be too easy, so of course it doesn't work.

I fail again.

I need help.

I need a Wiccan.

To explain these rituals.

To unravel these visions.

Celeste

✦

Winter is slowly loosening its grip and the days are growing longer. I plant some seeds in the flower box outside my window. This is a time that represents growth.

But later today, another will die.

They have to.

I meditate, closing myself off from the city around me, immersing myself in another world, another time and place. A time of misery and desperation, a place where an old man is stabbed through his broken heart and a woman is impaled in her cancerous stomach.

I focus on the rituals. The flames from the candles burning brightly as their souls move on.

They didn't know it at the time but I was saving them.

I sent them to a better place.

As I gradually filter out the dirt and scent of the exhaust fumes, the noise of vehicles revving and beeping with frustration, the constant hum of voices talking endless clichés and insincerities, I move ever nearer the white, the blankness I require to attain my next location.

To find out who needs me next.

With my mind clear, I begin the journey. My legs crossed and palms facing down, resting on my knees, my body remains motionless as my consciousness travels through the light at warp speed. A crossroad passes beneath my feet, then another, then another. I smell the grass, hear the trees blowing in the cold February wind. Another set of intersecting paths travels below me.

I sense the moisture and come to an abrupt halt as a wall of noise smacks me in the face. My eyes flit open, the noise from my travels now bleeding back into the murmur of reality outside.

I know where I must be. I can decipher my intuition.

But I won't know who I am there for until I arrive.

I do not need to stalk the hallways of the hospitals or aisles of the churches searching for desperation; it is always there. I just need to turn up. I can find the next victim when I arrive.

The nearest tube is Marble Arch on the Central Line, but I get off at Hyde Park Corner on the Piccadilly Line so that I can walk through the park. The bag over my shoulder contains everything I need, and is heavier than usual.

Crossing the road onto the central island, I am temporarily ambivalent about which way to walk. The park is huge, things look the same to the left as they do to the right; grey skies above, trees lining the roads and many intersecting paths. I find myself next to a sign that reads: 'You are here.' A red arrow points to the spot I currently occupy. A man about my age peruses the map next to me. He turns his head to say something arbitrary but instead just smiles, lifts his eyebrows as if to say 'Who knows?', then goes back to deciphering the shades of green on the board in front of us.

I notice that a path runs parallel to Park Lane and takes me around to the next corner.

That's the way I need to go.

It's where I'm supposed to be if I am to save another person.

I just know it.

Of course, they must die first, that is their fate; I cannot argue with that, another must end life on their knees. They will not thank me for what I do to them on this plane of existence, but they will realise in the next that I kept them out of an eternity in hell.

At that point, they can bless me.

It starts to rain. Nothing heavy. That light rain that you sometimes don't notice; it's not worth putting up a hood or opening an umbrella. It'll pass. By the time my foot touches the path I should be on, it has either stopped or I've just forgotten about it.

Ahead, I see a fountain. I could walk around the left-hand side; I could use the right. To the left, two young girls, seventeen or eighteen, are sitting on the stone ridge around the water. They are flicking their hair and talking as if they are chewing gum even though they are not. At first I don't notice the boy behind the home-video camera adjusting his tripod.

I choose the path to the left.

Intrigue diverts me.

The girls stop talking as I approach; the boy pretends he isn't there, thinking that, if he is perfectly still, I won't be able to see him. We're suspicious of each other. Perhaps it is a mistake to make my face memorable, to create a witness.

But, whatever they are doing, whatever they are creating, they don't want me to remember them either.

I walk past this filmic enigma and round the opposite end of the fountain, back on path.

I'm almost where I need to be.

I can feel myself being drawn forwards.

My pace increases. It's not excitement but it's some -
thing close. It's not anxiety either.

The end of the path is cut off with a red and white tape
as part of the ground is under repair. I step out onto the
cycle path, ducking under the tape, and in my haste I'm
almost run down by a gaggle of joggers.

In the distance I see crowds forming. Separate masses
around each independent orator. They are still too far
away for me to hear what any of them are talking about.
People queue to buy coffee from the stand to drink while
they listen. In the background a team of rugby players,
dressed in black and red, run some drills, oblivious to
what is happening right next to them.

What is about to happen.

One girl stands on a box, her blond hair as grey as the
English sky; she gesticulates passionately to a gathering
of two, who swiftly move on to the next spokesperson.

I smile in recognition.

It's her.

I'm just in time.

Talitha

❖

I'm not nervous about speaking in front of people, not even this many. I've done it before. But it's busier than usual today and the things I have to say seem to be too positive to care about.

Nobody wants to hear optimism.

Buoyancy is boring.

Twenty feet to my right, two men are tag-teaming a speech about the size of their penises. Apparently they think they are rather small. I don't know whether this is self-deprecating humour or whether they have a genuine affliction they wish to share, perhaps empowering other less-endowed men to embrace their lack of penile provision.

Whatever their motives, they are drawing the largest crowd.

I can't hear what the woman over the back is talking about, but she appears to be confusing gesticulation with passion.

I tell no people that they should feel privileged.

No crowd hears me say that life is for living.

I say purely to myself that each day is a blessing.

Then a man pronounces that his pubic hair is longer than his dick.

Fifteen people laugh.

I feel deflated. An elderly gentleman, too decrepit to climb on top of his soapbox, preaches the value of art. He quotes Nietzsche and two people listen. He coughs up phlegm and another joins his audience.

'Are you in yet?' a man cackles, and his spectators obligingly react with reverence.

I sigh as three men in their twenties buy a coffee from the stand and make their way over to the tiny dicks and their routine. I try again, 'I'm going to die.' Raising my voice is meant to attract more attention. I'm trying to shock.

It makes me look spoiled. Like I'm here just because I need the attention.

That's not why I'm here.

My eyes follow them as they each blow air into the small hole in the lid of their drinks that were probably only bought as hand-warmers. I start to listen to the schlong twins myself, not noticing the woman in the distance whose intent is clear. Her aim is direct.

She is closing in.

I shout across at the idiot horde, 'Size does matter.' Thinking I'm clever. But still, nobody notices, like I'm invisible. And now I've just ensured that my final words on earth are 'Size does matter.' Thank God nobody is listening to me.

I don't even see Celeste picking up her pace, darting straight for me. We are both unseen.

Nobody's noticed me all morning, so why should I be shocked that nobody saw this?

In a couple of minutes I will be dead and the woman who saw me from hundreds of yards away, the woman who locked her sights on my exact spot and honed in on it, the woman who sprinted towards me without me noticing, will be standing on top of my box talking, and still nobody will be listening.

It's all about location.

Celeste

—◆—

I place the undersized cauldron on her waste-of-a-soapbox. The one she is knelt in front of. I stand on the other side inside the circle I have cast. In the background I see the Marble Arch; closer still, a woman waves her arms and talks operatically.

I pour the sand into the cauldron that will hold the seven candles in place.

I light the first candle.

'Although it is now dark, I come seeking light. In the chill of winter, I come seeking life.'

Nobody is listening to what I have to say.

I light the second candle.

'I call upon fire that melts the snow and warms the hearth. I call upon fire that brings the light and makes new life. I call upon fire to purify with its flames.' I chant these lines, fixing my vision on the young girl.

I light the third candle.

'This light is a boundary between positive and nega-tive. That which is outside shall stay without. That which is inside shall stay within.' The crowd to my left laugh heartily. I'm temporarily angered, thinking they might be laughing at me, but they're not.

I'm invisible too.

With the fourth, fifth and sixth candles I repeat my fire incantation.

I bend down so that my eyes are at the same level as the girl's. She is dead now. My work is almost done.

I strike a match and hold the flame to the seventh and final wick. As it ignites, I remain low on the ground, visualising the seven tiny flames connecting to form one large light, aglow with purity.

'Fire of the hearth, blaze of the sun, cover her in your shining light. She is awash with your glow and tonight she is made pure.'

I see an aura of blue light outline the girl as the purification takes place; her eyes are closed, her mouth is pleading. Two joggers wearing oversized headphones bound right past us, safe in their endorphin-fuelled world. Ignorant.

Her aura still cleansing with a light only I can see, the candles still burning, I creak back to my feet, my knees aching. I can leave her now. Whoever she is, I will find out tomorrow.

Over by the number fourteen lamppost a man shouts, 'Shrivelled.' He squawks, 'meat and two veg, crown jewels.' He cries, 'twig and berries.'

I have three minutes until the number forty-four bus pulls up parallel to the Broadwalk.

My work here is done.

I can be proud of myself.

Another person dead.

Another person saved.

January

———◆———

I wake up on the floor, Mother's journals spread over me like a blanket.

But I haven't dreamed.

The Two did not return.

My preoccupation with the case has stopped me from wondering where Audrey is, what she is doing, who she is doing it with. It's working. But, for the first time in years, I also forgot about Cathy. For a moment, a brief moment, she just slipped my mind.

And I don't want to do that.

I do all of this for her, to find her. To find the person who took her from me and caused my family to disintegrate almost overnight. I don't want others to feel this loss, this guilt.

I look at Mother's journals and blame her for taking my thoughts away from my sister. Temporarily, I hate my mother again.

The concoction of wine and sleeping pills I had counted on to put me into a state of hibernation never materialised. I try desperately to stay awake so that I do not waste any more time. I have to read Mother's journals. I must understand Paulson's notes. I need to find a Pagan expert. Getting to a point of over-tiredness where hallucination becomes more likely. Where alertness sometimes descends into a waking catatonic stasis.

I haven't heard the phone that has been ringing constantly all morning, a worried Paulson dialling my home number, wondering why I have not shown up at work all day.

I don't yet know that the darkness outside is not early morning; I don't realise that it is the evening and that I've been asleep most of the day. While I lay here surrounded by the scribblings of a madwoman, a girl was dying on her knees at Speaker's Corner in Hyde Park, her face burned almost beyond recognition.

The doorbell rings.

I sit up too quickly; four journals fall off my chest to the floor, my brain throbs inside my skull and I grimace back to semi-lucidity. The sound of the bell pierces through my thoughts and stabs me between the eyes. I sweep the notebooks that have been keeping my legs warm throughout the night to the side, and endeavour to stand up.

It's too much to attempt in one movement. I feel confused and nauseous so drop to my knees, spreading my weight onto all fours and shutting my eyes to collect myself before another big push. My mouth flops open to suck in the stale air of my home-office, the saliva thinning and dribbling out onto some of the pages that are strewn beneath me.

I know what that means.

I need to get up.

The bell rings again and this time Paulson bends down, pushes the flap of the letterbox open slightly and presses his mouth into the gap.

'Jaaaaaan. Are you there?'

The few seconds of silence that follow his question are

133

broken by the sound of me dry-retching at the floor. But I am empty inside.

I try to speak. To tell him that I'm coming. But as I open my mouth again to do so I retch and taste bile as it burns in my throat. I need water.

I need to stand up.

'Jan, is everything OK?' he calls again.

At this point I manage to get to my feet, supporting my weight on the door handle to my study, and open the door that lets me out into the hallway, where I can see the fat silhouette of my colleague and only friend.

Noticing the change in light, Paulson pulls his fingers out of the letterbox, the flap springing shut, the noise reverberating through my head. He stands upright again, blocking more of the light from the bulb on the doorstep with his huge frame.

I break down the short journey to the front door by plotting three points along the way. Firstly, the table in the middle that the phone sits on. It's about half of the total distance but I will be able to rest my fragile weight on it to recuperate before stage two.

A deep breath and determination force my legs to wobble the distance; I almost collapse on arrival but am distracted by my weathered, sickly appearance in the mirror above the phone.

My eyes look black against my pallid skin but the bags under my eyes don't seem as noticeable as usual, like they have become my cheeks. Perhaps a consequence of my daytime collapse into sleep.

I thought I had turned a corner after Totty but it may take longer. I can't just forget the things I have seen, the events that have happened.

Next I aim my focus at the doorway to the second

reception room. Probably only four or five steps, and I'm motivated by wanting to escape my reflection. The rotund outline of my sergeant remains motionless as he waits for me to let him in.

As I hit my second target my right shoulder crashes into the frame of the door, cracking as it takes the full force of my momentum; chronic fatigue is affecting my depth-perception somewhat. I heave as I thud into position, but there is nothing to puke up; still I make a sound as if vomiting.

To get to point three, the front door, I rest my hands against the wall and guide myself along as if lost in the dark until I am face to face with the paunchy shadow at my door. I unhook the chain with my left hand and release the latch with my right.

The door scrapes open only about five centimetres, but that's enough to get a sense of the cold outside. Paulson's cheeks are red. He looks at me.

'Christ, Jan. You look like shit.' And he opens the door fully to let himself in while I turn and stagger towards the kitchen where the cold tap awaits.

He closes the door softly but it sounds like it slams to me. I'm not drunk or high or paranoid or delusional, I simply feel thrust into something foreign, very suddenly. I want to be myself. I want to rely on police work but the visions are changing, evolving, and they keep tripping me up. Initially Paulson follows me cautiously as I amble into the kitchen, but his phone rings and he stops to talk in the hallway while I carry on.

As I drink directly from the tap, I hear snippets of Paulson's conversation.

'Yeah. I'm here with him now,' he says, as if everything is normal. As if I'm copacetic.

'All day, I think . . . ' he lies. 'We're going over it now,' he misleads.

I hear his phone snap shut as he folds it back in half. I continue to slurp at the running liquid as he steps into the kitchen.

'What's going on?' he asks, sounding genuinely concerned yet annoyed at the same time.

I continue to suck at the tap.

'Look, Jan, I've covered for you all day. Murphy is beyond suspicious, I'm still not sure why you had to let him in on the whole ritualistic murder idea; I hadn't even had time to go through it properly myself.' He's right, I know he is.

He told Detective Chief Inspector Markam that I was out following a potential lead. He blagged to anyone who asked of my whereabouts, each one of them riled by Murphy who was planting a seed just as the man in the suit asked him to. The man who is many ranks above Markam. The one who wants me out and, for some reason, wants Murphy in.

I feel my stomach filling quickly but still I'm not hydrated, I can't stop. I start to breathe heavily, gasping for liquid. I sense Paulson sigh.

'You're going to need to pull yourself together, they've just found another body.'

I stop.

The tap continues to run in front of my face.

Of course there's another body, it has easily been twenty-four hours since my half-vision.

I push my face back towards the waterfall, this time not stopping as my mouth reaches it. I let the icy water run over my cheek, then my ear, the hair behind my ear. I turn my head to face the plughole and the cold water pounds the back of my head and neck, refreshing me, revitalising. I leave it there until it numbs. Then I pull my head out, stand upright facing my partner and brush the wet hair away from my face with my hands.

'We should probably get moving, then,' I say, trying to sound together, like I am cured.

'I should drive,' he suggests, not quite a statement, but not a question either.

And I know he's the one I can count on.

'I'll tell you all about it in the car.'

V

The front page of the newspaper this morning has no picture. It would be too graphic: the girl's face was burned so badly that her parents could just about confirm her identity.

They say she was set on fire.

They say it's the third in the series.

They say the police are working on some strong leads.

You shouldn't believe everything you read.

I haven't seen it yet. I'm still running.

This morning I decide to up the intensity of my training.

The last mile of my route is lined with lampposts. Between the first two, I jog at my regular pace. As I reach the second post, I break into a sprint, pushing myself as far as I can for the distance to the third marker. As I cross this line I slow down quickly into a walk. To recapture my breath before I start the process over again at the next pillar.

The final stretch before my flat works out to be a sprint leg so, as I hit the front door, I drop into a walk just as the stairs approach. At the time I'm thankful, but it makes the trip seem longer and I'm unable to start the recovery process. I try to breathe in through my nose and out through my mouth but it's difficult, so I stop on one of the landings partway up to stretch my calf muscles and put off reading the paper a few moments longer.

Every pore of my skin is excreting sweat; my forehead, my chest, my back are all covered in tiny warm beads of water, soaking or dripping onto my clothes. Even my palms are clammy. It's uncomfortable to hold on to the protective plastic that surrounds my morning tabloid.

I enter my flat, the scent of paint still fresh; a ladder I used to reach the ceiling still lies on its side. I'm too exhausted to digest today's current affairs and the emotional response it is bound to evoke, so I throw the paper across the room, landing it on the sofa where it bounces onto the floor and rolls to the far wall.

Stripping off all of my clothes in three swift movements has become routine; I leave them in a pile on the floor of the bathroom and step into the shower. It's scalding hot; the window and mirror steaming up instantly. Each hot droplet stabs into me, causing me an equal amount of pleasure and pain.

Then the pleasure outweighs the pain.

My penis shoots up, proud and strong. The hormones produced through exercise travelling straight to the tip.

I think of a time when the man I used to be was happy. With his wife. Before his son was created, before he died. With my eyes closed I clench a fist tightly around the solid protuberance.

With every tug I imagine her on top of me, beneath me, crouching in front of me. With every massage I long to be back with her. To be the man I was. With every stroke I tell myself that this day will come.

That I'd do whatever it takes.

To be a family again.

As I reach the climax, throbbing in my left hand, my

mind goes temporarily blank, eventually returning to the reality of my new life as V.

My life alone.

The Lord is my company.

I switch off the shower and wrap a towel around my waist. Not fully flaccid yet, the front pokes out slightly, showing my form as the excitement continues to diminish. I drip over the floor leaving wet, size eleven footprints in a trail to the living room, where I pick up the newspaper which rests against the skirting board.

In a break from routine I sit down on the sofa, opting to drip dry while I catch up on the national news. Of course, I am angered by the headline and the insensitivity of the article and the sensationalism of the events. But less so than before.

Desensitised, perhaps.

Maybe it's easier now I know there is a plan.

The Lord will stop this.

I lay the paper calmly on the vacant seat next to me and lean forward to the edge of my cushion. With one hand grasping the other, the air flowing freely between my legs and over my exposed torso, I ask the question.

Is it time yet?

What will you have me do?

I wait.

I listen.

I obey.

Remaining in my half-dressed state I reach for my Bible and begin to read. Flicking through the pages digesting the words, examining the meanings. I am told I will know which words I need, which ones I should use. I will know how best to use them.

That it is nearly time.
I still need the ladder lying in my hallway.
I need black paint.

January

———◆———

I tell Paulson everything.

I say that I no longer see The Smiling Man, that I think he was specific to Eames, or at least to that case. I say that now I have two children who appear to me, that they seem friendlier but still so sinister.

That I believe my mother.

That I wonder whether this is hereditary.

I relay the intricacies of all two-and-a-half visions.

And he listens, without questioning, interrupting or judging.

I don't tell him that I'm getting better at it. That somehow, somewhere within me, I knew the last location would be Trafalgar Square but was not certain enough in my convictions. That I could have done something about it if only I had considered it as a location rather than the method of killing. I still don't understand the significance of The Two, what they represent, what their part of the message means. I am not as confident as Mother in the things I see.

I don't tell him how much I need this case or that I am drinking too much.

Because he already knows this.

I explain to him that I just wanted to stay awake, so that I could avoid that dark dusty room that may hold all the answers but I cannot decipher as effectively as real life. I wanted to be alert, sharp, ready. Because I didn't want to be sat in a car driving to see another dead body; I wanted to be heading to a location to prevent another murder.

'Jan.' He speaks softly. 'I believe you. I mean, you proved this works as an avenue of enquiry on that last case.' He doesn't want to mention Eames or Audrey for fear it may kick me back a few steps. 'I just think that you need to combine it with . . .' He pauses to find the right words.

'Some actual detective work?' I ask, half joking.

'I wouldn't use those words, but you know what I mean.'

Of course, he's right. I'm too reliant on this ability, if that's what you want to call it. On the last case, when I was tracking Eames, I dismissed the visions to my detriment. I caught him, but I could have caught him much sooner – before he got to Audrey again. This time I have embraced them too fully. I need the balance but I'm struggling.

'Isn't that why I have you, Paulson?' I half joke, again.

He laughs. 'I guess so.'

We pass The Dorchester and other grand establishments on our way to the corner of Hyde Park, where the next victim awaits us.

This time she is not in the kneeling position; the candles are not alight. Her hair is singed and burned into her scalp, her face scarred and blistered, red and wrinkled. It doesn't follow the pattern. This seems like such an obvious way to get noticed, setting fire to some - one. The first two murders were far more discreet; you could understand how no witnesses came forward. But this, currently unidentified, girl was aflame in a crowded area.

Closer inspection will eventually confirm her cause of death not to be linked to fire or heat in any way.

The minuscule prick mark in her chest leads us to think that it might have been induced heart failure. That the fire was a by-product, perhaps even an accident.

That she was already dead.

'It doesn't add up.' Murphy joins us, suddenly appearing, his hands in his pockets, looking like a lost child. 'Seems like someone piggybacking on the back of the first two murders but not getting it quite right,' he adds.

'It's the same killer,' I say, putting Paulson on edge. He's already let his feelings be known when it comes to Murphy.

'You can prove that?' he asks, smugly.

'Not yet.' And I walk away from him to take a closer look at the girl.

I drop to one knee next to the body, which lies on the floor beside a wooden box. Seven tea-lights are strewn around the area; three are entangled in the matted hair. A small pile of sand lies next to the box; beside that, an upturned miniature cauldron of sorts. But the dirt around her is not displaced in any way; it doesn't look as though she struggled at all. You would expect to see traces of her flailing limbs, or a flat area of earth where she rolled over in an attempt to put out the fire, but there is nothing.

I reach my hand out to touch her face softly and have to remind myself why I am here.

'What happened to you?' I whisper, suppressing sentiment.

To my left I see the salt circle that has been present at

each crime scene. As I lift my head away from the grotesque sight below, something glows in the distance. Maybe one hundred metres directly ahead of me, two small figures radiate.

One boy, one girl.

Celeste

——◆——

I do not know the name of the girl who died, that is not important. What matters is that she is dead. That this is normal, cyclical, and that I helped send her to a better place.

The one I will come to know as V discovers the victim's name in the same way that I do, through the media. He is angered then distraught to find that this young girl has been burned. He cries when he reads that her face was disfigured and charred. He weeps at the loss of her soul.

I react differently.

Because I took her soul.

This morning, as V stands in his kitchen, stretching out his calf muscles, warming down from his exercise, his eyes glazing with a thin film of acrid tears, I too am taking deep breaths. Not to weep at the loss of an innocent life, I believe that Talitha Palladino will emerge again on the days and nights when our two worlds extend over one another, but to relax into my pose as I meditate on another successful journey.

He stands with clenched fists and tensed muscles while I sit, my hands resting on my knees and my palms facing the ceiling. My core is relaxed. I hum a chant of gratitude and hope for protection while he speaks gibberish and calls for more natural strength.

For he is the dark.

And I am the light.

V locks himself away from the world he thinks he is here to protect while I am more proactive. I want to find the next person to die. I am trying to picture the next location. I wish to save another.

I am one half.

He is the other.

I am the antithesis of everything he believes in, everything he does.

That is why he wants to take me. To capture me. To keep me with him.

He believes that I am the only one who must be saved and he is the angel to deliver me to justice.

January

I don't need to be asleep.

Standing at Speaker's Corner, Hyde Park, the third victim lying burned and unrecognisable in the dirt beside my feet, I see The Two in the distance. They are talking to each other at the corner of two bisecting paths in the centre of some playing fields on the parkland.

The boy, on the left, bends down and pulls something out of the ground. A box. A small tinder box.

I feel paralysed.

Can anyone else see this?

Paulson and Murphy are still standing ten paces away, arms folded, making the occasional perfunctory exchange, not seeing what I see, not noticing what is right in front of them.

They are the crowd that laughs at penis jokes.

They are the rabble that goes trick-or-treating.

They are the mob that rides the bronze lions.

The girl, on the right, delicately stretches out her hand as if to touch the box, then refrains and turns her head to me, releasing me from my paralysis.

Slowly, carefully, I straighten my legs, hoping not to alarm her, retaining my poise. She moves her gaze back to her partner.

My neck creaks delicately, swivelling around towards

my team. They do not react to the children. Only I have noticed. Just because I see it does not make it real. The caffeine, the booze, the lack of sleep, are designed to make me feel more aware but they mask reality. They dilute truth. They paper walls to keep my gut-reactions subdued.

Paulson and Murphy are still mumbling about I don't know what.

'Stay here,' I whisper in their direction, never averting my eyes from the ghostly image that, apparently, only I have noticed.

'What? Where are you . . .' Murphy trills.

'Just stay here. I need to look at this in a different way.'

They obey my command and continue their discussion, this time with a distracted eye flitting occasionally to me.

I start the walk away from the dead body, the dirt beneath my shoes crunching louder than I would like. I'm cautious. I don't want to spook the children. I just want to get closer.

Edging out of the lit crime scene, I set foot onto a darker path. My fellow detectives carry on their chattering.

My right heels drags. Only for an instant.

And the children turn their heads robotically in my direction, the boy's eyes flashing green.

I close in on them, feeling as though I'm gathering speed, but I'm not.

The boy leans into his friend and whispers something in her ear and she hugs him affectionately. He starts to walk away, leaving the girl on her own. I want to shout 'Wait!' but nothing comes out.

I turn back to see my partners, but they seem only partially interested in what I'm doing.

Two looking at one looking for two.

When I bring my head back round to the front, they are gone. Disappeared.

Evaporated.

Chased away.

I stop at the point where the roads cross.

So close.

Disappointed, I scan the area, the ground looks untouched. No footprints or obvious holes. The earth looks unmoved by their shuffling feet. I start to doubt myself. After the second victim, I thought I had pulled myself from the doldrums of my uncertainty over Audrey's departure and Mother's death. I was wrong. I needed this last kick.

I haven't slept for days but, still, something had to wake me up.

Looking back down the path I can see that Paulson and Murphy are making their way towards me. I turn away, focusing my efforts on squinting into the distance, trying to detect any moving figures in the woodland beyond. But they are long gone.

I will have to wait another seven weeks.

Twenty-first of March.

Ostara.

The next Sabbat.

Murphy asks what I've found.

'There is no sexual gratification in these killings,' I start, not knowing at first where I am going with this line of deduction. 'I just wonder whether this psycho watches afterwards. Whether they are turned on by the pandemonium.'

'Like it's part of the ritual and he has to watch it play out?' Murphy immediately suspects that the killer is male.

'The scattered geography would suggest random selection of these victims. The killer is drifting and taking whoever seems weakest.'

'It looks that way, Jan.' Paulson chips in.

'I just don't know whether I believe that.' His face screws up as I go against my own trail of thought. 'The ritualism goes against all of that. I think that location is key. What do all three crime scenes have in common apart from the candles and salt circles and victims on their knees? Why so public? What is in the vicinity which may help us pinpoint the way the victims are selected?'

My partners are silent, watching a show of January David neither has seen on this case so far.

I step through the middle of them, my arm held out perpendicular to my body, pointing back down the path from which we came.

'Look at this. See how the paths bisect one another forming separate crossroads? Think of the same design at Parsons Green. Is there something in that? Does this killer require such a thing as a component of the ritual? Could they have stood where we are right now, watching this poor girl burn? Were they in the crowd at Trafalgar Square? Did they stick around and go for a drink while we examined Lily Kane?'

There is silence.

I step back towards them and lower the level of my voice, my tone earnest.

'This is not a normal case. The killer is approaching the victims and taking their lives in an abnormal way. We cannot address this in an orthodox manner. We have to think differently about this one.'

It won't be too long before Talitha Palladino's parents see her again to confirm what they already suspect: their daughter is gone. I see her crumpled body being readied to be placed in a large black bag.

'Jan, I get it, think outside the box,' Murphy warbles, faking sincerity. He continues, 'But we can't ignore the tangible evidence, the crime scene, witnesses . . .' he trails off.

'I completely agree.'

Paulson smiles. Murphy is agitated. He wants to make a call and report back on my behaviour.

'If you can find a witness for me, Murph, that would be great.'

I look between them at the square of dirt where the boy and girl exchanged their message. I did not conjure the image. They were there. The Two were certainly there. I turn their appearance around in my brain, trying desper - ately to decipher their actions. Striving to gain ground on solving this case.

I think about The Smiling Man, and my sister, and Audrey. I think of Talitha and Totty and Lily. I think of the two children glowing in the park that only I could see. The pills still in my system, my vision pixelates for a second and, before I realise, more bile is involuntarily expelled into my mouth. I keep it closed and turn away, swallowing it back down, burning my throat.

Pull yourself together, January. This has to stop.

Back where we started, in the light, I watch as they bag Talitha Palladino.

Dead, she is insignificant.

'Everything all right, Jan?' Paulson queries.

I could try to explain.

But I don't.

Instead, I retreat, retracing my steps.

Talitha Palladino has been reduced to a chalk outline.

Murphy moans something under his breath.

Paulson follows me, ignoring Murphy.

The news crews are already arriving. Talitha Palladino's story will soon be aired to the nation by women with perfect hair and clean-shaven men. All of them using that soft sincere tone, counterfeit grief; conveying sadness solely through the use of their eyebrows.

'Wait up, Jan,' Paulson calls after me, his stumpy legs rubbing together, refusing to move at pace.

I fold in half, my stomach cramping. I try to disguise my discomfort; the want to heave. Paulson finally catches up.

Fifteen metres away, the crime scene is already surrounded by circus and hysteria and egocentricity and the circle of salt is the only part that looks untouched, undisturbed.

Paulson surreptitiously supports my weight and whis-pers, 'Come on, Jan, let's get you back.'

The moment of nausea passes and a calm ensues. Yet something of Talitha Palladino remains, lingering, in the air, in the puddles on the ground, hovering above the soil, in the flickering light-bulb filaments of the news crews.

I can feel it.

It's too close to the sensation I experienced after blowing out the candle set in front of Lily Kane.

Paulson walks me through the scene, trying his best to

disguise the fact that he is supporting most of my weight. 'Nearly there,' he reassures me.

Centimetres away from the spot where Talitha Palladino gave her final exhalation lies the salt circle, about half a metre in diameter, large enough for someone to kneel inside. Paulson, preoccupied with my near-stupor, accidentally disrupts a portion of the scene, the smallest part, almost insignificant. His left shoe nudges a section of the salt particles, breaking the circle. Instantly, a gust sweeps through the crowd, blowing the newsreaders' hair horizontally. Empty polystyrene cups shoot across the crime scene, the police tape rasps violently and the remainder of the salt is blown away, dispersing into the gravel, ready to dissolve with the next rainfall.

And I feel her leave.

This requires more than conventional detective work, but, for now, to keep Murphy and his backers pacified, that is exactly what I will have to do.

The Two can still find me when I am awake, so, now, it doesn't matter if I sleep.

They can get to me whenever they like.

To get them out of my head I must enter the mind of Celeste Varrick.

Ostara
March 2009

V

---✦---

I don't know why I have chosen these references. Perhaps I just know, maybe I am being told, being fed. Being used.

But something speaks to me when I read: '. . . the secret power of lawlessness is already at work; but the one who now holds it back will continue to do so till he is taken out of the way.' As I read on, I soon realise how appropriate this is, that it sums up everything I am doing though may not quite understand yet.

I paint the reference in large black letters on the glowing white walls of the room that nearly belonged to my son.

I flick to another page and read: '. . . the LORD your God is a consuming fire, a jealous God.' And things start to make sense.

The room now lies empty, made larger and more vacant by the wash of white over every surface. With the door closed, the walls are as black as the painted references.

This is how the Lord wants it.

This is how it must be.

Though I still have much work to do.

Before my Lord tells me to act, to take Celeste, two more must die.

One will die tomorrow.
The last on the first of May.
Then our work truly begins.
Then we bring justice.

January

———✦———

Following on from our research into the ritualistic nature of the three murders so far, we have managed to narrow down some kind of Pagan or Wiccan influence. I've arranged for an expert's contribution in the morning. I gave Paulson the task of letting Murphy know it is nothing to do with Satanism, and that, while different from anything we've seen before, this is far less sensational than that.

He shrugged and conceded that he was wrong; just gave in without question.

And that's why he shouldn't be a detective.

That's another reason he should not be part of my team.

The next Sabbat is tomorrow. Ostara. The twenty-first day of March. If I'm right, there will be another victim; The Two will come to me tonight and tell me where.

Leaving it in my hands.

Someone's life is in my hands.

Someone's death is in my head.

The Two will present themselves to me as I sleep on my bed. I've asked Paulson not to wake me, no matter what he hears.

He's staying with me.

We know they'll arrive tonight, we've worked that

much out; even Murphy knows when the next murder is due to occur. What he doesn't realise is that Paulson and I are using my visions as a bonus, to back up the physical findings. I can't ignore them but they no longer form the basis of the investigation.

'God, Jan, I hope you're right about this,' Paulson says, knocking back the last dregs of coffee from his oversized mug.

'Look on the bright side, if they don't come tonight, it means that nobody is going to die. I don't mind being wrong if that's the case.' But, of course, it's not. Graham White is lying in his bed tonight with his own problems, fighting off his own demons, hoping tomorrow will bring better fortune than today – like all of us. Only tomorrow, he becomes a victim.

I am afforded the right to have a guilt-free drink tonight; it relaxes me. It calms me enough so that I can sleep. Not that I need to sleep to see The Two, that is apparent now; I just prefer it that way. It's less real, less explanation needed if it is in the confines of my own home.

With Paulson staying this evening, as my back-up, my support, I decide to sleep in the bedroom for the first time since Audrey left. It's the bed that I was in when I first saw The Smiling Man, the place Audrey and I made love; it's a place that was just ours.

'Are you going up now?' Paulson asks.

'When is a good time?' I throw back, rhetorically.

I edge up the stairs slowly, one at a time, each step moving me into a colder part of this great house. I turn back to Paulson.

'I'll just put another coffee on, if that's OK. Wait down

here until you're done.' He looks like a child as he says this, waiting for some approval, some acknowledgement that what he is doing is correct. I throw him a nod and he slinks off to the kitchen to mix up another batch of Ethiopian coffee to keep him awake. Alert.

I half expect the door to creak open slowly, building the tension as I prepare to enter the room, but it doesn't, it glides open effortlessly, crashing into the wall behind, just as it always has. This recognition of past times fills me with a sense of ease and nostalgia. But that is short-lived.

Flicking the light on, I see that the room has not remained in the pristine condition that Audrey would have liked. It looks a little greyer, somewhat weathered. As though it has decayed along with me. The room has a constant five o'clock shadow, the walls are dulled, the bed has been having nightmares. The thin layer of dirt that appears to cover everything now takes me to the dust-covered floor in my visions and I tense up.

Then a ringing in my ears forces me to close my eyes.

I tilt my head to the side, put my little finger inside my right ear and wriggle it furiously. As though it might alleviate some pressure.

Then a sharp pain splits my forehead into two pieces and I move my hand from my ear to the front of my skull trying to block the stab, attempting to suppress the throb.

I open my mouth wide but nothing comes out at first.

Then I manage to release some pressure with a groan as I fall forwards onto the dank bed ahead of me.

Paulson hears my whimper but does nothing, just as he said he would, just as I told him to.

At the point my face comes crashing down onto the quilting, my plunge into darkness ends, the pain subsides instantly and the silence I seek is delivered.

Complete quiet.

With the exception of the shuffling feet.

There is no sense of the location for the next murder other than being inside.

The last thing I remember is the girl placing a cloak over the boy's head and plunging us all into blindness. I wake to see the swirling art nouveau pattern that Audrey picked out for the bedspread.

I have no idea how much time has passed, how long I've been out of it. The light in the room is the same. The smell is the same. I can hear the TV downstairs, a mumbled voice, some canned laughter. Perhaps I was screaming and Paulson turned it up to drown me out, obeying my request.

Pushing myself up from the bed, I feel refreshed, like I have rested for the night. When I get to the bottom of the stairs I can see that Paulson is asleep, sitting in one of the armchairs, the half-full cup of coffee in his hand now cold, the television blaring out some American sitcom.

'Paulson.' I speak softly so as not to shock him. But he doesn't even flinch.

'Paulson.' I say this at a normal level but evoke an identical response.

'Paulson!' This time I raise the volume and shorten his name to almost one syllable; the *s* hisses and he jumps awake. The coffee wobbles but he clenches and steadies it, preventing a spillage.

'Oh God, Jan.' He lets out a long exhalation to illustrate his shock. 'Is everything all right?'

'I've seen them,' I declare.

'You've seen them?'

'I've seen them,' I repeat, nodding in affirmation.

Paulson uses his left hand on the arm of the chair to lever his frame more upright and asks, 'And?' He pauses for a second, his eyes bulging as he leans forward for a response. 'What did they say? Do you know where it's going to be? Where the next murder will occur?'

I touch my forehead with my hand before swiping it slowly to the back of my head, pushing my hair flat. Rubbing the back of my neck as though I have slept all night in an awkward position, I look at the ceiling as if trying to recall something, trying to decrypt the message. I say, 'You know . . .' I trail off briefly and he edges his body forward even more. 'They're not just telling me where it will be, I can see that much now.' My partner holds his breath waiting for the next sentence to come out of my mouth. 'They are revealing something about each other. They are also trying to hide something of one another.'

'O-kaaaaaay.' He screws his forehead up to signal that he is hoping for elaboration.

'We already know when it will be. For the first time, I think they are attempting to convey who it will be.'

'Who *what* will be?' Paulson asks, just for clarification.

'The killer.'

'The killer,' he affirms.

'And the victim.'

'And the victim?' He accentuates the *and*.

'The killer and the victim. That must be what they represent.'

Tomorrow morning we meet with Alison, our Pagan specialist.

She can see what is happening. She understands the things that we do not.

She is too late.

Gray

❖

I lay in bed last night, awake, worried about what today would bring. Petrified at what the doctors are going to say about my nephew. I have to be brave for my sister, on the outside at least. I can't show how anxious I am – she needs a strong man around. What shows on the outside is seldom what is felt on the inside.

I would take his place if I could.

Before the day ends, my concern will cease.

My want will be heard.

Death is on my back.

Not far behind.

Watching.

I hate being underground: it makes me sweat, I get distressed, I panic myself into hyperventilation; but I hate buses even more, so there's no choice, really. The two men next to me speak in what sounds like French. They hold on to the overhead bar, their armpits aimed at my face, their laissez-faire attitude towards personal hygiene evident; a stench washes over me.

Inside, I gag.

Outside, I'm stoic.

I keep my breathing shallow so as not to inhale but have to give in eventually to prevent an anxiety attack.

I'm completely unaware that this is my last ride on the tube, that there was no need to waste my money on a return ticket.

That the next time I go underground it will only be one-way.

The Bakerloo line takes me to Waterloo. I make a wrong turn somewhere but still manage to get overground in the place I want to be. As I follow someone through the turnstile, grabbing my ticket as it pops up at the other side, I see a sign above me that points right towards St Thomas' Hospital.

That's where I need to go.

It's where I should stay.

And wait.

I make a dash for the exit. Stepping out onto the pavement, the sun on my face, I suddenly find myself in the middle of a gaggle of schoolchildren. All dressed in black apart from the girls, who wear yellow plaid skirts. The group parts down the centre and reconvenes on the other side of me before scuttling up the bridge. They are not moving fast enough to create a breeze but I turn noticeably cold.

I continue my journey towards the hospital. To my right, the giant Ferris wheel looms high in the sky between the dirtied architecture of the town hall and an office block. I wait at the traffic lights as the RV1 bus to Covent Garden swings around the corner.

Once across the other side I can see the multi-coloured glass rectangles that hang from the side of the Park Plaza Hotel. I run my fingers along the curved stone wall of the building next to me. I wonder whether it is difficult to hang pictures.

My face turns ashen at the sight of the hospital sign.

It doesn't look like a hospital. It looks like a tower block, or offices, or a car park. To the right, across Westminster Bridge, I see the Parliament buildings, I see St Stephen's Tower, I see history. Ahead, I see grey, I see depression, I see death. I see my nephew in an undersized coffin on my shoulder with three unknown, hired, pall-bearers, because his mother can't be expected to carry his body and aside from her I am all he has.

I see everything but the one person who can see me.

I turn my head away, trying to look at anything but the towering, dull edifice I am here to occupy for an hour.

The number 148 bus to White City.

The pink sign suggesting a trip to the Florence Nightingale Museum.

The oriental girl in strange, revealing attire.

Inside, I tell myself I'm too old.

Outside, I give her another sly glance.

I take a look at the blue sign on the building in front which reads: 'Westminster Bridge Consulting Rooms'. This is where I have to meet my sister to talk about her son, my nephew, and his illness. I bring my left wrist up towards my chin, look at my watch, back at the sign, back at the watch. I'm early. I missed a lot of the consultation last time because I took the bus and was held up. This time I have time to kill.

So I start to wander.

This is my mistake.

With each pace I get further from where I should be, with the last of my family, my responsibility; each step taking me closer to Celeste.

January

❖

'**V**ernal meaning youthful,' she says, with confidence. We all, myself, Paulson and Murphy, nod as though we knew this.

'Equinox obviously referring to a time of balance. This time between light and dark,' she continues. 'It is the point of the calendar before day is longer than night.'

I think back to my last recollection of The Two. This woman is making sense of my dreams; giving meaning to the thing which only I see.

Her name is Alison Aeslin. And she is not what I expected.

Her hair is not long, unwashed and straggly. Her skirt is not overly colourful and flowing down to sandal-clad, ringed-toed feet. Her skin does not appear weathered and dirtied from a lifestyle of outdoor cavorting. She doesn't smell like she lives in a field. She is not a cliché.

Alison Aeslin is smart, wearing a grey fitted jacket and tight pencil-skirt, which draws attention to her legs while hugging her buttocks into a perfect heart shape. It's the first thing I notice as I descend the stairs from the office and see her leaning slightly forward at the front desk.

'Ms Aeslin?' I ask, trying to disguise any shock in my voice at her appearance.

She turns her head towards me. Her face is beautiful.

Symmetrical. Straight blond hair that is cut into a bob, not a dowdy, ageing-lady bob but a high-priced, younger style. She uses her right hand to brush some hair away from the smooth skin of her face, and I'm drawn in by turquoise eyes.

'Detective Inspector David,' she replies, stretching out a hand as though this were the start of a high-powered business meeting.

I reciprocate the gesture, gripping her delicate fingers, restraining myself from allowing her to call me January. The coldness of her palms knocks me out of awe.

'Thanks for coming in. If you'd like to follow me upstairs to the office we can get started.'

We small-talk on the way up about the difficulty of her journey into the station, and I thank her for her help again, despite the fact that she has told me nothing as yet. I push the door open and usher her inside. Paulson and Murphy immediately snap to attention.

They introduce themselves as detectives.

Without further ado she launches into what sounds like an opening statement in a court of law. She explains that living life as a Pagan or Wiccan is often a search for balance within one's self, that the beliefs and practices prohibit harm to others. She says *we are all connected* and that it would take longer than this morning to fully acquaint us with the philosophy behind her belief.

And that's fine. I may need her more. I would like to get to know her.

'From the things I have seen in the paper and on the news, whoever is doing this doesn't really understand it either. They're abusing the things we believe and celebrate. Giving us a reputation that does not fit.' For a moment her passion looks as though it may boil over, as her eyes glaze with a thin film of liquid, but she steadies herself. 'It doesn't make sense.'

Most of the things she tells us complement our own investigations into the subject. Sometimes she adds something that we would have had to dig deep for, and other snippets stand out only to me.

She starts, logically, at the beginning.

'Samhain is a point in the year where we honour our ancestors; we acknowledge that death is part of life. We place a positivity on that journey into the dark. Life contains death but also the miracle of rebirth.' She articulates her points with a certainty and clarity you would expect from a business executive. We are all drawn in by her words.

She explains about the significance of casting a circle during ritual, but that the salt circle implies some sort of protection, which does not fit with the act of killing the young Lily Kane. I start to wonder whether the killer could have known their victim was carrying a cancer in her stomach. Could they have seen Lily Kane as the walking dead? Perhaps a hospital worker, doctor, nurse?

She accounts for the presence of the paraphernalia needed in a ritual to celebrate the cycle of life and death.

Not just death.

'But then that usually involves a red, a white and a black ribbon . . .'

She pauses, noticing the recognition on my face. The Two. The boy from The Two. In that first vision he held those ribbons and burned them.

She continues, '. . . but they were not mentioned in the press.' Her eyes fix on my face. 'There's often a herb. Rosemary, usually.'

I remain stoic. Giving nothing away. My mind jumps

back to the scent of the dust-filled room the night before Lily Kane was murdered.

In my first vision of The Two, they were telling me how this would start, they were illustrating the death and its ritualism. Not everything makes complete sense, but their message is clearer.

And so is the killer's.

'These missing details,' she continues, 'could show a lack of understanding of our rituals, they are not getting it quite right, but it may simply be a variation.'

When we discuss the death of the old man, Totty Fahey, she refers to Yule as the winter solstice, the shortest day, solar rebirth. She is unflinchingly upright when telling us that *we must remind ourselves that the world will be green again.*

We learn that sun talismans play a big part in the rituals of this festival, and explains their involvement in the crime scene, but we know these are Pagan or Wiccan. We don't know that there was holly at the location at the time of death because it had blown away, but Alison tells us that this is symbolic as the sacred plant of protection. Perhaps the killer is trying to protect him- or herself. Perhaps they psychotically believe they are protecting their victim; somehow preserving them.

Saving them.

If this is the case we are certainly dealing with a degree of narcissism that could imply the killer is acting out scenes that have caused them discomfort in the past; this time, they are the one who finishes on top.

'As above, so below,' she adds, gesticulating the directions with her icy hands – slightly out of character for her, so far, demure and contained demeanour.

'What did you just say?' I ask curiously. Paulson and

Murphy's eyes switch to my face for the first time since Alice walked in.

'As above, so below,' she repeats. 'This is a celebration of the sun but also our inner sun; our inner spark.'

I think about platforms in my vision of The Two.

Them below.

Me above.

Trying to tell me where the next victim would be slain.

I relive the moment I blew the candle out in front of Lily Kane and she flopped instantly, lifelessly, to the stone beneath. Did I blow out her spark? Am I somehow involved in these rituals? Are The Two making me think too esoterically? Warping the balance of the investigation?

Why has she not mentioned the flashing eyes?

Is she dismissing the salt circles as non-Pagan, non-Wiccan?

More answers breed more questions.

I want to talk to her more, not just about the case, but feel sudden guilt about Audrey. She is still my wife.

'This person might not even be a Pagan?' Murphy suggests, clearly hanging on to his Satanism theory.

'The details are certainly there to suggest that they are, or have a genuine knowledge of the practices and the way we approach rituals. It's just muddled,' our expert offers.

'Misused,' I add.

All four of us discuss the significance of killing in such public places. Alison suggests that some rituals are made for use by an individual, others are to be partaken by a group, and perhaps this bears significance. Maybe the killer feels they are involving those around the immediate area. Paulson offers that it is merely an affront to the authorities. Murphy half jokes that it is a challenge aimed at me.

I move the conversation on.

'We know that Imbolc is also known as the Feast of Bridget.' I try to show her that we have been researching this ourselves.

'Brighid,' she corrects.

'Sorry?'

'Brighid. It is the Feast of Brighid. Bridget is the Christianised version of the Irish fire goddess.' I can't gauge whether she is insulted or merely reasserting her authority on the subject.

'Yes. Brighid. I understand that they, you, Wiccan,' I fumble, 'burn an effigy of Brighid in much the same way that our perpetrator executed Talitha Palladino.' I feel I've rescued the situation somewhat.

She nods.

'It seems, from what you have told us today, that this was actually the first literal adaptation of a ritual.' I leave the question open for her to add something. I can see she wants to.

'Brighid is also the Goddess of Healing.'

I cut in on her, aiming my thoughts only at my team. I instruct them that this is the one constant in all the killings to date. That there is an element of protection and preservation with each of the scenes. It may be that the killer feels they are protecting him or herself, or that they actually believe that taking the lives of these people is somehow helping them, that they are being safeguarded.

They are improving the victims; purifying them.

Our Wiccan consultant for the day fidgets on her chair and we are all drawn back to the shape of her smooth, lean legs. She informs us that Imbolc is the women's festival, but we already knew that. Paulson and Murphy

172

both feel that the fact that lambs are being born and this Sabbat is often associated with milk is immaterial.

I, of course, am reminded of The Two, or lack thereof.

I want to ask her whether snakes are significant, but it will sound so left-field. I don't want to draw any attention from Murphy. I need to see her alone.

Alison Aeslin drops back into her sexy, self-assured stride as she unravels the intricacies of Ostara to the team, a festival of fertility that she herself will be celebrating later in the evening. Immediately, I imagine another literally translated death. A sex-related death.

And the phone rings to notify me that this was in vain.

I am too late again.

A step behind.

I excuse the team from Miss Aeslin's company; she will have to make her own way out. Murphy and Paulson speed out of the office, but I hang back for a second for one last question.

'What is the significance of the cross?' I ask, hunched over my desk, my head stooping low to the same level as her face.

She tells me that it may simply be the points on a compass. North, south, east and west. I had already thought of that. It is important within a ritual because you have to face the right direction. However, these bearings also have corresponding symbols of earth, fire, air and water, she informs me. It may indicate confusion. Mixing the Wicca way with Christianity.

She is correct, of course. She has been extremely helpful.

I wonder whether the earth, fire, air and water may link to the manner in which the victims died.

She has answered all of my questions.

I just haven't asked the right one yet.

The cross holds more gravity.

'Are you available should anything else come up?' I ask her, trying to remain professional.

She nods.

'There are a few other things I'd like to talk to you about, myself.'

She writes down her personal number and tells me to call at any time; she is here to help in whatever way she can.

I call in less than an hour.

Gray

❖

The first thing I do wrong is to head towards the hospital reception.

One of the signs on the wall reads: '24 Hour Accident and Emergency'. The map to the right shows all the sections of the hospital. Evalina Children's Hospital is highlighted with all the colours of the rainbow; this doesn't make it any cuter, it doesn't make it any better, it isn't easier to look at. Below this there is a section labelled 'Lupus Unit'. I walk around the corner to explore for myself, leaving the consulting room on the side of the road, keeping it behind me.

It's another hour before someone recognises that I'm dead.

It's another one hundred and twenty-three minutes until my sister finds out that I have a perfectly legitimate reason for not accompanying her again to the meeting.

The fountains and well-kept garden won't make the news any easier to take. Looking out over the garden, I see Parliament more clearly. The Union flag flutters at full mast.

I continue to walk. The hospital reception is just ahead. I look left as a woman exits one of the doors. The letters above it state: 'Pain Management Unit'. I try not to look, wincing at the possibilities that lie beyond that blacked-out glass door, and I pick up the pace.

The doors open automatically to the reception. I step inside and do a double-take.

To my left is NatWest Bank. To my right, a Marks & Spencer café. There are easily eighty people sitting at tables outside the café, inside the hospital, eating sandwiches, drinking tea, talking, laughing, like they have purposely ventured out for a fake al fresco dining experience. The doors swoosh behind me and I feel like each person stops what they are doing and looks up at me.

Like I don't belong here.

The automatic doors judder open again and startle me into glancing in the other direction. Everyone looks down, only one fixes her stare on me. I do not notice.

The reception desk looks like something you'd see in a hotel. The structure inside would fit happily into the Canary Wharf tube station. It must be deliberate. Anything to make you forget you are actually inside a hospital for sick children.

Maybe this is what I need.

This is where I should wait.

I tell myself it's not a hospital, that I am at a restaurant.

But my eyes catch a glimpse of another sign. It says 'Haemophilic Thrombosis'. It says 'Physiotherapy', 'Plastic Surgery'. It shouts 'Chest Clinic', 'Children's Eye Clinic'. It screams 'Radiotherapy'. My eyes, my stupid fucking eyes, look through the entire list of diseases, the word 'Children's' jumping out at me again and again, and I can't take it.

As I stagger away, back through the automatic doors, a woman with a twin pram, two girls inside, and a boy of around nine trailing after her, comes in the opposite direction. I see her yawn, as if she is here for a lecture, as if she is running a routine. I wonder which of her children is sick. Which of them is blind or deaf or riddled with leukaemia.

And I think of my nephew.

Inside, I'm crying.

Outside, I'm crying.

In these buildings full of anguish, I look the most desperate. I am the weakest.

I have been seen.

I jog back to the main road, away from the discomfort of the main building, but it's not far enough. I turn right, pacing parallel to the consultation room I'll never get back to, until I hit the corner and stop for breath. Through the fence is a dilapidated children's play area, still part of the hospital. Somebody jogs past me but I don't see their face. I look up at the sky for a moment; when I bring my head back down it's as if the world is distorted through heat haze, apart from the route I must now travel.

The path of desperation.

The trail of pious peril.

What I think is a sign is actually a trap.

What I think is fate is merely rotten luck.

I feel I am being enticed in a certain direction, like my limbs are independent from my brain, like I have no choice. I am being pulled by the cathedral and pushed by the silhouette that stalks. Somehow, I'm still aware of things around me.

I don't recall crossing the road but the lights in the tunnel stand out. They increase the blur around the edges of my vision, making this seem more like a dream than it is. Making it seem less like a nightmare.

Looking back at the crossroads by the hospital, the

shadow grows at the other end of the tunnel and my short-sightedness forces anything at that distance to a blur.

I look in all directions, trying to focus on what is real.

I remember a door with the sign '111 Westminster Bridge Road' and three people emerging with trays of sandwiches. I remember the boy in the black T-shirt with a sticker on his chest that says 'Pete'.

As I look back again it seems that everyone is walking in this direction. Ahead, nobody cuts against the grain.

I see a church in front of me on the opposite corner of the crossroads; the side of the building displays orange letters, each three feet high, in the windows, saying 'Offices to let'.

I ignore this church. It's not the right place. It's not the right one. The flow of people guide me past it.

I break away. Taking a road on the right and pulling out of the current. I look back. A figure moves faster than the others, dodging between them, unseen by me. Unseen by anyone. It passes and I feel at ease.

Safety in numbers.

The road is lined with red-brick flats. I hear a plate smash, I hear shouting, but I do not feel that sense of evil. I tell myself it is the hospital, it is the presence of death. I'm half right.

I want to reach the end of this street and turn right. Head back to the hospital. Wait for my sister and sick nephew. Face these facts.

As I hit the next road, an ambulance drives past, dragging me to the left, its siren sending me deeper into trance until I arrive at another crossroads. Until I arrive at St George's Cathedral.

The place that I die.

I enter the cathedral through the door on the right. A sign tells me that the left-hand door can slam and that I should be careful. On entry I can immediately hear the voice of a man, yet nobody is inside.

On each of the pillars that line the great central hall is a flat-screen television; none are turned on. Below each screen is a speaker; this is where the sound is emanating from. The acoustics mean that most speech sounds like a mumble, but I make out the word 'Amen' and then a chorus of singers.

Still I see no one.

I tread carefully, edging cautiously forward, trying to recall my last time in a place of worship. To my right a woman stares at a statue of Mary. A sign informs me that votive candles require a 30p donation. She takes three. Lights them, then performs her own mumble.

I walk in her direction; this seems to be where the sound is coming from.

The singing stops and so do I. Paralysed outside an empty altar. A holy woman of some kind walks past me, a nun, I suppose; she says nothing as she heads further down the aisle towards a larger room near the front of the building. Two elderly black women follow closely behind her, both holding plastic carrier bags containing I don't know what. Both from different supermarkets.

Again, the voice plays through the speakers, dreary and monotonous, trilling indistinctly, his congregation occasionally joining with their own murmured response.

And I move forward again.

To the next chapel.

Where St George waits to hear my prayer and watch over my demise.

Inside the chapel are what look like two large wooden seats with space to kneel and pray. Directly ahead is a marble statue of the saint perched on a box with curtains running the length of it; I step into the first seat and drop to my knees.

Inside, I do not ask why I am doing this.

Outside, I say, 'Dear God.'

I ask for him to take away the pain my nephew feels, I say that my sister needs a break, that he should cut her some slack. I offer to take on their suffering, to endure the discomfort and agony of my nephew so that he does not have to.

I forget my fear. And ignore what I am running away from.

For the split second I feel the blade penetrate, I feel like God has listened to me.

The moment just before I cease to exist, inside, I believe.

Celeste

❖

A round the corner, a congregation says 'Amen' and I settle myself in next to the dead man to complete my ritual. It is his time. A time of rebirth. I do not look at this as death.

At this point in the year I think of my father and his belief that he would be reborn after his death. In this building, any church, I remember my mother saying he abandoned his faith and would go to hell for his mistake. I recall that she let me watch over him knowing this, thinking nothing could be done.

Something can be done, Mother.

Look at me now.

I cleanse these people.

I save them from the hell you were frightened of.

A voice creaks through the speakers. 'Lift up your heart.' The followers moan a response in unison. He continues, 'Let us give thanks to the Lord, our God.'

His sheep sigh another few words in agreement.

I take a deep breath, inhaling the dankness of the cathedral, ingesting hypocrisy as I bow my head and pretend to pray. On the shelf in front of me I place my three small candles. The man to my left waiting to be saved. Waiting to be reborn.

I light the first candle, hidden from view, and recite my own verse.

'The wheel of the year turns once more, and the vernal equinox arrives. Light and dark are equal. The Earth awakes from its slumber and springs forth new life.'

In the background I hear, 'Holy, Holy, Holy Lord.'

All around, their drone reverberates.

At the back of the cathedral another woman drops thirty pence into a slot, takes a candle, speaks a few words to a replica of her Saviour's Mother and totters past us without a second glance. A man kneels in front of a red-gated altar and taps his head, heart and shoulders before immersing himself into prayer.

I light the second candle and say, 'The sun draws ever close to us. May the chill and darkness of winter be swept away.' I look over to my left at the man. I hear a voice proclaim 'Hosanna in the highest' and the priest rings a bell.

I command the man, Graham White, chosen as the most worthy to be purged, 'Rise. Step forth out of the darkness and into the light. Awaken once more in the arms of the Gods.' And I bow my head again in fake worship as a woman with an African headdress drags her feet along the floor on her way to join the laboured rejoicing around the corner, her plastic bag rustling as it hits her moving leg.

When she is gone, I light my third and final candle. The parishioners continue to purr at more uninspiring oration.

'The sky above us, the Earth below us. I thank the universe for all it has to offer and am blessed to be alive today,' I chant in a rushed hush.

I look over again at the one who must be saved and whisper, 'Welcome life, welcome light, welcome spring.'

A bell rings three times.

I take a moment to meditate on the three candles in front of me, ensuring that I do not catch the eye of the idol ahead, aware of the blasphemy and risk of a ritual in this location. But this was not my choosing. I do not decide who needs to be liberated, they do; with their plea for help and release.

I stand directly behind the man and finish my work, welcoming him. 'You have stepped once more into the light and the gods welcome you.'

And he is saved.

I exit to the sound of the Lord's Prayer; fifty people chant along, as yet unaware of the man in their chapel who was taken suddenly and returned a better person, finding his salvation in church but not in their Lord.

I hear them breathe 'Amen.' The word that signifies the end. A word that, to me, has come to mean 'thank God it is over'.

I thank no God.

January

For the first time on this case, I was not trapped in or by my intuition. I was able to move freely inside the latest vision of The Two, even setting a hand on the girl. In the cathedral, also for the first time, there is no salt circle. But that is all the information I have gleaned so far. It's all I have deciphered.

Nowhere in that vision of The Two was a location even alluded to.

But they were not trying to tell me that this time.

There was nothing I could do to save Graham White.

He was always going to die.

This time, The Two were trying to tell me who is committing these atrocities.

They've always been trying to tell me.

I call Alison and ask her to get here as quickly as she can.

I am still desperately hoping to understand this ability. Why, all of a sudden, I need this. I've solved my other cases before Eames without using it. I should be able to solve this case without the visions; they are another thing to contend with, another code to decrypt. It seems that, with each new appearance of my guide, whether it is The Two or The Smiling Man, the level of information and detail is evolving. They start by telling me how the murder will occur, then where, then who. Suddenly there is the possibility for interaction. Their evolution is happening at a different pace to my understanding.

Are they helping?

Are they even real?

Did they manifest themselves out of the desperation I have to find my sister?

I need to make them work in conjunction with my regular police deductions.

Mother's journal entry, two months after Cathy's disappearance, says, 'I give The Fat Man no peace. Now I can haunt *his* dreams.' I question her sanity, always, but she shows development. Perhaps we are not as similar as I thought.

I am standing in the light, blind.

Murphy, as always, thinks it's a copycat killing. The thing I am afraid of.

'It looks similar. The stab wound, public place, candle arrangement, all fit. He was found kneeling, I'll give you that.' He pukes his words out, self-satisfied.

'But...' Paulson chips in.

'But...' Murphy continues, congratulating himself already, 'there is no real sense of ritual. Sure, there are candles, there are candles all over this place...' One of the nuns scowls over at us like an irritated librarian as Murphy's voice begins to travel to further reaches of the holy building. 'But it just seems too easy. Somehow less accomplished.'

He looks at us both for acknowledgement that he is correct.

We say nothing.

'There's not even a salt circle, for crying out loud. I

mean, how easy would it have been to do that?' he continues, trying to prove his point, miming the action of emptying salt in a ring around his feet.

How can I say that know for certain that this is the next in the series? How can I say that I know it looks different, but my vision, my nightmare, my intuition, my torment, was different also? How do I explain to a non-believer?

He drones on, hoping one of us will eventually give in. 'Why, suddenly, inside a cathedral? It just seems so blasphemous and out of character.' I know he wants to end that sentence with 'for a Pagan', because he's still not convinced. He doesn't realise that smug rhetoric is not the way to put forward an argument.

He doesn't recognise that everything he does holds up the investigation.

Unless he is being intentionally provocative, unless derailment is his plan.

I tell him that two of the candles have burned out but one is still alight. I say that this would suggest that the candles were lit at different points in time; that it implies a ritual. A copycat would have just lit them all and left. They would have imitated ritual. I tell him that a salt circle may not have been required; as Alison Aeslin said, casting a circle in a Pagan ceremony does not always mean a literal circle.

I defeat him with conventional detective reasoning.

I don't even need to see Paulson's chubby face to know he is beaming with pride.

Murphy rolls his eyes up and to the right, as if peering into his mind for a prepared retort, but it's too late for that. I'm on a roll. I feel revived.

'The wound and positioning of the victim concurs,

absolutely, with the previous victims. The publicness of this slaying is exactly the reason I feel it is part of the same series. There are far safer, easier and less risky ways to bump off an ex or a lover or a business partner.' I'm starting to pace like a lawyer giving a final address to his jury, gaining confidence with each step.

Another ungracious look lands in our chapel from the nun as one of the constables seals it off by wrapping police tape around a pillar.

'The means, the location, the ceremony, all point to a continuation of this series.

Alison said herself that the slayings do not show a full grasp of the belief system she follows. It is being abused.' This time Murphy just rolls his eyes in resignation.

'This killer thinks of him- or herself as a visionary, killing weak people in a time of great distress. These victims are dotted around London so probably look random. But what is this guy's story? Why was he chosen?' They both stand in silence waiting for me to continue.

'I'm waiting for suggestions.'

'How are we supposed to know who he is?' Murphy chirps in with another attempted barrier.

'That's not the part of the question I am immediately concerned with, Murph.'

'The religious angle,' Paulson suggests. 'Maybe this is a two-fingers-up to Christianity. The killer may not even understand why if they're a confused religious nut.'

'How does that link in with the other victims?' I push back, not for an answer, just to get them thinking. Questioning. Murphy mumbles something under his breath about how this may not even be the same killer. I am preoccupied with the notion that the murderer may still be here, basking in the tumult.

I take my notepad out of my wallet and flick to the page where I have noted down all of the Pagan Sabbats. 'So . . .' I pause as I lick my finger to skim through to the correct page more quickly '. . . we have . . .' I add it up in my head '. . . forty days.'

'Forty days?' Paulson questions. Murphy still stares at the body of Graham White, his eyes flitting between where he now lies and where he knelt only moments ago.

'Beltane,' I respond assuredly. 'Beltane is the next Sabbat. It's the first of May, so that gives us forty days to figure out why this is happening and who is doing it. We have four victims and well over a month to piece this together before another innocent is added to the list.'

I feel like a leader again. I feel a little control returning. I feel stronger.

'What is this guy's story? Is he sick like the two women who have been killed or has he lost someone close to him like Totty Fahey.' My mind always comes back to Totty. He saved me. His tragedy pulled me from the dark abyss.

But I still feel I need to fully understand The Two. I need to continue working through Mother's scribblings.

Alison arrives through the cathedral doors.

Maybe she can help me with that.

Once she has had the opportunity to view the body, I take Alison outside with Paulson to discuss further. Murphy waits inside with the man we will come to know as Graham White and the one we will eventually know as Celeste Varrick.

Hiding in plain sight.

V

I prefer running in the rain. There's something refreshing about it. Cleansing, even. But the weather is starting to change; it's getting warmer. In the coming months it will be harder to breathe. In June I will have less energy and much more to do.

I'll have someone else to take care of.

For now, I've been advised to leave her alone. To continue the preparations.

Gail stops me in the hall, like she usually does.

'Morning, Sam. Keeping it up, I see.' She smiles and puts me at ease.

I don't recognise that she is flirting; that we've both always flirted.

I smile back at her and expect her to walk past to my flat but something is different this morning. She is stand - ing in the centre of the walkway, almost blocking me.

'I'm, er, having a few people over tonight for some drinks . . .' She looks down at her shoes for a brief moment.

'Oh, OK,' I say, interrupting her. 'That's fine. Not much sound travels through my walls,' I trail off innocently.

'No, no, no. I was just wondering whether you fancied coming over at all. Doesn't have to be the whole night. Maybe just for a glass of wine. Or if you don't drink . . .'

'I drink,' I laugh. 'Wine. I drink wine. Yes, I can certainly come over at some point, I'm sure.' I would only be drinking at home alone anyway.

'Great. Well, just come over . . . whenever. As long as it's after eight.' Her face lights up and she performs her trademark talk-while-you-walk-off routine that I am so used to.

I call back to her, 'OK. After eight.' But she has already disappeared down the stairs.

The rolled-up paper waits for me with the news of another London slaying. This time in a cathedral on the South Bank. The first time the killer has so overtly disrespected a specific faith. I read the article in its entirety, noting the profanity and irreverence; my naked body twitches as I peruse the journalist's words, leaning on the counter, performing my isometric stretches.

I know I cannot act. I want to. But that is not how it works.

My mind floats back to the meeting with Gail a moment ago. I'm lacking focus.

Why did I say yes to her invitation?

Have I forgotten why I am here?

The short spell of exuberance I felt in the hallway is blown away by the outrage I feel towards the article. Now I think about Gail again and pleasure returns. What part does she play?

Lord, why do I need her?

I should only want my wife.

Is this my temptation?

Is this my test?

This can't continue like this. Celeste cannot be allowed to take another.

I drop to my knees on the cold tile floor of the kitchen.

'*Das berinu mireca ol tahila dodasa tolahame caosago homida,*' I whisper, my hands clenched together in front of my mouth, my lips touching my left thumb as I speak.

This is my call for vengeance, for the manifestation of justice.

I spring straight up to my feet again in one movement. The message I receive is clear.

I must wait. It is not the right time.

Just one more.

I will witness Celeste with the next victim. I will see it with my own eyes.

Soon, we shall be together.

January

A lison agrees to meet with me.
This evening. Alone. At her place.

It is not a date.

'It's going to help me get in the mind of this…' I pause, not wanting to say *killer* or *psychopath*. She doesn't jump to my aid. '…this person we are after if I can experience Ostara genuinely.'

She buys into it and agrees.

I think I may just want to see her, to have that kind of company again. To break my current routine. To remind me of Audrey. I function better when I feel guilt. Self-reproach is my fuel.

I arrive at her place in South London wearing the same clothes I wore to work, my suit and shirt – no tie. That way it is still work; it does not look like I have made an effort. Apart from the bottle of wine.

I tap my knuckles loudly against the mottled window of her front door and look around cautiously to see whether anybody noticed. Two urban foxes creep past on the pavement. A figure descends from the stairs that lie directly behind the door. I hear her rustle the chain then she opens the door to greet me.

'Detective David,' she smiles, 'do come in.'

The sleek hair, perfectly applied make-up and fitted suit are gone. Her hair seems more natural, less styled, and her skin is somehow more pure. She is wearing dark blue jeans, which hold all the right shapes of her legs, and a simple white T-shirt, also tight but flattering. Her feet are bare and delicate.

I hand her the wine and stutter something about my gratitude to her for taking the time out to help. She thanks me but says we won't need any this evening.

She leads the way upstairs and I follow, my gaze fixed on the way her body moves from behind, remembering Audrey's legs and buttocks and back and neck.

And betrayal.

The hallway leads directly into a large kitchen area. Most work surfaces are covered with flowers. It seems excessive but I realise it must be part of the Ostara celebrations as the route down another set of stairs into the garden is lined with blossoms too. This is where she wants to take me first.

'I have beer or mead, if you are interested,' she offers, setting the wine down on an out-of-the-way surface. I remember that this is the traditional choice for drinking this evening and hope I haven't offended her with the wine.

'Mead would be great.' I don't like it but I think it may go some way to showing my commitment to this process.

I ask whether we will be going anywhere tonight.

'There are celebrations of all sorts. Some Sabbats I enjoy sharing with others, some I prefer to be solitary. If you'd like to get involved though . . .'

'Oh, er, thanks but I think I might get more from observation, you know?' I take a nervous sip of the drink, trying not to grimace at the bitterness.

'That's fine.' She smiles that faultlessly straight-teeth smile. 'Follow me outside.'

The yard outside is lit with white candles. It is paved, with a wooden table, six chairs and bench decorating it. There are several potted plants to add colour and a large timber rectangle full of home-grown herbs.

She lights a scented wood and incants words in different directions of her inner-city garden.

'I am offering the cedar to the four directions and praying to the Great Spirit,' she explains.

I nod in acknowledgement.

'The cedar not only acts as a purifier but it also attracts the good energies.'

This is the first time that she has really spoken in the way people stereotype this belief. Wishy-washy. Flowery.

I wonder whether the killer is performing something similar at this moment. Perhaps the taking of Graham White's life was the killer's purification ceremony.

'Any other questions?'

'No. It's all very clear, thanks.' I sip politely at the mead.

'Then, please, follow me back inside for the smudging.'

Inside she takes what looks like a wand and lights the edge. The distinct smell of sage is emitted and I follow her around the house as she waves her hand to force the smoke in the direction she desires.

'It's important to get it into the corners because energy gathers in these places and festers over the winter months. This drives out the negative entities and protects the area.'

I wish that would work on my mind.

I glean very little about the Wiccan life from watching her perform these rituals but I enjoy her company. Before I realise, she is topping up my glass and we are leaning against the kitchen cupboards talking about the case.

Her insights are valuable; I have a strong sense of the killer. But that is not why I am here.

Eventually, we slide our bodies down to the floor until I am leaning against the cupboard which holds her saucepans, one leg stretched out, the other with a knee pointing towards the ceiling. She sits cross-legged next to me, facing my profile.

I feel comfortable.

And I tell her about The Two and the things I have seen.

She does not judge.

'I'm standing up this time but half blind; only my left eye can see. Blinking furiously, I start to panic, maniacally shaking my head from side to side, hoping my right eye will kick in. As I look down towards my feet, I notice a line. A perfectly straight line that bisects my body, cutting half into light and half into darkness. I breathe to steady myself again.'

She nods and drinks beer from a tumbler, never taking her eyes from mine, allowing me to talk without embarrassment.

'I look ahead, my left pupil a speck, my right, a saucer. But The Two are not where they should be. They are closer this time. They are either side of me. To my left is the girl, I'm certain, five metres from where I stand, the closest I have ever been to her. She shuffles from her left foot to her right, the rhythm bringing my breathing back to an acceptable level. But I can only hear her.'

She cannot be seen.

'Ostara is a time of balance,' Alison observes. 'Black and white. Blindness and sight. But you already knew when the next murder was likely to take place so they must be trying to tell you something else.'

She believes me. She hears that I have vivid, cryptic visions the day before a murder is committed and she does not scoff or placate. She listens. She makes suggestions.

She helps.

I continue. 'The boy joins in to my right. In the darkness. Copying her tempo, he wears all black. He is the same distance away from me. I can see him. His eyes flash purple. They flash green. Yellow. In the air I taste sweetness. I taste sugar. Honey. Then the boy beckons me as he did before. I look left for the girl.'

'You feel safer with her?'

'Perhaps. Yes. Is that significant?'

'Maybe. At some point.' She sips her drink again.

'She is waving at me. Shaking her head in slow-motion. Exaggerating her movements as if talking in sign lan - guage. I can't see her, but somehow I know this.'

I explain how I attempt to move towards the boy and he drops down into the darkness ten feet for every step I take. All the while, staring at me, tempting me nearer.

'The closer you want to get, the further he falls,' Alison chimes in with her suggestion.

'I thought that maybe they were trying to tell me where the murder would take place. Somewhere with three levels or a lift, maybe. But that doesn't fit with the church where we found the victim. I couldn't feel the cold this time so I knew it was inside but that's it.' I gulp down half a glass of the mead I now have a taste for; my mouth is dry from all the talking.

Now more animated I move to my knees so that I face my new friend and I impart the final section of my vision.

'I take a step towards the light; my blind side. Looking back over my shoulder, I see that the boy has fallen to his knees and that his eyes are shut. The flashing has stopped. With each new step I take towards the girl I turn back, like an ant ensuring his path in the sunshine. The boy doesn't move. The gradient alters and I find myself moving downwards. Three steps. Four. My hands are stretched out in front of me and, on the fifth step, they touch something.'

'The girl?' she questions, open-mouthed.

I nod, bouncing excitedly.

'I look back to the boy. But he is gone. The girl waves her hands and shakes her head only centimetres from where my hand had just been. She is trying to tell me something.'

Gesturing to a blind man.

Screaming silently to a man who can't hear.

'As I turn back to the girl, the boy appears behind her, holding a large piece of black cloth. He lifts it up, illuminating the white figure briefly before me, then throws it over the girl, dropping us all into black and I wake up.'

I settle back down, sitting on my heels. Alison picks out the segments she feels she understands as Wiccan. The scents, the black cloak, the pursuit of balance. She suggests that, perhaps, The Two are not representative of murderer and victim.

'Maybe there are two killers.'

Disciple murderers could fit the profile.

But I do not get the sense from my visions that they are working together. It is their opposition that creates balance. The crime scenes also suggest someone working alone.

'Perhaps that is why the faiths seem so muddled,' she adds.

Alison is wrong about the case but correct about my visions. She has helped me unpick more of their meaning and place within the case.

In a position where our faces are so close, the alcohol coursing through our blood, a seemingly successful decryption of The Two's message, I feel I want to thank her, kiss her. This would be the opportunity.

But Audrey will not let me.

Beltane
May 2009

Celeste

—◆—

G od of the green,
    Lord of the forest.
  I offer you my sacrifice.
  I ask you for your blessing.

Tonight is a time when mortals and faery are close; the opposite to Samhain. This is the time of the green man, consort of the goddess.

  When we welcome in summer.

  The festival of fire and fertility brings with it another victim.

  Someone else to be saved.

You are the deer in rut,
    mighty Horned one,
    who roams the open woods,
    the hunter circling round the oak,
    the antlers of the wild stag,
    the lifeblood that spills upon the ground each season.

Tonight, on this final darkness in April, as we welcome in the dawn of the new month, myself and my captor are closer than ever, sharing this date, the importance of this time is equalled.

God of the green,
    Lord of the forest.
    I offer you my sacrifice.
    I ask you for your blessing.

Many rituals are taking place around the heath. Nobody sees me. I walk like a ghost. I work alone.
    Undetected.
    Undetectable.
    Behind me, a large bonfire grows, illuminating the night sky, ushering in the dawn. The women wear circles of flowers on their heads, some men wear antlers. The god of the forest has chased the May Queen around the roaring flames three times, and their passionate kiss has turned into something far more erotic. The on-looking partners, after banging their drums loudly and chanting, form their own coital partnerships. Some are merely covered with a blanket on the grass, some move further into the woods. Sometimes a man will leave with another man, and sometimes a woman will take a woman.
    I am in the wooded area with a woman.
    Laura Noviss.
    She is already dead.
    My ritual is almost complete.

In the darkness of the undergrowth, the man who calls himself V watches me. Wanting to take me now. Knowing he cannot.
    He tells himself that I won't get away with this.
    With the girl kneeling in front of me, shadowed by trees, I take the bag from my shoulders and empty the

contents. A white candle, a bowl, a bottle of water, five perfectly formed pebbles and a bottle of wine as an offering.

I feel him watching me.

And surround myself with an unbroken line of salt.

Now I am protected.

Because I believe.

'I am Celeste Varrick,' I pronounce out loud, 'and I stand before you, goddesses of the sky and earth and sea. I honour you, for your blood runs through my veins. One woman, standing on the edge of the universe. On this night, I make an offering in your names.'

I kneel down opposite the dead girl and place the large white candle between us. I dig a small hole, burying half of the candle and patting it tight so that it does not move and cannot fall.

I light the candle and make the offering of the wine, opening the bottle and pouring half onto the earth between us, the two women present. Again, I rise to my feet and call upon Isis, Ishtar, Tiamat, Inanna, Shakti and Cybele, the mothers of the ancient people.

'Your strength has flown through me,' I declare. 'Your wisdom has given me knowledge.'

The one who calls himself V digs his fingers into the bark of the tree he hides behind.

On this night of all nights his anger can transform into lust. Tonight, especially, all emotion ends in lust.

I drop back to my knees. I place the bowl in front of my circle and fill it with the water from my bottle.

A branch snaps in the blackness of the woods where the one I will come to know as V is invisibly pacing.

This is venom transforming into lust.

'I am Celeste Varrick and I kneel before you to honour the sacred that have touched my heart.'

I drop the first pebble inside the bowl and announce, 'I honour Lily Kane, who showed me the way. My maidenhead.'

I give her a short moment of silence.

I repeat the process three more times aloud.

I honour Totty Fahey.

I honour Talitha Palladino.

I honour Graham White.

All who have passed.

Each receiving their own moment of reflection.

With the fifth and final stone, I retain my focus on the girl ahead of me; she is my dark reflection. I drop the stone and silently, in my head, I say, 'And I honour you, for you are the most special of all.' I do not yet know her name. She was chosen only for her weakness.

I finish by standing and stating that, 'I am Celeste Varrick and I honour myself, for my strength, my creativity, my knowledge, my inspiration and for all the remarkable things that make me a woman. For everything I am now and yet to become.'

Looking to the sky, I feel the heat on my back and the top of my head from the blaze behind me. I sense the sexual desire and lasciviousness that breeds and multiplies around me in the grass. I tremble, a fulfilled shudder as the one who calls himself V sinks his gaze into my breast.

Hatred metamorphosing into a desperate urge.

I try to focus my attention back to the girl with no life in her, the latest victim, whose journey is just beginning. I attempt to meditate on the ritual and reflect on the feminine energy. Those around me are part of this ceremony without knowing. I need them.

With passions high I exit the circle, making myself vulnerable, and I run. Sprinting across the green, leaving my candle to burn out, vacating my altar, travelling in the opposite direction to the man.

He watches me disappear into the crowd, waiting for my golden hair to cease from shining as I pass the spitting embers of the celebratory inferno. And, when I am gone, when consternation gives way to rationality, he makes his way over to see what I have done to the girl.

He is there when I disappear.

He is seen when I am not.

For him I am the darkness and he is the light.

His eyes cover the entire scene and surrounding area. He looks over his shoulder at the merriment that continues on the heath, the participants unaware of the brutality that lies yards from their frivolity.

He bends down, blows out the candle.

And leaves.

Not everyone can be saved.

V

I lean against the back of the door to my flat; my forearms and hands rest against the wood, my head not quite touching the door, looking down at the floor between my feet. I feel relieved to be home.

The scene of Celeste Varrick's ritual still lingers in my mind, keeping me on the edge of seething rage and, alarmingly, carnal explosion. The confines of my own haven soothe me and I take a few deep breaths to attempt some calm.

But this is an important night.

And I can't shake this feeling.

Soon, I find myself rocking, unable to remain still. Incapable of focusing. I swing my hips from side to side. Left to right. Left to right. I rock back on my heels and tap my toes on the floor. I breathe again, out through my mouth, a long, drawn-out breath.

In through my nose. Then out through my nose. My nostrils flaring. My breathing hastens again, in through my nose, out through my nose, until I am panting and rocking and tapping my feet, until it builds within me and I release with a five-second clamour, pounding my fists rhythmically against the wood of the door.

Gail hears this from her apartment across the hall.

I run both hands over my face as I turn to the living

room, brushing my stubble in both directions, the bottle of Merlot on the table screaming at me.

I am gulping down the earthy claret liquid by the mouthful when somebody bangs against the door from the other side.

'Sam? Sam?' Gail's voice calls out in between rasps. 'Is everything all right?'

She waits a moment.

My eyes widen, as if I can see her through the wood.

I glimpse left at the room I will soon keep Celeste contained within. So she can no longer interfere with these people

Gripping the bottle by the neck in my left hand I stride towards the door.

'Sam.' She knocks again, harder this time. 'Sa—'

I open the door and drag her in by her blouse, creasing it instantly. She tries to open her mouth to ask me what is going on, but I have her inside the flat by this time, the door closed behind her. I press her up against it while forcing my lips onto hers.

Initially she tries to shake her head from side to side but I am too strong for her.

I release my grip on the bottle but it doesn't break as it hits the floor. I use this hand to grab hold of Gail's left leg, plunging my fingers around her hamstring and levering her knee up to my waist. Leaning my chest on her breasts puts more weight on her, pinning her back in position.

Overcome with lust, I force another kiss. She moves her head back as if trying to move away, but at the same time forcing her pelvis into me a little more. I thrust as if I am already inside her, pinning her sharply upright, her buttocks slapping hard against the wood of the door.

Using my left forearm to press her arm back, I grab a

clump of her hair in my fist and tug her head back to stop her moving. We look at each other without saying a word. Her eyes are glazed with a thin film of tears.

I release my grip slightly, allowing her to move her head freely.

Slowly, cautiously, her chin lifts as her mouth moves closer to mine. She takes my bottom lip in between her teeth, not tightly, not biting, just enough tension to grip it firmly, and pulls at it, all the time looking me in the eyes. With a quick jerk backwards she wrenches my mouth back to hers and we kiss passionately again. She kicks her right leg up and around my waist, her thighs like pincers gripping me, writhing against me, arousing me further.

I release my clasp of her arms so that I can unbutton my trousers. She uses her free hand to reach down in between her legs and rips her underwear ferociously to one side.

With my trousers now loose, Gail grips me hard and eases me an inch inside her before thrusting herself downwards until I am completely swallowed within her. She lets out a guttural pant as she comes crashing down.

This is not like the first time we had sex.

It is, in fact, the complete opposite.

But that night was not Beltane.

It was not Walpurgisnacht.

That night, it wasn't even sex. It felt more sensual than that, more emotional. There was a physical tenderness, an emotional maturity, taking into consideration the baggage that we both brought with us to the situation.

Tonight, we are just fucking. And, as we both land on the floor next to the wine bottle, panting, exhausted and bruised, I think of my wife.

And I weep.

And I blame Celeste Varrick for making me feel these things.

And this is the last time she gets away with it.

January

——✦——

It makes no sense. Tomorrow is not Beltane, it is not 1 May. Tomorrow is the day before Beltane. The last day in April.

So, why are they here?

I sneeze violently. The dust in this perpetual black box replicates pollen as the temperature proves warmer than usual. The sound does not echo.

This does not feel indoors.

Everything is black for a while.

I wait. Sitting down, legs crossed like a schoolchild, I don't need to reach forwards to realise that I am inside my invisible protective tubing. Alison believes that this represents the salt circle, that the killer may be trying to safeguard themselves or feels as though they are protecting the victim somehow.

I am learning to read all over again.

I'm not scared, I know that I just have to wait for the shuffle and, eventually, it comes.

I remember everything for Alison.

I can smell mown grass. The scent of flowers and wet cloth wafts its way through me. The dust and dirt being transferred from right to left only a few metres in front of me, but all is dark and I do not know which of The Two dances ahead of where I sit.

And I see two small lights flash green.

Then red.

Then white.

And I know it's the boy.

So I don't feel as safe as I did a moment ago.

Where is *she*?

Then it all happens quite quickly.

The boy drops to his knees, his eyes, a bright white, focus intently on me. I get up to my feet and his head tilts up to keep that gaze fixed on my expression. The warmth grows more fierce, as if he is radiating heat. My face starts to tighten. I start to perspire.

His head darts quickly to his right as if hearing a noise over his shoulder.

Then he looks back at me.

All the while, the heat increases, somehow making the dark turn to light.

His head looks over his shoulder again. Distracted by a sound.

I smell something burning.

The stench of recent fornication drifts by and sticks to the sweat beads that slide down my temples.

Then she appears. Running into the scene from my left.

She sprints straight towards the boy and I expect them to collide. He seems oblivious. His two bulbs are burned into my skull.

He does not see her.

As she gets closer to him, her partner, she avoids impact and instead chooses to run around him. Circling him again and again at speed. Punching her fists in the air, screaming her silent scream.

The boy appears to ignore her.

I sneeze again.

I smell red wine.

The boy reaches inside his pocket and pulls out a stone. As the girl continues to shout her silent profanities he launches the projectile in my direction. It hits my transparent barricade at the exact height of my face and I flinch. But no harm is done.

She continues to run rings.

He reaches inside his pocket again, pulls out another object, looks directly at me and launches it. Even though I am protected, even though I know he cannot harm me, my natural reaction is to recoil as it hits. My circle of protection seems to grow smaller.

I hear the sound of a rustling crisp packet.

I sniff in a combination of musk and dust.

The girl slows down and walks around him this time, her hands on her hips.

Again, he reaches inside his pocket and propels a rock in my direction.

Her pace increases to a jog.

The shielding squeezes in tighter on me.

Seconds later, a fourth missile impacts my safeguard and the girl stretches out her legs to full sprint once more.

I see light.

In the distance, a great light rises up, taking the darkness with it.

The boy kisses his fifth bullet. As he launches it, the white washes over him, the girl runs from it in my direction, following the rock. I see her pale face as it heads towards me.

She seems to be whistling.

I want to reach out to her but my arms are pinned to my side.

But the wave of light catches her first and I wake in bed sitting bolt upright.

My brain hurtles through the information we have uncovered and channels the musings of Alison Aeslin and her in-depth knowledge. The haze clears as I recall the intricacies of the Beltane goddess ritual, so similar to actions of The Two in my dream, and, for a brief moment, I entertain the idea that the killer may be female. I know the next victim is planned to be murdered at an outdoor location. There is quite clearly a sexual element to this so I flit back to the notion of a male killer. I still do not understand the flashing eyes but the visions are supporting the material evidence.

I look left for Audrey, to tell her everything is all right. To reassure her it was just a bad dream. But nobody is there. Of course. Just one of Mother's untranslated journals lying open on a double page with the never-ending, nonsensical sentence: maniswomanismaniswomanisman iswomanismaniswomanismaniswoman . . .

Celeste

⸻✦⸻

I arrive home just in time to see it. The dawn of a new day, a new time.

Standing in front of my bedroom window, I close my eyes and lift my head to the sky. In the distance, the sun is beginning to peep over the rooftops, ushering in the new season, bringing with it all the joys of fruitful loins and high-yielding fields. The light begins to hit me, firstly on my thighs and rising higher with every passing second.

With my eyes still shut, I place my hands at the top of my legs, stroking the brightness up my body. As it lifts, illuminating the once dark streets, I place both hands between my legs, gently caressing the May lustre towards my stomach, hoping it slows its steady ascent.

I leave my left hand where it is, working around in small anti-clockwise circles; my right hands strokes up - wards to my stomach as the effulgence creeps up my body. I grip my stomach tightly as the skin warms, half of me now awash with gratitude.

The line of darkness lifts above my breast; I feel it, this is change. I embrace my left breast strongly, working my fingertips across my heart to the right where I brush in softer, slower lines. My left hand continues, increasing in pace, bringing the pleasure I feel I deserve, the reward for my work.

My right hand moves up my neck, my fingertips touching my earlobes. The new day is near. This is birth.

I move my hand around the back of my neck, pushing my hair to the side, my palm edging across the top of my spine and up the back of my head; my thick hair drapes across the back of my hand and I comb through with my fingers, down my forehead, my forefinger and middle finger splitting either side of my eye, my little finger scraping my bottom lip down and opening my mouth. I suck in the sunshine.

I inhale the summer.

As my middle finger descends, it hooks onto my teeth for a short time as the movement of my left hand becomes more emphatic. I move it down my chin, the tip damp with saliva; it strokes down my neck, between my breasts and stops at my stomach, mimicking the other hand as it circles my bellybutton.

I push my knees together, squeezing my left hand tightly between my thighs as I near climax. Eventually, I relax again, opening my eyes to the new dawn; the sky is bright, it's a new age.

I look out through the glass at nothing, just brightness, just hope. I haven't tried to make myself invisible; my act has been on full view to anyone who cared to watch, but it was not about that, it was about embracing the moment.

I drop back onto my bed and allow myself to drown in the light. I make a promise for this new year, that I will continue my work with increased vigour. That I will search and open myself up to more people who have a troubled mind, an endangered soul.

That I will hunt these people down and save them from themselves, from their own desperation.

In those last moments when death is imminent, when they pray that there is a god, I will be there as their saviour, to let them know that there is worse.

January

---✦---

Paulson is still awake when I call, playing poker online, fleecing a legion of unsuspecting drunkards; he has eight different games playing at the same time on one screen, and still has the mental capacity to answer the phone.

'Jan. It's late. Everything OK?' he asks, not surprisingly sounding slightly distracted. I hear the tap of the keyboard as he sends the word 'unlucky' to AcesHigh39.

'It's tomorrow,' I say.

'It certainly is: 3.26 a.m. That makes it tomorrow, I guess.' He clicks once on the mouse to go all in on an Ace and a Five before the flop.

Everyone folds.

'OK.' I sigh at this late-night humour. 'Tonight, some - one is going to die. Tonight.' I pause briefly to allow him time to digest this information. 'Thirtieth of April.' I wait again. 'Not the first of May as we originally thought.'

In the game at the top left corner, BrumAndy1975 sends the message 'U SUK'.

'Fuck. The thirtieth? But . . .' He lets out a long breath. 'The whole Pagan thing . . .' He trails off again. 'Where does that . . .' Annoyingly, he can't seem to finish a sentence because he's too preoccupied by the £600 re-raise on table 145683235.

'Look, I don't know yet,' I hope that Alison might, 'but we need to get on this now. It's not making sense and the clock started ticking as soon as I woke up. So . . .' I hear a crashing as Paulson moves things around on his desk, collecting his wallet and keys and badge, shutting down his games or ticking the small box that allows him to sit out the next hand as long as he pays up the ante on his turn.

'I'm coming over.' He's already racing his way down the stairs of his house, focused on getting to me, deciphering the vision, catching this slayer.

I go to respond but he has already folded his phone in half, cutting me off to concentrate on getting here as quickly as possible.

I kill twenty-three minutes by drinking an overly peaty whisky and laying the various pages of the case file out onto the living-room floor. With a large blue marker, I start to write on the wall; I have no whiteboard at home and no one to tell me to do otherwise.

Paulson's tyres displace the stones in the driveway, alerting me to his arrival. I open the front door and wait on the doorstep for him, his steps making heavy going of the pebbles.

Seeing me waiting, he says, 'Better get the kettle on, eh?' I lift my glass up as if to say, *I'll be fine with this.* And I walk back in, Paulson following closely behind, eager to get down to business.

I am still writing on the wall when Paulson finally enters after brewing himself a pot of his favourite Mocha Java. I have set it up to look identical to our room at the station. I should have thought of doing this before but I never liked bringing work home with me when Audrey was here.

On the far left it says:

> *Lily Kane*
> *31 Oct, '08*
> *Samhain*
> *Parsons Green*

Below are pictures taken from the scene in black and white.

Next to this, in the same format, I have written:

> *Totty Fahey*
> *21 Dec, '08*
> *Yule*
> *Trafalgar Square*

I repeat for Talitha Palladino and Graham White:

> *Talitha Palladino*
> *1 Feb, '09*
> *Imbolc*
> *Speaker's Corner, Hyde Park*

> *Graham White*
> *21 Mar, '09*
> *Ostara*
> *St George's Cathedral, Southwark*

On the far right it says

?
1 May, '09
Beltane
???

On the adjacent wall I have taped a street map of London.
Each murder location has a drawing pin. Paulson stops
with his mug of coffee and stares at the green dots that
mark the four deaths so far, trying to find some kind of
pattern.

It looks like a lopsided trapezium.

There's nothing there to go on; it does not form a Pagan
symbol, perfect square or straight line.

This is the real police work. Elimination.

I don't even mention the intuition until he brings it up.

I turn around from the wall after adding the last dot of
punctuation. Paulson looks at me wide-eyed and sips at
his too-hot coffee.

'We need to turn these question marks into a location.'
I point at the three under the word *Beltane*. 'Otherwise
this' – I direct the felt tip at the single mark above the
words *1 May* – 'will become another innocent person's
name.'

I throw back the remaining few millimetres in my
tumbler.

'Tell me what you saw this time, Jan. What do we
know?' He drops his weight down onto the leather.

I stay standing.

'It's outside. It's definitely outside.' I explain the lack of
echo in my vision, the heat on my face, the smell of the
grass.

All of the murders have been outside with the excep -
tion of Graham White, but they have all been conducted

in an open environment with plenty of possible witnesses, but this isn't giving us huge insight into the mind of our killer.

We fixate on the scent of grass and decide that it has to be in a field. We rule out graveyards that have grassy areas because the volume of living people you'd find there would not follow the pattern of the previous four murders.

I move over to the map and cross off Hammersmith Cemetery. I scribble over Brompton Cemetery. I move east, colouring in any burial grounds or churchyards, any necropolis that is insignificant to our plight.

A line through St Luke's Burial Ground.

A cross through Tower Hamlets Cemetery Park.

A blot on Ladywell Cemetery.

'There's still a lot of green on that map, Jan,' Paulson points out, sipping his coffee.

But this is really only the beginning.

'Do you think one of the bigger parks?' he questions after a large gulp. 'Battersea Park and Regent's Park seem out of the area the killer has been occupying so far.' He stands up, walks over to me and taps on the map with his index finger. 'Maybe Green Park or St James's Park.' He draws an invisible line with his finger connecting all the pins and says, 'Those are the more populated outdoor spots in this vicinity.'

And he sits down, almost triumphant, like he has just solved the case.

'There's no pattern to these locations.' I wave a finger dismissively at the place where Talitha Palladino was executed.

'Yet,' he interrupts.

I ignore this interruption and continue, 'It could just

as easily happen at Regent's Park or Hampstead Heath or all the way over in Victoria Park, maybe even Greenwich. The killer chooses the location of each murder for a reason, whether it is part of the ritual or something to do with the victim. I think these are calculated. The choice of victim is more last minute. There is no line to link each location and no perimeter this person will stick to.'

Now that I have successfully deflated the both of us, Paulson asks me to recount my last intuition of The Two.

The doorbell rings.

Paulson is shocked that I called Murphy too.

I didn't.

It's Alison.

I retell the events of my mind.

Paulson interjects my story with repetitions of the elements he considers to be of interest or importance:

The scent of fornication.

Bulbs in his eyes.

Five pebbles.

Burnt wood.

Alison remains quiet, absorbing my words, making her own connections. She wants me to make more use of the visions; Paulson hopes for more conventional reasoning. I want to use them both.

I punctuate my story by popping two of my regular caffeine pills and washing them down with a swift glass of malt liquor.

'Careful, Jan.' I know he's worried that I'm about to erase my hard work over the last few months.

'There's no way either of us can sleep today, Paulson.' I shovel two more pills into my mouth and chew them, using my tongue to move them around, massaging the chalk into my gums.

'I know. I know. Just take it easy.' Then he downs the rest of his coffee, oblivious to the parallels.

An awkward silence ensues, and I click the pen lid on and off while perusing the map and the etchings on my living-room wall – the replica of my office wall that I have been staring at for months.

Paulson breaks the silence.

'Jan, if we have less than twenty-four hours, we could use all the help we can get, and Murphy knows you're marginalising him.'

I give him a look of resignation.

'We should put him to work before he does something stupid.'

He's right, of course. If there's one thing I know about Murphy it's that his ambition far exceeds his actual ability, but you don't always have to be the best at something to achieve the greatest amount. I recognise wearily that it's highly likely that, one day, I will be answering to him as my superior.

'OK, call him in. But not here. I'm not having him here,' I bark reluctantly. 'We've got all this at the station, tell him to meet you there, I'll follow shortly.'

Paulson edges forward on his chair, looking at me for confirmation that I mean now, right this second. I widen my eyes and raise my head a little as if holding my breath for him to get up and spring into action.

And he does. Because this is my investigation. I'm accountable. It will be done my way.

As he leaves the room to call Murphy, Alison speaks.

'I have an idea.'

'Wait until he leaves,' I instruct. I force a smile to make

the sentence softer than it was meant. Paulson returns and tells me that Murphy is already at the station.

'Get there. Get there now. Find out what he is doing and I'll be just behind you.'

He leaves without a word, pulling up the back of his trousers as he exits down the hallway and out through the front door.

I stand in front of the warm dented sofa cushion that Paulson has vacated, my eyes moving between the scrawled-on map and my handwriting on the wall to the left.

I almost knew where Totty would die. The Two were trying to tell me it was Trafalgar Square. Why are they now holding back? Why did they take this sensation from me?

There is no pattern. The pins, the blotches, the cemeteries and parks. They mean nothing.

Not every serial killer wants to be caught.

I say the words out loud to myself.

'Not every serial killer wants to be caught.'

I speak to myself.

'Not all vampires suck blood.'

'You want to hear my idea?' Alison asks sheepishly from somewhere behind me.

'Sure. As long as you don't mind talking to my back. There's something in here that I'm not seeing yet.' My gaze remains on the crime-scene photography pinned to my lounge wall.

She wants to recreate the Beltane ceremony. She knows it. She wants it to be used for good rather than the way the killer continues to abuse her traditions. I listen to what she has to say while observing the surrounding buildings at Parsons Green.

On a tall, oak block, stained with red wine circles, there sits a glass bowl full of polished onyx rounded stones. I'm not sure why Audrey bought this, perhaps to cover up the stains. I dip my hand inside and grab five of the tiny jewels.

The distance between Alison and the map on the wall is almost the length of the room; she doesn't want to influence it in any way.

She grips the first pebble in her hand and holds it to her mouth saying the words *bulbs in his eyes* quietly against it. Then she hurls it at the map as hard as she can. It tears the map slightly on Lancresse Road in De Beauvoir Town.

Useless.

I circle the church in Lily's and Totty's pictures with a red marker.

Alison repeats her process with the second stone, this time muttering *burnt wood* softly into the creases of her fingers. This misses the map completely, almost hitting me on the shoulder. So it repeats with the third stone. It hits a patch of water in Victoria Park and rips the map again.

I draw a red ring around the picture of St George's Cathedral for Graham White and another at the hospital he never returned to.

With the fourth pebble she mutters *scent of fornication* and launches it forwards. It cracks against some red lettering saying SW9. Not what she wanted at all.

I spot the health centre in the background of one shot taken where Lily Kane perished and mark it with my ink.

Alison closes her eyes with the final stone and just thinks to herself *five pebbles*.

Five pebbles.

It hits the map but I don't know where. She scours it for marks; the pebble now lies on the floor catching the light of a lamp. She runs her finger across the map, manically trying to locate the smallest of pockmarks.

'What if it hit the exact location the murder will take place in? What if it tells us where the killer hides? What if there is another message?' she mutters. What if there isn't an answer there?

What if you don't know what you're doing?

I think of Cathy and how ashamed she would be of her older brother if she were here.

It turns me cold.

But I need the guilt.

Help me, Cathy.

'Maybe it would work better if you threw the stones; you are directly connected to this.' She offers this so innocently. Perhaps three murders ago, maybe even two, I would have entertained this idea but I can't seriously pin my hopes of solving this case on the catapult of glass beads into a replica of the map in my office at the station.

And, more insensitively than I mean to, I respond, 'I'll stick to the actual clues if that's OK.'

She sits back down, hurt.

I stare at the photographs of Talitha Palladino, think - ing something is going to jump out at me. My eyes flit across to the map. I have forgotten that Alison is even here.

I take a step back in order to view all the information we have gleaned. The wall of death. The letters and images dancing around kaleidoscopically.

I make out a question mark.

Then another.

I see the word *Beltane*.

I think of burnt wood.

I see *1 May*.

I smell the grass.

The stench of fornication.

I'm reminded of cuckoldry; I remember unfaithfulness.

And, as the question marks begin to dissolve, pointing me in the direction of the heath that lies minutes from my house, I try to move my head closer to the picture of Talitha that is tacked up underneath her victim details.

Oh, January. You idiot. Of course there's a pattern. There's always a pattern.

The places of worship.

The hospitals and health centres.

The desperation.

This is how the victims are chosen.

V

I awake on the floor alone. Gail is gone. The passion of the moment was not followed by the same level of afterglow. That's not how it should have finished.

The half-full bottle of Merlot still lies on its side next to me, but the room is awash with a brilliant white glow blocking out the constant change of the traffic lights on the crossroads that normally perpetuates against my back wall. I roll from my side to my back to see the chain is not fastened on the door like it usually is when I go to sleep.

She let herself out.

I debate missing my run so as to avoid my routine morning greeting on return to the building. But that will make things awkward and I do still need her.

Things will be slightly different today, though. The newspaper headline will not be a shock. I was there, I know what happened. I witnessed the ritual.

I saw her.

She is Celeste Varrick.

She offered you her sacrifice.

She asked you for your blessing.

Flashes of my coital spontaneity start to flicker in my mind, interspersed with images of my wife. The only release from disgust is through prayer.

I roll over and get myself into a kneeling position, and I ask the Lord for guidance. I ask forgiveness of my actions, that only one woman occupies the space in my heart, that I crave only to be with her again and not with neighbouring temptresses. I say that I have realised my weaknesses and my full attention is on the task at hand.

I ask the Lord what he will have me do next.

I beg for more information so that I may fulfil the required preparations. I tell him I now know the face of the ritualist and implore that the time is near that I may stop her.

When I finally open my eyes, my body remains rigid, my knees magnetised to the floor, a statue of reflective genuflection. My Lord has confirmed that it is time. I am to take Celeste Varrick when the Sun is at the height of its power, on the longest day of the year.

She will call it Litha.

I will call it retribution.

The Lord extols my faith thus far but adds an exclamation.

My Lord declares that the time nears to capture Celeste Varrick, and that I will be reunited with my wife.

That there is still some work to do.

He informs me that I am to make a monster of her and in order to do that, I must first make a monster of myself.

On the summer solstice there will be a second victim, and this sacrifice will fall foul of the same ritualism that so disgusts me. He tells me that she will be another sufferer that is subjected to the ceremony of the previous victims.

He advises me that I will detain Celeste Varrick on this night.

He instructs me that, on this occasion, I am to perform her ritual.

I must demonise her.

Litha
June 2009

Annabel

———◆———

I'll try to be quick because it seems obvious that nobody is remotely troubled by my death; they are far more concerned with Brooke Derry, who gets to sit up in a comfortable bed and tell her tale.

And breathe.

I'm the one that nobody remembers, even though I died.

I was not ignored that day; people saw what was happening, they saw what happened.

That, this time, the victim was not the desperate one; it was the killer.

Look at me, Detective Inspector David.

Look at Annabel.

I'm supposed to be meeting a friend today, after my conference. But he will be late. Too late, as it turns out. I stop off at the Curzon Cinema in Soho for a healthy lunch of frosted carrot cake. The girl behind the counter asks if I would like a coffee but the sign over her right shoulder shows an enticing price for a glass of Prosecco Col di Luna. It's cheaper than the carrot cake, but I manage to stop myself from going for the two-glasses-of-Prosecco option.

Detective Paulson will question the two French ladies

behind the counter, but they won't remember specifics. I'm not the only person who likes a drink with their lunch. The place is filled with out-of-work creative types, tapping away at a laptop or catching up on the latest foreign cult movie, wearing their beards and their long hair and their homemade iconic T-shirts.

This part is not important, detectives.

Why are you looking here?

I use the toilet, wash my hands, gargle some water and spray down my throat with a minty freshener before exiting onto Frith Street.

I'm still fairly close to China Town so, as I start the journey towards my death, three or four oriental-looking people are travelling in the opposite direction. The third is a girl in a long thin jumper with a horrid picture of a panda on the front; she blows smoke into my face as we pass. She won't remember me so it's not worth asking her anything.

The next six people I pass are all taking a call on their mobile phone or typing a text or browsing the Internet; they don't see me; they have far less important things to be doing.

I pass a plethora of independent coffee houses, all boasting the best espresso and cappuccino. When the BT tower comes into focus above the buildings ahead of me, I know I'm almost there.

Halfway to dying.

The blue sign says 'Soho Centre for Health Care'.

It says 'Soho NHS Walk-In Centre'.

Outside the door is a pushbike with the words 'Ambulance Service, Cycle Response Unit' blazoned upon it. Seems somewhat pathetic.

Above the bike I read 'Westminster Community

234

Alcohol Centre' and I know I've arrived.

Detective Inspector January David, this is where your attention should be, not with the living girl who feeds you anecdotes, but here, where I first met my killer.

I leave after an hour of people sharing their feelings and showing off their achievements. I leave behind the tears and the excuses, the beatings and molested-as-a-childs, the bullyings and the addictive personalities. I walk out the door, leaving my executioner behind, for now, and turn right at the pharmacy towards Soho Square, where I never meet with my friend.

The sign next to the gate says that the park shuts at 21.30. I'll be dead by then; the detectives will have discovered Brooke Derry by this point.

And they think she's so important.

Because she gives them her description.

As I enter, I'm almost run down by a girl on a skateboard; her arm is already in a sling but she shows no fear as she attempts to hop her way up a kerb, unsuccessfully.

A black man in a fluorescent waistcoat says something to her to make her stop. As he turns round I see 'Park Service' on his back.

He sees me die.

I perch myself on one of the wooden benches near the entrance; the park is full, the weather is hot. People are having lunch or outdoor meetings or feigning a sick day or bunking lectures; the mood is relaxed and the spirits high. The woman next to me stares out at the differing cliques; she holds an empty yoghurt pot between her knees, occasionally running her finger around the rim in an almost sexual manner.

She is already gone when I die.

Do not question her.

Don't waste any more time.

Don't interrogate the blonde eating the baguette on the bench opposite; she is busy reading her book. Everybody people-watching, nobody seeing anything.

The weathervane points east but there is no wind blowing. My body points north.

Like all the other victims.

Make a note of that please, Mr David. Our bodies are the altar.

I will be facing the statue of Charles II.

While I wait for the friend who never comes, I wander around to the statue. It's not particularly impressive. I read the placard that suggests it was restored by Lady Gilbert in 1938; she didn't do the best job, it's still broken at the knee.

An elderly woman moves around the fractured stone until she is next to me. She looks me up and down and turns her top lip up at me as if to say, *Why are you here?*

She will remember my face but will be of no help in the investigation.

I look away from her but stand my ground. One section of the park is taped off while the sprinklers spray a patch of grass, wetting the outer path as it does so.

The woman behind me begins to talk, loudly.

'. . . used to be four, representing the four rivers. Water was brought down from Rathbone Place.' This is the information that January David will use, to fuel the Pagan influence.

Earth, fire, air, water, spirit.

This is not just the story of Brooke Derry.

It is the two of us.

I turn back to her and fifteen to twenty more pensioners are crowded around listening to her. Some stare at me unwelcomingly, as if I have hitched a free ride on their tour of this part of London.

'This hand used to hold a sword,' she yaps to her followers. She makes a joke and they laugh. One of the old men rolls up a copy of the *Independent* and places it in the empty hand of the statue.

They all laugh again.

I don't.

They turn to leave and one old lady climbs up and takes the paper out of Charles II's hand, tutting as she does so. She then moves on to the centre of the park where the guide squawks about the building that stands there.

The Gilbert family: blah, blah, blah.

Nineteenth-century hexagonal roof: yawn, snore, spit.

Place where Annabel Wakeman was stabbed and set fire to: sigh, groan, murmur.

In every direction I look, I can see a sign stuck to the side of a building saying 'Soho Square'. In one corner, outside the park, stands a Gothic-looking building, the Eglise Protestante Française de Londres. A nearby church is worth enquiring into on this case, but not with this murder. I am not the desperate one.

January David will also examine St Patrick's Catholic Church along the east side of the square, thinking it may be connected to the way Graham White was killed.

But this is so much different.

Unlike all the others, with the exception of Brooke Derry.

On one side of the central building, a local vagabond leans against a wall, slurring, hugging his bike. I take my own place against the set of wooden doors behind the shabby statue, open my bag, take out my bottle of alcohol and wait for my friend not to come and save my life.

January

❖

I know the killer.
  I understand her.

I'm inside her mind now.

She roams the hospitals and churches, stalking the desperate. She hunts them, picking the weakest, offering help, the false promise of salvation. She feels that she is rescuing them, delivering them from an evil only she perceives.

And now, thanks to Brooke Derry, I know her face.

But, until I have caught her, victims will continue to be taken.

Chief Archer calls, telling me there is another body and he thinks it might be connected.

I can't handle everything myself so decide to take Paulson with me to Soho Square to see the body of Annabel Wakeman. Archer hints that the site is pretty disturbing so I opt to leave Alison out of this crime scene and will explain it to her later. I get Murphy to come down to the hospital to watch over Brooke Derry; not that I think she is in any danger now, but it keeps him busy and out of the way.

Of course, when he arrives, we are not there to watch over him. The first thing he does is call his mysterious backer. Murphy tells him that we have a survivor, that she is conscious and has produced an accurate description of her assailant. He tells his handler that it is a woman.

He is then told to leak it out to the press. To get everyone behind this case and unite the country and the people of London against a common enemy.

And he doesn't even question it.

Even though he knows it is wrong and will be detrimental to proceedings.

That's Murphy.

He's done it again.

When we find Aldous on the Embankment at Lughnasadh in forty days, I will let him know that the seventh death rests heavily on his shoulders. That he is to blame. That I don't care what kind of support he has from on high, if someone else dies as a result of his stupidity, his ambition and his relentless mistrust of my methods, it will be on his head.

Whatever information he withholds, however he and his advocate hamper investigations, they hope that it will all rest on my shoulders. That's the plan.

The worst thing about his treachery is that, if he was more dedicated to his profession, if he wasn't so driven by a desire to progress so quickly through the ranks, if he was one of us, I wouldn't discount his input so much.

And then we would have realised that he was onto something from the very beginning.

Annabel

—✦—

I don't know Celeste Varrick. I know the man sat four seats away from me in a circle of anonymous, desperate losers, all dealing with alcohol or substance abuse; those who used these as a method for coping with grief. I know the slender, athletic, goateed man who finally spoke his turn, introducing himself simply as V and running through the catalogue of tragedies in his life that brought him to this place: his dead son, his estranged wife. I know the man that said he had found some solace in his faith and that it is guiding him back to happiness.

I know this man who purged himself of his demons in that protected setting, then drank with me in the afternoon before cutting a slit through my spine and leaving me incapacitated as the flames engulfed me.

Still, somehow, I got the sense that he didn't really want to do it. More that he had to do it. He wept. Silently. But he wept. Maybe that is the thing with murderers: they have a compulsion to kill; they feel compelled to act out.

I'm not an expert.

This is the first time I've died.

Maybe I made him do it. I told him I was looking for a way out of this desperate, solipsistic existence. I mentioned that I had tried several religions and self-help

241

methods. That I'd even dabbled with a bit of self-harm. I indicated, while taking a giant swig of red wine, that to forget is to heal. To not remember is to not know.

Now there is nothing.

No pain or feeling. I'm gone and it truly is the end. I see no light or man with white beard. Thankfully, I see no man with forked tail and horns either. Death is a different emptiness to the one felt in life. It is the essence of complete nothingness. No sound or light. No shadows. No future or present. Only life has history.

It is the essence of pain relief.

The quintessential cure.

So perhaps, if I had anything to feel in this lack of afterlife, I should be thankful.

V didn't kill me.

He saved me.

Just as Celeste would have.

Brooke

When he returns for the second time, I tell Detective Inspector David that I can't think of anyone who would want to harm me, that I don't have enemies. Sure, I have ex-boyfriends and some break-ups were more acrimonious than others, but this was not a man who did this to me. He quizzes me on my family, the people I work with or socialise with. He asks about the people at my gym and local newsagent and doctor's surgery. He wants to know where I could possibly have seen or been seen by the woman I described to the sketch artist.

How is my health? Have I been to hospital recently? What about church? Do I attend a church or holy building?

I want to say that a church is not a building but a gathering of like-minded people. Instead, I answer. Fine. No. No.

He needs to understand how I know Celeste Varrick.

I don't know her.

And she does not know me.

She doesn't need to.

A doctor enters, stating that I should really get some rest and the detective complies; there is nothing more I can give him.

'Detective,' I call out to him, my voice hoarse from the smoke. He turns around to face me at the foot of my bed. 'I never saw her face when she grabbed me, I've never seen her before today, but my mind cannot erase her image, it won't forget. She thought I was dead and she didn't look as though she cared one bit. She is a monster.'

I allow my body to go heavy and melt into the pillows propped against my back. When I wake up, a different man is in my room. He tells me his name is Detective Sergeant Murphy. He says he is working on my case. He informs me that the Detective Inspector and the large one who rode in the ambulance with me have been called to another victim, that the woman in the picture has taken another life as a substitute for her failure with me. Detective Sergeant Murphy has been sent to watch over me. To protect me.

'You'll be safe with me, Ms Derry,' he smiles confidently.

Now I am afraid.

The truth of my situation suddenly hits me.

Before I have the opportunity to ask him about this victim, his mobile phone rings and he takes the call, walking over to the corner of the room for privacy. I hear him say *sir* and assume it is work-related.

DS Murphy mumbles towards the wall for a while; I split my attention between his back and the window of the door that leads outside. Nobody walks past but I am on edge.

My apparent bodyguard turns around for a moment, looking at me briefly over his shoulder, and I pick up what he is saying. 'I'm not sure that is the best way to go about things.' His eyes soften as if notifying me that he won't be much longer, and he turns back to the corner to complete his murmured discussion.

'He won't find out about tampering with the evidence but this, this . . . I'm not so sure.' He rubs the back of his head with his free hand. 'Without doubt, he'll know it was me . . . And you can protect me?'

There is a pause and he looks over his shoulder again at me, rolling his eyes as if the person he converses with is merely a time-wasting hindrance.

'So this is definitely the move then? OK. I'm on it.' He hangs up.

'Sorry about that,' he apologises, and walks back over to me. 'Are you comfortable? Is there anything I can do?'

'I'm fine, thanks,' I croak. 'Maybe some water.' I turn my head to the empty jug and glass sat on the bedside unit.

'Not a problem.'

He picks up the jug in his left hand and heads for the door while simultaneously fishing his phone out again.

He says *Hi*.

He introduces himself as *Murph*.

He tells whoever is at the other end that he *needs a copy of the artist's impression faxed back to the hospital immediately*.

Then he leaves me alone for a brief moment scared that Celeste will return to finish her job. But she won't. They are all making a fuss over me for the moment because they don't yet realise I am the least important person involved in this case.

January

---◆---

C hief Archer is right; I do want to look at this.
Seeing her contorted body on the floor, charred beyond recognition, I'm taken back months to the vision of Talitha Palladino, the third person in this series of twisted murders. The scene has so many identical aspects to the location I examined after finding Brooke Derry. The candles, the wheel, the hay, the fire. But it's worse. It worked this time.

She is dead.

Completely dead.

I had hoped that the cycle had been broken, that the hole left in the Wicca calendar by Brooke Derry would somehow flush out the killer, draw her into making a mistake through desperation. I felt like I was starting to get inside the head of this butcher but there was no panic. Clearly. There was always a back-up, and she is lying on the grass in front of me, her skin tight and crisp and roasted.

Now Brooke doesn't seem to fit the mould.

A small top-floor flat.

A secluded ritual.

No possibility of a witness.

Alison will tell me that this occasion may have been a solitary ceremony but I start to worry about copycats.

That suddenly it has become much easier for a person to murder their partner, utilise some of these ritualistic elements and push blame onto the killer I am pursuing.

I may need to question Brooke Derry again. I feel like I am getting close to an answer, that I just need to find the right question for her, that the killer is close, that I am nearing a conclusion to this case.

I'm wrong.

And yet, the only thing I can be sure of is that another murder will take place on the first of August. It doesn't require an appearance from The Two to tell me that. It is the next Sabbat. Lughnasadh.

But I have to concede that I may need their help to stop it. I can predict the next location by combining my vision with the things I have learned from real evidence.

In the dead woman's wallet, we find remnants of a receipt from the Curzon Cinema. I send Paulson down there straight away to talk to people. Maybe she is a regular there, perhaps someone knows her. The time stamp has been burned away but it shows she ordered a glass of Prosecco, so you would assume it was late afternoon or after work.

The post-mortem will reveal high levels of alcohol and other substances in her system.

A partially melted debit card says *iss Annabel Wakeman*.

The scene smells similar to Brooke Derry's near miss, although not entirely the same. Her body looks remark - ably like Talitha Palladino's corpse at Speaker's Corner. To my left I see a Catholic church under reconstruction, with scaffolding erected around the front face. Over my right shoulder, another church. The vicinity of these buildings cannot be coincidence.

Ignoring the recently arrived fire chief, Archer, I think of Lily Kane, I think of Totty Fahey, I think of Graham White.

I see the sketched face of Celeste Varrick.

The photographer takes pictures of everything: the body, the ground around her, the statue ahead of us, the damaged building, everything is important. This will be useful.

To help see the things that we have not seen.

'Two in one day. When are you going to catch this guy?' Archer teases unpleasantly, his sarcasm laced with venom.

'It's a woman,' I say, not looking him in the face. Returning the favour.

'What?'

'The killer is a woman.' I bend down and pry open Annabel's pocket with the end of my pen.

'Oh. Well that has to be an even bigger kick in the nuts, then, doesn't it?'

'A killer is a killer, Chief Archer. Doesn't matter if it's a man or a woman, an adult or a child,' I reply dismissively.

I don't believe I would have been as coherent two or three months ago. I'm hoping that my activity around the body is indication enough that I do not wish to enter into debate.

He walks off, muttering to himself, 'Well, maybe you should get a bloody move on, then.'

There is more than enough evidence here to suggest the same murderer. The most important information now is the time of death. If this took place before the Brooke Derry attempt, then she is clearly trying to ramp up her death quota. If it happened after, then it could be more random. A desperate attempt to compensate for the earlier failure.

This is right. I can feel it now.

I'm close.

Nobody else has to die.

But the differences between the two victims found today and the ones which have come before start to niggle at me. Perhaps it can be explained away as an act of desperation causing the killer to make mistakes. Maybe Alison was right: The Two are not representative of killer and victim but instead signify two separate killers.

V

She cannot hear me behind the closed door. Celeste is caught, she has been detained and restrained. As I sit on my worn sofa, staring at the back wall of the flat changing once again from green to red, I cry.

Only the Lord witnesses my moments of pleasure.

And my moments of weakness.

Initially my tears fall silently through exaltation and relief. I've got her. The woman whose face will appear on the front of the newspaper, whose work I have been monitoring for months, waiting for the Lord to allow me to act upon my urge. I have her.

Gazing at the wall, I become engrossed in the flicking light show. Celeste's wails are absorbed into the white paint of her cell, only escaping under the door as inaudible murmurs. I drink to her futility. I toast my own patience. I think back to November the first and the line graph on the front page that illustrated the rise in London knife crime. I reminisce over the text explaining Celeste's first ritual the night before on Parsons Green.

I afford myself a smile of congratulation through my tears.

And then I think of the other thing He made me do.

I think of Annabel and my elation instantly evaporates.

I breathe in once more, a deep, deliberate breath; one

that seems like preparation for something more substantial. It is. I let out a noise like a feral pig that has just been shot through the lungs and is screaming the last air from its body. As though someone is slowly releasing the air from a balloon, my high-pitched lament elongates the words *Oh* and *No* into a note that harmonises with the hum of the city and drowns the muffle of the villain tied up in the room my son never got to sleep in.

Why would you have me do this?

But who am I to question? He is all-seeing. He is all-knowing. He sees my doubts.

My guilt is amplified.

I cannot come back from this. Sammael Abbadon has died too and only V remains.

V killed Annabel Wakeman to capture Celeste Varrick. This act bears no comparison to the misery caused by Celeste and the five lives she interfered with before today. She is the monster. She acts on impulse. She toys with fate.

V should not be punished for this.

V was working on behalf of the Lord; there was a higher purpose. The Lord sees the larger panorama.

It is not V who wails in self-reproach as the wall flicks from orange to green.

This is weakness.

This is the impotence that lost a man his wife and child.

This is the last part of Sammael.

I sit back and take another mouthful of alcohol. Whoever I am, I will be rewarded.

Lughnasadh
August 2009

January

──────◆──────

I don't know that V has Celeste locked in his makeshift jail cell. I don't even know who V is or why he feels obligated to act on behalf of the law. What I am aware of is that tomorrow marks the seventh Sabbat of this cycle.

And I don't want to get to the eighth.

The cycle cannot be completed otherwise we may never have another opportunity to locate Celeste. She must not be given the chance to conclude her work.

Higgs and his team are still running through hours of footage and logs from hospitals and holy buildings within the vicinity of each crime scene.

Alison is convinced that both rituals performed at Litha involving Brooke and Annabel show an understanding of Wiccan principles. I feel that the signature of the previous murders seems to have been forged. They were similar yet not quite the same to the trained eye.

I feel so close.

As I step up the intensity of the investigation, so The Two increase their involvement in proceedings. Last night, as expected, they visited again.

I'm stuck in traffic on the way to the station. My eyes are bloodshot and yellowing through lack of sleep, stress and booze, and the car hasn't moved for around eight minutes. I lean across to the glove box, hunting for some painkillers; the throb of my brain seems to be increasing with every passing minute that I am stuck in this jam, forcing my eyebrows lower as I grimace, flattening the lines on my forehead.

I grip my head, making my hand into a claw. The thumb presses on my right temple, the two long middle fingers on the left. I lower my chin to my chest and squeeze, hoping to massage the discomfort away.

The vice lifts my head back up and I open my eyes to view the traffic situation again.

I watch the traffic lights cycle through once without any cars being given the opportunity to move. It reminds me of the boy and his flashing eyes. I am seeing what he sees.

The light turns red again. We *stop*. I am suddenly reminded of the boy.

And I think again of his visit as I slept last night.

I am in darkness.

And I smell apples.

And dust.

I don't know whether I am asleep or awake, but directly ahead of me The Two are frozen in tableau. The boy wears a plain white smock; his facial features are obscured in their darkness; occasionally, his eyes flicker their spectral palette. The girl is decorated in simple black, her face bright white, angelic, glowing. As though one is the negative of the other.

She has her hand around his neck.

His feet are not touching the floor.

I wait for something to happen but they appear almost comfortable. He does not struggle; she does not waver.

256

They just look at each other square in the face, not in confrontation, not in abhorrence; it seems more like love. Like they are sharing a moment.

I notice a thin circle around the boy's dangling feet.

Then it erupts into flames as high as the boy's head, making him disappear into a cylinder of fire. The girl does not let go, she does not break her stare; she seems unaffected by the heat.

And she turns her pure, clean face gradually towards mine.

January

<hr/>

A loud honk snaps me out and I see that the cars in front of me have moved on and I crash back to reality, the light seeping through my windscreen erasing the image of The Two.

I drive off, but I can't stop thinking about last night – of course I would smell apples, this is Lughnasadh, the harvest festival. The Two are telling me this will be another fiery death, of that I am sure. It may be that their outfits, the smocks, are leading me towards the hospital. I know this already. Maybe Celeste has access to records, maybe she works for the health service in some capacity.

But it was the look, the look that The Two gave each other. Not one of fear or anger, but of trust and co-operation.

Perhaps the victims are all suffering in some way.

Maybe they have asked for this.

Maybe they have requested the help of Celeste Varrick.

To save them.

To be their saviour.

V

He tells me I must do it again. That it is all part of the plan.

That I made the agreement.

He says that Annabel was not the last, I must take another. But it is Celeste that is the monster, not me. And I agree, for that is the word of the Lord. This is the truth. I am the one who asked for the help. The Lord is merely my guide.

But that does not make what I have to do any easier.

Celeste takes lives without conscience.

She steals souls with no remorse.

She is everything that I am not.

In preparation I have researched Lughnasadh: its history, the prayers and rituals that Celeste would perform if she were not trapped inside the room that was meant for my son. Sitting on my sofa, I twist and shape a handful of straw, tying string in the appropriate places to fasten legs and arms to the body of my homemade figure.

I learn that this ritual, once again, involves fire, and I see an opportunity to increase Celeste's monstrous pro-file. I don't want to do it but I know that I must.

I draw strength from the family I hope to be with again.

My faith breeds courage.

With my tiny effigy complete, I pack my things into a satchel. A miniature bottle of wine, some bread and the knife I will use to kill Celeste's next victim; pretending to perform her next ritual.

I hope this is her last.

I hope our work is nearly done.

Dropping the hatch to the cell allows enough light in that I can see Celeste lying still in her confines. The scent of sweat pours out through the opening and I glimpse her now greasy blond hair draped over the side of the bed. She is not as appealing as the day I met her, the day I caught her. She has been weakened and sullied with neglect.

I know that she isn't going anywhere; her belief keeps her ensnared. I throw the bag over my shoulder and leave the flat, no need to double-lock it. I stand on the doormat for a few seconds, debilitated momentarily by my indecision. I take deep breaths, telling myself over and over what has to be done. I went through the same motions before I fulfilled my duty by taking the life of Annabel Wakeman. I didn't want to do it.

But she made it easier for me.

Deep down she had given up. She wanted to die.

I don't even know who is next on this list.

Until I get there.

As I arrive, I see a man resting his back against the wall to the entrance. He's in his forties, frail. Ill-looking. But that is given: we are outside a hospital. I don't want to know that his name is Aldous, I don't want to know whether or not he has children or a partner; this makes things more difficult. I just need to know how desperate he is to live. I only want to know how easy it will be to help him die.

I don't want to use the word *kill*; only Celeste says that.

He waits. And so do I. I see him check his watch. At first it is infrequent, once as he exits, ten minutes later, seven minutes after that. He starts to look around, is he waiting for somebody to pick him up? Someone who never comes. I watch as he coughs into a handkerchief.

He checks his watch.

Two minutes later he barks violently into the same piece of material, scrunching it into a ball when he is finished, containing whatever was hacked up – bile, phlegm, blood – and placing it back into his pocket.

He checks his watch again and looks to his left, then his right. His expression more anxious. His face asking for help.

With one last glance at his watch, he decides to hobble on a journey by himself. This is his mistake. He is vulnerable now. Once out of view of the hospital, he stops to look around again, this time over his shoulder. He is not looking for someone to meet him; he is making sure that nobody is watching.

He concludes that nobody is.

But he is wrong.

He reaches down into his bag and ruffles the contents around inside until he gets to the bottom, where he has hidden a box of cigarettes. I can't see the brand because his hand covers the box, but he pulls one out with his lips while simultaneously acquiring a lighter from his inside jacket pocket with his free hand.

The look of relief, of pure exaltation on his face, as he inhales the toxin that brought him here in the first place, is verging on orgasmic. His head tilts back in rapture, his eyes close; he holds the smoke in his lungs for several seconds. I wonder whether this is my opportunity to take him, piercing one of his lungs with my knife, holding my hand over his mouth so that he cannot exhale his poison.

I wonder whether I can do it.

What would Celeste do?

Then I start to grind my teeth. I blow air out through my nostrils, each time a little louder, each time with a little more brutality; tears begin to fall silently down my cheeks. It starts to rain. The man keeps his closed eyes aimed at the sky, allowing the droplets to bounce off his skin.

And, before I allow myself another opportunity to wonder anything else, my right hand has speared one of his lungs and my left holds his mouth shut. Just as I had imagined it.

Before I let myself ponder exactly who I have become, I have also sliced open his left lung, pushing the blade between two ribs and twisting on exit.

Before I have any chance to realise that Sammael Abbadon is never coming back, I whisper in the man's ear, 'Ssh, ssh. It's over. Don't fight. Go with it.'

I'm surprised at just how weak he is. He stops wriggling.

With tears still cascading down my face, my voice warbles slightly as I speak one last time to the dying man. I recite, *'Nonuci dasonuf Babaje od cahisa ob hubaip tibibipe.'*

Quivering through the incantation I end saying, *'Shemhamforash.* So it is done.'

He is now limp in my arms, giving in to his fate. If he'd wanted to live, he would have fought. If death wasn't easier, he would have tried.

He wants this.

I'm not a killer.

*

The rain is now falling heavily and everyone just wants to escape; their thoughts are on self-preservation. With life still left in the man, it is easier to balance him in a kneeling position; he doesn't resist. With his last gram of strength, he pulls the cigarette back up to his mouth, which I have now released, understanding he will not try to scream, and places it back between his lips, where it sticks as his hand drops back to his side.

I move around to the front of the nearly dead man, dropping down to his level. His eyes are still open. I expect to see the life draining from them but it seems he gave up long before I arrived. His look is vacant; he is not longing like Annabel. She wanted to die too, but there was a yearning in her eyes. I don't know whether this makes it easier or more difficult.

I take the bread from my bag and toss it quickly between his legs. I take out the candles, lighting the first one on the cigarette that sits comfortably in a groove of his lips; I light two more from this one and place them in the gap underneath the archway made by the crotch of his trousers. On top of these tiny flames, I rest the straw doll.

So it is done.

I leave the straw man to ignite and slowly burn into a larger flame that will eventually set light to the dead, kneeling man with a cigarette still in his mouth. As this happens, as those who splash through newly formed puddles as they pass by begin to double-take, as they start to register the scene of this man, under the bridge, burning before them, cars driving by on the road next to him, I will have arrived at the crossroads.

I will be calling for the Lord to appear to me in exactly the same way I did after Annabel had to be taken.

I say: '*Ilasa micalazoda olapireta ialpereji beliore: das odo Busadire Oiad ouoaresa caosago.*'

I say: 'Be thou a window of comfort unto me. Move therefore and appear. Open the mysteries of your creation. Be friendly unto me, for I am the same.'

On the other side of the crossroads, a woman looks straight through me. Her gaze pierces through my blood-shot, weeping eyes and I feel myself stop breathing for a moment. I catch my breath, blink, and she is gone.

This is the last, I am told. I will not be asked to do this again. I know that my focus should now be solely on Celeste. That monster, Celeste.

Soon, I will be rewarded.

I jog all the way home in the rain.

Shemhamforash.

So it is done.

January

❖

I'm still stuck in traffic when I should be meeting Alison.

She has helped me unpick and decipher these visions. Without her, I would never have been able to accept them for what they are. Now, I use her to keep me level. The truth is I've grown fond of her; I like having her around.

I'm close, I can feel it.

As I finally arrive at the station, I notice Alison's car is parked. She will be in the office alone with Paulson and Murphy; they do not know I have asked her to come in this morning.

It's becoming too much effort to dodge Murphy's suspicions; it's another thing to contend with while trying to solve a case. I know the visions have worth but I can't let him know that.

I sigh, unfasten my seatbelt and rest my head against the steering wheel, puffing out my cheeks and shutting my eyes for a moment.

I play through The Two's message in my mind, rejoining the scene at the point I was interrupted by the impatient driver earlier. I want to go into that office with something, an idea, an answer.

The fire still burns high but makes no sound. I can't

hear it crackle or hum and The Two have disappeared. But they are not far away.

The flames take on a certain beauty; altering shape as they caress the air that gives them life.

To my left and right, dust begins to move from side to side as the children start to shuffle their feet in unison; no longer independent of one another, their message is of an alliance.

I taste red wine on the back of my tongue and blood on the sides.

The blaze lights the left-hand side of the girl and the right of the boy. For a moment they are two halves. Until they emerge into full view. They are both carrying dolls made of straw, very simple human shapes bound with string. They look at each other in the same way that they did before, longing, affectionate. Just as they were while I was stuck in traffic.

Before she strangled him.

Before he was burned.

I notice that both of them have their toes turned in slightly; they fondle their dolls in an identical manner, like a warped mirror that conveys a reflection of every - thing you are not. Simultaneously they lift an arm each – her left, his right – and link fingers. Their other hands clasp onto the straw figures. The girl smiles. The boy does not.

She drags him over to her side and starts to skip around the bonfire. He reluctantly follows her, never letting go of her hand despite his apathy.

After the third revolution they stop at the side, count to three in their heads and toss the dolls onto the fire.

I smell burnt straw.

I feel moisture on my cheek.

The boy starts to smile, the girl's expression turns to a frown. They look at each other and, in an instant, she has used her strength to overpower him with a single blow that sends him flying into the fire once more.

It falls silent and still.

He does not scream.

She just stares into the inaudible blaze, expressionless.

As her head begins to swivel to the right to face the position I occupy, her mouth begins to open as if preparing for her silent shout but it is softer, smoother. Like she is ready to say something to me.

A giant knuckle raps against my driver-side window.

It's Paulson.

He bends down and peers in at me, now sat back in my seat. 'Everything OK, Jan?'

I click the door open. He steps back and I pull my weight outside. 'Fine. Just having a moment to myself before the day begins.

'The day began twenty-five minutes ago when your friend showed up unexpectedly.' He smiles but I can tell he feels put out.

'The traffic was insane. Roadworks. I was planning on getting in before you.'

'Well, Murphy is beyond suspicious. He's revelling in this,' he points out.

I roll my eyes, lock the car and we walk together to the office. I explain that I need some time with Alison this morning. 'You know what we need to talk about and I can't have Murphy around. I wish I could have you in there too but I can't run the risk with Murph, you know?'

He nods despondently.

*

Murphy smirks as I walk into the office, throwing a glance at Alison then back to me. Oozing his own particular brand of smugness.

Protected.

Controlled.

We stand there staring at one another for a few awkward seconds. I imagine picking him up by his throat.

Luckily, Alison disarms the situation with her mere presence. She is wearing a similar fitted power suit to that which entranced me on her first visit to the station. Her legs are crossed and she swivels ever so slightly on the chair behind my desk.

I motion for her to come outside to another room, leaving my detectives to fend for themselves.

The door shuts behind Alison and I find myself returning the smile she playfully threw in my direction, and for just a minute I forget about how much I hate Murphy.

Celeste

❖

He prevents me from saving any more lost and desperate souls.

I've been here for forty days now.

When you reside in the darkness, you don't see the setting sun or the passing of a moon, and it is difficult to grip time as it progresses. I only realise the duration of my stay when the one who is now known as V brings in the morning paper and slaps it down on the bed next to my face. The reverberation wakes me instantly.

Still in the darkness.

'What do you want?' I croak at the back of his head as he walks away towards the narrow strip of light the open door has created. I suck in the fresh air that creeps in.

He flicks on the light and I scream as my pupils shrink in the sudden glare. He doesn't even turn around when he speaks, like I am an afterthought to him. There is something different.

'Read, monster,' he growls, before disappearing round the corner for a few moments. With the door still ajar I can hear the clink of crockery, the running of a tap, and before I even have a second to glance at the tabloid by my right cheek, he is returning with a bowl of water.

He leans over me and places the bowl near to my shoulder. I can smell his sweat, and now the door is open

269

I take in his attire: trainers, a hooded grey jumper with a growing oblong of moisture running from his chin and spreading across his chest. Two continents of acrid perspiration under each arm.

He left me here alone.

He leaves me here alone.

In the beginning, I would fight against my binding in this situation, yanking against my constraints, gnashing my teeth towards his neck, fighting as best I could. But I soon realised that this would leave a patch of damp under my shoulder and an empty bowl at my head.

And he would not bring another one for hours.

So now I don't move. I let him perform his task in peace and lap at the bowl like a dog trusting that my master is not trying to euthanise me with tampered tap water.

He's right: I am a monster.

I drop my tongue into the cold liquid and pull some moisture into my mouth and repeat this until the bowl is half empty. When I roll back, he is waiting, watching. He stares a dead, blank look somewhere between me and the newspaper, as though he isn't really here. Like his body is in the room but his mind's somewhere different.

Like I don't exist.

I look down at the front page; it is dated 2 August, the day after Lughnasadh. I don't even look at the article. I have missed Lammas. I shut my eyes and begin to whisper to myself, asking for the fortitude to deal with my situation. 'Strength is found not in arms nor knife nor gun nor sword. It is found in the mind, it is found in the soul.' I hear him turn and his feet shuffle along the floor as he walks out the room again, plunging me back into darkness, leaving me, once again, shouting hysterically at a man who cannot hear me.

'I call on those who will stand and fight, those who will do what is needed, who make sacrifices on behalf of others. I call on those who die so that others may live.' I arch my back off the mattress, forcing myself up towards the skies, stiffening my body rigid and shout out, 'I call upon you to give me strength of heart, soul and spirit.'

I drop back down to the bed with a thud; the bowl bounces and empties the last half of its contents on the covers and I know I have another few hours of quiet contemplation and meditation before another bout of harassment.

How did I get to this place?

Where did it start to go wrong?

January

'It is completely black this time. No fire. And it's cold but there is no breeze. I feel exposed. My protective barrier is absent, so I know there will be no salt circle.'

There is no sound.

None.

'After five or six minutes, nothing has happened. I'm expecting something to pop up in front of me. I expect to smell the juice of an apple or detect the scent of straw or feel the heat from a bonfire, but there is nothing. No sound, no light, no scents, just an effervescent fear that my senses are slowly being knocked out one by one.'

Alison listens attentively as I work through the most astounding part of my vision. She sits across a desk from me as though I am ready to interrogate her about a crime. She leans her forearms against the edge of the table between us, forcing her jacket to open outwards into a broken triangle. I can see the form of her breasts through her blouse, the bottom of the triangle points down between her legs.

She knows I am looking.

'I start to walk, dragging my feet through the thick dust layer, but it makes no noise. I jump up, slamming my feet into the ground as I land, crashing them down mutely. I scream the silent scream of the girl in the black emptiness.'

I can still feel.

And this worries me.

I think about The Smiling Man stuffing my mouth with cigarettes, stretching my lips beyond their elasticity and suffocating me with the nicotine-drenched smoke. The consternation bubbles higher. The Two have changed, I have no protection and now I am walking in this perpetual black box.

And nobody can wake me up.

'A dot of light appears miles into the distance. No matter which direction I turn, it is still directly in front of me. I feel a compulsion to run. I have my sight. I can see, and the dot has become a blob of light. If I keep going it will become a smudge, before long it will be a beam, then a flood, and a flare.' I start to sit forwards as I gesticulate; the emotion of the story is clearly heightening Alison's own excitement. This mysticism turns her on.

'My mind tries to keep up with my feet as I stride out into a sprint, the half circle of blue-white brightness sprouting into a dome. The aroma of apples returns, the fragrant hay of other visits to this realm. My senses are returning. I see the two figures in collusion, their blur swiftly dripping into a sharp focus.'

'What is it?' She can't help but join in. Her voice is slightly higher as she speaks the word *what*. As though on the brink of orgasm.

'The Two are standing together, glowing in a white so white it is blue; they replicate the scene which only I saw in Hyde Park as Talitha Palladino's body lay charred and disfigured behind me.'

'You never told me about that,' she drones, dropping back a little in her seat.

'I never told anybody about that,' I try to reassure her.

'So what happened . . . at Hyde Park?'

'I'm getting there,' I lash out. It takes a second to regain my composure. Any molecule of foreplay has dissipated. Alison now rests back in her chair and we resume professionalism.

'My hearing restored, I hear myself panting. Forever is a long way to run. This time I am allowed closer and I slow my body and breathing down so as not to agitate them. It seems that they do not know I am here. That somehow they have a private moment away from my thoughts.'

That I am intruding on my own consciousness.

'I stop a short distance from where they stand together. I have nothing to hide behind but darker atmosphere. The crossed path beneath them is lit in a similar blue to their auras yet I see a dark spot between their feet. This is where the girl buried her box.'

Alison's eyes widen with intrigue at the mention of the crossroads, then augment into fear at the utterance of the buried box.

She knows.

'The boy moves in close to the girl and whispers something into her ear that makes her drop to her knees in front of him. He looks down at her but I do not see his lips move, yet she nods in agreement. He doesn't say anything again but she nods with more conviction. He lays his hand on top of her head, looks up to the dark sky above then disappears.' I notice that Alison is pre - occupied. Anxious. She wants me to get to the end of my story.

'The girl begins to cry. But I can hear her now. This is no longer a silent wail. I wait, not wanting to interrupt this time that should clearly be solitary. She cries and cries and cries on her knees. At first it sounds like disappointment or bereavement but it soon transforms into something far more peculiar. Like a weeping laugh. A bawling chortle.

As though she is happy. And, all of a sudden, she stands and walks off calmly into the distance.'

'And that's it? You wake up there?' she chimes in impatiently.

'I remain in my glued position, waiting for her to give me a sign, knowing there is more to the intuition, but she just disappears. Just like the boy.'

The Two have gone.

I am left alone with an illuminated crossroads and a black hole.

'With each step I peer around into the blackness, half expecting to see something, half prepared for an attack of some kind. But two steps pass, then five, then ten, and I find myself on the crossroads looking down at the dirt.'

'You see the box,' she affirms, knowingly.

I calm myself with a deep breath. I want to give all the information not a partial representation.

Continuing as though her interjections are inconsequential I tell her that I crouch down next to the spot where a hole has clearly been filled in recently. Not a large hole. Something big enough to bury a tobacco tin. Still, I worry, and judder my hand away from the earth before looking over both shoulders once more.

But they are gone.

This is what I am supposed to see.

It is time. I need to work for the answers.

Be an investigator.

I use my right hand to brush away the soft dirt that reveals the top of a metal tin. With the two longest fingers on each hand I create a moat around the tin, gradually getting deeper and deeper until I can create enough leverage to force it from its confines.

The apple perfume fades and with it the chill returns. The light around begins to diminish, slowly ebbing away until I am in spotlight. I flick the tin lid off and it hits the floor. But there is no sound; my senses are waning once again.

Inside, I find a small passport photo of the girl; a lock of her hair is tied around it. This is placed on top of a handful of dirt. I move the dirt to the side; underneath is another picture, this time of a baby. I bring the photo closer to my eyes to examine the minute features, trying to work out if it is a younger picture of the girl.

'That's when I feel a stab of ice. This then turns scorching hot inside me. I can't taste the blood that forms in my throat but I know that's what it is. The girl appears in front of me and drops to her knees shaking her head, telling me I have got it all wrong. She leans her face in close to mine and makes a soft "o" with her lips. She lightly blows on my face and my eyes open contentedly, confusingly, back into reality.'

I push back into my chair to signify that I am finished. The regaling of this conclusion leaves Alison's face ashen, terrified, and disappointed that she had not picked out the things she was brought in to locate.

She has been concentrating on the Wiccan element, the things she knows, when, in fact, it was the confusions in faith that she should have gripped hold of.

I have more information. I need to revisit every crime scene.

Nothing has changed; it's been there from the very start.

V

⬥

I still run in the morning. So that I have something that is normal, something from the life I am trying so desperately to get back to.

Before the Lord placed a condition on his help.

Before he made me do these things.

I hit the chrome button on my watch to stop the timer. A little sluggish today, slower than usual, but that should be expected. I lift my right arm and sniff under the pit; the scent is a mixture of dampness, citrus and the wine I gorged on yesterday evening. I'm sweating out the alcohol. Perspiring the badness. Evacuating sin.

Gail steps out onto her doormat, rummages around in her handbag, then locks her door. There doesn't appear to have been any awkwardness since that night of spon - taneous ardour. Our near-rape role-play. I don't even know if she heard me weeping, if she even noticed. We never talk about it.

'Oh, hey, Sam.' She smiles at me like a friend, like a neighbour. Not as a lover.

'Morning, Gail,' I call down the hallway as I release the stretch of my quadricep.

We start to walk towards each other, the window at the end of the hallway allowing enough light through to create an aura around her; she looks luminous. I become very conscious of my personal odour and ragged presentation in comparison.

When we meet in the middle she graciously pretends not to have noticed with her initial inhalation.

'Are you around next weekend?' she asks. No time for small talk; she can't hold her breath that long. 'I thought maybe we could have a drink, order some food in, maybe watch a film. If you fancy . . .' She trails off, playfully twisting her hair, diverting her eyes away in a sexually coy manner.

'Well . . .' I start, my slight pause snapping her back into her professional businesswoman persona, 'I'd love to.' She drops her guard slightly. 'I'm doing a little more redecorating . . .'

'More?' she interrupts.

'I just want to go over what I did before. I don't really like it that much any more. Probably just going to paint it white again.' I act as matter-of-fact as I possibly can.

'Okaaaaaay,' she responds, light-heartedly feigning suspicion.

'Shall we do it at yours so we don't have to inhale the paint fumes?' My cheeks blush when I realise I have said *do it*. Luckily my face is flush from a difficult workout this morning, so my childishness goes unnoticed.

She brings her smile back to the conversation, saying, 'Let's say seven thirty on Saturday, shall we?' Then her mobile phone starts to ring.

I begin to walk off so as to avoid an instance where we feel we should share an embrace or a moment of affection. 'Sounds perfect. See you then.' She just nods at me, fishes the phone from the depths of her bag and starts a new conversation on her way out.

I pick up the roll of paper from my doormat as I

normally do, step inside as I normally do, take off my trainers as I normally do, then unlock the door to my homemade prison cell, walk over to my detainee and slap the newspaper down next to her face aggressively to wake her from her slumber.

Normally I would go to the fridge, pour myself a drink and stretch against the kitchen counter while reading through the tragic headline prose. 'Celeste Slays Seventh'.

But things are not normal now.

And I don't need to look at the front page to know what it says.

My Lord asked me to kill one more time.

I've already killed too many.

He says we are nearly there.

That it will all soon be over.

January

Alison tells me that the woman I will come to know as Celeste Varrick is confusing Wiccanism. Demonising it. Fusing it with another belief.

All I hear her say is that Murphy was on to this from the beginning.

And I dismissed him.

'I'm as hazy about the ritual as this woman seems to be about Wiccan Sabbats, Jan.' Our relationship has moved to a point where she can shorten my first name in this way. 'Now I'm not sure whether you bury a picture of yourself or a loved one, the person you wish to save or see again . . .'

'So this may be a picture of her father or son or both.' This time I am the one interrupting the story, trying to add to my profile of this murderer.

'Maybe.' She brushes off my suggestion and returns to her recollection. 'The box should also contain hair, earth and, I believe, a piece of silver or something.'

I lean in towards her, urging her to get to the end.

'You have to bury it on the corner of a crossroads and incant some phrase to summon,' she pauses, looking for the correct words, 'not the Devil, but perhaps a minion of some kind. Either way, it is something dark. Something malevolent.'

This is the breakthrough we need right now.

We need to dig.

I thank Alison and send her down the corridor. She does not need to be a part of this next phase. She returns to work and I head back to the office.

Murphy does not see me approach and I hear him say, 'He's fucking losing the plot, Paulson. There will come a time when you have to choose a side. He will drag you down.' I allow him to finish. Undoubtedly he has been trying to poison Paulson's mind the entire time I was away.

I push the door open when there is a clear break between insults.

'Jan, everything all right?' Paulson asks, bringing his mug of coffee to his lips. Murphy starts, but says nothing.

'We need to start digging.' I say this out loud more to myself than either of them. They both look at me as if that is an obvious statement, as if I mean it in a metaphorical sense like digging up clues, but that's not how I mean it at all.

I want to recreate my vision.

I want to re-enact The Two at their crossroads.

I want to find the missing part to Celeste's dual ritual.

'We need to go back through all of the locations where the victims were found and dig. We need to find the nearest crossroads and excavate every corner.' Paulson still looks slightly baffled and Murphy had risen from his seat by the time I said the word *location* and started to walk out the room.

'Oh, now you've really lost it,' he jibes, turning his back on me as he heads for the door.

I snap.

As he reaches out his treacherous little mitt for the door-handle, I grip the right shoulder of his jacket and spin him around to face me. Then I take my other hand, clamp it around his neck and thrust him against the wall next to the still-closed door.

'Jan, be careful. What are you doing?' Paulson whimpers, concerned. I ignore him.

'Listen to me, you fucking weasel.' I have him pinned tightly; my face is so close to his I can taste his fear. My eyes do not flicker; they penetrate through the stare he is too frightened to divert. 'You do NOT walk out on me when I am talking. OK?' I wring his throat a little as I ask the question and he forces a pathetic nod. 'You do as I say. And right now you are coming with me and Paulson to every site where a person has been killed on this case and you are going to fucking dig. With your hands, if you have to.' He nods again. 'Good,' I say, somehow pushing him further into the wall. 'If we get there and we don't find anything, you can go off and report back to whoever is pulling your strings.'

'I don't know what you— ' he tries.

'Just shut up,' I jump in, emphasising the second *t* to highlight my disgust.

Paulson is behind me flapping, afraid that I've gone too far with Murphy. It's not the first time I've attacked him, though, and it probably won't be the last.

'Come on then, Jan,' he says from behind me, juddering. 'Let's get on to it.'

I release Murphy from his hold and he straightens his collar and shirt, his face showing enough frustration to suggest that he might strike back.

But, of course, he doesn't.

I push his shoulder around again to swivel him so he is

facing the door, the same way I would turn a criminal around to spread his hands on the car and search him.

'Let's go, then,' I order. And we tread down the corridor, down the stairs, across the Tarmac and gravel and into my car. None of us speaking.

And I drive us to Parsons Green where it all began.

There are leaves on the ground where the grass should be, but it's the same; this location will still always resonate with me as something sinister and foul.

We stand in the central spot where the paths bisect to form a crossroads. I shudder as the sensation from blowing out Lily Kane's candle returns while I view the space at which she was cut down. I allocate a corner to Paulson and another to Murphy. They start to dig at the earth with their hands. I do the same in one of the other corners.

A few moments later, Paulson calls out. 'Jan.'

I turn abruptly to look at him hunched over the hole he has made, his trousers riding lower than anyone would want them to at the back. 'I don't know if it's what you're looking for, but I've got something.' Murphy drops the handful of earth and makes his way over. I do the same.

Paulson turns around and polishes away the dirt from the item he has uncovered. A small tobacco tin. He gives it to me to open.

'This is it. This is what we came for,' I say, holding the treasure in my palm.

'What's inside?' Murphy finally pipes up, intrigued, remembering why he wanted to work on my team, forgetting what just happened at the station. We all forget for a moment.

I force the lid off with my thumbnail, all the time being

careful not to spill its contents. All three heads move together over the open tin as if we see its contents glowing. I sense the disappointment from my partners when they see a small mound of dirt, but that soon changes when I move this to one side and reveal the picture.

The picture is of a man. It is a colour photograph; he looks to be in his late twenties or early thirties. He has short dark hair and a goatee beard. This picture is wrapped in a delicate piece of hay or straw that has been tied into a bow at the front. The knot secures a smaller picture behind the one of the man. It is another colour photograph, this time of a baby. The baby is dressed in a white sleep-suit so it is difficult to tell if it is a boy or a girl. It has similar features to the man in the other photo.

'Could be the same guy as a baby,' Murphy offers. I respond with a short grunt of acknowledgement.

The only other item is a five-pence piece.

'It doesn't make sense,' Paulson speaks aloud the thoughts in his head. 'Surely it should be a picture of Lily Kane.'

'It will make more sense when we have the others,' I tell them both.

'Others?' Murphy asks.

'Trafalgar Square, Speaker's Corner, St George's Cathedral, Hampstead Heath and Soho Square.' I answer assuredly. 'We'd better get a move on.'

Not all of the boxes are as easy to locate. Trafalgar Square has nothing to dig up, by virtue of the fact that it is mostly stone and concrete. I eventually find it wedged into a crack of stone under a ledge of the north-west fountain. The soil inside is wet and the pictures water-damaged but it is clear that the contents are almost identical.

At Speaker's Corner, Paulson again discovers the tin in the earth, clearly having a talent for digging with his hands. It is not at the crossroads where I saw the apparition of The Two on Imbolc, 1 February, but at the site of the speakers where two paths cross one another, only twenty paces from the position where a charred Talitha Palladino was found.

Murphy finally pulls his weight, unearthing the fourth tin in a plant pot overlooking the corner of St George's Road and Lambeth Road, just outside the entrance to the cathedral where Graham White was found gutted on Ostara back in March.

Paulson then sniffs out the tin in the Hampstead woods and one in the flowerbed of Soho Square to complete our set.

Despite the success of our wild tin chase, time has crept along at an alarming pace and, while rejoicing at our collection of pictures and tins and thirty-pence total, a man named Aldous has been killed on the Embankment. I get the call as we head back to the station.

This is the killer's seventh victim.

There are only eight Sabbats.

Mabon is the last. It is in September, seven weeks from today. That is how long we have to put everything together: the rituals, the locations, the victims, the tins, the pictures.

We have so much to go on now but there is only one more death planned.

Mabon marks the end.

In order to crack this, I need to work backwards. From the time before Litha, when everything changed.

I must work from Beltane, back through Ostara,

Imbolc, Yule and the misfortune of the old man, Totty Fahey.

Back to Samhain.

Backwards.

To the very beginning.

Beltane
May 2009

Celeste

Tonight, at the Hampstead Beltane celebrations, I feel him.

I know he is watching me.

I can't see him, but I know he is there.

We are linked.

We have always been linked.

It isn't until Litha that I will finally see V's face. The moment that I turn around to the doorway of the flat as Brooke Derry, tied to a giant wheel, swings over a smoking pile of hay next to my sacred circle. Just before he wraps his giant hand around my throat, breaking my barrier of protection.

But that is seven weeks away.

I have not been caught yet.

Tonight, I run because I am frightened. Naively I think that my salt circle can protect me, but something on this night tells me it will not. I run. At times it feels so fast that both my feet are off the ground. The heat from the bonfire burns the right-hand side of my face as I dart past, dodging those who fornicate on the warm earth or fondle in the grass or writhe on laid-out blankets.

I remain at a sprint until the sense of warmth on my back has disappeared. I am far enough from the fire. Far enough from the carnal desire that reverberates through all those who celebrate on the heath.

Far enough from V.

Nobody sees me but him.

At the moment I feel safe, once I am sure I have not been followed, I turn around. The flicker of each flame gives the bonfire the appearance that it is living. The glow that it radiates seems to slow down everything around it. The speed that each flame dances across the burning mound of kindle is mimicked by the horned men who drape themselves in fur and emanate an animalistic sexual charge, drawing in the attention of prospective partners. I watch intently as the beautifully debauched individuals carousel around the central point, moving like liquid. Yet, far in the background, in the darkness of the undergrowth, one small flame remains still, but visible. To the left, a shadow emerges.

I take a quick step forward but manage to check myself.

I knew someone was watching.

Is this the first witness?

It creeps towards the solitary candle cautiously, look - ing around just as I had only moments ago. It walks like a ghoul, knees bent, bouncing steadily, its fingers gradually reaching out ahead of itself, aiming directly for the girl I left.

Always in darkness.

A menacing silhouette.

I am in the light.

Unseen.

Without realising, I am standing on tiptoes. My chin is leading me closer and closer to the action. On this night of heightened emotion, I am drawn to the danger of the situation, the unknown.

The grotesque figure comes to a stop and I imitate its movement.

I am the light reflection.

Its head turns horrifyingly slowly. I watch the contours of the shaded figure alter as it turns towards where I stand.

And I freeze.

He cannot see me; the fire is too bright. But I do not know this.

In the light I am invisible; in the darkness he is clear.

I see his aura glow just as his head snaps into a position aimed in my direction and I flee. In haste I drop my bag, taking four steps to halt my momentum before I return. My mind is racing, telling myself that he saw me, he saw what I did and pretty soon he will see the dead girl that I left behind.

Adrenalin courses through me, thrusting me forwards, filling my muscles with fear that will eventually manifest itself into a sensual pleasure.

Although I did not see his face, I felt him. And it is the exact sensation I will feel again as I turn to that doorway on the night of Litha.

That must be why I recognise him.

I know him.

January

━━━◆━━━

Alison Aeslin waits in my lounge while I shower upstairs in the en-suite I used to share with Audrey. It's early, Paulson is heading to the office where Murphy has already arrived; I make the water colder than I usually like to wake me up, keep me alert.

Hampstead Heath makes sense for a location based on my vision of The Two and type of celebration that goes with the Beltane Sabbat. I have immersed myself in understanding these Wiccan rituals since finding Graham White in the cathedral at the end of March. Nothing says outdoor sexual relations more than the heath. From our research and after talking repeatedly with Alison, the Beltane festival seems to revolve around fertility and sensuality.

This must be where the killer will strike next.

I return to the lounge clean and shaven, dressed in my work suit. Alison looks me up and down approvingly. For someone who rushed over here in the unsociable hours of twilight, she looks very appealing herself.

'Thanks so much for your help,' I say, trying to urge her out of the door.

'Oh, no. It was all you. I just threw some stones at a map.' She laughs and shakes her hair flirtatiously.

'You were here, and that counts for a lot,' I reassure her.

She smiles and stands up from the sofa. Standing opposite me she seems smaller than usual. Petite. Sexily coy. A moment of silence ensues which could lead down two different paths.

'I really need to get to the station,' I mutter.

There will be other opportunities for detours.

I arrive there after Paulson. Murphy was the first in.

I walk straight over to the wall, which contains the crime scene photographs and the list of names and dates that I replicated in my living room only hours ago.

And I explain.

I tell them that I think the vicinity of the hospitals and the houses of worship nearby are a pattern. That they are involved in some way, whether the victim visited them or they were killed in or near one. It spans across every scene. The killer is preying on the weak and infirm. I tell them that the implements used appear to, for the most part, correspond directly with some kind of Pagan or Wiccan ritual, and that these have been warped into something that is not used for good. Most of the rituals seem to have a positive agenda, whether for healing or welcoming new life or high-yielding crops or the advent of a new season. They have been twisted to bring about death and chaos.

Paulson and Murphy are both perched on the edge of a desk, nodding along to every plausibility.

'Murph, I want you to talk with the team on CCTV. Get them to collect anything from the hospitals, grab records too, see if there is any correlation between visitors, nurses, doctors. Paulson, we need the same for any holy building in the vicinities.'

'I've been here for hours looking into the Satanism thing, but it's all a bit messy and there's too much missing,' Murphy adds. 'You're right, Jan. This all just sounds like it fits.' I'm pleasantly surprised by his tone.

Then I say, 'And I think I know where it will happen tonight.'

Paulson sits forward on his perch so quickly that he almost falls out of his chair; his shoes slipping on the carpet in an effort to stop himself. Murphy, of course, does the opposite, sitting back resignedly and into his usual persona, no doubt secretly delighted that I am still showing some signs of my 'madness'. His puppet-master will be delighted to hear of this.

'And how do you know?' he swaggers.

Of course, I could tell him that The Two visited while I slept, and that I had a sense I was outside. I could tell him that I noticed a pattern while our expert, Alison Aeslin, threw a handful of stones at a map I have in my living room, which has an identical set-up to the room he is rolling his eyes in right now. But that is what he is expecting. It's what he wants. Something juicier to report.

I don't give him that.

I explain about the Beltane rituals that I have looked into, I tell them both about the fire and the sex and the horned masks. I talk about the altars and the earth and the outside world. And some more about fertility.

The Satanic elements pique his interest again.

I mention a church and the Royal Free Hospital, tapping my finger animatedly against their positions on the map. I talk of a spot between both of them and of outdoor sex. And Paulson guesses, 'Hampstead Heath.'

And I say, 'Exactly.'

*

I finally locate the fifth victim in the wooded area beyond one of the few Beltane bonfires that burns brightly this evening. Laura Noviss. Died on her knees. We are so much closer now, though, and it proves that my rationale is accurate, even if the timing is still slightly off. We are not called to the scene this time, we find it. Maybe next time we can stop it.

I feel something on the heath. Perhaps I'm getting carried away with the reading I have done, or maybe there is something to putting faith into the natural world. We can see it exist, we watch it grow and evolve. I may even be attuned to the celebrations in some way. But that is not what I feel.

I'm being watched.

V is here. So far the only witness, the only one who can identify Celeste Varrick.

He could tell us what he saw.

But he wants a different kind of justice.

He wants her for himself.

Ostara
March 2009

January

A t St George's Cathedral, where Graham White completed his journey to death moments ago, I start to
remember what it is like to be Detective Inspector January
David; to use nothing other than instinct and clear
thought to deconstruct a crime scene. This is what normal
used to feel like before normal was sullen, introverted
and inebriated. This is somewhere close to the person I
was before Audrey left.

I will be even closer to saving the victim by the time we
reach Beltane.

'That was great to watch, Jan.' Paulson smiles at me as
we talk outside the church doors, him smoking a quick
cigarette, neither of us noticing the person only a few
metres away pushing a small tin into a plant pot. A tin
that contains a picture of a man, a lock of hair, some dirt
and a silver coin. Neither of us noticing the completion of
the ritual.

My eyes are fixed on Alison who looks wonderfully
ethereal through the haze of smoke that Paulson exhales.

Murphy is still inside.

He continues, 'I think you put him in his place.'

'I'm just bored of the copycat theory. It's so easy. It's so
lazy,' I reply as Paulson blows smoke back over his
shoulder, checking that Murphy is still out of earshot.

'Well, you certainly laid that theory to rest.' He gives me a knowing look.

'Look, what matters is that we are on to whoever is doing this now.' The killer walks behind us, out the front gate, crossing the road towards the Imperial War Museum, and disappears. 'We'll be waiting next time.'

Paulson nods, inhaling the last of his cigarette before flicking it spiralling into the gutter.

It's the first time I have felt proud in six months, I can see that I am instilling confidence in Paulson too, reminding him of my prowess as an investigator not only as a seer.

And then Murphy joins us.

'There're still people inside the church, but the scene is blocked off, they won't be able to see anything.' Murphy steps outside, letting go of the door, which slams shut. He screws his eyes up as if to say *oops*. Paulson moves slightly to the left, allowing Murphy into our conversation.

Alison remains silent, listening.

'Jan, that was pretty weird in there,' opens Murphy. 'I mean, what is this all about?'

'The guy was cut open in a church. Each of the crime scenes on this case feels like that. All the crimes are deeply sinister, what did you expect?' deliberately speaking to him like he were a child. 'A darkness links these victims.'

'I agree completely that this is not a copycat killing.' Paulson and I look at each other, unsuccessfully dis - guising our surprise. 'I'm just not sure about the Pagan thing, though.' He doesn't even acknowledge Alison's expertise in this area. 'Maybe the Satanic angle fits . . .' He drops off, waiting for some kind of response.

I tell him that the rituals fit with Wiccan rituals and that the dates that the murders have occurred all fall on traditional Wiccan Sabbats. Alison nods. I tell Murphy that nothing so far has suggested Buddhism, Hinduism or Satanism, but it might be an idea for him to look into this area because Paulson and I have been focused on the evidence from the three crime scenes.

His response: 'Well, maybe it's something we're not seeing.'

Everything is a battle.

He is just waiting for my mistake.

V

Graham White is dead, never making it back to the hospital to meet his sister for their consultation, and Celeste is still free, able to roam the capital, still working out the next person she wants to save. Tonight, I am nervously attending a drink across the hall with my neighbour, Gail, and some of her friends I have never met. It won't be until tomorrow morning, when the paper arrives, that I will know all of the details of this latest crime; that I will be angered by Celeste's persistence.

So tonight is about enjoyment, if I can force aside my anxiety.

I'm not sure if this is supposed to be a date or merely a friendly gesture. Perhaps she never really expected me to say yes and I am not even welcome. She doesn't seem false, though. I think I have a decent gauge on her. But this is the first time in a long while that I have been out with a woman.

I haven't dated since my wife left; I hadn't dated anyone before her.

In some ways it is exciting, but I also feel that I am somehow cheating on her.

I shave, as I guess one should for such an occasion, ensuring my face is smooth and there is a perfectly straight line down either side of my goatee. I wear a shirt because she mentioned wine; if it had been beer then maybe a smart T-shirt would have sufficed.

I have a bottle of something red from Chile in my right hand, and I knock lightly on the door with my left.

'Sam. Hi. Glad you could make it.' Her teeth are perfectly straight; they look whitened, and even her eyes seem brighter. She is wearing a black dress that is short but not slutty; it certainly holds her in the right places, though. I feel slightly underdressed.

Then she says, 'You look great,' and it puts me at ease.

'You too,' I reciprocate, and hand her the bottle.

Gail's flat is almost the mirror image of mine. Her bedroom is tucked away behind the back wall of the living room, but her kitchen bleeds into the living room in a far trendier and more seamless, open-plan way, and the space I have been slowly transforming into a holding cell is actually her home office. She also has more than just a sofa in her living room, too.

But I am the only one here.

'I must look pretty keen,' I half joke, nervously.

'Sorry?' She lights a candle on her coffee table, finishing her room decoration that I must have just interrupted.

'Only that I am the first one here,' I try to clarify.

'Oh.' She laughs. 'My two friends were supposed to be here already but called to say they are delayed a bit. I'm sure they'll be here any minute. Take a seat.' She motions towards the cream leather sofa. 'Do you want red or white?'

'Er, I like red but if you've already opened a white . . .'

'No. No. Red is good. Just wait there.' She trots over to the kitchen area, where a bottle of red wine is already open, having been left to breathe a while. I watch her buttocks sway from side to side as she moves in her figure-hugging dress; there is no visible underwear line. She pours me a very large glass to get me started.

She is visibly preoccupied with ensuring everything is perfect; all the components of her abode help to create the ambience she insists on. The music is at a volume level low enough to speak over yet still appreciate and it isn't lyrics heavy, because that can interfere too. I keep the conversation going to show that I am at ease and enjoying myself. She flits between counting breadsticks, opening the oven door to check on food and pacing without any real agenda. I keep the conversation about her because my rather simple existence would probably come across as somewhat uneventful.

I'd rather not talk about me.

I don't want to discuss Sammael Abbadon.

'How many more are you expecting?'

'Just a couple. There were another two from work but they dropped out during the week.' She finally allows herself to sit down and takes two dainty sips of her own huge glass. I follow suit with a gulp.

'So, Sam, good day?' she asks, finally relaxing enough for a two-way conversation.

'Oh, you know, same old. Went for a run—' The phone starts to ring and cuts me off, which is lucky because I don't know how to finish that sentence.

She jumps up, placing her glass on a coaster, and wipes her bottom lip with her middle finger, then dashes over to pick up the phone.

'Oh, hi. Is everything . . . OK . . . right . . . no, no, that's fine, don't worry about it.' Her expression alters and the tension that has been in her shoulders since I arrived collapses with her deflation. 'Look, it can't be helped . . .

yeah, no worries. All right, then. Thanks. Bye.' She drops the phone back on the receiver and puffs out a sigh.

'Oh well, looks like it's just the two of us tonight. I've got enough food and drink for the entire building.' A laugh creeps out but it is more in resignation than anything else. She walks back to the table, knocks back all of her wine and says, 'Top up?' I still have half a glass remaining but I nod in support.

Someone more cynical might suggest that this was an elaborate ruse to get me into her apartment on my own, offer me free-flowing alcohol and delicious home-cooked food, then manipulate me into some kind of sexual scenario that is impossible to back away from.

We nibble on the snacks she has lovingly prepared for everyone who couldn't be bothered to make the same amount of effort that Gail has, and we drink. Three bottles of red between us and some shorts of an Ouzo-type drink a Lebanese client gave to her as a thank you. I don't even realise that we are no longer talking across the table; that Gail is next to me on the sofa, her knees bent and feet tucked up. It simply feels comfortable. Familiar, even.

After my second glass of what looks like aniseed-scented flour water, I compartmentalise my wife's existence. After the third, I cannot hear the Lord's judgement.

We don't get to a fourth.

Somehow, a playful caress of my thigh or chest manages to stick. A kiss follows and all the talking desists. Soon after, she is straddling me on her sofa. Not in an overly aggressive way or to show me that she is the sexually dominant one. It manages to be graceful, sensual. We just kiss like this for a short while, not like animals, not in a depraved or manic way; it is soft, like lovers, like partners.

I have only been with one other woman since my wife left and I was using her to help me move on.

I put my arms around her and sit forward, eventually rising to a standing position with her gripping my waist with her legs. Not forcefully, not squeezing me, they just hold me, hug me, and we continue to kiss. She weighs very little so I can support most of her weight in my hands. One is pressed against the middle of her back, the other hooks under her rear.

And I start to walk.

At first moving around the chair and then out of the living space towards the bedroom. I've never been here before but I know where it is. We have the same flat. She just has an office where I will hold my prisoner.

I lay her softly onto the mattress; now she can feel the extent of my arousal as I rest myself on top of her delicate frame. I kiss down her body, over the hills of her breasts and across the plains of her stomach. With my hands I start to lift the bottom of her dress to reveal her skin. (She is wearing underwear.) I look between her legs and know that if I continue with this, there will be no turning back tonight.

This will lead further.

A moment of pleasure for a lifetime of guilt.

Once again, I find myself at a crossroads.

Imbolc
February 2009

January

<hr style="width:30%; margin:auto;">

There cannot be a third victim.

This vision must hold the answers.

I am expecting to feel the same way that I did after the intuition concerning the whereabouts of the Totty Fahey death. Somehow I knew where it would be. Somehow I just understood what The Two were trying to tell me, cutting through their usually cryptic manner. The guilt of unknowingly allowing that to occur has been consistently ebbing away at my conscience since the candle went out.

And he did not fall.

I won't let that happen again.

But the vision of The Two, the snake, the milk, creeps up on me. I'm not even asleep when they decide to visit. Things are changing. They come to me in my waking hours while I stare out of a window at a police van, the siren sounding, the light rotating. And now I learn that they can be interrupted, that I can be snapped out of the situation by extraneous sources. On this occasion, it is Paulson returning to his desk, shouting for my attention from the other side of the room as he stealthily removes a packet of cigarettes and a member's card to an exclusive club from his locked drawer.

I fob him off, saying, 'I won't be much longer anyway. Might just take these home.' And I wave the wad of paper he printed off about salt circles and Pagan worship and Wiccan rituals and the eight Sabbats and I don't intend to read any tonight because all I can think about is getting back into that pitch-black dusty room and finding out what comes after the milk and where the snake went and why The Two have been reduced to a pile of clothes and where the next crime will take place.

I should have brought Alison Aeslin in earlier.

Talitha may still be alive.

I may never have reached Ostara to find Graham White on his knees in the cathedral. Laura Noviss would have made it across the heath.

I stop off at a pharmacy on the way home and pick up some pills to help me sleep. One bottle is traditional medicine, the other is homeopathic; I don't know which is best. Luckily the pharmacy is located within a super-market, so I also pick up a Merlot and Shiraz and pay for it all at the same till. The pharmacist gives me *a look* but still serves me.

I open both bottles as soon as I get in, and walk with one in each hand to the journal room, the pills rattling against the sides of their plastic containers inside my pocket as I move. This is either brave or idiotic.

Surely no more imprudent than sleeping the night on a bench at a crime scene or ignoring the clear warning of an imminent murder. Somehow I'm feeling much better. I'm emerging at the other side. I place the two tubs of pills on the floor next to my wine. This is not progress. This is not climbing out of the rut.

These are the times that I need Cathy.

I need my sister back.

The journals are piled around the room in no particular order. Sometimes it is more helpful to read through in a non-linear manner. I take a random selection of twelve and lay them out on the floor, three to my right running the length of my thigh and the same on the floor to the left. The remaining six rest on my legs, the spines bending backwards down my thighs and shins, the pages draping either side of my legs. A smorgasbord of Mother's doodles, thoughts, pictures and rants.

A random insight into the mind of a confused seer.

Below my left foot, Mother's handwriting says: 'The police are embarrassed. Help is drying up. Only Detective Lamont will listen.'

I take one homeopathic pill and a swig of Shiraz. I don't want to go in too hard.

Lamont? I can't remember his name from Cathy's case files.

This has to be investigated further.

I try to think of the last time I really looked at the paperwork that lives in my top drawer and I am filled with an instant, debilitating sorrow.

I glance at the homeopathic pills.

And take a mouthful of Shiraz.

The first entry in the journal on the floor to my left reads: 'I see how he is with Jan now. He won't speak to him. He blames him. It is our fault, though, we lost her.' I quickly turn the page to avoid any further mention of my father's feelings towards me, but the next page has an exquisite portrait of Cathy, drawn by Mother in blue Biro pen, using an accomplished cross-hatching technique I never knew she was capable of.

She looks just like I remember her. Those tiny circular cheeks. The unfathomably natural curl to her hair. The mouth that was almost always smiling.

I throw the tub of herbal sleeping remedy across the

room, bouncing it against the closed door, and reach for the hard stuff. The real drugs. I squeeze the pot tightly in my hand while examining the portrait again, swallowing some Shiraz. I look at her eyes on the page and feel like she is watching me not protect her again.

Squeezing tighter.

Two more glugs.

I shut that journal.

And launch the second tub of sleeping pills across the floor. This is not what Cathy would want to see. I should not be forcing myself to sleep, trying to find these spectres in my mind. I should be awake. Alert. Aroused. Searching out the real clues. The mistakes made by the killer.

On top of a box of journals, a foil-covered plastic sleeve houses four of my regular caffeine pills. I need to not waste time with idle rest. I take two washed down with my quaffable red.

On my thighs, the messages are in deep contrast. My left thigh displays another picture, this time a stick man with a large circular body. The skill level is the polar opposite of the incredibly life-like depiction of Cathy; it's as though a child has drawn it. I look at the date on the front of the journal and it is one year after the Cathy portrait.

'I called for January and Cathy to come down for dinner today,' the pad on my right knee says. 'Only Jan came down, of course. How did I forget she was missing, even for a second? What kind of a mother am I? Where is she, Fat Man. Stop your trickery.'

I remember this day. I recall entering the kitchen annoyed that she had dared to mention my sister's name. I recollect the anger and hatred I had for my mother as I stomped down the stairs, a dislike that evaporated as soon as I entered the room to find her broken down at her sink.

I understand now, Mother. I do it all the time with Audrey.

The next two pills fall down my throat with ease as does the remainder of the first bottle of wine.

This is what I wanted.

Time.

I do not sleep.

I do not dream.

I do not complete my vision, finding the answers to stop Celeste before she reaches Talitha Palladino. Because it wasn't a half-vision at the station earlier. That was everything I needed.

Totty Fahey snapped me out of my period of self-loathing and pity. Cathy helped by pushing me out of the dark well of my own despair. Talitha's death makes her available to stretch out a hand and pull me over the top, back onto the right track.

Talitha

❖

Don't worry, Dad.
    Don't worry, Mum.
  I can't feel the fire.
  I can't feel anything now.

The sound of the short-dicked duo speaking on the box across from where I stand and the mirth they evoke in their spectators has diminished. The last thing I was aware of was the sound of the woman aiming her words at where I knelt. Apparently I am awash with a glow and tonight will be made pure.
  I suppose that is true.
  I am dead.
  And on fire.
  The dot of light I think is heaven is nothing of the sort and soon turns to black as my body steadily topples forward from a slain kneeling position, the wind beating against my back causing me to lose my dead balance. As I lunge forward, unnoticed, crowds still chortling at infantile toilet humour, I knock the soapbox which nudges the cauldron Celeste left behind and dislodges the candles into my hair as I lie facedown in the dirt.
  My hair singes and clumps together in the heat,

eventually burning my head and face then setting fire to my clothing.

Don't worry, Mum, it doesn't hurt.

Dad, you knew this day was coming.

Nobody notices because I'm not making a noise. I'm not screaming for aid or trying to roll frantically along the floor to put myself out. I'm gone. So laugh at your dick jokes, bore yourself with Nietzscheisms, enjoy your coffee cup hand warmers. I'm not complaining. I exist only in memory.

And that will fade.

My awareness has fully disintegrated by the time January David arrives at the scene. I am non-being. I am nothingness. But that doesn't matter. There is no need for a witness in this case at all. Everything is laid out for you to solve.

Don't worry, Mum. Don't worry, Dad. The killer will be brought to justice in one way or another. I'm not in pain or stuck between two worlds.

I just outstayed my welcome.

It was too late for me to be saved.

January

✦

Talitha Palladino is the third victim. This time ritualistically burned.

Paulson and I hardly talk on the journey back to the house from Hyde Park Corner. I am trying to decrypt the image of The Two that only I witnessed. Paulson feels tested by my actions and is trying his best to stick with me, to support me. Murphy will clearly inform his puppet-master of the latest progress in the case, with particular emphasis on my state of mind. He will do what he has to in order to succeed. I can't believe he wants to take over the case, though. He's too lazy for that.

'You want me to come in, Jan?' Paulson asks genuinely.

'I'll be fine. Thanks. I think I will just go through those notes you printed off on the rituals.' He knows not to push this any further, although he wants to. I'm not going to do anything other than work a way out of this slump I have allowed myself to drop into so effortlessly; it has to be alone. I shut my passenger door, and Paulson reverses out.

The smell from Audrey's old office takes me straight back to Speaker's Corner. But first, I allow the cold water from the tap in the kitchen to run all over the back of my neck and head once more. Revitalising me. Hydration through osmosis.

I down one pint of water and fill the glass again, taking it with me into the living room where Paulson's print-outs lie in wait.

We already knew about the significance of the salt circles after researching them from the first two murders. The killer feels protected inside, as though they are untouchable while they complete the intricacies of the ritual.

Paulson has found lists of prayers and rituals that occasionally contradict one another. Some background on Paganism and Wicca and the spiritual aspect of this faith. There seems to be some opposition from the more established religions, which might hint at a reason for Lily and Totty being found near churches.

The most interesting things are the dates of the eight Wiccan Sabbats. Samhain, 31 October, was the date that Lily Kane was killed. Yule, 21 December, corresponds with Totty's demise. And tonight, 1 February, is Imbolc, and we have just scraped another victim from the dirt. According to this calendar, the next date falls in March. They call it Ostara. It falls on the twenty-first.

I know the date of the next murder but, maybe more importantly, I know that The Two will visit me on the twentieth. I can plan for their appearance.

I drink half the water in my glass, cleansing myself. I look down the list of Sabbats again. If there are eight, we are almost halfway through. Mabon is the last. We cannot allow this to get that far. It's my fault we even got to the third Sabbat.

I feel revived, lucid, energised.

I type one of the printed web addresses into my computer, which leads me on a trail of discovery, ending in the contact details of a practising Wiccan.

Alison Aeslin.
She will be important to this case.
She will be important to me.

Yule
December 2008

January

---✦---

For the first time ever, I wake up and I do not have to decipher my intuition. I understand the signs and the hidden messages that have consistently left me baffled.

I think I'm cracking it.

I think I can save Totty; there will be no second victim.

But I am still dazed.

The flames that bowed down in my direction were indicating another outdoor murder. This is the same winter wind that will blow away some of the clues at the real crime scene. But it is not until I am lifted high above the ensuing mayhem below that the location of Trafalgar Square registers.

I am atop Nelson's Column.

The circles of fire below represent the four plinths.

The lines that appear form the crossroads that the killer requires to complete their ritual.

The point at which these lines bisect each other is the location of the culling; the spot where the old man Totty Fahey will die.

I could prevent this from becoming another serial killing spree. I could take the team to Trafalgar Square, wait for the killer to arrive and seize them before any more blood is shed. The difficulty would be explaining how I know where someone is going to be murdered before it happens. I can only trust Paulson, I think.

Before I do that, I have to learn to trust myself. I can't be sure that I am right.

This entire case is about balance and that is exactly what I need to find. A line I can walk between the tangible and the esoteric.

It is well documented within the station that I have used my ability before, but people rarely talk about it. They tell themselves that I have a heightened sense of intuition; they discuss with each other how I always get the job done by any means available. But it is too embarrassing to the force as a whole to admit that this is real despite the hundreds of instances that exist on file of the police using so-called psychics on certain cases throughout history. I've never claimed to be a psychic.

I don't appear to have moved in my sleep; my fingers are still lightly draped around a half-empty tumbler. As I yawn in another morning, my jaw cracks, my routine headache creeps up on me and I'm aware that I really need to brush my teeth. But first, I grip the tumbler a little harder and knock back what is left, swilling it around and pushing it through the gaps in my teeth like an extra-strong mouthwash.

I tell myself that Cathy would be so disappointed.

I convince myself that Audrey had a reason to do what she did.

I know in myself that I should snap out of this lull; this cesspit of self-pity; but the truth is that I don't think I want to. I need to go through this fully. I need this pain and guilt and constant sorrow.

I need this hurt.

Maybe this is how I function.

Maybe this is why I do not believe it is Trafalgar Square, it's too early in the case; I don't have full confidence in myself yet. I don't believe I can save Totty Fahey. Because I have no conviction. I'm going to let this turn into another high-profile case with media coverage and pressure from my superiors. Because it would be more embarrassing to get it wrong.

Only one person has died so far. The killer's profile is sketchy at best and there is no pattern until Totty's death. He will ensure that I crack this case.

The image of the girl wagging her bloodied finger at me is lingering in my mind. This is something I am yet to decode. She may have been telling me not to trust the vision; she may have been telling me there is no point in trying to solve this case; she may be the reason I am not going to come forward with the information from this latest intuition.

But that isn't it at all. I'm just using her to excuse myself.

She is telling me I am wrong.

Totty

I can hear the voice of January David as he speaks to his partner in front of me telling him I am part of a series; that I have been killed in a similar way to someone called Lily.

At first, everything went black. I saw Celeste kneel down in front of me and dip her hand inside her bag and then there was nothing. Even the pain in my chest had gone. I'm not sure how much time had passed but I suddenly became aware of everything around me. I could hear the rhythmic speech of the woman in front of me, I heard a match strike and then a small dot of white light appeared.

It's still here.

It must be Pats.

My Pats.

But I can't seem to get any closer to her.

I don't feel the usual pain I get in my left knee or my lumbar region. I don't feel out of breath, either. Actually, I can't feel anything. I don't know what position my body is in at this moment, whether I am still kneeling. I can't smell anything either and all I can see is a speck of white against infinite blackness; I'm not sure I'm even *seeing* that.

I don't even really understand if I am hearing the

detectives or whether I am just aware.

I am simply being.

This is purgatory.

Then I am aware that January David begins counting.

One, one thousand.

Two, one thousand.

Three, one thousand.

And, on that final second, he expels an air that distinguishes the light I think I can see. He disappears my Pats. And all is black once again. I am no longer aware. I am no longer being. The light I thought was Pats, my Pats, is gone.

We are not together.

So it is done.

January

--✦--

For the first time in a long while, I leave the office before Paulson and Murphy.

The old man, Totty Fahey, is making me question myself and my sense of reason.

Before I even twist the key in the ignition, I have unclicked the glove compartment and am leaning across the passenger seat reaching for the bottle that waits for such occasions as this. But it isn't there. I don't even remember finishing it. In my desperation I displace some papers and the owner's manual, hoping a bottle will magically appear underneath.

I slam it shut but it flicks back open. I ram it harder this time but it bounces back again. Punching it several times doesn't seem to work either – it isn't until I calmly and slowly push the flapping door that it latches on peacefully.

My level of frustration now heightened, I slam my own door shut, twist the key and pull off with a screech, forgetting to fasten my seatbelt.

I sweat all the way home. My mind flits from the image of Totty Fahey, unmoving, to Lily Kane, falling to The Two and back to Totty. For a moment, I allow myself to think that it will be all right when I get home because Audrey will be there. But she won't. When will that feeling stop? I wonder whether Mother felt like this; whether this is how her breakdown started, longing for Cathy to be home again. And, at some point between these thoughts, I manage to look at the road, observe and ignore speed signs, and eventually get myself back to the gravel of my driveway without crashing or running down a pedestrian.

I speed into the house, forgetting to lock the car, leaving the front door wide open, and head straight into the kitchen in search of any alcohol. I don't leave wine in the bottle any more; every bottle that is opened gets finished. I pull a bottle of red from the rack. Instead of wasting time opening it properly I break off the top of the cork and use the handle of a wooden spoon to push the rest down inside the bottle.

And I swig almost half of it, molecules of stray cork occasionally making their way into my mouth. But, for those few pitiful moments, I forget how pathetic I am.

I place the crumb-filled bottle on the black granite work surface Audrey just had to have and finally close the front door. Only now do I remember how dwarfing the house has become. I take my wallet from my pocket and find the section that still has a picture of my wife. I contemplate tearing it in half as an act of petulant closure but opt out. I'm not brave enough for that yet. Not ready.

Instead, I walk back into the kitchen, grab the wine bottle by the neck and take it with me to the journal room where I can close myself off from this place.

The first page I open has a doodle of The Fat Man, the one that Mother believes can uncover the whereabouts of my sister Cathy. The one I am waiting to see. The next page mentions me.

'Jan hates me for saying anything. He looks at me differently. He'll forgive me when Cathy gets home.'

Again I consider tearing something into tiny pieces, but crumpling the pages violently has a similarly cathartic effect.

This is the kind of irrationality that I am avoiding by not telling Paulson about the last vision. Mother and I are different. She could not keep her desperation and fear in check. I won't end up like her if I don't let this strange ability control and define me.

I ponder this for a while, feeling a warped sense of uncertainty for not intervening and trusting my hunch. I could not have prevented an innocent person perishing at the hands of this madwoman.

Could I?

What must Cathy think of me?

Am I admitting to myself that she is dead?

Snap out of this, January.

You are not your mother.

You are much worse.

Samhain
October 2008

Lily

❖

It starts here.
  This is the beginning. Genesis.
  I am the first to be chosen.

When the stranger on the pew in front of me tells me that
they can help, I believe.

The stranger who will come to be known as Celeste
Varrick.

The recent revelation concerning my inoperable cancer
has filled me with a mixture of despair and hope. The
sudden realisation that I am definitely going to die – I
have months, no longer than a year – has brought me to
the conclusion that, actually, I want to live. So, if sitting
on this uncomfortable pew and talking to my clenched
hands, trying to believe that a higher being can hear me
and take over where conventional medicine has left me
stranded, helps me, I'll do it. If a complete stranger takes
up an equally uncomfortable seat in front of me and tells
me that she has a solution, I will listen. If a choirboy offers
me some magic beans, I'm just desperate enough to act
on it.

Celeste gives me a time to meet her in the centre of the
green outside and leaves, saying she needs to pick some
things up first. I remain in the church with the handful of

old folk that litter the adjoining pews, asking their God for answers, for absolution, for guidance.

It must work if they keep coming back.

Unless guilt is despair's twin.

The younger man at the front still has his head raised to the sky, standing opposite the iron rack of candles. I see his chin bob up and down, his cheeks tighten, but his voice is a whisper, a background hum. Quiet but intense.

I copy him. Projecting my voice to the heavens rather than the makeshift mouthpiece of my prayer hands. I tell whichever god will listen that I will make more of my life; I will give back, I will make amends, I will change my attitude towards others and myself. I say I will spread the word of God and the miracle of my rebirth. I whisper to the ceiling that I will do anything if I do not have to go through this. A woman three rows ahead of me obviously hears me and turns her head slightly over her shoulder as if spitting at me; disgusted that I am only now turning to faith because something is wrong with me.

I ignore her and press on with my negotiation.

Bargaining with the divine.

Pricing up my soul.

I wait. Remaining in a position of prayer, trying to believe that He exists, yearning for a response; some kind of sign. The spit-miming woman ahead of me crosses her chest, edges out of the long pew and exits, seemingly fulfilled. The man by the collection of flickering candles lowers his head as if God has spoken back to him. I look around to see the contentedness on the face of the tiny congregation.

Why do I not feel this?

Because I don't really believe?

I follow the spitting lady out of the church and the whispering candle man follows me.

At no point do I think about calling my parents, letting them know of my condition. Rebuilding a semblance of relationship even if only for a week. They probably wouldn't believe me anyway. I cried suicidal wolf too many times.

I don't know whether it is my own conscience or some celestial intervention but I suddenly, and ultimately, conclude that I have only two choices left: I meet with Celeste, to see if she is, indeed, my saviour; or, my second choice, I die.

When the one known as Celeste finally arrives at the crossroads, the decision has already been made for me.

Celeste

—✦—

This is only the beginning. I can save her. Lily Kane will listen to me.

Into my bag I pack a box of salt – this is for my own protection rather than Lily's – some chalk, three ribbons, one blue, one red and one black. I place the four stones into a protective, padded pocket on the inside then drop a handful of tea-light candles on top of my belongings. The lighter and matches are zipped in the waterproof section.

These are the tools of my ritual. They will begin the healing process for Lily Kane.

I sense my aura changing colour and a smile emanating from somewhere inside makes its way to my face.

This is my calling.

Lily will be my first.

Justice will play no part in these acts, all that is left to do is save these people from their hell.

My joy fades to frustration as I near Parsons Green. I'm slightly late. What if she thinks I am not coming? My crusade ending in futility at the very first obstacle. I jump off the tube and run up the path to the grassy area I said I would meet her at. The pub on the corner is bustling with positive drunken energy; children, parents, dogs, people of all ages have congregated in costumes to embrace the commercial Halloween celebrations.

And just by the oak tree near the centre of the cross-roads, as we had discussed, is Lily Kane.

Waiting.

Still.

And nobody sees her but me.

Lily

---◆---

The person January David seeks, the one he does not yet know as Celeste, is the last person that I see while I am alive. She is kneeling in front of me, that soothing voice fading into a muffled chant. Colour begins to drain from my peripheries until the only light I see comes from the solitary flame on the floor ahead of me.

Jump back five minutes to the time she was supposed to meet me.

I'm on time. I half expect Celeste to be waiting for me but she's not. I'm drowning in the fabric of my warm black coat; the children that use this place as a thorough - fare to the trick-or-treating terraces would be forgiven for thinking I am dressed as the grim reaper. My illness leaves me emaciated, pale and weak.

I stop in the centre where the paths cross each other and look around at the triangles of grass occupied by different cliques. I feel as alone as I always do. My hands are still cold in my pockets on this October night so I pull them out, clasp them together almost in prayer and blow warm breath into the opening as I walk towards the tree I was told to wait at.

I can see the blue sign of the health centre I visited this morning to receive my death sentence.

Seconds, maybe. No longer than minutes.

I turn back around to look at the church that offered me no answers or counsel. It looks unreal, lit against the colourless background sky.

As I bring my head down, I see a man walking towards me. The candle man from the church earlier today. I recognise him immediately and unconsciously smile in his direction. He reciprocates this friendly gesture.

I take my hands away from my face, preparing to shake his hand with a welcoming hello as he paces closer to me, the smile still on his face. I step forward off the slope onto the flat ground and say 'Hi.'

I'm still beaming.

He holds his grin.

But, as he reaches the light of the lamppost on the corner, I notice the tracks of his tears.

Before I have time to react, to feel compassion for the clearly saddened man of faith I noted earlier in the church, before I can turn my expression into something more appropriate, I feel the sharp, choking blow that closes my throat making it impossible to scream and difficult to breathe.

Soon after, almost in the same movement, the knife enters my cancer-riddled stomach. The agony blocked by the dent that closes my neck, a scream never materialises.

He lowers me to my knees, embracing me with a care you would not expect, and whispers into my ear. 'Ssh. Ssh. It's over. Don't fight. Go with it.' I feel the moisture from his tears wipe against my cheek as I descend.

And I let go of hope.

Jump forward five minutes to the moment that Celeste realises she is too late.

She has made a mistake.

As she blathers on, thinking she is helping, trying to

save my soul from a treacherous journey to hell it does not wish to take, I see the candle man from the church over her shoulder. He has already taken my necklace and buried something small in the ground only metres from where we are knelt. I watch him talk to no one. Deep in conversation.

Then he fades with the rest of my vision until only the flame remains and the voice of the person trying to save me, Celeste Varrick. The woman kneeling in a circle of salt, spouting wisdom about the natural world, unaware that just behind her is the man she will come to know as V, because her eyes are fixed in front of her at me, Lily Kane.

His first victim.

V

---✦---

At St Dionis Church on Parsons Green, I light a candle and look to the ceiling.

'Is this true?' I whisper to the heavens. 'Can we be together again?'

But the Lord does not reply. The same God I was raised to believe in, the one I would speak with to get through problems and anxieties, my constant, my comfort.

The one who took my wife and son from me.

And now He refuses to answer.

I am giving him one last chance, even though I was not afforded the same luxury.

I wait in silence for a while, hoping that this God will speak to me somehow, give me a sign that what I am thinking of doing is wrong or will not work, that my own desperation has led me to a dark precipice from which there can be no return. But a sign does not materialise; the voice of God does not penetrate. The only sound I hear is the whimpering of a young, emaciated, ginger-haired girl in the left-hand pews.

She will be the first that I take.

She will set me on the path back to my family.

For I have a new Lord, and he says it is so.

I continue to vent my aggression through softly spoken

venomous words aimed high, just in case He is listening but not answering. Perhaps I ask too much and God is effectively screening my call.

Leave a message, Sam.

Call back later, Sam.

From this point, Sam no longer exists.

There are several elderly ladies in the seats behind me who appear to be in communion with God. Their eyes remain closed as their mouths make shapes of guilt and desperation. I feel guilty. I am desperate. The noise from the other side of the church has ceased momentarily.

I am not here.

In plain sight I am invisible.

Only Lily sees me.

The soon-to-be-dead red-head is talking to a fellow parishioner in front of her. I didn't hear or see her come in. I stop my rant but keep my mouth moving as if still deep in contemplation. It is difficult to really hear anything in here because it all seems to descend into mumble but I pick out certain words. Most importantly, the ones which set out a time for their rendezvous and a location that I can end Lily Kane.

Allowing sound to pass through my lips again, I tell this phoney God that I renounce him, that he had no right to take away my child and destroy my marriage. I blame him. I tell him he can go and fuck himself. I tell him that everything I am about to do is his fault because when times were hardest he left me; that the single set of footprints in the sand is there because I am alone, not because he carries me.

I must, actually, say more than this because I look

around and both the women are leaving the building. Luckily, I know when they will return, so I can wait.

I blow out the candle that I lit on entry. He is dead to me now.

Celeste

———◆———

V has taken her.
    He got here first.

He always gets here first.

My short delay means that Lily Kane is already dead when I arrive. The frivolity seems to continue all around her with complete abandon. Young children are being walked right past her kneeling corpse, holding hands with their mothers, their other hand gripping on to a plastic bag full of confectionary.

On the earth in front of her a symbol has been etched with what I assume is condemning her to the under - world. She is the altar. Satan's prize. The first thing I do is rub this out with my foot, erasing the evidence that would help the police understand that I am not the murderer. Only I will ever know that this was here.

I may have been too late to meet with Lily Kane, but I am not too late to save her. To ensure her soul can be liberated. These are the ceremonies I perform every day, people come to me wanting to learn and perform a love spell, a wealth and weal spell, an employment spell or fertility spell. But not everyone knows how to ask to be healed, not everyone knows they may be protected or have their energy raised. These are the people I must locate and help.

I light a candle and speak again. 'At the end of that darkness comes light. And when it arrives we will celebrate once more.' I shut my eyes and open my heart out to this unfortunate creature before me, hoping that she is not in darkness now, that my ceremony is bringing her closer to a light, so that she may celebrate and embrace the cycle of life and death. So that her essence is not damned from whatever ritual came before mine.

In order for this to work, I must wait for the candle to die out naturally, eventually releasing her. There cannot be an interruption of this otherwise she will fall to the place her killer intended her to go. But I cannot wait around here and make myself culpable. Conventional law cannot be applied to this situation because this is not a conventional crime.

There is no point in calling the police or an ambulance, her body is dead, only her soul can be rescued now. That is my job. Balance. Equilibrium.

A couple walk their Collie through the green but the dog doesn't sense the evil that I feel so strongly. It must be working. Every person is oblivious to this. They do not see me.

I leave her. Nothing more can be done. Nobody knows I was here, that I have saved her. This is my calling. I feel it. As long as the candle remains alight, allowing for a natural burn out, my work is done. I am helping.

But all of my meditation, the circles I cast, the hand-fastenings, the healing ceremonies, they make no difference.

There is no redemption.

I am not protected.

I save no one.

They will never know that it was me, and that's fine. I'm not a serial killer. I don't wake up in the morning with an urge for malevolence. I don't have a hunger for malice against others. I do not crave the recognition for the things I am doing or will do in the future.

This is all part of a larger plan.

If I can just do this, there is something in return. I will be rewarded.

So, when I open the morning paper after my run and read the headline, I am not upset that one person in this hugely populated capital city has perished. I can't get upset about that, it was my doing; what I do get annoyed with is the report of tampering.

Somebody touched the body after I was finished.

Someone is interfering with me getting my family back.

I went to the crossroads. *I* buried the box with my photo, the earth, the silver piece. *I* summoned him. And *I* made the deal. It was up to me, only me, to do something to reunite us. It had to be my soul that was sold. It had to be me who committed these acts. This is the only way we can all be together.

And I won't let anyone stand in the way of my quest or the only god who would help me.

The article in the newspaper mentions certain items found at the crime scene, namely a circle of salt and a candle. The journalist refers to it as 'Halloween paraphernalia'. This writer believes that it is probably insignificant to the case and was more than likely left in the area by forgetful trick-or-treaters. It is significant for me.

There is no mention of the symbol that I left.

There is no reference to Lily Kane's deathly genuflection.

There appears to be more of a story in the items that this writer, and the police, allegedly, have determined as extraneous.

So, as I recover from my morning run, the one part of my old life as Sammael Abbadon, the aspect of my character that fools those around me into believing I am the same person I have always been, I pray to the Lord. Not for guidance or help but to ensure this does not affect our agreement. To ask whether I should be looking further into this and if I have permission to eradicate the problem.

My Lord answers. The agreement remains; whatever occurred after I had finished my work made no difference. It should be seen as a positive, now I have anonymity. But I do not have to act on it yet. I must stick to the job at hand.

There is a little way to go.

Yule
December 2008

Celeste

❖

I run to the top of the steps outside the National Gallery after realising I am in the wrong location to save the next person. Totty Fahey. V's second victim. This gives me the vantage point over Trafalgar Square to spot anything unsavoury and abnormal.

'There he is,' I say to myself. I'm not referring to the victim but the slender man with his back to me heading towards Totty Fahey. The one with the black aura.

I see what he is about to do. I am already taking the blame for his decisions.

I'm frozen. With fear or self-preservation, I'm not sure. But my inaction results in a private showing of V's second culling. I watch in silence as he effortlessly slides the sharp blade through the broken heart of the old man who instantly drops to his final kneeling position. Others laugh or converse at the action around them, whether the man on the plinth reading a broadsheet aloud or the idiot behind me spouting biblical drivel; but nobody cares enough to see an elderly man gasping his final breath, hidden in plain sight.

As though some lives are less worthy than others.

I bolt down the steps, jumping the last four. I must be quick but also not draw attention to myself, so I have to dodge people, sidestepping my way to the centre stone where Totty is now alone. Silently exsanguinating; draining of blood.

Not fighting.

The killer is now as invisible as his own victim. Only I am left.

He is the darkness and *I* am the light.

At first I drop down to my knees behind him, wrap my arms around his frail chest and place my hands over his wounded heart, but it has been irreparable for years. It's almost like he has resigned himself to death. Like maybe he wants to go.

He gives up before I do.

I move around to the front of him and physically restrain my own emotions. His eyes are still open and somehow, even though no tears are evident, he looks to be crying. His expression shows nothing, but his eyes speak a word to me.

Finally.

I spit on the floor and rub at the chalk symbol the killer left behind. Erasing evidence again. Not helping myself. I lay down my cloth, a twig of holly that will eventually blow away and a silver candle holder that will ensure the elements do not affect the flame. I recite a Yule mantra that I hope will keep Totty in the light as long as it takes to ensure he is rescued.

I finish the ritual on the man I believe to be dead and stretch upright.

'Pats?' he asks quietly, not spluttering but almost managing a smile, like he has seen something.

I drop back down to his level, perplexed at why he was chosen for this. I want to touch his face but my hands are covered in his blood. I move my face close to his and respond. 'Soon, sir. Very soon.'

But January David unknowingly ensures that the killer will get his way; that another will be condemned.

That Totty doesn't get to be with his Pats again.

V

---◆---

The look in the eyes of Lily Kane, the first person I ever killed, will live with me for ever.

First, her unsure scrunch of the eyes as she focused on the man she saw in the church earlier. Then her smile of recognition and advancing steps to greet me. Then the utter shock and disorientation as I pounded my fist against her trachea, her hands immediately reaching to the front of her neck in a futile attempt to uncollapse it, leaving her cancerous stomach uncovered, inviting my knife into it. Her eyes widening in the trauma yet showing no fear.

I can't witness that again.

The old man stands out. Every other person stares up at the plinth to applaud or condemn the artistic merit of a man reading current affairs aloud. The old man, Totty Fahey, as I will find out, looks across at the kids climbing the bronze lions; he peers up at Nelson's Column and I grip him from behind, locking his arms to his side and jabbing my blade through his chest. It does not slide through as easily as it did into Lily's stomach so it isn't until my third attempt that I pierce through to the heart.

He puts up less of a struggle than Lily did and I tell myself that he wants to go, that I am doing him a favour.

It makes it easier to twist the knife as I lower him, an almost dead weight already, to the concrete slab below our feet.

I'm helping you, old man.

Don't fight me.

He doesn't.

I tell myself that nobody really minds when old people die.

At the fountain I take the tin out of my inside pocket, wedge it into a nook at the edge of the water as there is nowhere on this crossroads to bury it, and call upon my Lord to inform him that I have carried out his wish.

Just as I will do after each kill.

Exactly as I did the night I first called on him for help.

'NIISO! bagile avavago gohon. NIISO! bagile mamao siaionu, od mabezoda IAD oi asa-momare poilape.' I mutter these words looking down into the water, the Enochian Key which refers to the emergence of a Satanic age; my eyes are closed, my voice inaudible to those around me.

I continue, 'Appear. To the terror of the Earth and the comfort of those who are prepared.' And we speak. I know that everything is going according to the plan; my work so far is pleasing. It is not supposed to be easy to do these things but they prove worthiness. Half of me does not want to.

My Lord informs me that a reward is due for the work I have done so far, I will see my wife again, but that I should also be prepared for another test at any moment.

Every day without my family is a test; every time he asks me to kill another person it is a test; every time I open the newspaper to find that someone is tampering with my work and may negatively affect my ultimate goal . . . that is a test. Having my family back is the final reward; until then, I believe the Lord is sending Gail to me.

But, of course, this is also his test.

Imbolc
February 2009

Celeste

V has taken two lives already. I have saved them. Everything is in balance.

He chooses these dates despite the fact he is not a part of this faith; this is not his way of life. He purposely sullies my beliefs.

And his own newly adopted half-ideology.

Imbolc is the women's festival, so it makes sense for this killer to set his sights on another woman for this occasion. This is the time for creativity, of the poets and their ideas. It is a time for us to whisper our secrets and our wishes.

I whisper to Brighid.

The secret of my abilities.

That I wish to save people.

Before they die.

I watch Talitha Palladino slump to her knees and I know I am too late again. He is behind her but his face is shielded by shadow as he utters his last words into her ear. I throw the strap to my bag over my head instead of having it rest on my shoulder, to make it more secure, so that I can run. In this split second, the killer has gone. Leaving his third victim in a position of prayer, waiting for me to salvage her spirit.

I arrive at the body out of breath – still more breath

than Talitha Palladino; adrenalin courses through me to make my heart beat faster – still less adrenalin than Talitha Palladino; my heart still beats slower than Talitha Palladino's. Drawn in the ground in front of her soapbox is a pentagram not too dissimilar from the one containing Baphomet, the Sabbatic Goat, that will keep me trapped in a cell until the end. I rub at it with my feet until the earth is flat and symbol-free. January David will never link it to Satanism.

Behind her a triangle has been crafted into the mud just as it had been for Totty Fahey, although his was upside down and represented water; this is the correct way and illustrates fire. I kick dirt into the miniature trenches that make the three adjoining lines and erase more of his work.

Performing my ritual, I am saddened to be here so late again. I cannot save her life, only her afterlife. How did nobody see this? Why do they not see me? How does the murderer make himself invisible? What strange power does he have? I ask myself these questions completely unaware that the killer is still here; he is always here talking with his God when I begin my healing ceremony.

Somehow, for now, I am invisible to him too.

He never looks back because he cannot face what he has done.

I walk away, leaving the girl on her knees, thinking I have saved her. But Mother Nature turns her back on me today. An imbalance is caused that rocks the purgatorial third victim, casting her into the fire. But all believers in a higher being will, at some point, be tested or let down by that in which they put their faith. It is how we deal with

358

the situation and the disappointment on our own that defines us.

The good will forgive as they expect to be forgiven.

The desperate will find something to fill the void.

In his despair, V turns to a faith which he manipulates for his own self-interest; he doesn't fully understand it. In their own anguish, the victims, unknowingly, turn to V. In the middle, I stand, to save them all from hell.

Ostara
March 2009

V

❖

They think they are getting closer after Talitha, but they have no idea what they are looking for. I hear them speaking; I stay in the cathedral to listen.

At the end of the row of pews, I kneel in front of a gated altar, speaking to my former God, taunting him, telling him that he has the power to stop these things if he will just speak with me. But I have conditioned myself to know that he will not enter into a dialogue when he is wrong; when he lets terrible things happen to innocent people.

The detectives do not want to disturb anyone wor-shipping in the cathedral, so I am left alone, much like the horde of parishioners in the chapel next to me who are oblivious to the scene that unfolds inside their house of worship. They continue blindly rejoicing a God that does not care and will not listen.

I smile to myself as I think this. Nobody can see my face as my back is turned in fake prayer. Nobody can see me as I walk right past them to complete my ritual. The perfect veil is openness.

The detective they all listen to, January David, is not my nemesis. We have no connection. There is no com-petition between us. He cannot feel my presence. He will not see me, until I want him to see me.

For all his hard work, he is doing nothing to get in the way of my plans.

It is only Celeste.

And I stayed while she interfered. I was here with her.

I wanted so much to turn around, to see the face of my enemy. As the bell rang to my right, there was a chant behind my back, in the chapel where I left Graham White; the moment I realise it is a woman. I could have finished things there, gone in behind her just as I did with the man she thinks she is saving. I could have slit her throat or severed her spine or punctured a kidney. But my Lord listens to me so I must listen to him.

I am not here to question.

I do not disobey the one who will bring me my family.

I think I hear the detectives leave, so I stand from my false prayer, metaphorically spitting on the altar. January David and the overweight detective are at the back of the church, passing the corner where the votive candles live. I head the same way, following them so that I can eavesdrop their thoughts on the case. I also want to see what my tormentor has done to interfere with my work.

As I look left into the chapel, one detective remains, standing behind the body, talking to somebody on his mobile phone.

'Yes. I got the phone,' I hear him say. 'Sir, it doesn't show any signs of voodoo. I think January is right about this.' He continues to talk to his superior, his back turned towards me so he doesn't know I am here. I am the only one around. I take a look at Graham's body flopped on the marble, my symbols nowhere to be seen.

She is trying to delete me.

'He doesn't think there's anything in the Satanic angle;

I think it's worth looking into, still. I can do that, sir. He seems to be playing this by the book, though.' He turns around and sees me staring into his space. He looks directly at me, the man who killed the person who is heaped on the floor below where he stands, not comprehending that he is closer to the truth than January David.

He twitches his head to his left, ushering me to move along. There is nothing to see here.

'Of course, sir. I should really go. He is outside with Paulson now and that woman. I . . .' He waits for the voice at the other end to finish and his eyes follow me out. 'Very well,' he ends, and hangs up.

I stop just before the exit and pretend to read an article on the wall about the Archbishop of Southwark and something else about the venerable Mary Potter. The detective passes behind me, forgetting who he has seen, preoccupied with his involvement in the debrief outside with his partners.

When I step outside, January David, the portly detective and the other one are huddled in a triangle; smoke streams out from one of the sides. A woman has joined them this time but I dare not look at her. I walk within a couple of feet of each of them, an arm's length, as I arc round to a plant pot against the wall nearest to the crossroads.

I hear them rejoice at their brilliance and how they are finally getting somewhere on this case, then I block them out to summon my Lord. We talk only a short distance from the gaggle of detectives, but only I can see the Lord.

Because I believe.

He tells me that I am doing well, that tonight I should indulge myself.

I think about Gail and whether this means her.

I should be thinking about my wife.

My Lord lies that the next will be the last; that I am to carry on the way I am.

Hospitals and churches are the key. In no other places will you see such high levels of desperation and questioning. It is simple to pick out those who are willing to fight to the end, and those who are on the verge of giving in or have already lost the will to live.

I sensed it immediately today as I jogged past Graham White.

Calculated randomness.

My Lord merely requires a number of souls.

I get to decide whose vitality I will gift.

It isn't murder if the person wants it all to end.

I am not a killer.

Beltane
May 2009

Celeste

—✦—

Today is the last time that I am free of the one who now refers to himself only as V. After saving Graham White, I have managed to weave my own story into his diabolical scheme. The next victim is planned for today, Beltane, but he knows I am coming. He understands my intentions and he wants me here now. He needs to see me. To digest everything about Celeste Varrick as he watches me from the shadows.

So that he can capture and devour me at Litha.

For the one known as V, the killing must be the easiest part. Now he has to think ahead of his next murder.

I think that somehow I know this. That I am attuned to this inevitable peril. I am beginning to understand this killer. I know him. I feel maleficence as I enter the heath; it draws me to another girl's death I am too late to prevent; it is then masked by fear and heightened sexuality.

He only presents himself in the image of a demon to me, yet he will know my true face. Maybe that is why I will end the Beltane celebration with a simple act of selfish gratification. My only act of pleasure.

In some way, without me even knowing or understanding, V forces me to a climax.

This is really the end of my quest.

*

From the time I decided to help Lily Kane, all paths were going to lead to this moment. The time when V would come to know me. This very instant where he is now in complete control of my destiny. When his Lord will give him the green light to capture and keep me.

To use Brooke Derry as bait.

Litha
June 2009

V

I expect them to find Annabel first. So that they will be distracted by her while I take Brooke Derry. That is my plan; that is the Lord's wish.

It doesn't happen this way, because the police are too busy waiting for something to happen rather than preventing anything.

Reactive detectives; I'll have to remember that.

After I grab Brooke from behind and render her unconscious, it is just a case of riding the lift to the top floor, tying her up, lighting the kindle and leaving her to be found. The scheme was never meant to cause her real harm; she was supposed to be found alive. I just needed her to look dead for Celeste.

She knew this. It was role-play for her. Sexual, almost.

I finish the preparation and leave. Exploiting my training, I run down the stairs, out the building, across the road and up the many flights of stairs that lead to my flat. I can see Brooke's front door from my living-room window.

And it isn't too long before I recognise the eager impishness I witnessed of Celeste at Beltane in the woods of Hampstead. Her hair flails dramatically behind her as she thrusts her elfin frame through an opening in the door.

I'm unaware of how she knows where to find me, but it doesn't matter any more.

I have her now.

Thank you for allowing this, Lord.

I will not let you down.

I reverse the process, this time speeding down the stairs of my building, jumping the last three steps of each flight. I launch myself out onto the pavement and across the road, ignoring the use of the traffic lights. My heart beats faster than Talitha Palladino's. Soon I am at the top of the stairs and I can hear her voice as she acts out her pathetic rituals, interfering with my plan.

Getting in the way of my family's rightful destiny.

Her mistake is her blind faith. Thinking she has been sent to help these poor victims. She doesn't even check to see whether Brooke is alive. She assumes that Brooke is already dead, that her body cannot be saved, only her soul. Celeste simply launches straight into her mumbo-jumbo routine, lighting a candle, chanting at the walls. Brooke will be able to hear all of this and I want that. She will remember as much of the woman as she can. I will be too quick taking Celeste for any kind of meaningful identification. The police will put down any vague recollection of a man in the room as confusion – if she even remembers me, that is.

Watching her from the doorway, I feel a similar arousal to that which I experienced on Beltane as I stalked her from the shadows of the undergrowth. There is some-thing stimulating about looking at someone who doesn't know you are there. Part of it is excitement that the Lord has decreed that this should now be her fate after months of begging.

Celeste is my only victim I take real pleasure from.

I now know her and she knows me.

But I haven't been told to make her into a monster yet.

I haven't been told that I must kill her.

That, on the evening of Mabon, I will have one final test.

January

Although the death of this victim, Annabel, seems more brutal and the ritualism somewhat diluted in comparison to the other five, it is not a copycat killing. There are elements that only the police and the killer know.

Not everything is shown on the map.

Lily Kane was slain in full view of the St Dionis Church on Parsons Green. Previously that day she had attended the Parsons Green Health Centre for biopsy results. It's such a small building that it doesn't show on the map. Our investigation led us to this information anyway, but it wasn't until all the crime scene photos were placed side by side that a picture began to form.

Talitha was killed at Speaker's Corner, Hyde Park. We know of her life-long struggle with a heart condition, but what we didn't see was her vicinity to St Mary's Hospital to the north-west, and the six churches and one synagogue over to the east of the spot she was murdered.

Totty Fahey had been to the church of St Martin-in-the-Fields before his life was taken; we know that from the programme found in his coat pocket, we see it in the background of a photo where he kneels, deceased.

Graham White was brought to his knees inside a cathedral, never making his appointment at St Thomas'

Hospital, never finding out that his nephew would make a full recovery. It seems quite obvious that the danger grows with each victim. That whatever comment Celeste Varrick is trying to make about science or religion, her motives become clearer as her ambition grows.

This is part of the reason I knew it would be Hampstead Heath on Beltane and not Green Park, Battersea Park or any of the other populated greeneries around the capital; it is so close to the Royal Free Hospital. There is a link between the vicinity of the hospitals to the churches; the proximity of helplessness to desperation.

She is starting to show her hand, whether through desperation or a need to prove herself.

A mistake has been made somewhere along the way.

So when Paulson returns from the cinema having gleaned nothing of importance from the staff and patrons, it doesn't matter because his travels have unearthed the biggest clue of all so far. Tucked behind Watson's Pharmacy, on the corner of Frith Street, is the Soho Centre for Health and Care.

A building so small it also does not show on our map.

Annabel's scorched remains lie crumpled between this miniature hospital and the two churches around the square.

I feel close to Celeste now. My mind jolts to the little girl in my intuitions. The link between the two of them.

But, just as I start to understand her, just as I begin to place myself in her mind, she is taken and, now, I have something else, something new, to battle with. As a result of her capture, I am one step back.

I should be listening to my mother.

With the information Paulson delivers, I am certain that this is the work of Celeste Varrick. It fits her modus operandi. It slots nicely into her series. So now I want to speak to Brooke Derry. I want to know everything she remembers, because she is the anomaly.

She either holds the answers or she makes us ask the wrong questions.

She was never supposed to die.

There is nothing more we can do here tonight. I exit the square at the corner of Greek Street and enter Milroy's of Soho to buy myself a bottle of their own brand expensive whisky. The cashier tells me, 'You're the second gentleman to buy one of these today. Usually only shift one per month.' I nod and fake a smile to avoid any further small talk.

It would be impossible for me to know that he was talking about Sammael Abbadon. That his security camera shows the face of the man who managed to capture Celeste Varrick before even I have. The man who has really killed all these people. The one we should be looking for on the CCTV footage rather than the invisible woman.

In my mind I am searching for a female. Celeste Varrick. The person performing these sadistic ritual killings across London. I don't yet realise that Annabel Wakeman was disposed of by Celeste's captor.

That I am no longer just searching for a single assassin.

There are two.

From the beginning, there has always been two.

I need to speak with Brooke again.

V

With a bottle of whisky in my left hand, I exit onto Charing Cross Road and make myself invisible in the crowd. There is no time to dwell on the thing I have just done. The ritual I have just performed. The woman I have left behind. The bottle is for later.

To celebrate.

And commiserate.

In a couple of hours I will have apprehended the real harbinger of warped Pagan mysticism.

This time, I don't stand back and idly watch her. My Lord says that it is time.

Finally.

V

I run up the stairs to the top floor where Celeste is incanting something gibberish that she feels will have an effect on Brooke Derry, the girl who hangs in front of her. The altar. We have found each other.

I reach the top without feeling out of breath; Celeste's voice travels down the corridor, polluting my ears with her sacrilegious rambling, stirring up the anger and passion I felt on Beltane as she did the same.

I wait outside the door, trying desperately to block out the forlorn face of Annabel, to control my legs from shaking as the adrenalin pumps through my body, strengthening me for the next struggle that lies ahead.

The doorway has been left open because she thinks she is safe in her little circle of salt. With five victims already, she thinks she is untouchable.

I don't share her beliefs.

She is not safe from me.

Her voice taunts me closer. 'Tomorrow the light will begin to fade as the wheel of the year turns over and over.'

I crane my neck around the side of the door enough that my left eye can see her kneeling from the side. She looks straight ahead at Brooke Derry and continues.

'Today the sun casts three rays. The light of fire upon the land, the Earth and the heavens.'

She turns her body within her circle so that her back is now facing Brooke and proclaims, 'The mist rolls in bringing rain and fog, the life-giving water without which we would cease to be.'

I edge into the doorway, prepared once more for what I have to do, what has to be done. Her body turns again for the last section of her ritual.

I stand face to face with Celeste Varrick. The woman who will soon be front page news.

Her eyes grow large as our gazes meet, a look of surprise with a mien of recognition.

'You,' she mouths.

'You,' I snarl back through an anxious smile and take a step forwards.

Desperately, she tries to finish her ritual, she speeds up the remaining verse, almost making it sound like one word.

'Beneath my feet is the Earth, soil dark and fertile.' I step again towards her. 'The womb in which life begins.' Another step nearer. 'Will later die then return anew.' And she breathes deeply thinking she has won. She doesn't even back away from me because she truly believes she is untouchable within that pathetic ring of condiment.

With a one-inch thick line of white dust separating us we stand upright opposite each other. I can smell the juniper smoke vapour rising to my right, her left. She can taste the red wine on my breath from this distance. She thinks she can sense my energies.

Misled, she looks deep into me. I see the tendons in her jaw tense before she speaks.

'Leave this place.' She talks sternly, confidently, keeping the pause between each word the perfect distance to assert some authority over me. She pushes her chin forwards ever so slightly, but noticeable enough that she is closer, deliberately more threatening, and whispers 'You cannot win.'

In the purest of reactions, as if her tongue stimulated the fibres of my left deltoid muscles, causing my arm to lift itself up independently of my conscious thought, my hand is now wrapped around her throat.

Her beautiful eyes bulge in shock and she looks down, trying to comprehend why a line of salt on the floor has not prevented me from touching her. I see those eyes scanning her periphery, searching for a break in the barrier.

There is no gap.

I just don't believe.

Not in her. Or what she is doing.

She is so afraid to leave her perceived protective haven that she doesn't kick her feet or flail her arms or try to shake free from my grasp, she just accepts it.

To my right, Brooke Derry swings over a growing cloud of smoke. She twitches but does not open her eyes.

'I am not here to hurt you.' I try to speak eloquently, exaggeratedly pronouncing every *t* so that the message is clear, but I do not loosen my grip.

Celeste's eyes show confusion.

I use my other hand to bring the cloth to her face, covering her mouth and nose.

It is seconds before she is on my shoulder, unconscious.

I don't even feel her weight; the epinephrine secreted throughout my body inflames my muscles with temporary superhuman strength and stamina. I even have enough to free a hand and check Brooke's pulse.

She will be fine.

I'll call it in.

I take Celeste down in the lift and out of the building without anybody asking questions. Some people may notice something but do not enter into dialogue. They soon neglect the memory of what they have seen the instant they remember that they are the most important person in their own life.

We are only outside for a short time before I enter another lift to take her up to my flat, to her new home.

Two buildings down.

Nobody sees the two of us together; I feel certain of that.

When January David is called to the scene on my street, I already have the person he is looking for. When he combs through the crime scene, Celeste Varrick is crying out for help she will never receive.

When he is at Soho Square, I am sitting on my sofa, emptying the contents of another bottle of wine. Avoiding Gail's late-night knock at the door.

And, when Detective Inspector January David sits down tonight on his own, torturing himself about how another person has died on his case, when he lifts his first tumbler of Milroy's whisky to warm his throat and numb his brain into momentary abstraction, I will be toasting him with the same tipple and devouring it for the same reasons.

I want this to be over now. I need it to be finished.

I ask the Lord to fulfil his promise, so that I may stop this. So that I may have my life back.

My Lord tells me that the hard work still lies ahead.
I lift my glass.
Cheers.

Celeste

---◆---

I don't move, at first.
  It takes a few seconds to realise that, actually, I can't.
I'm bound, and not just physically.

I drip slowly through all the emotions I should feel in this situation: confusion, denial, hysteria. I shout obscenities at the tiny rectangle of light on the door in front of me until it opens, revealing the bearded chin of the man who has taken me.

This is the point I realise I am not in police custody.

This is when I start to remember what happened.

And the rectangle that only displays a mouth and chin suddenly opens out into the image of an entire face in my mind. The face of V. The man I have been trying to save these people from.

In the darkness of my cell, more and more images light up inside my memory as V kneels outside the door uttering an Enochian Key, believing it is a way to summon his Lord and communicate on a personal level. A flash of his slender frame and dark, piercing eyes creeps into my consciousness and I recall the feeling of his hand around my throat. This dissolves into the vision of the gargoyle-like figure I witnessed in the woods at Beltane, skulking around the girl I had tried to save, creeping around in the shadows undetected. It flits further back in time, eight months ago, when I saw him in the church on Parsons Green at Samhain, lighting a candle, whispering to the ceiling.

He's been with me from the very beginning.

He has no real faith.

He is the desperate one.

Paranoia is the next emotion to set in. Why am I still alive? Why are we linked? Question after question materialising. What does he want from me? Why am I here? What is he going to do with me? My insides go cold at the thought of my probable death, and I say my own prayer for protection and safety to counteract his, hoping I can save my own soul in the way that I have tried with every one of his victims.

But the minutes drag into days, and weeks pass before I learn that he is continuing his killing spree in my name, and those weeks have to turn into months before he finally explains it to me. Three months must pass before my destiny is confirmed and revealed to me in the most peculiar way. Only then will I know why my capture was so important, my containment vital and my eventual conclusion inevitable.

Mabon marks the year's sunset and foreshadows darker times that lie ahead. This Sabbat foresees the future for both myself and V. Life throws many decisions at people, but none as tough as this Mabon, 21 September. The only choice is whether I die or whether V dies. Until this moment arrives nothing that either of us do or say or believe is of any significance.

Only one of us can survive Mabon, and it has to be me.

For I am the light and he is the darkness.

I am right and he is wrong.
He is blindness and I am sight.
And he will kill again at Lughnasadh.

V

---❖---

I summon him.

'. . . be thou a window of comfort unto me. Move there - fore and appear. Open the mysteries of your creation.'

This is the same plea I utter after each sacrifice, once I have buried the box that bears my image. This is the same invocation I use to receive my next objective, to check on my progress.

'. . . Zodoreje, lape zodiredo Noco Mada, hoathahe Saitan.'

And I wait for him to appear.

Just as I have with every person whose suffering I have extinguished.

Just as I did for the very first time the night before Samhain, when he appeared to me and listened, telling me that there is always a way to get what you want in life, that there is always some price to pay, but that I could one day be part of a family again.

I never actually see him, much as I never hear his voice; he does not materialise in front of my eyes in any guise, neither as monster nor as beautiful woman, as some legends would have it. It is a sense. The awareness that somebody or something is there with you, that they are on your side and that they hear you and act.

I feel the pain in my knees crunching into the hard wooden floor as I perch outside Celeste's cell. There is no sound coming from inside. My eyes are closed yet still I sense the changing colours on the back wall with every rotation of the traffic lights below. While I wait I allow myself a moment to drift into my possible future.

Am I finished?

The atmosphere in the room changes. It smells the same and the temperature is constant; it's more like the air is thicker or the walls are closer together.

He is here.

And he is pleased.

We talk, not with words or signs, but we converse. I convey my thoughts over the five people who have perished; the one that lies in hospital and the real villain that is shackled in the room to my left. He pacifies me with words of encouragement, that all has gone according to plan, that Celeste has made no difference to the outcome of any of the chosen ones.

Time appears to stop in his presence; the pain in my knees is eradicated; no sound but his voice can be heard. Once I register the changing lights, the muffled sound of a car stereo and the arthritic sensation in my kneecaps, I know that I am once again alone.

My bones crack as I push myself back to my feet. Still, Celeste respects the quiet. I drop down onto the sofa with my glass of red wine and allow myself a moment of relaxation. To my left is an empty, clean tumbler. Between my legs, the bottle of whisky I bought as a reward after sending Annabel Wakeman into the next life. I knock back the wine and swap glasses.

As I split the seal on the whisky bottle, Celeste jumps full force into another bout of blasphemous bellowing and her futile struggle to escape the confines of her circular trap. I don't even flinch; this is my moment, my latest reward for completing the Lord's work. One step closer to my goal.

I pause for a moment of reflection then, in my mental calendar, I write a reminder.

'August first, take another. September twenty-first, Mabon, reunite.'

I sip at the warming liquid, close my eyes in satisfaction, allow the final remnants of tension to release themselves from my shoulders, down the remainder of the glass, fill it again and slouch back into the comfort of my chair.

This is my routine until I pass out.

I will miss my regular run tomorrow.

Brooke

---◆---

The crash of the flimsy door to my hospital suite startles me from sleep. My first thought should be that my attempted murderer has come back to finish the job. Instead, the tall, ragged, tireless figure of January David bounds towards the foot of my bed. Detective Sergeant Murphy swiftly folds the sheet of paper showing Celeste's sharp features into his inside jacket pocket, hiding his second act of treachery on this case, and stands up almost to attention.

'Do you know her?' The rumpled detective grips the bar near my feet and his eyes pierce mine.

'What?' I look to the side at the nervous Murphy for support.

'Come on, Jan . . .' he tries to come to my aid but a single finger is held up in his direction, instructing him to stay out of it.

'Do you know her?' He repeats the question slowly, wrapping his mouth around each word, pausing as though placing a comma between every remark.

'Who?' I project a confident confusion, suppressing my anxiety at his line of questioning.

'Don't give me that. You know who.' He lowers his finger and I suddenly feel ganged up on. Even Detective Sergeant Murphy seems to be waiting for my answer.

'What? The woman—'

He doesn't allow me to finish my question. 'The woman you described to our artist. Do you know her?'

I find enough strength after a decent period of recuperation to force myself forwards supporting my own back, leaving the crumpled pillows behind me.

'Of course not. She tried to fucking kill me.' I screw my eyes up in apparent disbelief at his ludicrousness. How far will this go before he leaves?

'Are you religious in any way? Do you have a faith?'

'How is that even relevant to this or the last question you asked me?' I move my focus towards Detective Sergeant Murphy, trying to bring him back onside.

I watch Detective Inspector David noticeably withdraw, take a calming breath and redress the situation. DS Murphy fidgets next me, tugging at his jacket as if straightening himself out from a long car journey; he is trying to disguise the object in his pocket.

'You've been under some stress.' He tries a soothing tone, which comes over as patronising. I humph. 'I understand that. But if you have anything you want to say to us, maybe something you had previously for - gotten, now is the time to say it.'

I don't even give his words a chance to hang in the air as though I have anything to consider.

'Get out of my room. That's the only thing I want to say to you. Get out.' And I lower myself back into the pillows and turn my face away from him.

He calls for his partner to come outside with him. I don't turn my head until I hear the door close again. I watch them outside through the window. January David looks calmer as he speaks with DS Murphy, he seems to be reasoning with him. No doubt asking him to come in here and see whether I know the woman from the picture he has folded in his pocket. Because I trust him more. He is my confidant.

I don't know Celeste Varrick.

That much is true.

They both look at me through the window of the door leading into my alleged place of safety like I am an attraction at an aquarium. Only DS Murphy comes back into the room, shutting the door behind him.

'Look, I'm sorry about that, he's very passionate about—'

'Is this some kind of good cop bad cop thing?' I ask, dismissing him.

'That's not a real thing, this isn't a film.' He comes across as genuine so I let him back in a little. 'Look, he goes about things the wrong way sometimes. I believe you. But if there is anything else that you think you remember that you may have left out of your statement to Detective Inspector David earlier, then now really is the best time to say something.'

A silence creeps over the room for a beat.

To avoid any misunderstanding.

'There's nothing else,' I admit. 'I don't know who she is.

'That's good enough for me.'

He stands in the spot his boss stood only moments ago and tells me that all he wants is to catch the woman who did this to me. He wants justice for the things she has done to the other five people who were not as fortunate as I was. Then he apologises and asks me one more time whether there is anything I may have forgotten. *For Detective Inspector David*, he says, palming off the blame.

I give him a look that says *I won't answer that question again.*

'Then all that is left to do is give you more time to rest while I get this picture to the press. We want everybody to know what she looks like. The people have a right to know who this monster is.'

'Won't that scare her into hiding?' I ask innocently, displaying fear that she will know it is me who has identified her.

'This kind of person cannot stop what they are doing by themselves. They need to kill. The only way to prevent any more deaths is for the police to apprehend her.'

His logic makes sense. I'm not an expert on the psychology of a killer but it sounds right. I tell him not to be long, I don't want to be left on my own. And I agree for him to contact the newspapers with the image I described.

Making my input on the case even less valid than before.

Making myself useless.

Safe, yet without purpose.

Though I was taken off the wheel, I am still the one to be sacrificed.

Lughnasadh
August 2009

Aldous

—◆—

I'm not unhappy. I don't want to die. I don't leave the consultation in the hospital thinking that I would be better off in the ground. I don't want to get followed along the Embankment, stabbed and set on fire, just because I am dying anyway. Just because there is no hope.

I want to live the last moments of my life, no matter how long that is, to the fullest. Isn't that what anyone in this position wishes for? There's nothing I can do about it now but enjoy myself.

I wait until I am out of sight of the hospital; it feels confrontational to light up a cigarette after receiving the news about my lungs. V is watching me. He sees this act of defiance as a reason to take my life from me. He thinks I don't want to be here.

That's his consolation, his justification.

He lies to himself to excuse his behaviour.

This is not the work of the Lord. It is the obsession of a desperate, selfish individual.

I suck down the toxic, nicotine-drenched smoke and close my eyes with delight as I blow it back out through pursed, smiling lips. I swallow another mouthful of the fumes that are killing me and set on my way.

There is a brief moment, before I disappear from the

world beneath an underpass, when I have the opportunity to contemplate my family for the last time. Before he takes them away from me in a bid to get his own back.

I care for them. I love them all. My parents. My son. My two younger brothers. At least I don't have to break the news to them about my illness, I've avoided that pity party. Although, I'm not sure I was going to tell them anyway. I've refused treatment. I don't want to be a drain on the system when there are youngsters who deserve the medical resources far more than I do. I want to be able to smoke and drink and eat the food I want without judgement, without people thinking I shouldn't because it will mean I can live three weeks longer.

Three more miserable weeks.

But none of this matters. I pass into the shadow of the overhanging bridge, away from the bright grey sky which shouldn't be here at this time of year, away from any cameras that may be able to record this event, and I start down a much shorter road to my death.

The blade pierces me deep. At first it feels like an inconvenient insect bite, but that melts away when the knife is pulled out. The man behind me is strong, he holds my body tightly into his and whispers into my ear not to fight. That I should just go with it.

I don't know what choice I have. I had already made the decision to go with death, but not this way. This is not on my terms. This is not happening as a consequence of something I have done to myself.

So I drop to my knees.

Air is sparse and my lungs must be filling with blood because it feels like drowning. V still holds me close from behind as though he is caring for me, like we are friends, comrades on the same battlefield. I lift the cigarette back to my mouth but I cannot inhale, I can't taste the blood. I am numb both physically and emotionally. I don't even feel him dig the knife in and retract it another six times.

I don't know that he throws some kind of homemade doll at my knees, that he scatters a handful of candles on the floor before setting fire to the doll and then myself. I'm dead. He has not performed a ritual of healing, he is not trying to save my soul from eternal damnation. He is a fake. A fraud.

I do not hear the detectives arguing when they finally reach me because Celeste's ritual was not performed correctly. It was not performed at all. There was no candle left for January David to extinguish. When he blames one of his colleagues for my death, I do not hear this because all is black and silent. I can't hear them fighting or pushing one another up against the wall because it is not important. Nothing is now.

I see no heaven nor hell nor purgatory.

V does this for nothing.

Celeste saves no one.

Or maybe it only exists if you have faith.

And I have none.

Mabon
September 2009

V

The door is open to the spare room now, so anybody could hear her scream.

But they will hear me first.

That's when Gail is supposed to come across the landing and bang at my door asking if everything is all right, just as she did on the night before May. She will hear a woman howling; that's when she will confirm my story.

She is not allowed to die.

All of the lights in the flat are out; the back wall of the living area changes from green to red. I move across the room, grab the holy book in my right hand and move over to the window. People slither by on the streets below: couples, groups of young men jostling and teasing each other; a girl trying to look older than she is stands outside a shop-front with a cigarette waiting for whoever.

The wall changes from red to orange.

And back to green.

I walk over to the kitchen and take a sip of red wine. A scream startles me.

Celeste is awake.

Her cell door is open.

I snatch at the phone, dropping it in my haste, it rotates in the air, in slow-motion, but I catch it, upside down, before it hits the floor. Before it disturbs her.

With my index finger trembling, I tap the '9' button three times.

A woman asks me what the emergency is.

I whisper into the mouthpiece. 'She's here, in my flat.'

'Sorry, sir, can you speak up?' she asks, annoyingly.

'The woman from the front of the paper. The woman that killed all those people . . .'

'Sir?' She prompts me for more information.

'She's in my flat. She's here now.'

'Can you tell me your address, sir? What is your name?'

'She's here now and she wants to kill me.'

And I leave the phone on the floor. The voice at the other end calling 'Sir' over and over and over again.

Celeste

———◆———

Three months today. That's how long I've been here. At first I couldn't keep track of the time, he kept the door closed, kept me in the dark. It wasn't until he showed me the newspaper that I was sure.

I started counting on the second of August.

The day after Lughnasadh. After he killed Aldous Harman and made it look like a cut-price Pagan ritual.

The day he told me why he still needs me.

I awake from a deep sleep to a triangle of slow-flashing light in my room, and the scent of wet paint. I bring my hands up to my face and rub the sleep from my eyes. It takes a few moments to realise that I am no longer bound. That I am sitting up.

Before the awareness sets in, I notice that the walls are now blank. The biblical references have been erased, the writing has been hidden.

I can't hear him.

What has changed?

Am I free?

I shake my legs. My ankles are not shackled to the bed frame either. I bring my knees up to my chest and wrap my arms around them, forming a ball. I rock back and forth for a short while. It feels so liberating to be small, to not be stretched out and straight.

This is a small gratification. My solitary moment of pleasure for the last thirteen weeks.

A floorboard creaks.

He's out there.

I stop rocking. I stop breathing. The bedsprings cease squeaking.

All is quiet again.

Cautiously, I rotate myself back to a kneeling position, moving through the ruffles of the quilting as silently as possible. The light flashes back to red and the point of the blood triangle lands at my bedside. I peer down at the lit floor, examining everything in the light, making sure this is not a trap, prudently edging sideways one inch at a time.

Until I hit a wall.

An unseen barrier.

There was never any need for the satin knots around my ankles and wrists. There was no benefit to having me bound in that position other than discomfort and torment. I've been trapped the entire time.

The triangle changes to an orange colour and I look up at the ceiling. Not everything has been painted over.

I temporarily lose control and the only thing I can think to do is scream in frustration.

Of course I am not free: he still needs me.

Within a second he is standing in my doorway, his shadow elongated, surrounded by green and then a more terrifying red.

He smiles at me and looks to the ceiling.

I stand on the bed and start chanting. Spitting as I do so. Forcing every ounce of venom and malice towards my captor.

I pray to the Dark Mother.

'Day turns to night and life turns to death, and the Dark Mother teaches us to dance.' I bounce up and down, turning around and around in a pseudo-trampoline dance, adrenalin masking the agony of having been tethered in the same constricted position for so long.

A knock at the front door shocks him and he looks back over his shoulder, yet still leaves the door open.

I incant louder. 'Hecate, Demeter, Kali.' I pierce him straight through the eyes as I shout, 'Nemesis!' He is stalwart in the doorway. Unflinching.

I raise my hands out to the sides as if summoning something up from beneath the floorboards. 'Morrighan, Tiamet, bringers of destruction, you who embody the Crone. I honour you as Earth goes dark and as the world slowly dies.'

This prompts him inside the room.

Closer to me.

I sense him being drawn in.

Closer. Closer.

I feel strong. Stronger than he is.

As he stands on the threshold of the ring that contains me I look him up and down, eventually returning to his eyes. At this moment I realise that he has to die tonight.

He cannot leave this room alive.

January

❖

This is the end.
    The final Sabbat.

Tomorrow is 21 September and Celeste will want to complete her year with another murder. Tonight, I expect to be visited by The Two; tomorrow, I expect to catch her before she kills, and put an end to this pantomime spree.

We still do not know her name to be Celeste Varrick. Nobody has come forward with a positive identification; there have been several false and misleading identifications including one woman of a different race, one who was thirty years too old and one who had died several years before. The frustration is that we know what the killer looks like and when she intends to strike again. We just don't know where she is.

Because she has been captured.

Because I have been so wrong the entire time.

We are chasing a ghost.

Paulson found the tin containing the pictures in a bin a few metres from the spot that we found Aldous's frail, burnt body on the Embankment at Lughnasadh. It takes our collection to seven boxes, fourteen photographs and thirty-five pence. This all adds up to no-idea-where-the-next-death-will-occur.

I had an idea, albeit unconfident, that Totty would be

taken at Trafalgar Square. I worked out, from the visions and the evidence collected, that Laura Noviss would die on Hampstead Heath, but didn't quite make it. This is the time to gather everything. To get that one flash of inspiration.

All of the information that we have gathered so far is now spread across two walls in the office – and replicated on two walls of my living room. Each victim's name is printed in bold letters; below is the Sabbat and date they were killed. A picture of the victim and several photos of the crime scene are tacked up below this, and their corresponding tin is placed on a table in front of their details.

This is how we always set out our information on serial cases.

This is what works.

'There is no way of policing all of the hospitals and churches or places of worship in London. We don't have the manpower.' I stand in front of the display of death and preach to the room: an attentive Paulson; a handful of junior officers who are excited to be thrust onto such a high-profile case, and Murphy, who has somehow wangled his way into staying on my team despite the fact that I have strangled him and pinned him to the wall of this very office. We almost came to blows again after finding a deceased, kneeling Aldous Harman seven weeks ago.

'You don't think it will happen somewhere within this triangle?' a junior officer pipes up, his finger drawing three connected lines in the air as he traces a shape from Hampstead Heath, down to Parsons Green and across to St George's Cathedral.

Beltane to Samhain to Ostara.

Everybody's eyes flit over to the map on the wall that

is stuck with green drawing pins stabbed into the spots where Celeste's victims have perished.

The young constable continues, 'It just looks as though everything is contained within this area.' I feel the anticipation in the room as the group awaits my response, Murphy hoping I slip up somewhere along the line.

'Thank you . . .' I stand, looking at him, my hand held out in front of me, waiting.

'Higgs, sir. Constable Higgs,' he finally chips in.

'Ah, yes, Constable Higgs,' I repeat. 'Thank you, Constable Higgs, great work with the CCTV footage. If we concentrate only on the area within this triangle, that is still a hefty chunk of land to monitor. It is important to look for patterns but not force a pattern if there isn't one there. The next attempt may be in Highbury, which does fall outside the triangle, but would form a rather nice square to contain all of the other murders within. Also, we could make a triangle from the Beltane killing, down to Lughnasadh and across to Ostara, but that would leave Lily Kane outside the shape in Parsons Green.' I draw imaginary shapes with my finger along the contours of the map.

'So it could be anywhere on that map?' Another junior presents himself as Barnes.

'I'm saying that it could very well be within this triangle but that we should not discount the area outside the triangle without a strong idea of why we should stick within this shape. She,' I point at the sketch of Celeste, 'is a contradiction. On one hand she falls into the category of a visionary murderer, probably hearing voices in her head, she picks these victims at random from a variety of locations. Yet she also falls easily into the mission-oriented type. She targets her victims; the infirm, the faithful, the desperate. These killings are planned. They should be in a concentrated location. But they are not. If we remain within the area of the pins we need to be certain of the reason to do so. To venture outside we also need some solid evidence.' I see Murphy gazing in my direction, seemingly resigned to my new-found clarity of thought, my restored deductive lucidity.

I look away, giving him nothing.

'So, somewhere in London,' Murphy utters, trying to undermine me. His immunity is obviously directly proportional to his level of bravery.

'All crimes that we investigate happen somewhere in London, Detective Sergeant Murphy. We know when she will strike next; we are trying to determine the whereabouts. So if you feel you have something to offer like young Higgs here, then please help us pinpoint a location.' My retort leaves him silent, uncomfortable and fumbling for words.

Despite my outward confidence, everything still feels upside down. My intuitions have, so far, been an extra dimension to my detective work; they would back up the tangible evidence I had collected doing my job in the conventional sense.

Where I once used my visions to add confidence to my detective work, I now use my work to help justify the visions. They just won't quite tessellate.

And I haven't had a clear sense of the location since I failed to save Totty Fahey or Laura Noviss; it's as though I am being punished and The Two are becoming more and more cryptic with each victim's location. I feel I can decipher other meanings from their clues, especially with Alison's help, but the whereabouts of the next attempted murder is still proving elusive.

The contradiction in personality traits either leads to

someone who is being deliberately psychologically ambivalent or, as Alison keeps reiterating, there may, in fact, be two personalities, a team of murderers. I feel close to the killer now and my gut tells me these crimes were committed by one person.

Then Higgs nervously offers another query. 'But, sir, could you, I mean, er, do you have, maybe, er, a . . .' He stalls a little while looking for the right word – 'better' – then he leans his head in my direction as if letting me know this is not the word he really means. '. . . a better idea than anyone of where the next attempt will be.' He wipes his forehead with the back of his hand when he finishes. I know what he is hinting at.

'Well, of course, myself, DS Paulson and DS Murphy have all been on the case since the beginning.' I don't give in to his line of questioning, but he is persistent if nothing else.

'I mean, with your, um, extra insight.' He delivers the words *extra insight* in the same way he uttered the word *better* only a few moments ago. The room falls quieter than silent.

'By that you mean . . .?' I trail off, wondering how he will phrase his next sentence or whether, in fact, he will shy away. This is a test.

'I think we've all heard that you have some kind of . . .' He pauses for a second, ready to put on his *extra insight* voice. '. . . psychic ability.' Murphy lets out a snort and several pairs of eyes jump over to him.

I strain a laugh myself. 'Don't believe everything you hear in training, lads.'

'So, you're not psychic, then?' Higgs persists. While it is slightly irritating that he won't let things go and he has a seemingly endless amount of questions, I feel myself warming to him, and wonder whether he would be an interesting addition to the team one day.

'I've been very lucky with a couple of hunches in the past that have helped me crack some high-profile cases.' I feign modesty. 'This has developed into rumour of supernatural abilities, but it is nothing of the sort,' I lie. 'Some detectives are rather procedural and fastidious' – I look at Murphy and his entire body sighs back at me – 'whereas I use a certain amount of intuition and risk. It is different but it's not psychic or spooky or anything other than an alternative way of looking at things. That is what we need to do for this case.' I brush it off and the whole room buys into my yarn. All except Higgs, who cannot conceal the suspicion in his eyes.

I like that.

But then I start to wonder whether he too has been placed here to try and trip me up. To make me proclaim that I am led by dreams of smiling men or dancing children.

'Anyway, enough talk about that. What do we know for certain?' I dismiss the talk of my ability because I don't want to encourage speculation; this case requires the conventional now. If my intuitions are telling me anything it is that I need to be more proactive and not sit around waiting for the answer to somehow make its way into my mind while I sleep.

Yet still a part of me is yearning to get home, to speed up time to The Two's final visit.

Ideas are bandied around the group for hours; marks are made on the map; conclusions are drawn about where the next attempt definitely won't be and where it possibly may occur. Some points are intriguing and insightful; others are ludicrous and heavy-handed.

And none of it really matters because we are trying to get into the murderous mind of Celeste Varrick, a woman who has never committed such a crime, whose only real offence is the neglect of the people she is trying to save spiritually when she could be rescuing them physically. A selfless woman whose faith drives her to do good.

A woman who may herself be the final victim at Mabon.

I send them out of the office once I sense their grey matter dehydrate, telling them to be back in here for 6.30 tomorrow morning. That they all need more ideas because it will be going down tomorrow at some point and I will be issuing our plan of attack for the day.

I'm left with Paulson and Murphy.

'That was productive, Jan,' Murphy says sincerely. 'If we'd have done this a little earlier you never know what might have happened,' he adds, eroding his attempt at being genuine.

'There have been a few obstacles on the way, but we're back on track now.'

Naturally, I'm alluding to his treachery and covert operations, but the main obstruction to this case isn't Murphy's ambition or even the fact that we are searching for the wrong person entirely; it has been my own ego. But I'll never admit that.

Murphy grabs his jacket and heads towards the door to leave. 'So, back here in the morning for a final brainstorm, unless you dream something up in the meantime?' He says *dream something up* in the same voice that Higgs said *better* and *extra insight*.

I just look at him, my eyelids hanging as if on the verge of sleep. He opens the door and takes a step out, swinging the left side of his jacket around and slotting his arm in coolly.

'See you in the morning, then.' His voice fades out as he walks off, feeling pleased with his insubordination.

'That fucking guy . . .' Paulson stops himself short, speaking through gritted teeth, shaking his head in frustration.

'Ignore him. It doesn't matter.'

'Thinks he can get away with anything all of a sudden,' he continues under his breath.

'Just forget about Murphy, we've got a job to do now and it's more important than his annoying self-interest. OK?' I rein him in.

'You're right,' he says resignedly. 'Back to yours, then, I guess.'

I've pulled myself out of the slump that Audrey so effortlessly left me drowning in, but I still want Paulson there when I snap out of the vision, for no other reason than logistics. I don't want to waste a second. I can't wait twenty minutes for everybody to reconvene at the station. I don't want to squander even a second on the phone calling it in.

I just need to start my journey towards Celeste the moment I awake.

The evening drags. Paulson and I stare at the information covering two of the walls in the living room for most of the night; sometimes in discussion, often in silence. We eat a take-out curry; he drinks coffee, I limit myself to four glasses of Scotch.

Paulson is on alert.

I need to sleep.

By 22.30 I have rescinded the cap on my drinking and

polished off another two large glasses, hoping it will help. I try to sleep in the leather chair, not wanting to waste the time it would take to walk down the stairs from the bedroom.

By 23.20 I'm worried, and anguish over sleep is the worst thing for anyone who has suffered with insomnia.

'Half an hour left of the day,' I slur in the direction of a pensive Paulson, who is rubbing his excess chin fat as he tries to piece the pictures and words together.

'Stay calm, Jan. You don't have to be asleep, remember. It'll come,' he reassures me. This has become a habit of his recently.

'You're right.'

And I take a deep breath, slumping further into the sofa cushion.

But he's not right.

Midnight passes, which officially makes it Friday.

The twenty-first of September.

Mabon.

I am still awake at the time when TV channels stop airing programmes with sign language in the corner. Paulson is sweating profusely.

'Maybe nothing is going to happen today,' Paulson suggests half-heartedly. 'Maybe we have more time.'

But he's wrong.

I feel abandoned. Like I am being punished for allowing this to continue for so long. As if I abused my powers when I didn't stop Celeste at Trafalgar Square or Hampstead Heath.

Does this mean that my ability has vanished?

How will I ever find Cathy?

I hold on to the hope that The Two will visit at some

point today, whether this is during a short power nap or they decide to cripple my eyesight behind the wheel of a moving vehicle. I need them. But until that moment arrives I will have to locate Celeste the orthodox way.

But The Two are never going to visit me again. They have given me every clue that I need to solve this case. I should know that Celeste is not the killer. I should have stopped this already.

In a few hours I will be back at the station, working on a way to unearth the innocent woman who has not killed anybody. The one only she knows as V, who I will know as Sammael Abbadon, will be receiving his final instructions; he will finally understand why he has kept Celeste Varrick alive in his room for the last three months.

The Two will not help me with any of this because the fate of Celeste Varrick has already been decided.

There is nothing I can do to save her.

She is long gone.

V

I need to fill my day with activity.
To make the time pass.

To distract my thoughts temporarily. For today is the day I have been working towards. I will be reunited.

I awake early. Again my cheek is embedded into the sofa cushion where I spent the night, the pattern from the fabric imprinted into the side of my face. It is 6.33 a.m. and I want to ask the Lord what he has in store for me today; what my final challenge will be. But I don't want to seem desperate, even though that is the only emotion I can muster.

In the corner of the room are my trainers and a mound of sweat-drenched clothes from yesterday's run. I pick up the tracksuit bottoms, sniff at them and snap them like a whip to straighten the legs out. They are still a little acrid and damp because I left them scrunched together but I don't want to waste any time looking for clean clothes; I just want to get outside, run, and kill some time.

Delaying my despair.

I jog lightly to the end of the road to warm the muscles in my legs and stop at the corner where I use the railing at the junction to aid with my isometric stretching. All the time trying to think of nothing, but all the while picturing my wife, my son, wondering what the Lord has in store for Celeste, how I have used Gail. Not once does the taking of seven lives enter into my consciousness.

As though they were expendable.

Necessary. Each one a stepping-stone.

A matter of self-interest.

Looking down at the stopwatch on my wrist, I see the screen has only just ticked over into its sixth minute. Silently, I ask the Lord why he has slowed time today. Should I be using this deceleration for some final contemplation?

I turn left and forget everything I see, smell, taste and hear for the next forty minutes. I don't recall whether I kept a constant pace or sprinted between certain lamp-posts. I don't know whether I sped up at the final straight back to my building or if the journey up the stairs to my landing was walked or bounded two steps at a time. I don't even remember what I thought about the entire time. I only slip back into humanity when Gail's front door slams shut and the realisation that I have to deal with the situation I have created for myself punches me in the gut.

'Oh, morning, Sam,' she says, sounding shocked to see me even though this exchange has become part of both our daily routines.

'Morning,' I pant, alerting me to the possibility that I did, in fact, complete my run by leaping up the stairs.

'End of the week,' she offers.

'Yeah. Been a long one. Friday couldn't have come any sooner,' I give back, not lying but not telling her why the week has dragged so much for me.

'Maybe we should toast the weekend this evening . . .'

I love how forthcoming she is and I fleetingly allow

myself to forget the mission and indulge in flirtation. 'Cocktails at seven?' I suggest, not really thinking about which cocktails I can make or whether I even have the equipment to perform such a task; it just seemed like a suave thing to say in response to her playful suggestion.

'Ooooh,' she says, pursing her red lips and raising her left eyebrow as if I hinted at something sensual. I feel the top of my penis begin to press against the soft fabric at the front of my tracksuit bottoms as I start to get hard imagining her lips wrapped around me, her eyes looking up at me to gauge my pleasure. 'It's a date.' She smiles at me and I see her eyes dart down, noticing my excitement.

The awkwardness that follows with Gail not knowing whether to kiss me goodbye jolts me into reality. Who does she think I am? Who is she to me? Why did I allow such a complication?

She carries on walking, like she always does, but turns back saying, 'Have a good morning,' as she quickly glances down at my increasing bulge, purposely making it obvious she has done so. Her final, lingering, tease.

I am already unlocking the front door as Gail disap-pears around the corner and down the stairwell. In my haste I decide to kick the rolled-up newspaper through the doorway and across the floor, stopping as it whacks against the back of the sofa. I close the door quickly and lean my back against it as I reach my hand down into my tracksuit bottoms and grip hard, tugging five or six times until I have coaxed full arousal, my hand beating against the inside fabric aggressively.

I take my hand out and admire the triangle of tracksuit jutting out in front of me before ripping them down and grabbing hold again, using my other hand to take off my sweatshirt until I am standing completely naked.

I picture Gail bouncing on top of me but an image of my wife creeps in. I try to imagine the sounds that would come from Gail's mouth if I bent her over and inched myself inside her anus or gripped the back of her neck, forcing her to take in more than she could handle, choking her, bludgeoning her throat to the point of gagging. Then I see my wife's crying face.

And I don't know who is thinking these things.

Is it V?

Is it Sammael Abbadon?

Still gripping hard, I move my hand back and forth, back and forth, but I know I cannot close my eyes and imagine what I would do to Gail so I move over to the cell door and open the flap to reveal Celeste lying spread out on the bed. The noise wakes her but she doesn't move her body, just her eyelids, and she stares directly at me through the open rectangle, my eyes wide and glazed as I continue to tug faster and faster.

It takes a few moments for her to register what I am doing but she starts to scream obscenities at me as I continue to masturbate with my eyes fixed firmly on her form. It is not that I find her sexually attractive; it is that I don't think of anything or anyone else while I look at her and the only way to quell this sexual thirst I am feeling is to finish what I have started. I don't want to, but I have to.

This is who I have become.

It's too late to turn back now even if I want to.

It fills more time.

'You filthy fucking bastard,' she screams at me with venom. It all just helps me focus.

Her insults are incessant and relentless but I don't think of Gail. I don't think of my wife. I don't think of anything. Even though my eyes are pointing directly at

Celeste, I'm not even sure that I see her. At this moment I see nothing and feel nothing. It's the best place for me. All of us, invisible.

Then I climax. Shooting into the door of her cell, I groan as I do so and Celeste expels a drawn-out 'No.' She must feel abused. Part of me thinks I should care, but the part that should feel this way is dead. I drop down to my knees, my face now at the same level as the mess on the closed door.

Celeste cries on the other side.

I manage to whimper, 'Shut the fuck up,' but it isn't loud enough for anyone to hear but me. I just don't have the energy. I don't know who I am.

My penis starts to go flaccid as I talk to the Lord, mumbling my usual mantra, asking him questions about why I am acting this way, why I have changed so drastically. I ask him what he will have me do next. I can't hold out any longer.

This is all I have left.

Let me have this. So much has already been taken from me.

He tells me that this will all be over this evening; that it ends tonight; my work is almost done. One more person has to die but that I do not have to go anywhere for that to happen.

Then he tells me that I have to make a choice.

I must decide who I want to be with the most.

Celeste

❖

When the flap opens, I know he's back; it can only be him. I've given up all hope of anyone else finding me. Somehow, I know it ends today.

This time he is not coming in, though; he just watches me through the hole in the door. I don't understand what he is doing; he just gazes vacantly in my direction. Is he coming in? Will he bring me water?

I have been keeping track of the days since he showed me the newspaper article that proclaimed my alleged monstrosity, my lack of soul and compassion; my contempt for mankind and those who follow a deity or entrust themselves to science. The utter fabrication of a personality I do not possess.

I have not seen the sky for three months. I have not breathed in fresh air or basked in the changing of seasons, but I have been counting my meals and my bowls of water since the false revelation a tabloid journalist puked onto a page about me and I know that today is 21 September. For me, this means Mabon, the autumnal equinox, the time when the Earth Mother enters her third trimester; when witches walk between the two worlds. For the one I have come to know as V, this is a date for homicidal lunacy; another opportunity to ravage a belief that is not his own and sully the name of good-natured fellow Wiccan brothers and sisters. Without realising, he manages to besmirch his newly adopted faith through a lack of true understanding. He merely cherry-picks its relevancies and exploits them for his own gain. Not a true believer. A part-time plastic capitalist.

I know something terrible is going to happen today and the possessed look in his eyes only confirms that. Deep down, I have always known that it would be me who would suffer the most when this moment finally arrived. I could never win. Good does not always prevail.

Then I notice he is wobbling, almost vibrating; his eyes are fixed but the small amount of fat on his cheeks is shaking. His expression seems to change from anger to tedium to pleasure and back to rage.

And it clicks with me what is happening.

Despite being on the other side of a locked door and only being able to see a cut-out section of his face, knowing what he is doing to himself, where his hands are, I feel as if he is touching me. Like he is close to me; breathing on me.

I shout at him.

Because I want him to get off me.

'You filthy fuck, get away from me,' I shout, my voice squeezing through the rectangle and beating him in the face, but his eyes continue to move through vexation, vapidity, indulgence.

Red.

Amber.

Green.

I proceed with a barrage of obscenities; it didn't work for me when he first captured me and it won't work now but it is all I can think to do. And then I hear him finish and I see that final look of relief in his eyes. I've seen that look before on men as I stare up at their sweating torso once it finishes jackhammering away between my legs. Every man pulls that same face.

He drops down out of sight, probably onto his knees again, praying to his fake Lord that he uses to excuse the things he does and I can think of nothing better to do than cry.

Even though he never touched me, I feel raped.

I lie on the bed wanting desperately to curl into a ball and shut myself off from it, but my wrists and ankles are still tethered leaving me outstretched. After several minutes of self-pity I am thrust back into the truth of my situation as the gap of light goes dark and my assailant re-emerges.

'Don't worry,' he says in a low monotone, 'not much longer. It'll all be over tonight.'

And he locks the shutter, plunging me into my pitch-black confinement for the final time.

January

———✦———

'Just because it hasn't happened yet doesn't mean that it won't happen at all.' I reassure Paulson that my intuition remains intact, despite The Two vacating the black room in my mind. 'You're going to have to stick tight to me.'

I should be thinking about the last time, and the time before that. I should be recalling all of the messages that The Two have attempted to convey to me throughout this case. I should clear the pictures from the other two walls in my living room and write down all the information from every vision.

The boy's traffic-light eyes.

The circles of candles.

The light and the dark.

Blindness and sight.

Imbalance between The Two.

I should write all of these things across the walls and then combine it with the actual police work. The way each person died, the situation of a holy building, the proximity of a hospital at every scene, the ritualistic elements, the fact that every murder was committed in front of a huge crowd.

Blindness in plain sight.

With the exception of Brooke Derry, who still lives. And breathes.

I should disregard everything that she has told us. She is not the anomaly that helps prove the rule. She is not Audrey. What she says is not as important as where she was found.

I should combine all of this information while I have the time, before I am supposed to return to the office and appear knowledgeable and experienced and competent in front of my expanding team. And then I should amalgamate it with everything I have learned from my mother.

Maniswomanismaniswomanismaniswomanismanis womanismaniswoman.

I cannot rely on one skill without the other.

I must be a detective, a seer and a son.

Proactive.

A dreamer.

A brother.

But I'm still not ready. I can't just decide one day that I have escaped the trench I allowed myself to fall into when Audrey left me; I am still drinking, I think about her every day: what she looks like now, whether her hair is any different, what she is like as a mother.

Whether there is a way to get her back.

Do I really want her back?

So I don't go over the images of the boy and girl who have plagued my mind since October, because I am too concerned with the fact that they have not shown themselves to me this evening. I run them by Alison over the phone to see whether I can spark anything in her mind she may have forgotten to mention. I block out my mother's journals because I won't focus on the important information contained within them, only the portrait of my innocent sister, her face depicted in the way I have always remembered it. All I have is the evidence that every other detective would have at their disposal and right now that just looks like a blurred retrospective catalogue of my ineptitude.

'You want to stay here and work through it, just in case?' Paulson offers.

'No. No. Let's just head into the station and wait for the team. Try to put something together before they get there for the brainstorm.' I try to hide my deflation but Paulson sees right through it.

Right now, more than anything, we are going to need a little bit of luck.

V

---✦---

[illegible faded text from previous page bleeding through]

As I cut the material that binds Celeste to the bed, I am still unsure about whom I should choose. My Lord tells me that I have always known but even at this late stage I am in a bewildering state of ambivalence.

She doesn't wake up but it doesn't matter if she does; her strength has diminished, her muscles deteriorated and the circle painted above her will keep her trapped in here while I make a decision.

I am already late for my proposed date with Gail by fifteen minutes; it will be another fifteen minutes before she comes to knock on my door. I have quarter of an hour to decide everyone's fate and, apparently, I already know the answer.

I creep out of the room so as not to disturb Celeste's rest; she will need her strength soon, and I leave her door ajar and unlocked for the first and final time. Anybody could hear her scream, but it doesn't matter any more.

Nerves start to take hold of me and I find myself shaking, but not because I am frightened or anxious; perhaps it is excitement and anticipation of the denoue-ment; the culmination of my work.

My hands wobble as I collect together the trinkets I took from all the people that helped me along my journey. Lily Kane's necklace, Totty's watch, a bracelet

429

from Talitha Palladino and a photo from Graham White's wallet. My body trembles and goes cold as I sweep them all into a pile ready to leave in Celeste's cell.

Maybe that is why I drop the phone.

'The woman from the front of the paper. The woman who killed all those people . . . She's in my flat. She's here now. She's here now and she wants to kill me.' I leave the phone on the floor, the woman's voice at the other end still calling out to me.

It won't be long until they get here and I can already hear Celeste moving around, discovering her new-found sense of false freedom.

Still, I tiptoe, despite having complete control over the situation and anything that is going to happen. I hear the bedcovers rustle as she moves with more freedom, aware that the painting she has been forced to stare at for two months is a trap. It works on her because she believes. This will be her downfall.

Tentatively I push the door open with my hand while protecting myself behind the wall, not revealing myself.

Just in case she doesn't believe.

Because she may have escaped the circle.

She may want to kill me.

Because she wants to be the one that survives this.

The door glides open quietly and I almost hear an intake of breath coming from inside. With a handful of victim curio I step into the doorway; the light from the street and traffic behind surround me in an ever-changing aura. I am faced with the woman who every - body in the country has already sentenced to a life of imprisonment. She is kneeling on the bed, her long thin arms draped by her sides, seemingly as strong as the day I took her.

We glare at each other in silence for a short while until she starts to snarl. The memory of our encounter this morning is still burned onto her retina, the scars reopened at my full appearance. I watch her shoulders rotate forwards and she leans into a position of poise, her arms resting in front of her, fists clenched on the mattress, like a bulldog exuding its prowess.

Ready to pounce.

I startle her by throwing my pile of souvenirs across the room; they slide along the floor and hit the wall on the other side, spilling in all directions. She only glances at them, momentarily allowing herself an opportunity to wonder. Then she snaps her head back towards me, straightening her legs a little and lifting her backside up, then down. Up, then down, savagely pumping energy around her muscles.

Her growl gains volume and the shriek travels out the open door and across the corridor to Gail who is waiting impatiently for my arrival.

This alerts her.

She runs down the corridor and bangs on my door. She asks whether I am OK in here but all she hears is screaming. The pounding on the front door ceases and Gail runs back to her own flat to notify the police. I take the lock off the front door so that she may enter easily on her return.

So that she may be my witness.

I take a final glimpse of Celeste through the open doorway.

And the decision is made.

My Lord was correct; I always knew.

I choose my son.

January

In an act of desperation, I decide that we should narrow our search down to the triangle of pins that mark the outer reaches of our murder map. I order a handful of junior officers to call larger hospitals within this vicinity to inform their security to be extra vigilant. They need to call the Royal Marsden, Royal Brompton, St Pancras hospital. They need to call the hospitals that have already been involved in this case: the Royal Free Hospital, St Thomas', Lister Hospital. I tell them that they need to personally visit the ones on the list that we have narrowed down due to their close proximity to churches or mosques and open parkland. Anything within close range of a crossroads.

It's the best that I can come up with.

I still haven't had a vision.

I tell Paulson that we will once again be retracing the steps of the killer. Going from one scene to the next. Getting inside her head even further. Really, I have a theory that The Two have not shown me where the next murder will take place because it is going to happen at a location we have already been. Guided by guilt, I tell myself that it has to be Trafalgar Square, and at the very least you are always guaranteed to have a crowd. But I am doing what I tell the juniors not to do. I am forcing a pattern that does not exist. There seems no other viable option at this time.

I am trying to atone for Totty Fahey.

Murphy finally relents on his idiotic news bulletin idea after the majority agree it provokes widespread hysteria and the last thing we want is a group of vigilantes running wild through the parks and hospitals of the capital; staking out holy buildings and causing diversionary havoc.

The team works swiftly and efficiently, checking in with me once tasks have been completed and updating me with progress. Paulson and I travel back to where it started at Parsons Green. It's a waste of time; Celeste is not coming back here. I don't have a feeling or sensation or connection to Celeste when I stand on the spot that Lily Kane died. I just want to get to Trafalgar Square and put things right.

I save it until last because the attempt is more likely to happen at night. If Yule is the year's midnight, Mabon is seen as the sunset. So I believe Celeste will wait until dusk.

When we arrive at the venue of Totty's final breath, it yields the same results as every other location. I had hoped she would come back to the place that I failed.

Then it hits me.

She will return to the place that *she* failed.

Brooke's apartment.

The pin that was not pushed into the map. It does not form any kind of pattern, it was merely missing. The key to solving this case was not to look at the things we can see, but that which we cannot.

Paulson and I jump back into my car and head for Brooke's flat. I call Alison en route and explain to her. She tells me that she is right by that location and will see me when I arrive.

I finally get that one piece of luck I have been waiting for all along, the spark of inspiration.

My phone flashes the name *Murphy* and I have to pick it up.

'Jan.' He speaks urgently before I even have a chance to answer.

'What have you got, Murph?' I leave all animosity out of this exchange.

'Two calls have come in. One from a man saying the woman from the newspaper is inside his flat and wants to kill him. Another from a neighbour who says she can hear screaming.'

'Fuck. What's the address?' I ask, sitting upright in my seat, Paulson's bloodshot eyes peering back at me, his mouth open and ready to ask a question.

Murphy tells me that he is already on his way there.

And the animosity returns. He wants the credit for this one.

But the address is so close to where Paulson and I are that we should get there first. We're heading in that direction anyway.

It is the same street as Brooke's apartment.

Celeste is returning to her Litha foundering.

For one joyful, minuscule moment of time I forget about Audrey, my mother, the disappearance of The Two and my yo-yoing popularity within the force. The only thing I am concerned with is saving the man that put in the call and ending Celeste's reign of terror. I hang up without saying anything else and tell Paulson to push his foot through the floor, we can stop this.

I call Higgs and tell him to get himself and some men

over to Brooke's address still; she has more to explain, they need to bring her in for questioning. Then I redial Alison with the details of the new address.

'Wait outside,' I instruct. 'We are a couple of minutes away.'

She does not wait outside.

Celeste

—✦—

I hear something, and that is unusual because no sound gets in or out of this room when the door is closed.

Then I notice it is open.

The door has been left open.

I lift my head off the bed slightly to expose my other ear to any noise coming from outside my cell. He is whispering something; I can make out the faint murmur and assume he is deep in prayer so place my ear back to the mattress.

Now I am awake it registers that my shackles seem loose too. The material is still tied around my wrists and ankles but it is not as taut as it has been. Perhaps the one known as V is allowing me one last night of comfort before I join his list of victims.

Slowly, carefully, I pull down my right arm, hoping the loop has become loose enough to free a hand, but as I pull down my arm keeps on coming, and with it the fabric around my wrists. I move my other arm to my side.

My hands are free.

My feet are no longer tied to the bedstead either so I bend my legs, bringing my knees up, gripping around them with my arms and curl into a ball; the feeling of movement is better than anything I have experienced: like a blind person regaining sight.

I'm aware that the bed sheets are rustling as I move but, at this moment, I don't care. I can fight back. I am liberated. I feel my strength return and flip myself onto my knees to praise the Earth, to praise my own fortitude.

For I am right and he is wrong.

He is the blindness and now I see.

The slender, solid figure of the man only I know as V appears in the now fully open doorway, the lights behind him illuminating him like the demon I saw on the heath.

He says nothing.

He just stands there like a ghoulish harbinger of death and torment. For some reason, I start to snarl at him, pushing myself into an offensive pose. My monster ready to take on his.

I scream at him, 'Come on. Come on.' Growling like a Dobermann. Over his shoulder I see the front door to the flat juddering as a woman bashes her clenched hand against it, calling his name, asking whether he or everything is all right. He doesn't even flinch. He steps inside the room, following the handful of jewellery he flung across the floor, and the hairs on my neck prick up. The light catches the side of his face for a split second and I see him almost smiling.

Then he stops and pulls out the knife.

This is the end, I tell myself.

Only one of us will walk out of this room.

The rapping against his front door ceases as his neighbour retreats to her apartment and alerts the already-aware authorities. And he leaves. He backs out the room, the knife still in his right hand, and moves over to unlock his front door with his left, leaving it accessible to anyone who wishes to witness the climax of his infernal scheme.

He tiptoes ghoulishly past the door opening without even looking back in at me. I am stunned into silence. He wishes to take a final drink. A solemn toast of gratitude for what he is about to receive in return for his work as evil's delivering angel.

There is nothing I can do.

The door is open but I am unable to penetrate the protective circle he has encased me within. I lay back against the mattress which has been my home for two months, tucking my knees against my chest. Grateful for this minute amount of freedom.

The triangle of light turns to green.

Then red.

Then black, as a figure steps into the doorway and casts a shadow along the floor.

It must be time.

But the silhouette is not the one who now calls himself V.

It is a woman.

She peers into the room, glancing at the trinkets taken from each victim which are spread across the floorboards. She smells the unmistakable aroma of drying paint. And she steps into the shadow of my prison, the amber light now pouring back inside.

I notice that she sees the ruffled covers on the bed and creeps silently towards where I lay.

Her face is close enough to pick out features yet she does not acknowledge mine.

It is not Gail.

She will not return. The police have instructed her to remain in her flat for safety.

The woman I do not know touches the bed sheets and glances up at the pattern which keeps me detained in a circle of prevention.

She is not here as a witness.

This is not a rescue operation.

She stands next to the bed and looks right through me.

V

---✦---

By the time January David arrives, I should be gone. With my son.

That is my choice.

Standing in the doorway, I will have one last moment to back out; to kill Celeste instead. To get back with my wife. But Gail has made me realise that I haven't gone through all this to get my wife back, to be in a family I have already been a part of. It is to start a new family with my boy. To be at peace.

I run through the list of people that I have taken on my quest to be reunited; the lonely, desperate people at the end of the line. Those with incurable diseases or debilitating illness. Those who have lost faith in almost everything. Those who will try anything not to feel the way that I do every day.

Those people like me.

My God abandoned me when I needed him most; my wife left, taking my only strength and happiness with her. I sought the answers through the natural highs of exercise and the beauty of alcoholic numbness. Loneliness can make people do things that normally they would not.

They become somebody else.

I became V.

The soul of Sammael Abbadon seemed a small price for the chance to regain the greatest of lost happinesses.

I think of the first tin that I buried, the night before Samhain last year. I remember each one I concealed thereafter, completing the set tasks each time with this ritual, and the one so obviously hidden beneath the loosest of floorboards in this cell ready for the detectives to unearth and draw their conclusions. Another box filled with earth and silver and a picture of me. They will believe that I was Celeste's ultimate prize.

I know what I must do.

This is not suicide; it is renaissance.

I knock back the last mouthful of red wine I expect will ever pass my lips and place the glass gently on the work surface I usually reserve for stretching my calf muscles out after running.

I feel I have done everything asked of me. It is Celeste who will be blamed for these deaths; I will be rewarded.

Gail is expected to arrive at the moment my mission concludes. I have planned it that way. But she is not my witness.

I smile as I take a step towards the room where my son never slept, and remember the day he was born. I slow my breathing down, counting in my head: inhale, one and two and exhale, and one and two. I think back to what I felt on the night before I took Lily Kane's suffering, when I convinced myself that someone out there was listening to my woe. When I told myself that I could sense a presence on that crossroads and they spoke to me, letting me know that everything would be all right, that if I took in the Lord on that night, righteousness would prevail.

The height of my own desperation when I believed I was talking with a God.

The night I gave in to temptation and was delivered unto evil; a force that promised me salvation in exchange for something I should have held more dearly.

I draw the knife once more as I edge closer to the room that holds Celeste, my enemy, my patsy. She will believe this is meant for her, that I mean her harm, that she is the punctuation mark to this fabled spree. But I could never kill Celeste. She does not fit the profile. To me, she is already dead.

The people I have donated to the Lord are ones I feel were worthy. I stalked the sick and dying in hospitals, the lonely and confused at focus groups, and those, like me, fickle with faith if it provides the answers they long to hear. It is easier to take someone who is near death through sickness or age or has contemplated their own demise or has nowhere left to turn. Celeste is content and rounded and benevolent. I could not take that away.

Sammael Abbadon could not take that away.

So I must die.

My choice, after I obeyed the tasks set out by the Lord I thought was listening to me, after I sought out and took the last breath of seven hopeless strangers, was to take the life of Celeste and rekindle relations with my estranged wife or to end my own existence on this plane and be joined for ever with the son I never had time to know.

I will think of only his face as I swiftly arc the pointed weapon down through my own stomach. At first, I won't even feel the pain; I will drop to my knees with a thud before the ice-cold blade turns to white heat and the tendons in my arms tense frantically, trying to make me release my grip.

We will be together soon.

I shut my eyes for the final steps and speak inside my head.

Lord, I make her the monster. I falsify her actions and make them more heinous so that there is no question of her guilt. People must see her and believe in an instant that she is capable of these atrocities. That she planned them, they were premeditated and they were all for her own gratification. They must see this innocent woman and view her as a ghoul. Her culpability will be unquestionable. When my wife reads about this, she will know where I have travelled.

I will be with my son and my wife will remember me as a good man.

In doing so, Celeste will become the anguished person she so desperately wanted to save. She will become Lily or Talitha. She will end up as Graham or Annabel.

Or me.

I open my eyes at the doorway, prepared to complete my task. But things are not set out as they are meant to be. This is not right.

Celeste is not in her bed.

She is not contained within her circle.

She stands opposite me, trembling.

'How did you get out?' I ask pointedly. My eyes are unblinking. My hand, unflinching. The blade dances from red to green.

She does not answer.

'How did you escape the trap, Celeste?' I ask again, making a subtle advance inside the cell.

'I'm not who you think I am.' She finally speaks. 'I am not Celeste.'

She is trying to trick me.

I point my knife at her from across the room.

'You have mistaken me, sir.' She whimpers, holding her hands up, her palms in my direction, as if this will save her.

'Shut up, Celeste. Shut up.' I spit as I say these words, the revulsion forcing its way out through my mouth.

'My name is Alison Aeslin.' She begins to cry.

I take the dagger into both hands and lift it high above my head.

And Celeste screams.

January

———✦———

Paulson pulls the car up to the kerb around two hundred metres from the building where we found Brooke Derry, and I jump out before the car has even come to a complete stop.

Alison is not waiting outside for me as I requested.

I have already leapt up the first six steps before Paulson has reached his arm over to release the catch on his seatbelt.

I can hear someone screaming a few flights above me.

A female.

So close.

I turn the corner and a woman in a short black dress with no shoes hangs out of her doorway at the end of the corridor. She is visibly shaken, drawing in breaths between tears.

'Ma'am,' I say as I approach the door before hers, the door which leads to a trapped Alison Aeslin, slowing my approach cautiously so not to cause her alarm.

'I heard him cry out but that was ages ago.' Her voice is shrill and piercing as she tries to hold back her anguish. Paulson is working his way up now, cursing yet another flight of stairs.

'Please go back into your flat, ma'am.' I urge her back inside with a flick of my wrist. 'It's safer in there.'

445

I take a step back from the door of the address that Murphy gave me – he is still on his way – and plant my feet to set myself.

My back is almost up against the wall opposite but I have enough room, so take a step forward with my left foot, raise my right knee to my chest then thrust my foot forwards at the door.

Alison screams.

Then I hear a man shouting back at her.

I hear a crack and wonder whether it is the wood from the frame or a bone in my leg. Paulson only has one set of steps left; I can hear him panting. Murphy is still in his car on the way here. I push my foot into the floor, applying pressure on the heel and the ball to check for any damage; a shooting pain went through my shin as I connected with the wood but everything seems to be in place.

'Saaaaam,' the woman whimpers to the side of me, still ignoring my order; her distress is a little off-putting.

'Get the fuck inside now,' I shout down to her manically, more to relieve frustration than anything else, maybe to shock her into shutting up.

I check the door to see how much I have loosened it but as I fiddle with the lock it opens. It was unlocked. Paulson finally rounds the corner as I push the opening wide enough to fit through. I wave a finger in his direction and mouth *get her inside.* He passes behind me and deals with the hysterical neighbour.

And I move in.

I see the wall ahead of me change colour from green to red and my mind flits to the eyes of the boy in my vision. They were showing me where the killer was, what he saw.

The room is light enough for me to see that there is

nobody in here with me, it is clear. The next room is on the left and the door opens inwards. A triangle of light that mirrors the back wall points me inside.

I hear a man's voice speak sedately, 'Come forth from the abyss and grant me the indulgences of which we speak. By all the Gods of the Pit, I command that these things shall come to pass.'

And Alison's sweet voice whimpers, 'I don't know who Celeste is.'

I move around the corner.

He has a knife held above his head.

V

Her tricks won't work.

That Wiccan claptrap she spouts has no effect.

Celeste stands in front of me, her eyes glazed with false tears of anguish and hardship, telling me that her name is Alison. Lying to me. Lying to herself.

I hear Gail calling out to me.

Why are you staying away?

You need to witness this.

Nobody in this room can die without a witness.

There is a crash against the front door as though somebody is kicking at it or ramming their shoulder into it. I have unlocked the door. Turn the handle. Come in and observe.

Celeste screams at the sound of the encroaching visitor, thinking she has the upper hand, that she is going to be saved. I tell her, once more, that her cries for freedom are futile. That she is already dead.

The latch clicks the door open and I know that my spectator has entered, they will soon see what I want them to see. They will find Celeste to be the monster they had imagined her to be.

I stand opposite her and lift my dagger aloft.

'By all the Gods of the Pit, I command that these things shall come to pass.'

I arch my back slightly to gain more leverage with the downward thrust of the blade but before I am able to complete my ritual and return to my family, January David grabs my wrists and pulls me backwards onto the floor.

Celeste

———◆———

I am still here.

Hidden in plain sight, just as V has been this entire time.

The shadowy figure leaping up and down on the bed in the background of the action is me, Celeste Varrick. The long, dirty blond hair bouncing around as this ghost reaches for the ceiling is mine. I am that presence.

Not this impostor.

I watch as he calls her a name she does not recognise and rejoice at her distraction. I aim to rub away a part of the painted star and symbols above me. If I just disturb them enough, I can leave this circle. I can get out while he cannot see me.

V is not startled by the banging behind him, I see him smile, like this is another part of his scheme; everything is how he wants it to be.

Until January David enters my cell.

He pulls V's arms at the wrists, rotating his shoulders backwards and forcing him down to the wooden floor with a thwack; I feel the pain as his head collides with a floorboard and cease my acrobatics.

Despite the pain, he does not let go of his weapon.

The detective attempts to pummel V's knuckles into

the ground to force him to release but V is strong, his mind is unstable but his will is intense.

'Go! Get out now. While you can.' I shout to the other woman V has been calling Celeste. 'This is your chance,' I continue.

But she does not listen.

She stands steadfast, ignoring my advice, panicking as the two men grapple each other for supremacy.

I look back at the men and V is atop the detective, straddling his chest, forcing the dagger towards his neck from above. The detective uses all his force and training to keep the blade from piercing through his windpipe. He twists V's wrists so that the point of the blade faces away from him, he holds the weight of the killer above his chest.

The woman who is not Celeste, she is not me, shrieks, 'No. January. No.'

Why does she not leave?

Why will she not listen to me?

Does she not want to be saved?

I can save you, Alison Aeslin. I can restore balance. Just as I did with Lily and Totty and Talitha and Graham and Laura.

January David uses V's own weight against him, for - cing him sideways, taking himself out of danger. But V will not loosen his clasp on that sacred dagger.

The men are now standing. Detective David has my captor pinned against the wall, the knife now pointing at V's chest as they both push in opposite directions, cancelling one another out.

He does not want to kill V, he wants answers. He wishes to get to the bottom of this case. That is why he tries to, once more, force the blade to the side, the light from the streets bathing them in a warm red glow.

Get out, woman. Leave them be. You can live. It is too late for me.

The light dims suddenly as a larger-built man appears in the doorway just in time to witness January David plunge a seven-inch blade through the heart of the man who has been killing for a God who promised the world.

V gags or coughs or loses breath, or does all of these things at once, letting out a noise I have never heard before; a long guttural bellow as he does so. His scream sounds like two voices at the same time, one much lower than the other. And slides down the wall onto his knees. I drop down onto the mattress, mirroring his movements; he sees me again.

He knows that this is over. I watch him as he speaks one final time in his mind.

He pulls the knife from his chest, twisting it as it exits his body, increasing the size of the entry wound and the blood begins to flow even faster, heavier. He drops the knife onto the floor and lowers his arms back to his sides, slumping his buttocks in between his lean calf muscles so that he balances in a kneeling position, his eyes fixed on me as the life drains from him.

January David comforts the woman, holding her, while his partner in the doorway stares on in disbelief.

I don't know what to do.

Am I safe now too?

Should I care?

V's mouth moves slowly like a goldfish blowing bubbles as if he is trying to say one last thing. I manage to move my head forward a little, trying to determine his words. The only thing I can make out is that the word has a *b* in it somewhere, because his mouth makes that shape. The movement gets slower and slower as he nears his final breath, a puddle forming in front of him just as it did when I tried to save Totty and Lily.

Then his lips stop moving and a sweet smile creeps onto his face, his eyes still open, looking in my direction but not necessarily at me.

The blood-drenched knife on the floor dances from green to red.

And I feel completely paralysed.

We are darkness.

V

Against the wall, January David grips my hands, which hold the handle of the dagger, and twists, forcing the tip of the blade away from my heart, aiming it sideways, towards my shoulder at the worst.

He is not my saviour.

It is too late for that now.

I wish I had not gone for a run today, my strength is waning. It takes one final surge of adrenalin to cancel out his efforts, to guide the sharpest point of the blade back towards my tensed left pectoral muscle. Another exertion backs the knife away from me and closer to my adversary, just as he did to me on the floor only moments ago.

He uses all of his weight and the power from his legs to nullify my own efforts.

And then I release.

I relax.

And the force is freed in the direction of my heart like the energy being liberated from an elastic band catapult.

Slithering down the wall, I drop to my knees and speak one more time with the Lord I have never seen but have been in the presence of; have never heard but has spoken to me; who asks me to prove myself but only ever appears in my mind. I tell him that I have done everything asked of me and now I wait on my knees for my reward.

I pull out the knife, spilling more crimson onto the wood beneath me, and still he does not come. He does not answer. But my own wretched distress keeps me holding on until the end. This is my last hope. My final misguided chance.

The end draws closer and I begin to understand the peace that comes with passing. It doesn't feel like a conclusion but an introduction to something new. I smile as the darkness makes its way towards me, mouthing the word of my son's name as I believe him to be near. This is how Lily must have felt. And Totty.

All of them.

I see Celeste's face one last time as she kneels on the bed across the room from me like my echo. I am her shadow. The blackness draws in, closing the aperture of colour beamed to my retinas. I say his name one final time.

My son.

'Jacob.'

And this life stops.

January

---·❖·---

'Call an ambulance!' I yell at Paulson, holding Alison in my arms.

'I'm not sure there's anything that can be done, Jan.' He screws his face up in uncertainty.

I know there's nothing that can be done but this is what we have to do.

'Speak to Higgs too. Make sure he has Brooke Derry. She is going to fill in the holes in this story.' I drop straight into the role of an investigator.

Murphy pulls up outside the building. He'll be up here soon. I want to deconstruct this scene before he gets the chance to interfere.

'You're safe now,' I speak softly to Alison, rubbing her shoulder for comfort, 'it's over.'

Paulson flicks the light switch and I feel the need to cover my eyes as the brightness crashes down. Alison nestles her head further into my chest.

My eyes adjust to the new conditions and I pursue the areas of the room I could not see before; my breathing still heavy from combat.

The man on the floor is definitely dead; I can see the amount of blood he has lost. His position is the same as the other victims. There appears to be jewellery splayed out across the floor – the personal trinkets taken from each of the victims. Paulson mouths at me from across the room.

'Salt circle.'

There are no candles this time but there is a symbol on the ceiling, a large circle with a five-pointed star in the centre and what looks like a goat inside that.

Paulson sees me lift my head to view it and moves his mouth silently again.

'Pagan talisman.'

He's right, but not in this case.

He's making the pattern fit the theory.

I beckon him over to support Alison while I pick up the remaining details from the scene.

'Listen, Alison, I am going to leave you with DS Paulson for a moment. I need to check on the body, make sure there are no more surprises. I will be in the room. OK?'

She nods and composes herself but refuses to look up.

I place two fingers on the kneeling man's neck, but can't feel a pulse over the sensation and sound of my own heartbeat. I never expected to.

Murphy arrives with a junior officer and stands speechless for a moment in the doorway.

'What happened here?' Murphy finally pipes up.

I ignore his inane question and bend down next to the spot where I had V pressed to the wall. I recall almost stumbling on a loose board while we were in conflict. Using my keys, I dig into the grooves at the edge of the wood and lever it out of its slot. Murphy and Paulson look on in anticipation as my grazed hand slips into the black hole and retrieves a small tobacco tin that we know will contain a five-pence piece, some dirt and two pictures. We will come to know that they depict

Sammael Abbadon – one as a child and one as a younger man.

This is it. The eighth and final box.

'Nooooooo. Saaaaaam.' The hallway woman has finally given in to temptation, ignoring everything Paulson just explained in her apartment for her own safety. She falls heavily to her knees, screaming Sammael's name as he kneels in front of her, his body only part-filled with blood, not responding.

'For Christ's sake, Murph. How did she just get past you?' It all happened too quickly for him and the graphic nature of the scene temporarily stunned him.

We have seen worse.

'Paulson, get her out of here. Find out what she knows. Get her to identify this man.'

He escorts her out again, leaving Alison slouched and vulnerable.

I remain in the room piecing together the last details of the case that Sammael Abbadon has cleverly arranged for us to conclude that Celeste is in fact the serial killer we have been searching for, and that he was going to be the final innocent on her list. That she has been working towards his death from the very beginning.

I think about the moment his strength seemed to just evaporate and the blade pierced through his sternum.

He was always going to die tonight.

Perhaps he wanted to. He became like the victims he had taken.

It was supposed to appear as though Celeste had been preparing for this moment, the last Sabbat on the list, and she did not want to share it with anyone. So, instead of culling Mr Abbadon in a public place like the others, she kept it as a private moment between the two of them.

None of it was true.

He has failed.

The picture that Murphy leaked was nothing but a hindrance.

The woman in the picture was not the killer; the killer is the man on his knees in a growing mere of blood. The man whose heart I thrust a knife through.

'Murph, you need to wait here for the photographer and forensics. I'm going to take Alison to the hospital and then home. You think you can handle things here?'

'Of course, Jan.'

'Paulson is just down the hall, he'll come back with you to the station. Brooke Derry is on her way in for questioning. I'll meet you all there later. OK?' It's not really a question but I know how he responds to direct orders.

Alison finally looks up at me with a wary warmth and I half smile to let her know again that the worst is over.

'I'm going to take you out of here but I need you to look at one thing before we go. Do you think you can do that?' I am speaking too quietly for anyone else to hear but Alison. I point towards the symbol on the ceiling and ask whether it is Wiccan.

Her head cranes up slowly and she squints her bloodshot eyes at the painting.

'Parts of it are, yes. But in its entirety it would appear to be a devil's trap.' Her head drops a little from the emotional exhaustion.

'A devil's trap?' I urge her to continue.

'It's allegedly used to trap demons or evil within its circumference. Once something passes within the circle it

459

cannot then get out unless the trap is erased or a gap is made within the circle. Can we just get out of here?'

I look up at the insignia once more then directly down at the ruffled bed beneath. Whatever he was trying to trap he was going to tie to this bed.

But there is nobody there.

Forensic evidence will show that the only person to sleep on the bed is the man who now kneels dead opposite where it stands.

Not Celeste Varrick.

There was no Celeste Varrick. Not here.

At Litha, the man who only knew himself as V, who the rest of the world will know as Sammael Abbadon, never caught a woman by the name of Celeste Varrick. He trapped himself.

V

I am not with my son.
   It was a lie all along.
I'm nowhere.
I'm no one.
I fucked up.

Seven people have died at my hand, eight if you include my own pathetic suicide, and all that exists is blackness and nothingness. I wasted my life and have now wasted my death.

God did not speak to me, the Devil did not make a deal; he did not strike a bargain. None of this happened. Desperation spoke to me and I answered. Hopelessness struck a deal and I was all ears. Misery, torment and loneliness were the things I believed in. Disheartenment and agony were my faith.

After cutting Celeste's hands free, I knew that I was going to be the one to die, and she would have to suffer with living. I buried the box, painted the devil's trap, faked a protective salt circle for nothing. To condemn innocence.

Perhaps there were darker forces at work, but we were not working symbiotically.

I wanted my wife to read the newspaper tomorrow and see the story of Celeste's capture; the article praising the efforts of the police, in particular the work of January David's team, but she will not read this. She will not shed a tear for the man they call Sammael Abbadon, the one they should refer to as the final victim.

She mourned his death the day our son died.

The son I misguidedly performed this elaborate routine for.

Maybe Celeste could have saved me. Perhaps shown me that there is a light. Because there was no light as the last of my breath was expunged from my lungs, as the gush of blood eventually turned into a useless drip of seeping life force. Nobody met with me, not my son, not my father and certainly no Holy Spirit.

This whole exercise, the entire plot of my life for the last year, soaking up the voices and instructions to kill and maim and make into a monster; the heinous burnings and sacrifices and stabbings all in the name of self-interest to reunite with a family I never knew, deserved or cared enough for when I had the chance, all of these things have not led me anywhere. I have not progressed or moved forward; it has only helped me reach the conclusion that I knew already, the deduction that dropped me into a deluded alternative life, that friends and family who have passed before you are not waiting with open arms, you are not greeted by the Lord in any form when you die, no matter what life you choose to lead. There are no gates, no stairs leading up or down, there is more and more non-being and nothingness.

And nobody is listening. Not to me.

Nobody has ever been listening.

Nobody has ever been there.

January

✦

I've come full circle.
Completed the twelfth step.
I know who I am.

At the beginning of this case, I allowed myself to believe; it was always my scepticism that kept me sharp before. For almost a year I have not been Detective Inspector January David, I have been my mother. Accepting wholeheartedly the extravagant and eccentric idea of spiritual guides above everything else. Falling into the trap of so many beliefs where everything else is wrong and only your own dogma holds the truth.

My mind was narrowed.
I feel I may be punished.
That the visions will stop.

The last year has not always been about this case, it has not even been about finding my sister; it has been the grief of losing Mother and my father and Audrey leaving and being completely at the mercy to a strange power that I didn't want to accept then ended up over-accepting.

Then it became about finding a belief again.
In myself.

And now I feel I have a renewed sense of vigour, a hunger for this profession and the crusade to find Cathy.

It is due in a large part to the support of Paulson and the arrival of Alison so serendipitously into my life.

The doctor tells her that she needs to rest and prescribes some low-level Valium to help her sleep tonight. He also provides the details of a private professional dealing with post-traumatic stress. I inform her that the force will foot the bill after everything she has done to help.

She says very little in the car back to her house. I am so desensitised from the things I have seen that my demeanour remains unaltered. It disturbs her to see that stabbing a man through the heart has not had some profound effect on my state of mind.

He was a killer.

He stopped pushing the knife away.

'I'm so sorry you had to see that, Alison.'

I want her to know that I am here for her, that she can feel safe around me. The way I always imagined Audrey felt.

'I wish I'd just stayed outside like you said.' Her face is expressionless. There is no response to this that will elicit something positive; I simply tense my lips and say nothing.

We continue to say exactly nothing until I pull up to the kerb outside her front door.

I start to get out so that I can walk around and open her door, help her inside her home. But she stops me short.

'It's OK. I can handle it from here,' she says, looking at me sullenly.

'It's no trouble. I can make sure . . .'

She cuts me off.

'Look, you've done enough already. It's fine. I'll go

straight to bed and take these pills. There's no need to worry.' She opens her own door and stretches her left leg to the pavement.

'Are you sure?' I don't want to push her either way; she is in a delicate frame of mind.

'I'll be fine. I just need to sleep this off.' She lies and edges out further before my voice pulls her back.

'I'm sorry. I'm sorry for the way this all ended. I'm sorry you saw those things. But I'm not sorry you got involved. You helped get to the bottom of this case. You helped me.' I pause to give this last sentence some resonance. She just stares at me half-vacantly. 'The case is over now but that doesn't mean I am not here to help you. If you need me . . .'

She jumps in again.

'I think it's probably best if we leave it be for a while, don't you?'

This is not really a question. I want to remind her of that night in her kitchen, I want to ask whether she can refute any connection we had, I just want her to say that it doesn't have to stop here.

'I need some time.' And she kisses me on the cheek before fully exiting the car.

It's the last time I see her.

Paulson greets me as I return to the office.

'I wasn't sure we were going to make it for a while there, Jan.'

'By *we* do you mean *me*?' I chip in, smiling. He opts to laugh too, instead of committing himself to any response, but I know that he was worried for the majority of the case; for me, for himself, his own career. And he was right to feel that way.

465

'So what did you get from the neighbour?' I get straight to work. I want this to be over.

'Er, Sam. His name was Sam. Full name, Sammael Abbadon. He'd lived there for as long as she had rented her apartment. They'd just started seeing each other. He was some kind of fitness freak. He'd arranged for her to come over for cocktails this evening, but obviously things didn't turn out that way.'

'And what have you pulled up on this guy? Has he got a record? Is he some kind of deviant? Evangelical miscreant? Why was he out for these people?'

'Well . . .' he starts but Murphy walks in.

'Did you tell him?' he asks Paulson excitedly.

'Tell me what?' I join the conversation.

'Oh my God. You haven't told him yet.' He shuts the door behind himself and starts to reel off information from the Brooke Derry interrogation. How she too had been fucking this Sammael Abbadon. How she would role-play with him. How he would bend her over and make her look at a picture of another woman while he took her from behind.

'And get this. She reckons she never knew he was going to kill anybody.' Murphy throws his arms up in cartoon disbelief.

'So this was some kind of role-playing game for her? For them?' I quiz.

Brooke does not fully comprehend the severity of her situation.

'And a bit of a stretch at sacrifice,' Paulson weighs in. 'Do any of these people actually understand their religion?' He sighs heavily.

Brooke Derry was never meant to die. She was used. Told that it was part of some ritual or sex game where she just had to tell the police that she saw a woman in her apartment. She would then describe the woman in the picture that Sammael Abbadon would make her look at while they screwed. A picture of the wife who left him. That spiritual Wiccan whose womb could not develop their son properly. Whose beliefs could not bring him back or save their marriage.

Whose remains will be found under the same floor-boards I pulled the last tobacco tin from and identified in the coming weeks.

'Where's the wife?' I ask next, logically.

'That's what I was going to talk to you about, Jan.' Paulson looks serious. 'She's gone. She doesn't have any family left, really. The only person who knew her said she was trying to make things work with her husband and he was keeping her away from everyone. People just stopped seeing her around.'

We all seem to take a pensive moment, threading together the final strands of the case.

'I've asked Higgs if he can try to locate her but I'm not hopeful. Her name is Celeste Abbadon but, if she is still alive out there, she may be taking her maiden-name, Varrick.'

I recall the killer talking to Alison as Celeste; she mentioned it at the hospital.

And it starts to make more sense.

With all the evidence at my disposal, I can now form an accurate psychological breakdown of the killer; it doesn't matter that he is no longer alive.

I empathise with the desperation he must have felt losing two people so close to him but it can either manifest itself into something positive or it can warp your sense of reality. For Sammael Abbadon he was left alone and delusional. He found solace in something that he felt could give him answers, could bring his son back to him. He treated it in the same way his wife would have treated her beliefs, the faith he so openly rejected and, judging from each crime scene, detested and abhorred.

Celeste was not really with him, she was never there. She was at once the substantiation of his guilt and the reflection of his conscience; he would take a life but she would save a soul. He wasn't really killing anybody, he was rescuing them. He was doing his Lord's duty in order to gain a free pass back to the child he had never truly known.

When he let the knife pierce between his ventricles, he was allowing himself to be sacrificed but he was killing Celeste a second time.

'Thanks, Paulson. That's great. And well done with Ms Derry, Murph.' It sticks in my throat to say this to Murphy and he will use this success to claim a large portion of the credit for the case, but these things are out of my control.

An hour later, in the office, I look at Paulson and Murphy getting a head-start on some of the paperwork, and they are less tense, relaxed even. Paulson will undoubtedly celebrate in his own unique and depraved way, while Murphy can gloat to his sponsor that he has completed his covert mission.

I do not allow myself this luxury.

Serial killers do not have consciences; they do not all wait for a three-month break between stories to begin their murderous sprees; they do not always give the lead investigator time to recover from the strains of such a case; they do not care about leaving enough of an interval for personal convalescence.

468

It starts again tomorrow.

And I will soon know that something else is coming.

My intuition has not left me.

But it has changed.

I leave the station alone, heading back to my own car with its distinct odour and dented seat that tessellates perfectly with the contours of my body. I start the engine and lean across to the glove box.

I deserve this.

Not everything changes.

I think about sleeping in a bed tonight and not allowing myself to just melt into a stupor on the lounge carpet. I think about going into work tomorrow, even though it is Saturday and I am not supposed to be there, just to refresh my memory on Cathy's case, to look into the Lamont character that Mother mentioned in her journals. I want to catalogue the journals; I want to go through them with some chronology.

I want to sort myself out.

Get organised.

Find Cathy.

Move on.

But life is not sequential.

I pull into the drive and turn out the lights. Everything looks as it always does. But I feel something. Perhaps I am forcing intuition. Maybe I don't want to stop.

I just want to feel something.

I turn the key and push the door open, noticing immediately that I left the light on in the journal room. I can see a strip of white beneath the door, and I sigh. When I close the front door I have another foreign sensation. That I am being watched, that somebody is here with me.

I move into the kitchen and flick on the light; prepared

for anything my fist is clenched. But nobody is inside. I fix myself a glass of water because I don't need any more alcohol today.

Because I think I will sleep easy tonight.

I know that the living room is still covered in pictures and scribbling from the Sammael Abbadon case, and I don't want to be reminded of that.

I don't want to move backwards.

I decide that I will go straight upstairs to the bedroom and rest, but the detective in me, the sceptic that is returning, the eternal cynic, has to look around the house.

This feeling can't be nothing.

I'm right.

There is somebody in my house.

In my living room.

A girl. A young girl.

She is leaning with her hands over her eyes and her head resting against the wall. As if she is counting.

I don't need her to turn around, though.

I know her face.

It has been thirty-four years, but I know what my own sister looks like.

'I was in the kitchen getting us some juice. Cathy was outside counting to thirty. When I went back out she wasn't there. I was in the kitchen getting us some juice. Cathy was outside counting to thirty. When I went back out she wasn't there.' I repeat these words in my head just as I did to the police officer all those years ago. Stating the facts.

Telling it exactly as I remember.

But what is true is not always what is fact.

What is genuine is not always what is real.

But at this very moment, I believe.

Acknowledgements

Continued gratitude to Random House for the chance to write every day and a job that never feels like work. Huge appreciation, once again, to everyone at Century and Arrow who have got behind January David, this book and the writing.

Thanks, in particular, to Natalie Higgins for all your support since the first book and to my editor, Ben Dunn, who showed me that good is not good enough. We completed this journey together.

To Sam Bulos, agent, friend, confidante and sounding board, thank you for your patience, belief and encourage - ment to write the stories I want to write in the style I want to write.

Thanks to Brendan Patricks, whose very magic directly inspired so many aspects of *Girl 4* that I could not acknowledge it until this book.

Chuck Palahniuk, who started all this, who said, 'I know this because Tyler knows this', who unknowingly gives me something to aim for, thanks is not enough.

Special thanks to my mother, who brought me into this world and hasn't stopped supporting me from that moment. I am where I am because you are who you are.

To Phoebe and Coen, my light and my courage.

And to my wife, Francesca, my great inspiration, my

hero. You make everything easier. You make me believe. But you can't get me into an early-morning writing routine.

THE POWER OF READING